LIGHT AS A
FEATHER

LIGHT AS A
FEATHER

Previously titled Light as a Feather, Stiff as a Board

BY ZOE AARSEN

SIMON PULSE

NEW YORK LONDON TORONTO SYDNEY NEW DELHI

For DSK

This book is a work of fiction. Any references to historical events, real people, or real places are used fictitiously. Other names, characters, places, and events are products of the author's imagination, and any resemblance to actual events or places or persons, living or dead, is entirely coincidental.

SIMON PULSE
An imprint of Simon & Schuster Children's Publishing Division
1230 Avenue of the Americas, New York, New York 10020
First Simon Pulse edition October 2018
Text copyright © 2013 by Zoe Aarsen
Originally published in 2013 by Lovestruck Literary as *Light as a Feather, Stiff as a Board*
Cover photograph copyright © 2018 by Awesomeness, LLC. All Rights Reserved.
"Hulu" is a trademark of Hulu, LLC. Title design copyright © 2018 by Hulu, LLC. All rights reserved.
All rights reserved, including the right of reproduction in whole or in part in any form.
SIMON PULSE and colophon are registered trademarks of Simon & Schuster, Inc.
For information about special discounts for bulk purchases, please contact
Simon & Schuster Special Sales at 1-866-506-1949 or business@simonandschuster.com.
The Simon & Schuster Speakers Bureau can bring authors to your live event.
For more information or to book an event contact the Simon & Schuster Speakers Bureau
at 1-866-248-3049 or visit our website at www.simonspeakers.com.
Cover designed by Sarah Creech
Interior designed by Tiara Iandiorio
The text of this book was set in Adobe Garamond Pro.
Manufactured in the United States of America
2 4 6 8 10 9 7 5 3 1
This book has been cataloged with the Library of Congress.
ISBN 978-1-5344-4403-4 (hc)
ISBN 978-1-5344-4402-7 (pbk)
ISBN 978-1-5344-4404-1 (eBook)

WELCOME TO WILLOW
POPULATION 4,218

PROLOGUE

LOOKING BACK NOW AT THE NIGHT OF OLIVIA Richmond's birthday party, my original expectations for the night were so innocent, they were pitiable. It was the second week of our junior year of high school, a week before the Fall Fling, and the most pressing issue on my mind was whether or not a cute boy would ask me to go to the dance.

Violet had suggested that we play a game, and it seemed so simple. There were no rules to learn, no cards to deal, no need to split into teams.

She hadn't mentioned that in her game, she was always the winner.

Or that playing could cost you your life.

CHAPTER 1

U M, HELLO. YOU DID *NOT* MENTION THAT HENRY would be home this weekend," Candace said, interrupting Olivia's sidewalk monologue about her pursuit of the perfect dress for the Fall Fling. The search had begun over the summer. Olivia could picture it in her head, and after having heard her detailed description twice during our after-school trip to the mall, we could all picture it in vivid detail too. The dream dress was the color of vanilla buttercream frosting, not so yellow as to be summery, less formal than a homecoming gown, and not so white as to be bridelike. Ecru would do, or eggshell, or any pale variation on white that would show off Olivia's glamorous tan, obtained by rowing each morning at summer camp in Canada. Even my daily runs in Florida beneath the blazing sun hadn't rewarded me with a tan as dark as Olivia's.

We were walking to the Richmonds' house from the bus stop a few blocks away. Our plan was to sleep over at Olivia's house that night to celebrate her birthday, and the straps of my overnight bag, which I'd carried with me to school that day and afterward to the mall, dug into my shoulder. It was the first week of September, and although I'd known Olivia, Mischa, and Candace my entire life, I'd only been hanging out with them since the beginning of the semester. There was no way I would have been invited to any of their birthday parties during our freshman or sophomore years, and I was highly aware that my admission into their group and consequential new popularity was due to the complete transformation I'd undergone over the summer. Just as I was still getting used to boys who'd never looked at me before suddenly checking me out, I was still getting to know my new circle of friends.

Olivia was the last among us to turn sixteen, but none of us had our own wheels yet that September. Mischa shared a car with her older sister, who seemed to always have custody of it. Candace's divorced parents were denying her access to wheels until she picked up her grades when report cards were released at the end of the semester, one of the few things upon which they agreed. Taking the bus home from the mall was hardly desirable, but it was less nerdish than having a parent pick up all five of us in an SUV curbside outside Nordstrom. We were in high spirits that afternoon after having slurped down sugary lattes at the mall, dropping our parents' money on earrings and paperback novels just to have purchased something to carry back to Olivia's house. Leaving the mall empty-handed felt strange and wasteful. I had bought a pair of chandelier earrings I thought might be cool for the Fall Fling, *if* any boy were to ask me within the next week.

Olivia looked down the block toward her house, where Candace's eyes had spotted Henry's blue pickup truck in the driveway. Olivia's angelic button nose wrinkled, and she put one hand on her hip as if objecting to her older brother's presence within the three-story house. "Ugh. I didn't know *he'd* be here," Olivia replied.

"Who's Henry?"

Violet Simmons was new in town. Only a girl who had moved to Willow over the summer could be ignorant of Henry Richmond's identity.

"My *brother*," Olivia informed her with disgust.

"Her *totally hot* brother," Candace added. Candace had a big chest and a loud mouth. Her last name was Cotton, which was abundant reason for every kid in class to crack up whenever a substitute teacher read roll call in homeroom and announced her name as *Cotton, Candy*. She wasn't as pretty as Olivia, but from a distance if you kind of squinted at her when the sun was shining in just the right way, you might believe it if she told you she was a runway model. During my two weeks as an inductee into Olivia's popular circle, I had been endlessly amused by Candace's gravel-voiced musings and observations. Candace suspected that Mr. Tyrrell, the biology teacher, was probably a good kisser. She had been suspended from school for three days at the tail end of our sophomore year, back when I was still the old version of McKenna, for getting caught by Coach Highland under the bleachers during gym class with Isaac Johnston. Candace said exactly what she thought, and even though she was hilarious, I was a little terrified of her. It was likely that Candace thought about nothing but fooling around with boys, every second of every day.

"You are so gross, Candace." Olivia rolled her eyes.

But Candace wasn't alone in thinking Henry was hot. I'd had a crush on Henry Richmond since just about the second grade, way back when it was still the custom in our small town to invite every kid in your elementary school class to your birthday party.

Henry was two years older than Olivia and had just started college at Northwestern. He was majoring in sociology with the goal of getting into law school after undergrad. I only knew all this because I had practically committed every single photograph and mention of him in my yearbook to memory. Last year, it was likely that Henry had never even noticed me any of the times our paths had crossed in the hallway at school, when he was a graduating senior, already accepted at Northwestern with a generous scholarship, and I was an unremarkable sophomore. It was just as likely that if he *had* noticed me, he never would have remembered me as a chubby-cheeked second grader sitting at his parents' dining room table, singing "Happy Birthday" in the dark to Olivia when she turned eight.

"I think it's sweet! He came home for your birthday," Mischa said. Mischa was the complete physical opposite of Candace. Mischa was petite and nimble, the school's star gymnast, with perfectly straight, thick brown hair that hung down her back to her waist, heavy and glossy. She was sharp-tongued and chose her words carefully, but in our two weeks of fast friendship I had gotten the distinct feeling that there was always a storm of thought going on behind her eyes.

"He did *not* come home for my birthday," Olivia corrected Mischa. "He's probably home because of his stupid foot."

Henry had been on the school's tennis team, bringing Willow High School its only state title in tennis in over twenty years. He had played most of his senior-year season on a stress fracture in his fifth metatarsal, and only after he won the championship in Madison did he go to the doctor and start hobbling around the high school in a soft cast. At graduation, he crossed the stage on crutches and

Principal Nylander slapped him proudly on the back. I only knew this because I'd been at graduation, even as a lowly tenth grader, as part of the color guard team. I'd held my huge white flag throughout the entire commencement exercise in the hot June sun, watching Henry Richmond, a little in awe of his height, his auburn hair, his twinkling green eyes.

I would be lying if I said I wasn't pretty excited about Henry's presence in the Richmond household the night of Olivia's slumber party. As we approached the house, where we'd be setting up camp in Olivia's carpeted basement for the night, my heart actually began to *flutter* at the prospect of catching a glimpse of Henry. Of having a chance to peek into his bedroom.

As we marched across the Richmonds' front lawn, all carrying our shopping bags from our mall excursion in addition to our backpacks, the glass storm door of the house opened and Henry stepped out onto the Richmonds' front porch.

"Well, look who's finally home! It's the birthday girl," Henry called out to us. The keys to his truck dangled from his index finger.

"Why are you back, nerd?" Olivia asked him, thwacking him with the backpack she pulled off her shoulder. He deflected it expertly, accustomed to their lifetime together of play fights.

"I wouldn't have missed your little princess party for the world," Henry teased, looking us over. I felt color and heat rising in my cheeks under his gaze as he reviewed us, a collection of the prettiest sixteen-year-old girls Willow High School had to offer. Surely he knew Candace and Mischa from their years of friendship with Olivia. He was probably, at that very moment, realizing that one familiar face was missing from his sister's gaggle of giggling friends:

Emily Morris, the redhead with the big pout, had moved to Chicago over the summer.

"Yeah, right." Olivia smirked. "So, where's my present?"

"My *presence* is your present," Henry joked. "And besides, your birthday is *tomorrow*. So even if I *had* brought you back something really cool from campus, you'd have to wait until the morning to find out."

I thought about the silver earrings in the shape of ribbons that I had brought with me, wrapped and tucked away in my backpack to give to Olivia in the morning as a gift. I'd spent the majority of the money I'd gotten from my grandparents and relatives for my own birthday on them.

"Meanie." Olivia replied.

"Henry, you already know Mischa and Candace. This is Violet, and McKenna," Olivia said, nodding her head at each of us as she made our introductions.

"McKenna," Henry said, repeating my name, looking me over from head to toe with those green, *green* eyes. In the months that had passed since Henry had graduated and school had let out in the spring, I'd gone to Florida to stay with my dad and his wife, Rhonda, who was a registered nurse. She had helped me lose the twenty pounds of baby fat that had kept me shopping at plus-size stores throughout junior high and the first two years of high school. When I'd returned home to Wisconsin, my mother had studied my new appearance and had finally relented about the cost of contact lenses. I was glasses-free for the first time since the third grade, when it had been determined that I was nearsighted. According to Olivia, I was practically unrecognizable. Her opinion probably should have offended me, but because I knew she thought I looked amazing, I was flattered by it.

"I remember you. You live over on Martha Road, right?"

This sudden attention from him was enough to make me stutter and stammer. If I had known when Olivia first asked me to spend the night at her house that Henry would be there, I might have chickened out entirely and made up an excuse about needing to go out of town with my mom.

"Yeah," I managed to reply. The fact that he knew which street I lived on probably shouldn't have surprised me; the year that I was eight, *everyone* knew where we lived. Everyone used to drive past. But I guess I was surprised that he still remembered, even after so many years.

"Cool," Henry said, nodding without smiling. There was a moment of awkward silence, when I feared that all of us except Violet were thinking the same thing. It was the reason Henry might have remembered me since childhood, something no one in town spoke of often, and something I preferred not to think about much. Thankfully, no one said a word.

You're McKenna Brady, that girl . . .

"I have Packers tickets for tomorrow," Henry announced, breaking the silence. "Me and Dad are going to the game after my radiology appointment."

"I *knew* it," Olivia said to all of us. "See? He's getting X-rays. He doesn't even care that it's my Sweet Sixteen."

"I can't help it if football season happens to start on my little sister's birthday," Henry teased. "Now, if you'll excuse me, Mom dispatched me to run some errands in town."

It was almost six o'clock on a Friday night, the early September summer sky a lazy shade of periwinkle. The weather was still aggravatingly warm, a dry kind of warm that made it impossible for me to focus in class because my brain was convinced that it was still summer break. It was warm enough that Olivia had instructed all of us to bring bathing suits to her party just in case we felt like jumping in the pool before dinner. I wondered if that was still on her mind—that dip in the pool—because although I had worn my new bathing suit a few times in Florida while down at my dad's condo, I had never worn it yet around people who I actually knew in Willow. The thought of debuting it in front of Henry thrilled me, and made my heart beat dangerously fast. My weight loss was recent enough that I still kind of couldn't believe my own eyes when I looked in the mirror. It always kind of felt like at any given moment, the pounds could just appear back on my frame unexpectedly. The Richmonds were wealthy, or at least financially comfortable to the extent that I was pretty sure Olivia's mom didn't clip coupons out of the Sunday paper for dishwashing liquid and frozen low-cal dinners like my mom did. It was safe to assume that there would be a cute economy car with a bow on it in the Richmonds' driveway waiting for Olivia in the morning. I found myself fighting a sudden surge of jealousy. I'd turned sixteen in July, and I'd known with certainty even months before my own Sweet Sixteen that there would be no car provided to me by my parents.

As the engine of Henry's pickup revved behind us, Candace muttered, "When it's *my* birthday, can your brother be my present?"

* * *

An hour later, as we all floated in the pool and conversation had once again returned to the upcoming dance, I watched distractedly as dark, angry storm clouds rolled in from the south. I was lingering in the deep end of the pool, treading water, keeping one hand on a pink floating lounger and one eye on the glass sliding door that led to the Richmonds' living room. My friendship with Olivia was too fresh for me to ask for any information about her brother, and I was too insecure in my own new attractiveness to think I might stand any kind of shot with him. For all I knew, Henry had resurrected his high school relationship with Michelle Kimball, the girl he had dated throughout his junior and senior years. I had heard they'd broken up at the start of the summer, knowing they'd be going to separate colleges in the fall. Michelle was good friends with Amanda, Mischa's older sister, so I assumed it was best to keep my interest in Henry suppressed.

"We're going to Bobby's after the dance, definitely," Mischa was saying, drawing my attention back to the girls in the pool and away from the possibility of the door sliding open and Henry stepping out onto the patio. "Amanda and Brian are driving me and Matt. Is Pete going to have wheels?"

Violet perked up at the mention of Pete's name. I doubted that anyone at school had clued her in yet to the fact that Olivia and Pete were practically an institution. They'd been into each other since fourth grade. If there was any guy in all of Willow who was definitely off-limits, he was the one. Violet must have figured out by the night of the party that being befriended by Olivia was the equivalent of winning the social lottery. Showing interest in Pete or challenging Olivia's status would have just been foolish. Our town was so small that it wasn't as if there were many other girls who would want to hang with you if you had Olivia, Candace, or Mischa as an enemy.

Mischa was extremely fortunate in that Amanda was a senior who happened to be dating the captain of the varsity football team. Even though Amanda was always putting their shared car to use, Mischa never had to walk to school or ride the bus because Amanda drove her everywhere. Amanda's own popularity had poured the foundation for Mischa to follow in her footsteps. Amanda had been the captain of the junior varsity cheerleading team and that year was the captain of the varsity team, as nimble and athletic as her younger sister.

"That's the plan," Olivia mused lazily, watching her own long, platinum-blonde hair fan out in the water. Pete was a junior, like us, and had just turned sixteen and gotten his license. His parents had bought him a black Infiniti, and he rolled into the parking lot every morning at school like a king. Bobby's was the one and only twenty-four-hour diner in town, the place where cool high school kids congregated after school and football games. Even the McDonald's and KFC in Willow closed at ten o'clock at night. Before junior year, I had never had the nerve to step into Bobby's other than on a weekend morning with my mom for breakfast.

"So, what's the plan? Should we drive together? My stepdad is going to freak if I tell him I'm driving with Isaac alone," Candace said. She was sprawled on her back on the other floating chaise lounge, one that was an aquamarine shade of transparent blue, letting her arms drift across the surface of the water. Candace, for all her boy craziness, sort of had a boyfriend. Isaac, the guy who had been partially responsible for her sophomore-year suspension, was a senior that year. He played defense on the football team and was a big guy with a booming laugh. I would have liked him immensely if it weren't for the fact that as recently as five months earlier he had teased me callously about being a "dog" and a "cow." So far, during my junior year, he hadn't dared to utter a single insult at me. That was the power of being pretty, I was finding: not having to constantly dread childish insults being lobbed at me. Isaac wasn't very bright, which seemed to bother Candace, even though she wasn't exactly being invited to join National Honor Society either.

"Well, we have to figure out what these two nerds are going to do," Olivia said, nodding at me and then at Violet.

Violet and I exchanged glances across the length of the pool, both momentarily hating each other. Neither of us had a boyfriend, or any solid prospective dates for the dance. Because my attractiveness was so new, boys who had known me since kindergarten weren't sure what to do with it just yet. To them, I was still McKenna Brady, the smart girl, the girl liked by parents and teachers, the girl with glasses and braces who had lived through that thing back in third grade. I could have no way of knowing if any of them were ever going to work up the nerve to be the first boy to acknowledge that I'd changed by asking me out, even though I was all too aware of their eyes on me in the hallways at school. I could have taken matters into my own hands and asked Dan Marshall, a somewhat friendly junior whose locker was next to mine, or Paul Freeman, who had offered me his algebra notes when I'd been out sick for a week at the end of sophomore year. But asking either of them to be my date would be like an admission of defeat.

Violet was a source of intrigue throughout the high school. While it was not uncommon for people to move away from town, like Emily, and disappear from the world of Willow forever—despite earnest promises to write letters and send e-mails—it was a rarity for anyone new to appear in the student body. Willow just hadn't been the kind of town to attract new residents for at least a decade. It was far enough away from Green Bay that commuting was almost an hour-long drive for parents who had jobs there. For a long while in the eighties and nineties, there was a pretty big tourism business geared toward the nature lovers who wanted even more autumn leaves and clean air than were offered by Wisconsin Dells to the south of us, or by Door County, to our east. But there was no real reason for anyone to *move* to Willow. There was no major corporation offering high-paying jobs anywhere nearby. There wasn't any big scientific research laboratory attracting the families of high-profile scientists. The beach along Lake Winnebago was rocky and surrounded by woods, not anything at all like the white sandy beaches in Tampa, near my dad's place. However, I guess one could make the argument that Willow was a decent place to live if you were really into boating culture and happened to live in Wisconsin.

So the fact that Violet was new in town was enough to make her an instant celebrity at Willow High School. The fact that she was also gorgeous only added to her fame. Violet had a heart-shaped face with very wide-set crystal-blue eyes, which looked eerily iridescent because the brown hair framing her face was so dark.

She was porcelain pale in a town where every other girl made a point of showing off her summer's worth of tanning efforts in September, pushing the limits of the high school dress code with short shorts and tank tops to expose as much bronzed flesh as possible. Even two weeks into the school year, none of us knew her very well. She kept to herself and refrained from gossip, most likely because she didn't know anyone at school well enough yet to contribute. She was a hair twirler, a lip biter, and seemingly a daydreamer, drifting off into her own thoughts often at lunchtime until she heard her name called as a command to rejoin the conversation. Everything about her was a little girlish and romantic, right down to the tiny but chic antique locket she wore around her neck.

And the fact that she was new in town meant that boys refrained from approaching her, just like they shied away from me.

"You should ask Jason," Mischa told me when she surfaced from her underwater bolt across the pool. "He told Matt he thinks you're hot. He'd totally say yes."

The Fall Fling, and absolutely every detail related to it, was terrifying to me. I had never danced in public before, other than at my cousin's wedding. Feeling pressured to find a date by a deadline, or else, was also a first for me. In this case, I wasn't even sure what the *else* might entail if no one asked me to the dance. Olivia's wrath? Banishment from the popular group? There was no way of knowing. There was only an increasing despair rising in my chest that the night of the dance would arrive, and I'd still be dateless. There was already a lavender cocktail-length strapless gown hanging despondently in my closet. I wouldn't wear it to the dance the following Saturday night, but I had no way of knowing that in Olivia's pool the night of her party.

"If he thinks I'm hot, then why doesn't he just ask me? I don't like the idea of doing the asking," I grumbled.

"Oh, come *on*, McKenna! It's not the Middle Ages. You can ask a boy out," Candace scolded me. "You don't even have to ask him outright. Just linger around his locker and ask him if he's going to the dance and if he's asked anyone yet. He'll get the picture. Boys just need to be pointed in the right direction."

"That's not very romantic," I said. Why couldn't my life be just like Olivia's and Candace's, with boys approaching *me?* The fear of being rebuffed and maybe additionally even insulted was something neither of them had ever experienced.

"What about Trey Emory for Violet?" Mischa suggested. Olivia squealed.

I felt a chill run up my spine and sensed dread filling my stomach. Trey Emory was a senior who might as well have been from another planet. He didn't play on any sports teams, didn't go to football games, and mostly kept to himself, other than his occasional outings with the skateboarder guys who often ditched classes to smoke cigarettes near the service entrance of the school cafeteria. He smoldered of danger and mystery; he had an actual *tattoo*. Teachers despised him. Even though he'd been placed in remedial classes most of his life, he had won a statewide high school bridge building competition and was taking Advanced Physics.

And he just happened to live next door to me.

There was no particular reason why any of my new friends would have known where the Emory family lived, or that every once in a great while, Trey and I would exchange solemn waves from our bedroom windows if we'd just happened to catch a glimpse of each other before closing our blinds at night. Once, toward the end of sophomore year, when I was still the old, unpopular McKenna, we stepped out of our houses in unison on a morning when it was pouring rain. He hadn't even really asked me if I wanted a lift. He had just flashed his keys and then lingered in his driveway with his engine idling until I worked up the nerve to dash through the sheets of rain and climb into the passenger side of his crappy, banged-up Toyota Corolla. We had ridden together all the way to school in silence after I awkwardly managed a "thanks" as we'd pulled out of his driveway.

"Oh my God, *totally!*" Candace agreed. "He's a freak but a *hot* freak."

"Who's Trey Emory?" Violet asked innocently.

"You *know* who he is," Olivia taunted. "He's that smoking-hot senior guy with the dark hair who wears the green army jacket every day."

"*That* guy? He gives me the creeps," Violet complained, leaning back in the water to soak her hair again.

Trey and I were kind of friends in some very strange and abstract way, but I dared not leap to his defense. I had a suspicion that an admission of our acquaintance would not be well received.

"Yeah, so? I still wonder what's under that army jacket," Candace continued. She really was incorrigible.

One of Violet's slim, lily-white legs kicked up, breaking the surface of the water and creating a little ripple that spread out in a circle around her, drifting toward the rest of us. "Whatever he's got under there, I don't want it coming with me to the dance."

It bothered me a little that Mischa had suggested Trey as a potential boyfriend for Violet rather than for me, and I was a little relieved that Violet had dismissed the idea. It was probably because I'd known him for so long that I felt a little possessive about him, even though he'd never given me any reason to believe he was into me.

* * *

Hours later, after pizzas brought home by Henry and an ice cream cake served up by Olivia's parents with a cheesy group performance of "Happy Birthday," all five of us occupied the Richmonds' basement in our pajamas.

"Yawn," Candace declared as we flipped through Netflix options.

It was barely eleven o'clock on a Friday night and we were already out of fresh gossip, Fall Fling chat, and songs to which we could emulate moves from music videos. On the last two Friday nights at that hour, the five of us had been tumbling out of movie theaters, giggling and squeamish after watching horror movies.

"What about *Blood Harvest*?" Mischa suggested. Mischa was the one who especially loved scary flicks. . . . She loved being terrified out of her wits.

"Bring it," Olivia commanded from her blanket nest on the couch. One of her deeply tanned legs poked out from beneath the striped wool blanket she had spread across her body. The warm summer evening had turned into a chilly autumn night, and Mr. Richmond had come downstairs with us after pizza to light a fire in the fireplace. I sat on the floor near the sofa, as far from the fireplace as I could get, paranoid about flames, as always.

"I love Ryan Marten," Candace commented during the movie's opening sequence, during which Ryan Marten, a Hollywood heartthrob portraying a vampire, arrived at a farming community with his loyal clan just as the town was preparing for its annual carnival.

Candace reached into the bag of mini pretzels that Mischa passed to her and popped a handful into her mouth. "I can't imagine any guy as hot as Ryan Marten ever coming to this sad-ass town."

"Hey! Pete's as hot as Ryan Marten," Olivia objected.

Candace dramatically rolled her eyes at Olivia across the couch. "Yeah, whatevs. Sure he is."

I smiled nervously up at both of them, not daring to comment. In my own opinion, Pete Nicholson *was* every bit as hot and sexy as Ryan Marten, and just as untouchable as the famous action star too. Pete looked like an Olympic sprinter or something. He was so tall, his facial features were so perfect; he seemed entirely out of place in our town. In Willow, most guys were built like linebackers and were preparing for futures in which they would take over the failing family farms from their dads. Mischa's boyfriend, Matt, was cute, but he was as tiny and compact as she was, herself. He wore baseball caps backward and threw gang signs like a rap star, even though the closest thing to a gang he belonged to was the wrestling team. Candace's on-again, off-again boyfriend, Isaac, had a square jaw and probably would have been considered to be good-looking at any American high school, but it was easy to envision the kind of soft-gutted, sunburned farmhand he would be in as few as ten years. There were a lot of men in our town who looked just like Isaac someday would, with faces prematurely wrinkled from long days on a tractor in the hot sun, and dirt beneath their fingernails even at fancy restaurant dinners on Sundays.

Violet was looking down at her hands in her lap. She had rarely mentioned boys or contributed to conversations when boys were the topic in the two weeks since she had entered our world. I wondered if maybe she had decided that the only boy Willow had to offer worth her interest was Pete.

"Were there a lot more cute guys in your old town?" I asked her suddenly, realizing I couldn't even remember where it was she had told us she had lived before.

"Sure," Violet replied. "I mean, not *so* many. But my last school had three thousand students, so you know, it's just simple math that out of fifteen hundred boys, there would be more than one or two cute ones."

Three thousand students. Our high school had barely three *hundred* students. There were fewer than eighty kids in each class, with the most in the senior class and the fewest in the freshman class. "Fifteen hundred boys," Candace repeated dreamily. "I can't even imagine so many boys under one roof."

"Where are you from, again?" Olivia asked Violet.

"Lake Forest," Violet said. "Outside Chicago."

I'd only been to Chicago once. My mom had gone to college there, long before she'd met my dad when they taught together at the University of Wisconsin–Sheboygan. She'd been a graduate student teaching Introduction to the World of Natural Science as a requirement for earning her master's degree in biology, way back when she still wanted to be a veterinarian. He'd been an established psychiatry professor, ten years her senior, already having an established taste for girls younger than him. My poor mom wouldn't realize until she was no longer a young girl that his preference wouldn't change. I felt a pang of guilt suddenly for leaving my mom home alone on a Friday. Before I became popular, Friday nights were when we watched all our favorite British sitcoms together until our faces hurt from laughing. She was probably relieved to have some time to herself, but I still felt uneasy about it. I felt a little sorry for myself, because I was the only girl in the basement who felt the burden of her mother's loneliness like a weight pressing down on my chest.

"God," Olivia muttered. "I can't wait to get out of this place and live in a real city."

We all lost interest in the movie quickly, none of us particularly caring about the plight of the citizens in the town being invaded by vampires since all we wanted was for Ryan Marten to have more screen time. I was starting to get a little sleepy, but I knew very well what happens to the first girl who falls asleep at slumber parties. I stood and stretched, and excused myself to go upstairs to use the bathroom. "Me too," Candace announced, and followed me up the stairs leading to the kitchen.

"One of you can use my bathroom on the second floor," Olivia called after us.

We reached the top of the stairs and I suddenly felt strange—like a burglar—in the Richmonds' house. I could hear a television on upstairs. The ice cream cake had already been cleaned up by Mrs. Richmond, and the kitchen was quiet other than the buzzing of the stainless steel fridge.

"Olivia's room is to the right at the top of the stairs," Candace told me as she stepped into the bathroom off the kitchen and flipped on the light.

I remembered the approximate layout of the Richmonds' house from when I'd played there as a little kid. As I walked down the hallway toward the front of the house, where I could ascend the staircase that led up to the house's second floor, I stopped to peek through the front windows at the driveway, where it looked like a red Toyota had been parked next to Henry's truck. The Toyota had a big pink bow on it. I immediately looked away, feeling guilty about having spotted Olivia's grand birthday present before she did.

On the way up the stairs, I heard a door open on the second floor, and music leaked into the hallway. Suddenly, Henry was at the top of the stairs, smiling at me. We crossed paths in the middle of the staircase, and he was carrying a plastic cup in his left hand, presumably on his way down to the kitchen for a refill of whatever he'd been drinking.

"Hey," he said.

"Hi," I replied, realizing in a hot panic that I was wearing very, *very* short red shorts and a tank top as pajamas that I hadn't really intended to model for any boys when I'd stuffed them into my backpack earlier that morning in preparation for the slumber party.

"You shouldn't sweat the Fall Fling so much," he said.

"What do you mean?" I asked, blushing furiously, hoping he had not overheard our discussion in the pool.

"It's just a dumb dance," he said, his eyes locking with mine intently. "Just a bunch of idiots clapping their hands to bad music. It's not the end of the world if you don't go."

"Well, that's a relief, because I don't think I'm going to go," I said, only aware as the words left my mouth of how true they were.

"I mean, you *could* go," Henry backtracked, studying my face. "I mean, I *might* happen to be back in town next weekend for my last radiology appointment. It would be kind of fun to be back in the high school gymnasium one more time. It would also be kind of fun to spy on my sister and ruin her big night of romance. *If* the only thing keeping you from going is not having a date, that is."

My heart was beating awfully fast. I felt like I might have been starting to perspire under his gaze.

"Are you, like . . . asking me to the dance?" I asked with a confused smile, desperate to not be making a pathetic, wrong assumption. If I did, and if Henry told Olivia that I'd jumped to a silly, hopeful conclusion about him asking me out on a date, I would *die* of embarrassment.

"I guess I am," Henry said. "I mean, if that's allowed. I guess since I'm not technically a student at Willow anymore, you'd have to ask *me*."

"Uh, okay," I said, having a hard time believing that this was actually happening. That Henry Richmond was actually *asking me*—me—*out*. "Olivia might get kind of mad, though. You know, about you being there, as you said, to ruin her big night."

Henry smiled his killer megawatt smile. "Come on, McKenna. She'll get over it. It'll be fun. I know my sister pretty well, and I think she'd rather have you come to the dance with me than not go at all. So, what do you say?"

"Yes, okay. That would be awesome." I couldn't help but grin so hard my cheeks hurt. "You can get my number from Olivia to, like, make plans."

I danced across Olivia's dark bedroom, taking care not to step on any of the discarded clothing or shoes littering her floor on my way to the adjoining bathroom. It might have been the happiest moment of my whole teenage life, being asked to the Fall Fling by a *college guy*, way, way cuter than any of the guys who still went to Willow High School. I smiled at my own reflection in the mirror over Olivia's bathroom sink. My nose was peeling a little bit from my fading tan, and my hair was wavy from having air-dried after the quick shower I'd taken before dinner. I was going to have to remember to thank Rhonda for the millionth time for making so many salads for me over the summer, and for dragging me with her to Pilates.

As I washed my hands, I wondered if Trey Emory would be going to the dance. The mere thought was so ridiculous that I rolled my eyes in the mirror. Trey would not wear a polyester suit and dare to show his face in the high school gymnasium, or do the step-and-clap dance beneath red and black streamers. Dances were not something a guy like him would be into, which made it all the more preposterous that Mischa had urged Violet to consider going with him. It would just never happen. But I wondered what he'd think if he heard I was going with Henry Richmond. It was possible he wouldn't care at all.

Back in the basement, the movie was ending, and Candace was turning off the lamps on both sides of the couch to make the setting spookier for ghost stories.

"You first, Mischa," Olivia insisted. "Mischa tells the best ghost stories," she informed Violet.

Mischa's eyes began glowing with enthusiasm. "Okay . . . What about Bloody Heather?"

"Oh, man," Candace whined. "You always tell that one. I've heard it, like, a million times."

"Yeah, but Violet's never heard it," Olivia said.

I had a vague idea of the story they were talking about, but I couldn't recall ever having heard it in detail either. Ghost stories were one of the many things that kids who had older siblings heard before everyone else. Important information about dating was another one of those things. I didn't have older siblings, and my only older cousin, Krista, had moved away from Willow with Aunt JoAnne and Uncle Marty when I was in seventh grade.

"Okay, okay," Candace relented. "But tell the abridged version. If you tell the whole thing, it'll take all night."

I wasn't in the mood to hear a ghost story; I was still so excited about my exchange with Henry upstairs that I could barely sit still. It had already crossed my mind that despite what Henry had said, Olivia was going to be furious if he actually came to the dance as my date. Mischa might be upset too, if there was a possibility that her older sister might assume I was trying to push Henry's ex-girlfriend further out of the picture. One trip upstairs to the bathroom had complicated my night infinitely, I was realizing as the initial rush of excitement passed.

Mischa dropped her voice mischievously to a low whisper as she began excitedly telling the story. "There's a stretch of Route Thirty-Two that passes the St. Augustine Cemetery. It's way out past the airport, and my family used to pass it every summer on our drive up to our summer home near Lake Superior—"

"What ever happened to that summer house? We should totally go up there over Christmas break," Candace interrupted.

"My uncle Roger lives there now. Stop interrupting," Mischa scolded. "Anyway. So a couple miles before the cemetery, there's this little bar called Sven's. It's just a crappy little sports bar, you know the kind, with fluorescent beer signs in the windows. So, my mom's boss goes in there one night after work last winter to watch the Packers game. Has a couple beers, probably shouldn't drive home but figures it's okay because he doesn't feel drunk and everyone in the bar keeps saying a blizzard's on the way. It's December, and already dark out, and the roads are empty because of the weather forecast and also because it's just farms in every direction up there."

We were all listening carefully, leaning in to be able to hear Mischa better. The television was still on, but playing music videos on mute.

"So he's driving along, and snow's falling. At first, there are just a few tiny flakes that he sees in his headlights, then the flakes start getting fatter, heavier. He's so busy watching the snow, he almost doesn't even see this girl walking along the side of the highway. From the back, she looks young, you know, like our age. She's carrying her shoes in one hand. He wonders if he's seeing things. The snow's getting heavier, and this girl isn't wearing a coat, so he thinks maybe she's in some kind of trouble and just needs a ride home. So he lowers his window and asks if she needs a lift."

"The girl gets into the back seat of the car and pushes all his flyers over to the other side of the seat. My mom is a real estate broker," Mischa explained for Violet's information, not realizing that I'd also never heard her tell this story before and benefited from the explanation. "So, her boss's car had all these open-house flyers in the back seat. He really wants to know why this girl is wandering outside in a snowstorm, so he checks her out in the rearview mirror. He said she was pretty, and she wasn't shivering at all even though she was just wearing a sweater. There were snowflakes stuck to her eyelashes, and she didn't even seem to notice."

Mischa's lips began to hint at a smile; I could tell she was enjoying how tense we were all becoming, hanging on her every word. She began slipping in between the present and past tenses in her haste to push the entire story through her mouth, telling the story as if it had just occurred days ago.

"He asked her where he could drop her off, and she gave him some street address and some directions on how to get there. He pulled up in front of the house that matched the address she gave him, then looked in the rearview mirror again and almost had a heart attack. Because this time her whole face is bloody. Like her nose is bleeding, her eyes are bleeding, there's blood gushing out of her mouth—"

"Ew!" Olivia shrieked, even though she'd heard Mischa tell this story before.

Mischa continued. "He swerved his car and it went off the road into a ditch. And when he checked to see if the girl was okay, she was gone. He got out of the car to see if maybe somehow she'd jumped out of the back seat. But she was nowhere. It was like she'd never existed at all." She paused for dramatic effect, her eyes sparkling. "Except all those flyers in the back seat of his car were drenched with blood."

"Wow," Violet said solemnly, believing every word of it.

"He got his car out of the ditch, drove all the way back into town in the blizzard and went straight to the police station."

"This is the best part," Candace informed us.

"So he stumbled into the police station, heart pounding, sweat just, like, pouring off his forehead because he was terrified that he was going to look into his rearview mirror and see her back there, bleeding all over the place again. He ran up to the cop at the front desk and was like, *The craziest thing just happened. I saw this girl walking along the side of the road. I asked her if she needed a ride*, and the policeman just looked at him, and was like, *And then you looked in your rearview mirror, and she was gone.*"

I got a chill. It was a dumb story, but Mischa was doing an admirable job of making it scary.

"And my mom's boss was like, *Yeah! How did you know?* And how freaky is this? The cop was like, *We get people in here every winter, saying the exact same thing.* It turns out, a real girl had been hit by a car while she was walking home from Sven's during a snowstorm *forty years ago.* Whoever hit her just left her on the street to die in the snow. So, the legend of Bloody Heather is, the ghost of this girl only appears to people leaving Sven's, driving home past the cemetery when it's snowing. It's only men who see her."

"Good job," Olivia commended Mischa. "What about the story of the six white horses?"

"God, no!" Candace protested. "That story is soooo long."

Violet sat upright on the floor and folded her hands in her lap. Calmly, in a quiet voice with one eyebrow arched, she asked, "What about Light as a Feather, Stiff as a Board? Have you guys ever played that?"

Olivia rolled her eyes. "Geez, not since middle school."

"I don't like that." Candace shook her head. "I don't like the idea of messing with spirits. Too scary."

"It's not spirits," I interjected. "It's group hypnosis. My dad has written papers on this. That's why it works better for younger kids than for older people. The chanting hypnotizes everyone playing the game." The game involved one participant making up an elaborate story about the future death of another participant, who would stretch out on the floor. All the other players would kneel around the girl lying down, sliding their fingertips underneath her body. At the end of the story, which was usually either remarkably gory or silly enough to inspire giggling, everyone but the girl lying down would chant, *light as a feather, stiff as a board*, while raising the reclining girl toward the ceiling using nothing but the slightest bit of pressure from their fingertips. I could never figure out exactly how it worked, because during my own childhood, the handful of times when I'd played the game and the hypnosis had been successful, the body had been raised effortlessly over everyone's heads. Inevitably, the state of hypnosis would be interrupted by one of the players, ruining the effect for everyone, and the body of the unfortunate girl who had been lifted into the air would crash down to the floor.

"I don't believe that at all," Candace told me, making me feel kind of like an idiot for having spoken up. "Something weird happens during that game. It's scary as hell when it works."

Violet smiled and shrugged. "It was just a suggestion."

"Let's play!" Mischa insisted, pulling a pillow off the couch. "I want to be the storyteller first."

Olivia's phone buzzed with a new text message. "It's Pete," she announced. "It's midnight. He wanted to be the first one to wish me a happy birthday. Isn't that sweet?"

We all agreed that it was quite sweet, and Mischa decided that Olivia would be the first subject in our game. I had a queasy feeling about participating even though I knew in my head what my father had told me was true. There was nothing occult or mystical about this game. But for me, making up stories about death scenarios didn't feel right. Death had already visited my home in my lifetime, and I didn't like the idea of tempting it, even just for the sake of a game.

Olivia lay on her back with her head balanced on the pillow that rested upon Mischa's knees. I knelt along Olivia's right side, facing

Violet, who positioned herself along her left side. Candace dropped to her knees at Olivia's feet, tickling them lightly to make Olivia kick and squirm before Mischa got started. Olivia accidentally kicked a little too high and knocked Candace in the chin.

"Ow!" Candace wailed.

"No tickling!" Olivia bellowed.

"Quiet, everyone!" Mischa commanded with authority. "Everyone must be very serious for this to work! I mean it."

Without exchanging any words, we all agreed to settle down. Mischa waited until the only noise in the basement was the crackling of the fire. We could distantly hear the talk show being watched upstairs by Olivia's parents two floors above us, the fuzzy applause of its audience. Mischa placed her fingertips on Olivia's temples and began concentrating on a wholly original description of Olivia's future death, which was how the game went.

"It was the night before the Fall Fling," Mischa began in her scariest storyteller voice.

"Not the night before *the dance*," Olivia complained. "Can't I at least die the night *after* the dance so I have a chance to fool around with Pete one last time before I die?"

Candace smirked. "You've already fooled around with Pete plenty."

Violet and I blushed. The full details of how much Olivia and Pete had fooled around so far hadn't really been disclosed to either of us yet. We were juniors in high school; naturally we were curious about who among us had gone *all the way*. I had barely gone any part of the way, except for a few chaste kisses I'd exchanged over the summer with a guy named Rob who lived in the same condominium community as my dad and Rhonda. I didn't know anything about Violet's history with boys, but she looked as uncomfortable as I felt.

"Quiet!" Mischa ordered. "I'm the storyteller, and I decide! Okay, fine. It was the night after the Fall Fling. Olivia Richmond had been grounded by her parents for staying out way past her extended curfew the night of the dance, having innocently fallen asleep in the big field behind the high school track beneath the stars with Pete. No matter how many times Olivia insisted to her parents that she was only guilty of being sleepy, they wouldn't believe her, because they knew their daughter and her boyfriend were total horndogs who couldn't keep their hands off each other."

"You're gross," Olivia said without opening her eyes.

"The problem with being grounded," Mischa continued, "was that Pete had told Olivia he wanted to show her something very special that night, the night after the dance. So Olivia waited until her parents fell asleep, and decided to sneak out of the house to meet him down by Shawano Lake."

Candace made an insinuating *ooooh* noise, earning herself a frown from Mischa.

"She got out of bed and changed out of her blue satin pajamas and into her skinny jeans and the totally amazing cashmere sweater that her best friend Mischa had given to her for her sixteenth birthday."

"Nice touch," Candace whispered off to my left.

"She raised the window of her second-floor bedroom and climbed through. But the fabric of her skinny jeans caught on a rusty nail in her window frame. She forcefully jerked her leg to try to break free, and in doing so lost her grip on the drainpipe and fell forward.

Her pants tore, and she tumbled to the ground, breaking her neck in the fall. However, she did not die instantly. She writhed in pain, struggling to breathe, paralyzed, until dawn. She drew her last excruciating breath as sunlight broke over the horizon.

"Two days later at the funeral home, to the horror of her friends and loved ones, Olivia's body rested in her coffin, *light as a feather, stiff as a board.*"

"Light as a feather, stiff as a board," we all chanted in unison, our expectant fingertips beneath Olivia's limbs gently pushing her heavy body upward.

"This isn't working," Candace said after about five iterations of the chant.

"I don't feel anything happening," Olivia announced. She opened her eyes and sat straight up.

"Can I try?" Violet asked, looking directly at Mischa.

"Sure," Mischa said, handing her the pillow that she'd been balancing on her knees.

Something about Violet's demeanor changed when she switched places with Mischa. For the first time since I'd met her, she seemed fully present instead of distracted by a daydream. And for the first time that night, she seemed genuinely thrilled to have been invited to the party.

CHAPTER 2

OLIVIA RICHMOND HAD EVERYTHING ANY GIRL could ever want. A beautiful house, perfectly straight blonde hair, a handsome boyfriend, and a close circle of friends. She began her junior year of high school with everything in the world going for her. She had even just received a brand-new red Prius for her Sweet Sixteen, and everyone at Willow High School knew she'd be named homecoming queen that fall."

I dared not look up to try to catch Violet's eye, but her mention of a new red Prius had caught my attention. How had she known that there was a red Toyota parked in the Richmonds' driveway at that very moment? Had she guessed?

Violet was a noticeably different kind of storyteller from Mischa. She didn't attempt to make her voice sound spooky or scary. Her voice was steady, confident, and she told her story solemnly, as if it was factual. Time seemed to slow down as she assembled the tale. I could hear the Richmonds' grandfather clock ticking at the top of the stairs, hear Candace swallow quietly, two feet away. Olivia's breathing was rhythmic but shallow, and her eyelashes fluttered as if she was dreaming. Violet's locket threw little glimmers of light

33

around the basement as the flames in the fireplace reflected off of it.

"The night before the Fall Fling, when the Willow High School football team was clear across the state claiming a victory over the team in Kenosha, Olivia was pulling together the final details for her big date with Pete. She had already found her perfect buttercream-colored dress, and a pair of earrings that would look fantastic dangling from her ears, just barely brushing her tan shoulders. But she was still missing the perfect pair of shoes to match her dress, and time was running out. She announced to her friends after school on Friday that she was going to drive to the mall in Green Bay in search of the perfect pair. After combing the mall and settling on a pair of shoes that weren't ideal, she found that the brand-new car she had received for her birthday wouldn't start in the lot. She tried and tried to start its engine, but it just stalled.

"As heavy storm clouds filled the sky, Olivia accepted a ride back to Willow with a classmate from her high school who happened to recognize her car in the mall parking lot. They began the long drive back to their small town down the wooded rural highway as Olivia's mind filled with thoughts about the upcoming dance, as well as the new complication of having to get her car towed out of the mall parking lot in the morning. The raindrops falling from the sky turned to hail, and before Olivia and the student behind the wheel even realized what was happening, they were hit head-on by a speeding truck whose driver didn't see them swerve into his lane. Olivia's ribs were shattered, her internal organs splayed out across the front seat of the wrecked car. Her right arm was severed and discovered twenty feet away from the automotive wreckage after the hailstorm. Both of her legs were crushed beneath the crumpled dashboard, pinning her into the front seat, preventing her escape even if she had remained conscious long enough to try to crawl away from the wreck. When the truck driver was able to bring his truck to a skidding halt and rushed to the car to see if either passenger had survived, he had to turn away, because Olivia had also been nearly completely decapitated. Her head dangled from her shoulders by a few cords of muscle and chunks of skin, having been knocked clean off her spine.

"Three days later, as her shocked family and the grieving town of Willow assembled for Olivia's wake, her body lay in a closed coffin, *light as a feather, stiff as a board.*"

I was in such a state of awe from the gruesome detail and calmness with which Violet had brought an end to Olivia's life with words that my mind wasn't even focused on whether or not the game would work. An odd feeling of static had fallen across the room, and out of the corner of my eye I could see that the fire in the fireplace was blazing higher and brighter than it had all night, even though an hour ago when I had gotten up to use the bathroom, the logs were already glowing red, lit from within. This unsettled me so much that I remained silent as my friends repeated after Violet, *light as a feather, stiff as a board.* As I joined them in chanting and Olivia's straight body, her mouth frozen in a frown, lifted as if it were weightless, I was genuinely frightened. An uneasiness had slipped up against me, a sensation that someone—or *something*—was patiently observing us.

"Light as a feather, stiff as a board," we chanted together slowly, ever so slowly, lifting Olivia's body with our fingertips inch by inch. I became increasingly aware of my desire for the trick to fail. *It's only a game*, I reminded myself.

We nimbly climbed from our knees and onto our feet when we

had raised Olivia to the level of our eyes. From there we continued to lift her, from the height of our hips until she was level with our shoulders, her arms crossed over her chest, her silvery blonde hair dangling toward the ground.

"Holy . . ."

It was Candace who broke the spell. We were snapped back to our senses, and before we had an opportunity to even feel the full weight of Olivia's body in our hands, she had dropped to the ground with a *thud* and was rubbing her behind good-naturedly. Relief washed over me.

"Thanks, guys!" she teased, not at all hurt in her tumble back down to the carpet.

Despite the fact that we had all played the silly game before when we were younger, and had experienced the effect firsthand, everyone but me was delighted with our small success. It was as if Violet had cast the spell on us so skillfully, so thoroughly, we hadn't even had to exert an ounce of thought toward making the chant work.

"That was amazing!" Mischa exclaimed, her entire face ignited by a smile.

Unlike my excited friends, I was troubled by everything that had just happened, from the precision of details that Violet had chosen to the ease with which we had raised Olivia off the ground. Something in the basement—something about Violet—was different. The gruesome story she'd told had been so realistic that it seemed more like she'd been recalling a memory than inventing a tale on the fly.

It was kind of like becoming aware of a tiny splinter in my finger that didn't necessarily hurt, but refused to be ignored. Since the first day of school I'd been under the impression that Violet was reserved, maybe even shy, but her turn as the storyteller in the game revealed that under the right circumstances, she could be captivating. Maybe she had just been pretending to be introverted since we'd met her, and it took her a while to warm up to people. I could understand that—I was shy around adults I didn't know well—but that still didn't explain how Violet had known about the Prius in the driveway. I couldn't grill her about that in front of Olivia and ruin her birthday surprise, but I also didn't want to play the game anymore.

"Who was the driver?" Olivia asked. "I wouldn't just accept a ride home from Green Bay with *anyone*."

"And you skipped the part about where Olivia buys her dream dress," Mischa teased Violet.

"Yeah. It would be helpful to know where I'm going to find that dress," Olivia said.

Violet blushed, her alabaster skin heating up into a deep pink. "Sorry, I'm not a fortune-teller." She looked directly at me and added, "Just making up stories here."

"Do me next!" Candace insisted, dropping down to her knees on the floor.

We reassembled our little circle, my friends eager to see if Violet could deliver the phenomenon with such conviction a second time. A warning voice in my head urged, *Don't do it again. Not another person.* However, I was a little afraid that my reluctance to participate was going to annoy the others. I'd been waiting since elementary school to be welcomed back into Olivia's circle of friends, and I wasn't about to blow it by acting babyish about a spooky game. "Okay, we all have to calm down and focus or it won't work," Violet reminded us as she adjusted Candace's head on the pillow in front of her knees on the floor.

She drummed her fingertips on Candace's temples and stared up at the ceiling, lost in thought. "Candace Cotton. What should we do with Candace Cotton?"

As soon as the story came together in her mind, the expression on her face changed. Her gaze steadied and she looked down at Candace, who dutifully closed her eyes and crossed her arms over her chest as Olivia had done. Olivia had assumed Candace's position down near the feet, and had daintily placed two of her fingers beneath Candace's heels, her palms facing the ceiling. Candace took a deep breath, preparing herself for Violet's terrible story, her chest heaving toward the ceiling as she took in air, and then sinking back toward the floor as she exhaled.

"It was October, and Candace's family was far away from Willow on a spur-of-the-moment vacation. Candace was excited to show off her new bikini at the beach, and to swim in the ocean for the first time. The waves were mild that day, so she blew off her parents' insistence that she try her luck with a surfing lesson instead to wade out into deeper water on her own. At first she stayed close to the shoreline, not venturing too far away from where her brothers were building sandcastles on the beach. The water was warm and tempting, not nearly as cold as she had been expecting, so she waded in deeper, to her hips, and remained there until she felt confident she could handle herself in the stronger currents.

"After she disappeared, her brothers told her parents that they saw her walk straight into the deeper currents, right at the waves, as if on a mission. Unafraid, as if she was daring the ocean to come and take her. They said a wave washed over her and the ocean just swallowed her whole, enveloping her in blue and carrying her away. Her body washed up three days later, two miles down the shore. Foul-smelling seaweed was tangled up in her hair. Fish had nibbled away at her eyeballs and lips."

I felt Candace twitch above my fingertips at this horrific description of her own body.

"As her devastated parents identified her decomposing body at the coroner's office, its stink was unbearable. It lay on the metal autopsy table . . . *light as a feather, stiff as a board.*"

"Light as a feather, stiff as a board," we repeated.

Unbelievably enough, Candace's body, heavier and larger than Olivia's, lifted just as easily as Olivia's had. I did not dare to look up at the other girls raising Candace with their fingertips for fear of being the one to ruin the thrill, even though my heart was racing in terror. We only got Candace about two feet off the floor before she startled and we dropped her.

"Oh my God, that was crazy!" she shrieked, throwing her hands to her face to press her own cheeks. Her eyes were glossy, watering with excitement. "I could actually feel you guys lifting me!"

All my friends were bubbling over with enthusiasm then, thrilled with our success. I was quiet and smiled in an effort to appear like I was having fun, but I was really wishing that someone would pull out a game of Twister or suggest that we do something— anything—else. Violet had become the party hero. The warm rush I'd felt surge through me during my encounter with Henry upstairs had abandoned me completely. My limbs were cold with fear, the same kind of nervous fear that overtook me when I watched horror movies. An enjoyable fear, but a sensation that I hoped wouldn't last long. Self-conscious, I wondered if I was the only one who was a little freaked out by the grotesque details that Violet was so easily able to conjure as elements of her stories. Maybe she was some kind of sociopath and we'd somehow overlooked her mental disorder over the last two weeks, distracted by her big, innocent blue eyes and long lashes.

"You're so good at this!" Mischa exclaimed.

"I'm okay," Violet admitted. Her comment sounded to me less like a humble-brag and more like she truly didn't want any of us to make a big deal of her storytelling talent.

"I've never even *been* to a beach before," Candace said, "other than at Lake Winnebago, and that doesn't even count. But it was so *real*! I could practically smell the salt water as you were telling the story."

"This is so much fun! I'm so glad you suggested doing this," Olivia gushed. Suddenly, she pointed directly at me. "Let's do McKenna next!"

"No, no," I said, holding my hands up in protest. With reluctance I had watched the others receive their stories, but I wasn't eager to hear one of my own. "That would be too weird."

"Come on, McKenna!" Candace egged me on. "You have to. We're all doing it."

Violet's not doing it, I thought to myself.

I found myself stretching out on the floor among them all, easing my head onto the upholstered couch pillow. Violet's fingertips grazed my temples, cool pressure against my head, touching me so lightly that I could barely feel her skin against my own.

"Oh," Violet said suddenly, the second her fingertips touched my temples. She sounded surprised. "This is going to be a tough one." At my feet, Candace's eyebrows shot up her forehead in alarm.

Mischa and Olivia exchanged concerned, knowing glances. "Why?" I asked, looking straight up at Violet.

"Usually when I play this game, I get a good idea as soon as I touch someone," Violet explained. "But I don't have any ideas for you. The only thing I can think of is fire, but it doesn't feel right. I mean, I can tell a story about fire if you want. But I don't know if it's going to work."

My heart began beating furiously fast and I wanted to sit up and bring an end to the stupid game right there and then. I knew it wasn't fair; Violet was new in town and couldn't possibly have known how eerie her words were. For me, the party was over. I wanted to call my mom even though it was after midnight and ask her to pick me up immediately. But I couldn't do that. I was sixteen, not a baby, and I couldn't even find the strength to sit up and relieve Violet from having to tell my story. I desperately didn't want Candace, Mischa, and Olivia to think I was too chicken to play.

"Don't tell a story about fire," Olivia said finally, with tenderness in her voice that suggested she knew how much that would terrify me. "Anything but that."

"No! Tell it!" urged Mischa. "Wouldn't that be *so scary*, if McKenna were to die just like—"

"Stop, Mischa," Candace commanded, silencing her. "That's totally messed up."

The basement was quiet for a moment as the girls' eyes locked. Without a single word uttered, I sensed Mischa back down. I looked

41

up at Violet, and flinched when I found her looking directly down at me with an expression that told me she knew *exactly* why I couldn't stand to hear about my own demise in flames. She knew about Jennie. I was certain of it, and it chilled me to the bone. I sat straight up, bolting away from her, my concern with popularity temporarily forgotten. "I don't feel like playing anymore," I announced in a shaky voice.

"It's okay," Candace assured me. "Mischa can take her turn."

"Yeah, I'll go," Mischa volunteered.

Mischa readily stretched out on the floor and gently set her head upon the pillow. I took the position at her feet, wanting to distance myself as much as possible from Violet. I was barely paying attention as Violet told the tale of Mischa's death, something about choking and turning blue.

Instead of devoting my thoughts to the story, I found myself wondering about Violet. Who was this girl, really? Was it normal to have such control over this type of game, to be able to hypnotize one's peers so casually? Had she observed more with those huge blue eyes than we had noticed since the first day of school? Did she know more about all of our lives than she was letting on?

Perhaps because of Mischa's eagerness for the game to work like a charm, we lifted her higher than anyone else, barely breathing, we were so charged up as we raised Mischa's tiny body above our shoulders, level with our eyes, and then over our heads.

It was a buzzing from Olivia's cell phone on the coffee table that broke our concentration. Luckily for Mischa, we caught her before she fell five feet to the floor.

"Wow, you were really high up there, dude," Candace informed Mischa as Olivia bolted across the basement to grab her phone.

"It's Pete!" she whispered to all of us. "He and Jeff Harrison are—"

Bam! Bam! Bam!

A loud knock on the basement storm window from the backyard made all of us jump in the air. Mischa screamed, and we immediately heard commotion on the second floor as Olivia's parents sprang into action. As soon as Olivia realized that the source of the knock was handsome Pete, squatting in her backyard with another member of the basketball team, Jeff Harrison, she erupted into giggles. Candace clutched her chest dramatically as if she were having a heart attack. I was still too rattled by the intensity of Violet's game to be amused, but I was relieved that the boys were there. Their unannounced visit meant that we were probably done playing.

We heard the door at the top of the stairs open and we all froze.

Olivia made hand motions to Pete to back away from the window. "Olivia, what's going on down there?" we heard Mr. Richmond call from the top of the stairs.

"Nothing, Dad!" Olivia chirped back in reply. "Mischa just saw a spider."

"Must have been some spider," Mr. Richmond said in a tone that suggested he knew she was lying.

Mischa and Olivia both suppressed giggles with their fingers. "It was," Mischa called over her shoulder.

"Get some rest, girls," Mr. Richmond encouraged us. "It's after one. Busy day tomorrow."

"Okay, Dad," Olivia said, clearly just wanting him to go back up to the second floor and leave us alone.

She waited until he climbed all the stairs back up to the second-floor master bedroom, her head nodding slightly as she counted his footsteps, before dragging a chair over to the window to slide it open.

"Pete, what are you *doing* here?" she asked, standing atop the chair as the rest of us watched.

"Jeff and I were driving around and I thought it would be fun to stop by and wish you happy birthday in person," he told her, putting his hand up to the window screen separating them. His eyes wandered the room as he made notice of all of us in attendance. Violet nervously chewed her lower lip. When she'd packed her pajamas for the party, she probably hadn't been expecting that Pete would see her wearing them, just like I hadn't expected to run into Henry while wearing mine.

"That is so romantic," Candace muttered to no one in particular.

"That's totally sweet, but you guys have to get out of here! If my dad hears you, he'll call the cops!" Olivia cautioned.

Pete vowed to leave quietly, but only after Olivia figured out how to remove the screen so that he could kiss her through the window. She fumbled with the screen in the window frame until it fell forward and silently hit the grass of the backyard, and lifted herself on her tiptoes so that Pete could lean through the open window and kiss her.

"Isaac would *never* be that romantic," Candace grumbled.

An hour later, we snuggled into our blankets, finally ready to go to sleep. I spread out my sleeping bag on the floor, turning my back on my friends as I heard them all begin to breathe more deeply and then snore.

I couldn't sleep. Everything about Violet's contributions to the game, including her suggestion that we play it in the first place, was troubling me. How had Violet, who hadn't gone upstairs all night, known that Olivia's parents had bought her a red Toyota? Was it possible that someone in our tiny town had told her about Jennie, even though the subject was an odd one to share with anyone new at the high school?

My eyes began to burn with tiredness, and I noticed the time on the cable box near the television was 3:31 a.m. Suddenly, I sensed that I wasn't the only one awake in the basement, and turned to find Violet sitting up on her sleeping bag across the room, rubbing her eyes.

"Sorry if I freaked you out earlier," she whispered, careful not to wake the others.

"It's okay," I lied, because that's what girls say. It wasn't okay at all, but after her impressive performance, I was a little afraid of offending her. I rolled over, turning my back to her once again. That night I barely slept, unable to shake the suspicion that the fire in the fireplace that had burned so wildly while we were chanting had never burned itself completely out.

CHAPTER 3

I N THE MORNING, OLIVIA RUSHED THROUGH THE
front double doors of her house to squeal in delight in the driveway at her new red car.

"Oh my God, I love it! I totally love it!" she exclaimed repeatedly, throwing her arms around her father, and then her mother, and
then her father again.

None of my friends said anything about how trippy it was that
Olivia'd received the same make and model car that Violet had mentioned in the story she'd told just a few hours earlier. If Violet was
surprised by this element of her prediction coming true, she didn't
show it.

Mrs. Richmond made us all pancakes in the shape of the first
letter of our first names, which was kind of a childish treat, but we
all enjoyed it anyway. I devoured my misshapen *M* in silence, still
unsettled by the game we had played the night before. Thankfully,
Henry had left the house to drive to his appointment for X-rays
before we had even stirred awake. I wasn't in the mood to flirt or
act bubbly; still freaked out by Violet's game, I wanted to repack my
backpack and rush home in the safety of daylight.

When I emerged from the first-floor bathroom and began my descent back down to the basement to retrieve my overnight bag, I heard Olivia uttering the words "sister" and "fire." I knew immediately that she was debriefing Violet about my life story, and in an odd way I was flattered that Olivia even still remembered it. All the events she was relaying had occurred right around the time I had fallen out of favor with Olivia and Candace and the other girls who had been considered to be the prettiest and friendliest back in elementary school. I couldn't blame them for allowing our friendships to lapse when we were little kids. What had happened to my family was so terrible that parents wanted to keep their own children away from us, as if distance were a preventative measure to keep tragedy from striking them, too.

My footsteps on the creaky stairs interrupted the story, and both Olivia and Violet smiled awkwardly when I reached the basement. Only Candace turned and nodded at me with sad eyes, confirmation that I was indeed interrupting exactly what I suspected.

"We're going to go see *Blood Harvest 2: The Reaping* this afternoon," Olivia announced cheerfully, her offer laced with falseness. "Do you want to come with?"

"I can't," I lied smoothly. "I'm going shopping with my mom to look for stuff for the dance."

I was thankful that I hadn't previously announced to my new friends that the lavender dress had already been purchased, some information I'd held back on sharing just in case a date never surfaced.

That was the day that summer settled comfortably into fall. The temperature finally dropped noticeably by ten degrees and a sharp scent of dry leaves crept into the air, overpowering my town's summer smells of freshly cut grass and honeysuckle bushes. I rushed home on foot, not wanting to have to wait for my mom to arrive at the Richmonds' in her station wagon. My mom put other parents on edge. She was lucky to escape Willow on the three days each week when she taught in Sheboygan, where the only people who had known her long enough to remember about Jennie were the other professors who had been at the university as long as she'd been teaching there. Within town limits, everyone her own age remembered not only the story but the headline that appeared the next morning in the *Willow Gazette*: ONE CHILD DEAD IN TRAGIC HOUSE FIRE. A lot of kids I knew had divorced parents and lived with their moms after their dads left Willow to find new jobs, pursue new wives, and start over with fresh rules in a new game. But only my mom inspired awkward kindness everywhere she went. Even the checkout girls at the grocery store smiled a little wistfully when handing over her change.

The walk was nearly two miles, but I hurried, eager to get home to my own familiar bed to catch a few hours' worth of sleep. Thinking about Jennie exhausted me, and I wasn't happy that her memory had been dredged up so close to the Fall Fling, when my life was rapidly changing in a brighter direction. There were entire stretches of days sometimes when I barely thought about her, and then, of course, when I did, I felt guilty. It wasn't even accurate to say that I missed her; it had been so long since she'd passed away that I hardly remembered what it had been like when she'd been alive. By that autumn, I had lived on my own just as long as I'd lived with her, my life split in two distinct halves: With Jennie, and After Jennie. What had replaced the hollow longing that immediately followed her death was a distinct uneasiness, an undeniable but intangible sensation that somehow nature had messed up. Somehow, the wrong twin had been reclaimed.

"Nature doesn't make mistakes," Mom was fond of saying when talking about her profession, teaching future botanists and biologists about Phasmatodea, stick bugs that could blend seamlessly into their surroundings, and earthworms that aerated soil.

But what if . . . I could never prevent myself from wondering. *What if it did, just once?*

My mom liked to comfort herself by saying that when Jennie died, that was the beginning of the end of my parents' marriage. My dad, in her opinion, just wasn't *man enough* to help her through the tragic loss of a child. Truthfully, I think my dad would have packed his bags and headed down to Florida as soon as my mom started finding gray hairs, even if we hadn't lost Jennie the previous year. What made his attention wane wasn't the second empty bed, covered in its pink bedspread, untouched next to mine even after we moved into our new house, or the closet full of dresses and leotards that were several sizes too small for me but that my mom wouldn't consider giving away. It was my mother's refusal to move on, to accept, and the wrinkles that formed around her eyes during all the nights when she stayed up late, drinking tea on our porch, wanting to be sure, *completely sure*, that all the electrical appliances were turned off before she climbed into bed for the night. For all his advanced knowledge of the human psyche, my father couldn't understand why he could forgive my mother for her paranoia, but couldn't overcome his own revulsion toward her aging process.

He seemed to think having a younger woman in his life made

him appear cooler to me, but his attempts to keep up with Rhonda's interests were embarrassing. At sixteen, I already questioned his authority, his decisions, and his expertise far too frequently for his liking. Rhonda had turned twenty-seven that summer when I had been visiting in Florida. "Ha!" my mother had exclaimed at that. My mom had just turned forty-one.

Autumn was my favorite time of year, despite it also being a season of a lot of unhappy memories. Among them were the anniversary of Jennie's death, and the anniversary of the following year, when Dad boxed up all his clothes and crammed them into the hatchback of his car for the three-day drive down to Florida. Colored leaves in the trees and dry crunching beneath my shoes made me nostalgic, but comforted me. Wisconsin is basically the autumn capital of the world, in my opinion. At no time of year was it prettier in Willow, and never did it feel more like home.

I reached our corner and passed the vacant lot where our old house used to stand. Mom had insisted that we use the money from our insurance company to buy the only house for sale on our block at the time our first house burned to the ground. Morbid? Yes. But at the time Mom was grieving; she couldn't stand the thought of Jennie's spirit being alone on our old street, with us hypothetically all the way across town carrying on with our lives. It was a little weird to walk past that empty corner every day, but the perimeter of our old house's foundation had long since been obscured by dry, overgrown grass. In the eight years we'd been living in the house at the other end of the block next door to the Emorys', Mom had never once considered moving away. The lot on the corner had become town property, and every once in a while someone on the town board had an asinine idea about putting a park there. The proposal would always be shot down by no fewer than twenty mothers who vowed they would never let their kids play on slides and swing sets on the site of such a horrific event.

"Hi, honey!" Mom called when she heard me enter the house through the side door in our kitchen. Our storm door had a way of banging twice due to its busted spring—*clap, clap!* She was in the living room, reading the newspaper as she liked to do on weekends, still wearing her glasses and drinking a mug of coffee I knew she had probably made hours earlier when she had gotten up to walk the dog. "How was the party?"

"Fine," I said. "Olivia got a brand-new Prius."

"Randy and Beth always have spoiled that girl. Start dropping hints with your dad," Mom instructed me. "Brand-new cars are not really within my realm."

"So," I announced, setting my backpack down on the table behind our sofa and smiling at her, "guess who got asked to the dance next Saturday."

"Get out of town!" my mom exclaimed. In her defense, she taught a bunch of college kids, so she was always eager to practice what she thought was cool slang. "Who? Wait! Were you guys hanging out with boys last night?"

"No, *Mom*," I said. "We were in Olivia's basement all night, just like I said we'd be. Her *brother* asked me."

"Henry? Isn't he a little old for you?"

One of the curses of living in a small town was that everyone's parents knew every kid at school. All of our families picnicked together, coached in the same little league, carpooled to the ice-skating rink.

"He's only two years older than me. Not a big deal," I insisted, even though in my own heart I thought it was kind of a *huge* deal.

A huge enough deal that I was still a little apprehensive about how Candace, Olivia, and Mischa were going to react. Olivia was relatively easygoing and nice to most girls at school, at least nicer than the stereotype of the blonde, rich, popular high school girl. Candace, on the other hand, could be vicious. Mischa had a tendency to respond in social settings in a manner directed by either Candace or Amanda.

My mom wanted to know all about the party—which movies we'd watched, what kind of cake Olivia's mom had served—but I was eager to file away my memories of the party and not think about them again. I announced that we hadn't slept much and that I wanted to take a nap, and headed down the hall to my room.

I drifted off to sleep on my own bed, my muscles aching with sleepiness from not having been properly rested the night before. As I recalled the strange feeling that had come over me when Violet had told her stories, the hair on my arms stood straight up in my warm room.

Of course it wasn't evil spirits that were levitating the bodies, I assured myself. That was just crazy thinking. I didn't even believe in ghosts or spirits or poltergeists, evil or well-intentioned. I had spent a large part of my childhood wishing for a message from the spirit of my twin to no avail. If Jennie hadn't been able to figure out how to cross the divide of energy separating the living from the dead to communicate with me, then why would a random spirit—who didn't have any particular reason to be interfering with the sixteenth birthday party of a girl in a boring part of Wisconsin—bother to contact us?

But still, it was weird, I thought.

I slept soundly despite the daylight hour. Dreams began and ended without reason, as they often did whenever I fell asleep at an odd time of day, or slept too late in the morning.

I dreamed briefly of a birthday party, one of our own. I couldn't be sure which birthday it was, perhaps when we turned five, but in my dream it played back in my memory like a fuzzy Super 8 home movie, muted. Jennie and I wore matching paper party hats, pink cones held onto our heads with slim strings of cheap white elastic. We were dressed as we often were around that age, with Jennie in blue and me in red, my mother's primitive technique for keeping track of which twin was which. Jennie and I beamed and leaned forward in unison to blow out our candles. Olivia was there, very small for her age, and solemn-faced. Cheryl was there too, smiling and in pigtails. My father moved around the table in our old dining room with his video camera; my mother cut our cake and placed neat slices on paper plates with the Barbie logo printed on them. In a lucid moment after this memory closed out of my dream, I promised myself that I'd ask my mom when I woke up about which year we'd had a Barbie party.

What might have been minutes later just as easily as it might have been hours later, my dream shifted into one that was significantly darker. I was suddenly out on our old lawn in the dead of night, freezing in my paper-thin nightgown, feeling the blazing heat of the fire engulfing our house singe my bare arms and face. Neighbors were lifting me, carrying me farther away from the house, and sirens interrupted the quiet of the night, delivering firemen to our house far too late to make any difference in our future, with their hoses and yellow suits. I could never remember in my dreams or waking life how I'd ended up out on the lawn. What had awakened me so late at night and inspired me to leave the house?

In my dreams, as clearly as in my memories, I could see my parents' writhing silhouettes, black against the raging flames behind them, emerge through the front door of the house. My father's striped pajamas had caught fire. A fireman threw a heavy safety blanket on him and wrestled him to the ground out on the lawn to stifle the flames as my mother, her face caked with black soot, wildly searched the crowd that had gathered to watch the midnight spectacle. She looked so deranged, so unrecognizable with her hair mussed and her face smeared, that all I saw was the white of her nightgown and her frantic dark irises darting against the whites of her eyes. When she saw me in the arms of a neighbor near the fire truck, she ran toward us on bare feet across the crunchy, frozen grass.

"Where is she?" she had asked me in a strangled voice, shaking me by the shoulders. "Where is your sister?" In the eight years that had passed since the fire, I couldn't remember anymore if I had actually seen Jennie wave at me from the front window as flames devoured the curtains, or if I had imagined it. But whenever my daydreams or nightmares brought me back to the moment when my mother asked me where Jennie was, I saw her there in silhouette, the details of her face lost in shadows. She was aware, as the fire swallowed her, that I had made it out alive. If she had actually made her way to the window as I believed she had, she must have realized that she was going to die alone, without me, which was probably more terrifying than reaching the end of her life. I'd never had the courage to ask my mother if Jennie's body had been found in what had been our bedroom, or somewhere else.

In the years since the fire, I had come to realize after running those terrible moments through the processor in my mind hundreds of thousands of times that my mother had no idea when she first saw me which twin I was. All she had assessed in the frenzy of the emergency was that only one twin had made it out of the house. In my dream I felt nothing, neither fear, nor horror. Perhaps I had been in shock that night, suppressing all my memories of sensation.

For the first half of my life, my entire identity was shared with Jennie. Everyone who saw us assumed that we were two halves of a whole, nonexistent without our other half.

"My, they're so cute," people would comment. We weren't. We were average-looking, and chubby with chipmunk cheeks. The year that Jennie died in the fire, we were both missing our front teeth. It was our identicalness that was cute and memorable, not our features. Had I not been born a twin, people might have said behind my mother's back that I was a homely child.

"They're so well behaved," people would compliment my mother. But we weren't that, either. We fought and bickered constantly. We were always jealous of the attention the other twin received from our parents. Whatever toy was being played with by our twin was the only toy in the house we wanted. We had duplicates of every toy in the toy chest, but even that wasn't the solution to the problem. More than anything else in our toy chest, we fought tooth and nail over our Lite-Brite sets, so violently that eventually Mom claimed she had donated them to homeless children (even though after Jennie died I found both boxes hidden away in the garage).

Tricking our parents and teachers was a never-ending source of entertainment for us; we would swap clothes, swap name tags, and insist on being called by the other twin's name. My mother cautioned my father on a daily basis that she was on the verge of a nervous breakdown, being home with us all day long while he was off teaching lectures on campus. Naturally, throughout my whole life people have suggested that I read books and studies about identical twins sharing telepathic powers, secret languages and codes, inexplicably having the same habits. I had no recollection of us sharing any such special connection before Jennie's death. I remembered only her presence and a sense of comfort in having her near. Being a twin made me acutely self-aware; I didn't need a mirror to know how ugly my scowl was when I was angry. I could still remember crying to my mother, *Tell her to stop making that face!* whenever Jennie glanced at me with her brow-furrowed frown, because I thought it was hideous and I knew I was capable of looking exactly the same way.

After the flames had been extinguished, the chief of the fire department approached my mom and dad and they exchanged words quietly, too far away for me to overhear. My mother collapsed into my father's arms, and we were all driven in a police car to the hospital in the next town over, where we were assigned separate rooms and monitored for smoke inhalation. I was told by a doctor that my mother had been sedated and that I would be able to see her in the morning. Nurses brought me tomato soup and allowed me to stay awake, watching cartoons, until the sun peeked over the horizon. I was eight——too young to understand death. Too young to understand that Jennie was gone—*gone*—and I'd never see her again. For at least a year, I kind of expected that one day I'd wake up for school and suddenly she'd be back, unharmed and fully restored, her old self as she'd been before the fire. Special twin connections aside, somehow that night in the hospital I'd already known factually that Jennie was dead. I didn't remember any of the concerned nurses informing me, but I knew.

The next afternoon, my mother sat next to me on the edge of my bed, her eyes swollen from so many hours of heavy, drugged sleep. My father stood stoically behind her, his hands on her shoulders.

"Jennie, we have something to tell you that's going to be hard to understand," my mother began.

I opened my mouth to correct her, but I hesitated. I had an opportunity to switch, I realized. I could have let them go on believing that I was Jennie, and that McKenna had perished in the fire. But as an innocent, naïve eight-year-old, I didn't see any value in that. My instinct to correct the incorrect was too great. "I'm McKenna, Mom," I corrected her.

I was too young to know that parents really do have favorites; they can't help it.

Even the medical chart that dangled on a clipboard at the foot of my hospital bed had my name listed as Jennifer Laura Brady. Had it been wishful thinking on my parents' part when my intake form had been completed, or just an innocent mistake? I had never dared to ask.

When I woke up, the sun was low in the sky, suggesting as I yawned and stretched that it was almost dinnertime. My dream about the fire ended where it often did, at the hospital. For a few more minutes I lay still in my bedroom remembering how for almost a year after the fire, my mother would sit alone on our front porch every night, her eyes fixed on the empty, singed lot on the corner as spring heated into summer. I drifted out there one night and sat down beside her on our porch swing. "I could be Jennie if you'd like that," I offered earnestly. Her bereavement was that severe. I was willing to do anything, even sacrifice my own identity, to make my mom right again.

"I don't feel like cooking. What do you think about going to Bobby's?" Mom mused as I opened the fridge and lingered there, reviewing options. Showing my face at Bobby's with my mom on a Saturday night would have been mortifying when I was still the old McKenna. But now, after a momentary hesitation, I agreed. Sleeping through the day had rendered me starving, and there was nothing in our fridge that could compare to a giant chef salad at the diner.

As we stepped outside our house, Trey was pulling into the driveway next door in his sputtering gray Toyota. I had a split-second flashback of its interior: the squishy front seat and the faint smell of pine from the air freshener that dangled from his rearview mirror. My first instinct was to look away and pretend as if I hadn't heard his engine shut down a mere ten feet away from me. But then my mom had to be a huge geek and wave, making a friendly exchange unavoidable.

"Hi there, Trey!" my mother called out as Trey climbed out of his parked car.

"Hi, Mrs. Brady," Trey replied. My mother still went by *Mrs.* even though everyone in town knew my dad had taken off seven years before. Without saying a word to acknowledge me, he nodded at me with a dismissive expression that told me everything I needed

to know: He thought my ascent into popularity was deplorable, he was disappointed in me, and the social rift between us had deepened.

"He's a handsome guy, that Trey," my mother said once we settled into our own car and were putting on seat belts. "I never would have thought he'd turn out so cute; he was a goofy-looking kid. What's his story at school? Girlfriend?"

I could see what she was trying to do. The uncomfortable truth about Trey was that I doubted he'd have any romantic interest in me even if our wildly different friends wouldn't have made it socially awkward for us to be together. After all, he knew where to find me. The thought made me strangely sad because I'd crushed on him pretty hard in elementary school when he'd acted like an older brother toward me. I had no idea what kind of girls he was into, but I was pretty sure I wasn't cool enough for his liking—which didn't even matter, because I had Henry Richmond on my mind.

"He's a total *freak*, Mom. Girls avoid him."

My mother started the car's engine and then told me coolly, "Freak? I don't like this new habit of yours of looking down on everyone else at school. Ever since you started spending time with Olivia and Candace again, I don't think you're aware of how critical you're being. You weren't like this when you hung out with Cheryl."

Ugh, of course my mom wouldn't understand that I couldn't both be popular and retain strong ties with my unpopular friends. And she'd never in a jillion years understand why I, a normal, functioning teenager, could never be in a romantic relationship at Willow High School with Trey Emory, even though, as Candace had rudely pointed out the day before, he was really hot if you could overlook his strangeness. I remembered him being a serious smart-ass when he

was a kid too. A long time ago, he'd put a lot of effort into making me laugh.

While we were at Bobby's eating, I felt a buzz emerge from my purse and checked my phone to find a text from a number I didn't recognize. It included a photo attachment. The photo was of an X-ray, and accompanying it was a message that said, Cleared for dancing. Henry.

Saturday nights in September served as my reminder that I hadn't completely escaped my previous life. Everyone at school knew I didn't have a boyfriend, but I was still relieved not to have been observed by any witnesses driving home from the diner with my mom as the sun was setting. While Friday nights so far that school year had been girls' nights—sleepovers, trips to the movie theater—Saturday nights seemed to be reserved for boyfriends. Candace and Isaac were surely bumping around town in Isaac's truck, probably up to no good. Probably even Matt and Mischa had plans to go to the movies or split a pizza at Federico's.

Olivia was the kind of girl who enjoyed constant social stimulation, so even though she was out on a romantic birthday date with Pete, she texted me, Candace, Mischa, and Violet throughout the night with updates, including a picture of the gold necklace that Pete had given her as a gift with a pendant in the shape of an O for "Olivia."

A year ago it would have been ridiculous for me to have thought there was a chance I'd have a boyfriend before the end of high school, but now I had started wondering if I might have my own Saturday-night dates in the near future. Maybe by July, when my seventeenth birthday rolled around, there would be some cute guy in the pic-

ture with a sparkle in his eye, like Henry, who'd surprise me with a romantic gift. After all, a year ago it would have been crazy to think I'd ever be invited to a party at Olivia's house. I lay on my stomach across my bed reading a magazine, when my attention was caught by a flash of light outside my window. I got up and raised my blinds for a better look, and once my eyes adjusted to the dark, I saw Trey sneaking around in his own backyard with a flashlight. His bedroom light was still on, and I could see directly into his room across from my own bedroom window. Lights were still on in the front of the house, where his parents and younger brother were probably watching late-night Saturday comedy shows. Trey crouched down, and appeared to be digging for something beneath the bushes that lined the fence separating the Emorys' yard from our own.

Unable to suppress the urge to talk to him—even though I couldn't remember the last time we'd had an actual conversation—I raised my window and whispered, "What are you doing?"

I heard rustling, and then suddenly Trey was standing upright again, his flashlight dancing across the aluminum siding of my house until it came to rest on my face. Instinctively, I shielded my eyes.

"One of the stray cats my mom feeds had kittens back here," he whispered back loudly. I could barely hear him over the crickets chirping.

"Hang on," I called out quietly, suddenly really wanting to be a part of whatever he was doing. I pulled a cardigan off the back of the chair at my desk and slipped out the back door of our house through the kitchen. Outside, I opened the gate to our own backyard and then opened the gate to the Emorys', joining Trey in the chilly dark next door. He was crouching again, leaning over with his flashlight on but resting in the grass, pointed away from whatever he was inspecting. His black faded T-shirt rode up his back, revealing his bumpy spine and just the tiniest bit of the top of his butt. I caught myself blushing for even absentmindedly checking his body out like that, grateful that at least it was dark enough that he wouldn't notice my shame.

"There are six of them, I think," he whispered at me without turning to face me. I squatted down next to him to try to get a look. Sure enough, a small calico cat was stretched out beneath the Emorys' white azalea bushes, which were still oddly in bloom since warm weather had stretched so far past the end of August. "Look at the little gray one."

There were six furry blobs, possibly more, snuggled up against the mother cat, nursing. The calico cat blinked at us with bored gold eyes.

"How did you know they were back here?" I asked quietly, not wanting to alarm the mother cat.

"I heard meowing from my room," he replied. "I thought about bringing some cat food out here, but it might freak out the mother cat if I get too close."

We watched in silence for a few minutes, mostly relying on the light of the nearly full moon. I thought about how odd it was that we were inches from each other, our elbows ever-so-slightly touching, actually interacting after years of carrying on our acquaintance in silence. The strangest thing was that it felt like years hadn't passed since the last time we'd hung out like this. Like it was the most natural thing in the world for us to both be peeking under his mother's flowering bushes at midnight.

"You should leave a can of food back here for her," I urged him finally. "Just don't put it too close under the bushes."

"Good thinking," he agreed, and slowly stood up. He walked across his backyard and silently entered his own house through the back door. When he returned, he had already opened a small can of fancy cat food, and rejoined me near the bushes to set it down a few feet away from the mother cat. The smell of salty salmon caught the mother cat's attention, but she made no attempt to abandon her tiny kittens to investigate its source.

"I'm afraid to leave them out here alone for the night," he admitted finally with a small laugh.

"Cats have kittens in suburbia all the time and they're just fine," I assured him, not really believing my own words. Wisconsin was filled with plenty of nocturnal wildlife that might pose a threat to a mother cat with six kittens to defend. Before our dog, Moxie, got old, she was constantly killing invaders in our yard and dropping their carcasses on our back stoop: a dead possum, a dead raccoon, a dead squirrel, or a dead chipmunk.

"I might sleep out here," Trey announced suddenly. "Just to scare critters away, you know? I tried to move the mother cat earlier, and she flipped out. I don't think I can get her and the kittens into my house."

There were scratch marks on both of his hands, presumably from his attempt to pick up the mother cat. I was amused, but touched, that he went back into the house again and returned with a sleeping bag and a pillow.

"Aren't your parents going to think it's weird that you're sleeping outside?" I asked. I was starting to get really cold, and I had seen my mom shut off the light in our living room, most likely signifying that she was turning in for the night.

"My parents already think I'm really weird," he said matter-of-factly with a shrug.

We stood eye to eye, and I was bursting with things to say. Trey Emory cared enough about a feral cat and her newborn kittens to sleep outside in the yard. It was totally weird of him. But also totally endearing. What else did I not know about the boy who slept fewer than fifty feet from my own bedroom every night? We stared at each other in silence for a long moment, during which I wondered if he was working up the nerve to say something to me just like I was trying to find the right way to tell him that I wished we hadn't grown so far apart over the last few years.

Then, without warning, he reached toward me and brushed my hair back from my face, tucking a lock behind my ear. "Good night, I guess," he mumbled.

My face must have betrayed my shock at feeling his fingers graze my cheek, because he smiled bashfully and apologized. "Sorry. That was weird, wasn't it?"

"No, not weird," I assured him, although the unnaturally high pitch of my voice exposed my lie. My thoughts ran wild; had he meant that to express that he liked me? Or as more of a big brotherly way of saying good-bye? A formality? I assumed the latter, but I couldn't tear my eyes away from his.

"Nah, it was weird. I should have totally gone with a handshake." That was the sarcastic side of Trey that I remembered from when I was a little girl, the way he had of teasing me that made me tingle from my head to my toes.

I rolled my eyes at him. "A handshake would have definitely been weird." Without thinking through the implication of my words, I added, "A salute might have been better. Next time, maybe a salute."

"Right," he agreed, holding my gaze and nodding. "Next time."

I looked back over my shoulder on my way toward the gate leading me out of the Emorys' yard just once, and saw him already busying himself with the task of spreading out his sleeping bag a few feet away from the bushes. My heart swelled before I remembered that I had an actual, real text message from Henry Richmond on my phone in my room. I was going to the Fall Fling with one of the cutest boys to ever graduate from Willow High School. I couldn't be bothered with any kind of silly crush on my next-door neighbor.

In the morning, my first impulse of the day was to peek out the window to see if Trey was still outside. But I had slept in a little late; and there was no sign of Trey in his yard.

I spent the day trying to banish him from my thoughts, but couldn't stop wondering what the chances were that he was thinking about me, too. There had been something between us that I couldn't explain exactly, just like I couldn't explain what had happened in Olivia's basement on Friday night.

The only thing I knew for sure that weekend was that even though I was excited every time my phone buzzed with a new text from Henry, I couldn't wait to see Trey again.

CHAPTER 4

SOMETHING FELT DIFFERENT ABOUT MY WALK TO school on Monday morning.

Perhaps it was because the summer heat had subsided, or because I was hopeful that I might run into Trey in the hallway. For the first time that year, there was a spring in my step, as if I couldn't wait to fall back into the routine of classes and put the strangeness I'd experienced at Olivia's party behind me.

Before classes began, Olivia approached me in the hallway.

"My brother said he's taking you to the dance," she said, and I couldn't tell if she was happy or upset about that. "It's cool."

I breathed a sigh of relief. "Really? Because if it's not, I can ask someone else. Honestly, Olivia. If it's going to be awkward for you, I'll ask Dan."

Dan, with his buzz cut and endless freckles, was all the way at the end of the hall, out of earshot. He had already gathered up his books for first period and told me to have a good morning.

"Don't be silly! Of course it's cool. You and my brother make a cute couple. Candace might be a freak about it, but ignore her. Henry thinks she's a windbag."

Having Olivia's blessing made me feel much more at ease about going to the dance. "What about Mischa?" I asked delicately. "Do you think she and Amanda might think I'm stepping on Michelle's toes?"

Olivia wrinkled her nose. "Michelle already has a new boyfriend at the University of Minnesota. I wouldn't worry about that."

In the cafeteria at lunchtime, conversation had returned to the football game on Friday in Kenosha and whether or not we'd all take the bus across the state to cheer for our team. The verdict was that we would go to Kenosha because Candace was insistent that we support Isaac, but we would not stoop so low as to ride the bus with the gross freshmen and unruly sophomores.

"I can drive," Pete offered. "We can fit five in the Infiniti." He looked around our table and counted heads with his finger. "One, two, three, four, five," he said, pointing first to his own chest and then to Olivia, me, Candace, and Jeff. Although Jeff was tall and played basketball with Pete, he wasn't especially cute *or* funny. I had a feeling that by the middle of the week, Olivia would pressure Pete to make Jeff ask Violet to the dance just so that no one would be left out.

"Amanda and I have to ride with the cheerleaders on the bus," Mischa informed Violet. "You can ride with us if you'd like. It'll be fun." Violet was sitting at the far end of the table eating yogurt, and she nodded.

I had never been to a football game as a spectator before. As a member of the color guard, I had always sat with the band in my unattractive blue uniform, waiting for performances on the field. It had never really occurred to me before that I might one day sit up in the stands eating hot dogs and popcorn with the cool crowd from school. While I wasn't much of a sports fan, the thought of the game and riding to Kenosha in Pete's car put butterflies in my stomach.

After lunch, I walked back to my locker with Candace, who had been uncharacteristically quiet for the past hour. Of our small group of friends, I was probably the least close to Candace, but our lockers were along the same wall in the same hallway, so from time to time I found myself walking alongside her, usually with little to say.

"I've been meaning to tell you something," she said in a low whisper as soon as the others had walked down the hall in the other direction toward their own lockers to exchange books for the afternoon session of classes, "about Friday. There was something weird with the story Violet told about me when we were playing that game."

I stopped walking for a second, so startled by the abrupt way in which Candace had gone from cheerfully making plans in the cafeteria for Friday night to instantaneously serious when she brought up Olivia's party, returning me to the state of discomfort I had experienced in Olivia's basement. Maybe I hadn't been the only one who'd felt a little too scared to have fun during the game.

"Yeah?" I asked, not wanting to volunteer my own unpleasant memory of the party.

"Violet said during all that stuff about being in the water that I went out into the waves far away from my *brothers*. I don't *have* any brothers. I have two half brothers from my dad's second marriage, but I'm pretty sure I've never mentioned anything about Dylan and Jordan to Violet. I mean, they live in Green Bay. I barely ever see them."

I frowned. I had known Candace since kindergarten, and *I* didn't even know that her dad had two sons with his new wife. Both of Candace's parents had remarried, and I only knew about her younger half sister, Julia, who was in eighth grade.

"That *is* weird," I agreed, wondering if I should confide in Candace about my own astonishment surrounding Violet's knowledge of the red Prius that had been parked in the Richmonds' driveway the night of the birthday party.

Just then, I looked up to see Trey approaching us. My involuntary reaction was to smile and raise my hand to wave, but a nanosecond after we made eye contact, he looked away and walked past me as if I didn't even exist. I blushed, completely humiliated. I had definitely overestimated whatever we had shared in his backyard, and I was ashamed at the force with which my heart was beating inside my rib cage. Fortunately, Candace hadn't noticed my momentary distraction; her eyes followed Trey down the hall.

"Nice," she whispered to me conspiratorially with a wicked grin. We reached my locker, and Candace lingered while I twisted my combination open, her books pressed against her chest. Her focus returned to Violet and the events of Friday night. "Do you think Violet's been like, *spying* on us? I even went through my Instagram to see if maybe she saw pictures of them, but I don't have any up there."

I realized that Candace's concerns about Violet were rooted in regular everyday life, not in the realm of supernatural powers, as mine were. It was ridiculous of me to think that maybe Violet had ESP or some kind of special communication with ghosts.

"Maybe someone just told her," I suggested. "Like Olivia."

Candace frowned, unconvinced. I could understand why. Olivia didn't concern herself with the details of anyone else's life. She existed in her own little perfect world, blissfully ignorant of the trivialities of everyone else's plights. "I don't know. I just think it's weird."

Violet was in my first class after lunch, US History, taught by Mr. Dean.

"Class, I know that around this time of year the only election on anyone's mind is for homecoming court. But I'd like to remind you that Student Government nominations are due this Friday, and I'd like to encourage all of you to consider running for class office," Mr. Dean said. He was the faculty administrator for Student Government, overseeing the elections and assigning tasks to the four officers of each class. Student Government was something that rarely crossed my mind; Olivia was always our class president, and Michael Walton, a brainiac on the Mathlete team who everyone knew would eventually be our class valedictorian, was always vice president. Tracy Hartford, the biggest gossip in the junior class, was always secretary, and Emily Morris had been treasurer since freshman year.

When the bell rang and I was gathering up my books, Mr. Dean said, "Miss Brady? Can I have a word with you?"

Violet raised her eyebrows at me on her way out of class, wondering why I had been singled out by Mr. Dean for a one-on-one.

I approached Mr. Dean as he erased his notes from our class on the chalkboard. Our homework assignment over the weekend had been to write an essay on Thomas Paine's pamphlet *Common Sense*, and I hadn't done a fantastic job, since I'd been so preoccupied with thoughts of Trey, Henry, and the strangeness of Olivia's party.

"Yes, Mr. Dean?" I asked.

"I wanted to ask if you'd given any thought to running for the role of junior class treasurer," Mr. Dean said. "I think you'd be a natural."

I was confused as to why he'd think I'd be a natural at anything. The only class in which I really ever stood out as exceptional at all was art, and I didn't have any reason to think that elderly Mr. Dean with his suspenders and bow ties was swapping stories with Miss Kirkovic, the far younger and cooler art teacher. Besides, I had already overheard that Jason Arkadian, who was one-half of our high school's measly debate team, had turned in a nomination form with five signatures in order to run for the office. Jason was hardly as popular as guys like Pete and Isaac, but still, people knew who he was. He'd never been called a cow, hadn't lost a twin in a horrific tragedy that everyone in town had heard about. Basically, I had a hunch that a victory over him would require a lot of work.

"I am terrible at math," I assured him. "I don't think I'd do a very good job of managing class finances."

"But you're well-liked. You're friendly with everyone in your class," the old man countered me. "The junior class treasurer is a very important role. You'd be in charge of raising funds for the junior class trip."

Every year, during the first week of May, the junior class went on an overnight trip, usually to either Chicago or Minneapolis. The previous year, the junior class Student Government had organized a daffodil sale and a chocolate sale, both of which had underwhelmed, and the funds raised had fallen so short of the goal that kids each had to contribute two hundred dollars to partake in the trip. I didn't want to entertain the idea of running in the election, but Mr. Dean's suggestion that I try already had me thinking about all those leaves I'd seen on the ground on my walk to school that morning. I could organize a student service to rake leaves and shovel snow, the two tasks that *everyone* in Willow needed help with most urgently. "I'll think about it," I assured him, and rushed off to gym class.

In the hallway outside the history classroom, Cheryl was waiting for me patiently. I was disgusted with myself for the way in which I had been treating her since the beginning of the school year. Cheryl was so mild-mannered, so genuinely sweet. She was the kind of girl I was sure would come into her own away at college; she'd find an intellectual boyfriend and finally be recognized for her academic potential. But in high school she was a girl with big, clunky glasses and the wrong style of jeans.

"Hey," she said shyly. Poor Cheryl. I hadn't officially put the brakes on our friendship but she knew the score. I sat with my new friends at lunch and had partnered with Mischa in chem lab instead of with her, at the time insisting that Mischa really needed my help whereas Cheryl would get a good grade in chem lab on her own. "I was wondering what you're doing on Friday. My mom got tickets to the Lamb and Owl show in Madison, and I was thinking maybe you might want to go."

My heart sank. Cheryl knew that I loved the folksy duo Lamb and Owl from New Zealand. I'd had no idea that they were doing a US tour and I was suddenly both jealous that she had tickets and enraged with her for buying them in what was obviously an attempt to rekindle our friendship. Cheryl didn't like them nearly as much as I did. Ditching the first away football game of the year to venture downstate with Cheryl and presumably her mom or dad to a hipster folk concert would definitely not go unpunished by Olivia and Candace.

"I would love to," I lied wistfully, "but I might have to be here late after classes on Friday for a meeting that Mr. Dean was just telling me about. And then I usually stay home on Fridays. With my mom. You know, this time of year."

I hated myself for using Jennie's death as a way to get out of having to go to the concert, but the excuse rolled off my tongue with such ease. Immediately Cheryl's face fell, a mixture of disappointment that I was rebuffing her offer, and shame that I had called her out on forgetting that it was the most emotionally trying time of year for my family. As soon as I saw her reaction, I regretted my choice in excuses, but it was too late to rescind my lie. I wasn't sure what I'd say if she found out I had gone to the game with my new circle of friends, but I knew I'd feel guilty if she did.

"Oh my God, McKenna, I'm so sorry," she apologized. She looked as if she might start crying. "I completely forgot. I just miss hanging out, you know? I thought it would be fun to go to the concert together."

My heart was kind of breaking. I didn't have much experience in ending friendships, and I wished there were a way that I could invite Cheryl into Olivia's circle too, but high school just didn't work that way. I was disappointed in myself. But I wanted to belong. I wanted to go to the Fall Fling on Henry's arm and not have to ever worry about being called "cow" by any of the idiots in the junior class ever again. I wanted memories of being popular to look back on by the time I left

Willow for college. In an odd way, after the grief-saturated childhood I had endured, I felt like I was owed two years of popularity.

"It's okay, Cheryl. Maybe we can hang out next weekend," I offered, knowing in my heart that I'd make excuses the following weekend too.

Outside on the track, with all of us dressed like clones in our red-and-black gym suits, Olivia and Mischa blazed past us, taking their laps far more seriously than me, Candace, and Violet. Candace tuned both me and Violet out by adjusting her phone endlessly, skipping songs that didn't suit her that afternoon and singing along off-key to those that did. I wished I'd brought my phone outside too, to relieve me of having to make conversation with Violet. We walked casually to the annoyance of Coach Stirling, our shadows stretched out on the gravel before us.

"About Friday," Violet said softly. She appeared to be nervous, and was fiddling with her locket. "I think I owe you an apology for what I said. I didn't know about your family. I felt really awful all weekend, but I didn't want to text you or anything because that would have made it weirder."

"It's okay," I replied, not especially wanting to talk about Jennie outside on the track on such a beautiful fall day, with a crisp breeze blowing. "You're new in town. How would you have known?"

She bit her lower lip nervously, as she often did, and I thought judgmentally that if she weren't so pretty, it would have been easy to categorize Violet among the anxious nerds and self-conscious dweebs of our school. "I don't want to sound like a total freak, but sometimes

I see things. I mean, I don't talk about it with people, like, ever. But like I said, I feel really bad about saying I saw a fire."

I felt the day slowing down around me like a special effect in a movie. I wasn't sure if I had heard her correctly. Was she implying that she had some kind of psychic abilities? Perhaps my suspicion hadn't been so off base.

"Um, could you elaborate on that?" I asked. "You can't just say something like that and not explain."

Violet shrugged as if what she had just said wasn't a big deal. "You know, like, stuff. About people. Not, like, X-ray vision or anything. But I just get sort of a vague impression of something that happened to them, or is about to happen, and I never really know what it means. When I touched your forehead, I smelled fire and I saw smoke. I didn't know that you'd already survived a house fire," she said apologetically. "Please don't tell anyone else. I know I sound like a nut." My walk had slowed down to a snail's pace. I couldn't really believe what Violet was telling me, but at the same time, I *had* to believe her.

"So . . . Olivia's car?" I dared to ask. "You mentioned in your story about Olivia that her parents were going to give her a red car for her birthday. Did you know that when you said that, the red Prius was already parked in the Richmonds' driveway?"

Violet wrinkled her nose, obviously stressed that I was grilling her. It wasn't my intention to be tough with her, but I naturally had a lot of questions. "No, I didn't know it was already up there. She'd said she wanted a Prius, so I just made that part up. Lucky guess."

"That is really, really weird," I told her. On one hand, I was grateful that Violet had opened up to me. On the other hand, she was completely freaking me out. "What else do you know . . . about me?"

She only dared to look me in the eye for a second before her eyes darted up at the sky to avoid my stare. "Nothing, really. That's it. Just the fire. And . . . you have a dog? Something slow and spotted and furry."

Moxie was a Brittany spaniel, and those days she was somewhat slow, hobbling around on her arthritic legs. I nodded to acknowledge that I did indeed have a dog, but I didn't believe Violet for a second.

Violet knew more, much more. But if I were to tell my friends, they would think I was crazy.

And somehow she knew enough about *me* to confide in me, I guessed because she probably already sensed that I was onto her.

What I was wondering more than anything—but didn't dare ask—was, if Violet had been able to sense the fire that had killed my sister, then were the stories that she'd told about Olivia, Candace, and Mischa also somehow based in reality?

"Mr. Dean thinks I should run for class treasurer," I told my mom as I was stirring noodles around on my plate at dinnertime. I was being abnormally quiet at the dinner table as I thought about Violet and everything she had admitted to me out on the track. It wasn't like me to be reserved at mealtimes, but I definitely didn't want to confide to my mom that I suspected a friend of having supernatural powers. She would have been on the phone with my dad, asking him to evaluate me, in a heartbeat.

"Treasurer? Why treasurer? You'd make a better class secretary," my mother said, never one to encourage me to pursue anything I didn't really have my heart set on. *Save your energy for the challenges that count,* she liked to say.

"I can't run for class secretary, I won't win. Tracy Hartford always runs for class secretary and wins every year. I can only run for treasurer because that's the position I'd have a shot at," I elaborated.

My mother poured a little more cold spaghetti sauce out of the jar and onto her pasta. "That's not the attitude of a winner," she chided me. "I didn't even know you were interested in Student Government. Who else is running?"

"Jason Arkadian," I said, swirling my spaghetti around even more.

Explaining to my mother that there was no possible way my fellow students would vote for me over Tracy, and that if I chose to challenge her for her role of class secretary I would suffer certain public humiliation, was futile.

"Well, does Jason Arkadian really want to be the junior class treasurer? Wouldn't you feel bad if you denied him that opportunity just because it seemed like fun for a few days?" my mother asked me critically. She just didn't get high school.

"No, because I'm interested in it too," I admitted. Now that Mr. Dean had suggested it, all of the planning and possibilities associated with the election offered my brain a safe haven from more disturbing thoughts of Violet and her strange visions. I could lead a successful fund-raiser; I was pretty sure of it. I had never known Emily well, but had gotten the sense that she'd run for office just because Olivia had. I wouldn't even have to try very hard to do a better job than she'd done. "I would have to organize a fund-raiser to pay for the class trip in May. I already have some ideas."

My mother stared at me across the table as if an alien were sitting in my chair instead of me. "You're serious about this."

"I am," I told her.

"Well. If you're into it, then I'm into it. It'll look really great on your college applications. What do you have to do?"

I told her I'd have to formally announce my nomination on Friday at a meeting after school. As soon as the words left my mouth, I realized that attending that meeting might actually complicate my trip to Kenosha to see the game. I felt a little better about declining Cheryl's offer to go to Madison. I hadn't been completely lying to her after all about having an obligation on Friday after school that would prevent me from going to the concert.

"I'll pick up some poster board at Walgreens tomorrow. But I really wish you'd consider running against Tracy Hartford. Her mother has the biggest mouth," my mother complained.

That night as I did my homework, I left my blinds raised intentionally because I could see that Trey's were still open over the fence. I couldn't see him stirring in his room, but his lights were on, suggesting that he was still awake. It had bothered me all day that he'd ghosted me in the hallway, although considering what Violet had told me during gym class, I suspected I had bigger things to worry about. Henry texted me, making my heart rate speed up to a *thud-thud-thud* when I read his message asking me what color my dress for the dance was. He was renting a tux and wanted to make sure the cummerbund matched, so that we would look like a real couple. I wondered if he'd buy a corsage. My mother would be absolutely floored if a boy showed up at our house with a corsage to slide onto my wrist.

Finally, around one in the morning, I was too tired to even keep my eyes open any longer, and got up to lower my blinds. The moment I stood up, I looked through my window and saw Trey looking right back at me. This time, I stopped myself before I waved. I wouldn't be made to feel like an overeager fool twice in one day.

For a moment, neither of us looked away. Trey finally nodded at me, acknowledging me. I looked away first, and closed my blinds. I shamefully wondered what might have happened if I'd left them open while I changed into my pajamas. Would Trey have watched? Would he have wanted me to know that he was watching? Even just imagining the possibilities made my cheeks burn and my heart race. Why was I even thinking about flirting with Trey Emory?

That night, I was kept awake by thoughts about Violet and who she was, if she was as innocent as she seemed, and if she knew as little about me as she claimed. And then even more thoughts about Trey, and if he hated me, and if so, why. I shouldn't have been thinking about any of these things, I knew. I should have been smiling to myself in the dark because I had an election campaign to plan, and Henry Richmond was thinking about me. He had my phone number, and I'd be seeing him on Saturday night.

"Check it out, guys. I think this is it."

Olivia stepped out of the dressing room modeling the dress she had found on the rack at Tart, one of two cool boutiques at the small

mall in Ortonville, the next town over from Willow to the west. That mall was nowhere near as big as the one in Green Bay, but we had decided to drive over on Wednesday after school to see if perhaps Olivia's dream dress could be found there. Candace's mother owned a nail salon inside the Ortonville mall, and Candace insisted that we avoid that hall of stores so that her mother wouldn't know she was shopping instead of doing homework.

"Whoa. I think that's the one, dude," Candace said, slurping on her frozen chocolate latte through a straw.

The dress—strapless and cream-colored in a shade that was just dark enough not to be too summery for September—fit Olivia perfectly. It was covered in a layer of delicate eyelet, and when Olivia spun in front of the mirror, the full skirt swung around her knees as if she were a princess in a Disney cartoon.

"I kind of love it," Olivia announced. "It's not really what I was picturing, but it might even be better."

"It's hot," Violet assured Olivia. "You should buy it just in case it's not here later this week."

The numbers I saw on the price tag made me gasp when I saw them in a flash before Olivia returned to the dressing room to change back into her jeans and silk blouse. I wondered if Violet recognized the dress that Olivia would carry home in a bright pink bag from Tart that afternoon. Did it look exactly the same as she'd envisioned it in her prediction of Olivia's death? Violet had been uncharacteristically lively and talkative on the drive over from Willow, and I suspected that she was intentionally avoiding eye contact with me.

Once back within town borders, Olivia dropped Mischa off

first, because she had to go to gymnastics class with Amanda. Violet insisted on being left at the library, where her mom would pick her up after work. I was surprised to be the last one remaining in the car other than Candace, who rode shotgun in the red Prius. Being the last one to get dropped off was sort of like being the last one who Olivia hoped to get rid of.

I decided it was as good a time as any to test my plan to run for class treasurer against Olivia. I announced it casually, as if I were still kind of kicking the idea around.

"Are you sure you want to do that? I mean, Student Government is *so boring*. It's the worst. I only ran for president because my dad really wants me to try to get a scholarship to the University of Wisconsin." After stewing over the possibility of winning the election, by Wednesday I was sure I wanted to run. More important, I was sure I wanted to win. It was odd that in the two days since Mr. Dean had encouraged me to run for office, I'd gone from not caring about Student Government to feeling like my life couldn't go on if I didn't win.

"Totally," I said. "It wouldn't be boring for me. Don't think I'm a freak, but the more I think about it, the more I'm into it."

Olive exclaimed, "You are definitely psycho! But meetings will suck less if you're there. We should run together, like running mates!" Having not only Olivia's approval, but her enthusiasm as well, solidified my resolve to run. Participation in the election went from being a high-risk gamble of my social standing to a necessary step in my certain victory with just a few words from Olivia.

"Oh my God, you guys are so political," Candace complained. "What am I going to do in this dump of a town when you're both passing bills on Capitol Hill?"

"Marry Isaac and have, like, fifty kids," Olivia joked.

We pulled into my driveway and my chest ached a little when I saw that Mom's car wasn't there. She was probably still on her way home from Sheboygan. Entering a dark house by myself was my least favorite part of any day, because it was then when it hit me hardest that if our old house had never burned down, I probably never would have had to spend any time alone. At least Moxie would be happy to see me, even if only because I would let her out to go sniff things in the backyard.

As I gathered up my backpack and opened the back door of the car to climb out, Olivia said, "So, Violet still doesn't have a date for the dance."

I froze. Olivia's tone had gone from funny and joking to threatening just like that. How was it possible that it was Wednesday and Violet still hadn't worked up the nerve to ask someone? Didn't she know that Olivia and Candace wouldn't permit her to attend the dance alone? Going to the dance with girlfriends was fine for girls who weren't in the popular circle, but it was absolutely not going to be permitted by a girl who was expecting to be named homecoming queen in a few weeks.

"Has she mentioned anything to you about going by herself? I mean, I know she said she has a dress, but that would just be . . ." Candace trailed off, looking for the right word. "Pathetic."

I shook my head, wanting to distance myself from Violet's dateless state as much as possible. "No, she hasn't said a word," I claimed.

"Well, if she says anything, could you, like, discourage her from going to the dance alone? I mean, obviously she can do whatever she wants, but that would be really weird," Olivia said.

I let myself into my house through the back door with my keys, feeling uneasy despite the fact that I knew Henry's interest in me would prevent any such conversations about *me* from being had behind my back. But Olivia and Candace would have turned on me as quickly as they'd turned on Violet for any little reason. It was stressing me out to think about it, but it was becoming evident that having a real boyfriend was going to be more important in securing my popularity than even winning a Student Government election. Henry had only asked me to one measly dance; he'd given no indication of actually wanting to be my *boyfriend*. Homecoming was going to pose the same problem all over again.

Moxie limped over to the back door to greet me, her tail wagging, and I petted her and stepped out into the backyard with her to watch her stretch her legs. The sun was already setting even though it was barely seven o'clock, yet another reminder that summer had passed. I heard the Emorys' back door open, and felt what seemed like a bolt of electricity shoot through my body when I looked over the fence and saw Trey stepping outside carrying a can of cat food.

"Hey," he said unenthusiastically, crossing his yard to where we had seen the mother cat with her kittens under the bushes near the fence earlier in the week.

"Hi," I said, trying to sound as casual as he had sounded.

He disappeared as he crouched down to place the cat food beneath the azalea bushes, and I shifted uncomfortably, wanting to say more. "How are they doing?" I called over the fence, wishing I could cure myself of the desire to have Trey pay attention to me.

A moment passed before Trey stood up again and replied.

"They're all right," he said, looking right at me over the fence. "One didn't make it that first night. But the other five are already getting kind of bigger."

The thought of a kitten not living through its first night of life took my breath away with sorrow. Grief filled me, as familiar a sensation as hunger or sleepiness. "That sucks," I said, my voice cracking a little. I hadn't realized I was so close to tears over the loss of a little cat that I'd never even touched.

Trey frowned, looking down at presumably where the mother cat was beneath the bushes, and then agreed, "Yeah." It wasn't quite dark out yet, but it almost was, and our solemn conversation was punctuated by the early chirping of crickets. The moon was already high in the evening sky, just a fraction of a crescent.

Trey looked quickly over his shoulder toward his own house and then back at me. "That's weird," he said.

"What?"

"Do you feel that? It feels like someone is watching us."

I looked around, very aware in that instant that he was right. It *did* feel like someone was with us, watching us, just like it had felt in Olivia's basement the previous Friday night, when we had been playing Violet's game. I knew it was ludicrous to even consider, but Violet had told me that she saw things when she touched people, things about their lives that she otherwise couldn't have known. I wondered if it was her who was watching us right there and then. I felt the little hairs on my forearms raise with goose bumps. The feeling was unnerving and made me wish that Trey and I were both at least on the same side of the fence.

"Yeah," I admitted. "I feel that too."

Trey looked as if he was about to say something more, but then we both heard the engine of my mother's car, and her headlights blasted the aluminum siding on the Emorys' house as she pulled into our driveway, country music playing on her stereo.

"See ya." Trey waved, dismissing himself at my mother's arrival. He returned back to his house through its back door, and I clapped my hands to summon Moxie.

"Moxie! Come on, girl," I called. My beloved old dog's ears perked up and she limped back toward me as quickly as she could. Mom went inside to set down the bags of fast food she'd brought home.

I waited for Moxie to climb up the stairs onto the deck. In the kitchen, she whined when she caught a whiff of the foil-wrapped burgers on the table. "Was that Trey you were talking to when I got home?" Mom asked.

"The Emorys have kittens in their backyard," I said, dancing around the matter of my having been talking to Trey.

"He could use a haircut, that Trey," my mother continued, blocking my attempt to change the subject and handing me a plate. "You and Jennie used to always play over at the Emorys' when you were little. They had that great swing set. Trey took you girls on the school bus for the first time when you started first grade."

I unwrapped my hamburger in silence, not wanting to remember back that far. I vaguely remembered the three of us in the Emorys' yard, pumping our legs on the swings, soaring higher and higher. Jennie used to say she wanted to touch the sky.

"I always used to think that one of you girls would marry Trey. The three of you were as thick as thieves back then. Mary Jane used to let that boy run wild. He would absolutely refuse to eat the crust on bread whenever he would stay here for lunch, because she always used to cut it off for him—"

"Mom," I interrupted her coldly. "I really don't want to think about it."

The words were out of my mouth before I thought them through, but they were accurate. I didn't want to remember. It was just too weird, made me too nostalgic, to remember back to what it was like to run up and down Martha Road with Jennie. We roamed the neighborhood during summers when we were kids, and the memories were flooding back of bicycles toppling over, skinned knees, hide-and-seek up and down the block, climbing over fences.

Mom made a serious matter out of squirting ketchup and mustard onto her burger and then setting the bun back on its top, trying to prepare her response for me with care. "I'm sorry, McKenna. It's just that time of year. As soon as the leaves start to change, I can't help but remember what things were like when you girls were little."

Choosing to ignore her, I handed Moxie a significant chunk of the meat from my burger. "I don't have a crush on Trey. So just . . . stop thinking we're going to get together. It's not gonna happen."

Later that night as I waited impatiently to fall asleep, all my apprehension earlier that week about Violet and the game had abandoned me, and my thoughts were completely devoted to Trey Emory. In both of my recent encounters with him, I hadn't thought to look closely enough to see what color his eyes were. Light, I was pretty sure. Green or blue? I couldn't recall. He hadn't been wearing the army jacket earlier that night, and I'd been so surprised to see him in the yard that I hadn't even noticed while we were talking. I was thinking about his biceps, how they had been a little more noticeable than I'd been expecting beneath his tight black T-shirt. I was wondering if he lifted weights, and if so, where, and why he went to such great lengths to hide his jacked arms beneath his ratty jacket.

I wasn't thinking about the fact that Olivia had found her dress, but still didn't have a pair of shoes for the dance.

CHAPTER 5

O N FRIDAY MORNING, I STOWED MY PINK cashmere cardigan in my school bag in preparation for the game in Kenosha later that night.

"I'm going to be home late tonight," I informed my mom in the kitchen, where she was correcting papers submitted by her students with a red pen between her fingers, ready to strike.

"How late?" Mom asked, barely looking up from her grading task.

"Somewhat late," I replied smartly. Kenosha was a three-hour drive from Willow, and the game started at seven.

Even if it ended promptly at nine, which I was sure it wouldn't since I knew from past experience that the halftime show would last at least twenty minutes, the earliest I could possibly expect to be home again was midnight.

"Can you define 'somewhat'?" Mom asked, finally putting her red pen down, adjusting her glasses, and looking at me.

I rolled my eyes, knowing that she was going to make a big deal about my being out past midnight. "I'm going to the football game with Olivia and Candace. It's supposed to start at seven, but I'm sure it'll start late. And it'll be at least two hours long, and it's all the way in Kenosha, so I'm going to miss my curfew if we stay for the end of the game."

"I don't feel very good about you being out past midnight, McKenna," Mom told me. "Who's going to be driving?"

I hesitated, not really wanting to divulge that we'd be in Pete's car. Pete's *expensive* car.

"Olivia's boyfriend," I replied.

"And how old is Olivia's boyfriend? Old enough to buy beer?"

It was becoming difficult to resist the urge to groan and tell my mom she was being ridiculous. "Mom. No one is going to be drinking beer. I don't see what the big deal is. You let me go to all the away games last year with the band and you weren't a huge freak about it."

My mother sighed as if she couldn't stand to hear another word come out of my mouth. "McKenna, I liked you a lot more before you were fabulous. I want you home by midnight. End of story."

I exhaled loudly to let her know that she was ruining my social life. How was I going to tell an entire car full of my friends that I had to be a party pooper and get home before everyone else?

At lunchtime, the entire cafeteria buzzed with excitement. The football team, including Isaac, was loud and obnoxious, obviously getting psyched up for the game that night.

"We should leave no later than three forty-five," Pete told us. "I have basketball practice for an hour after class, but after that, we should all meet in front of the library."

I breathed a sigh of relief. Whatever orientation Mr. Dean had planned for those of us wishing to run for student office couldn't *possibly* take more than an hour. "You're going to the Student Government election meeting, right?" I asked Olivia, really wanting for us to attend the meeting together, kind of innocently hoping that she hadn't been kidding about us running together as a team.

"I'm not sure," she said, wrinkling her delicate button nose. "I have a small crisis on my hands. I still don't have a pair of shoes for the dance tomorrow that matches my dress. I mean, I have a pair of white heels from my uncle's wedding, but they totally clash. I was thinking about making a mad dash for the mall after school and then meeting you guys at the game."

My stomach began to feel queasy. If Olivia wasn't at Mr. Dean's meeting, then how serious was she about running for class president again? What if Mr. Dean wouldn't let her run because she had so casually disregarded his required meeting? What if Michael Walton saw an opportunity to surge past her and snatched the coveted role of president from her, and I had to spend the rest of junior year listening to his sniveling narrative about the lack of adequate recycling bins in the cafeteria?

"Oh my God, Olivia, that's just like the story Violet told," Candace announced, her eyes enormous.

Violet, at the end of the table, turned in our direction. "The story was just silly," she murmured.

It was indeed strange that it was Friday, the day of the big game, just as Violet had started her story about Olivia's fictitious death, and Olivia was talking about going to the mall, just as she had done in Violet's story. I got a little chill thinking back to what Violet had told me on the track after Olivia's party, about how sometimes she saw things.

"What about the dance?" Olivia asked Violet suddenly, as if it had only just then, in that second, occurred to her that Violet had not yet confirmed a date. The topic of the similarities between the day's circumstances and those described in Violet's story was banished. "Who are you going with?"

Violet's face brightened and her eyes sparkled. "Didn't I tell you guys? I'm going with this guy from my church. He goes to St. Patrick's in Ortonville."

Mischa raised an eyebrow at me, and I looked away, not wanting Violet to observe our doubt. She definitely had not mentioned this mysterious guy before. Olivia, never a skeptic until she had irrefutable reason to be one, looked genuinely surprised. "Really? That's awesome! What's his name?"

"Mark," Violet offered. "Regan. I think he went to public school in Willow until around fifth grade before his parents switched him to private school."

"I remember him," Candace announced in a bored voice. "I remember him in first grade eating uncooked pasta when we were supposed to be stringing it together as necklaces for our mothers in art class. Curly hair, dimples?"

Violet nodded.

"Interesting. I can't picture what he must look like now," Mischa commented, peeling the dimpled skin off an orange.

I tried to remember any curly-haired boys from elementary school in our grade who had switched to private school at some point, but there were so many names and faces flooding my memories of kids who had moved out of Willow that Mark Regan didn't come to mind.

"Cool," Olivia said with a genuine smile, relieved of having to chastise Violet for failing to spark an interest in a boy before the dance. "Is he coming to the game tonight?"

Violet shook her head. "No. He's on the St. Patrick's football team and they have their own game in Ortonville tonight. I might go to that instead of ours. I mean, if that's okay with you guys."

Consensus around the lunchroom table was that it was okay for Violet to attend the game in Ortonville instead of riding to Kenosha with the rest of us. Olivia was pleased that the risk of Violet showing up alone at the dance had been mitigated. She and Pete wove their fingers together across the table, beaming at each other in a way that only the most popular kids in school can smile when they're also in love. No one could ever be more perfect than Olivia and Pete.

After eighth period, I rushed to my locker, eager to get the Student Government meeting with Mr. Dean over and done with. I still felt pretty anxious about the possibility of a dark horse entering the race and stealing my chance at victory. There were an odd handful of people in the junior class who could do exactly that: any number of guys from the basketball or football teams, one of Tracy Hartford's friends from the softball team or French club. I didn't want to simply assume I'd win, not even for a second.

Olivia appeared next to my locker, already carrying her books in her canvas monogrammed bag over one shoulder. "I talked to Mr. Dean," she informed me. "He told me since I've already run for office before, I'm excused from today's meeting."

She was smiling like she had a wicked secret, waiting expectantly for something.

"Oh," I replied, unsure of why she remained standing there, next to my locker, as I stuffed my backpack with books I wouldn't touch again until Sunday afternoon.

"Sooooooo," Olivia said, dragging the word across an entire octave of notes, "will you come to the mall with me?"

I closed my locker and twisted the lock. "Olivia, *you're* excused from the meeting, but I'm not. I have to go if I want to run, even though it's just a dumb requirement." Under any other circumstances, I would have abandoned whatever plans I'd made for myself to partake in anything Olivia asked of me. But Olivia already had everything; she didn't really *need* me to forfeit my shot at holding class office to go shoe shopping with her. Still, I felt like refusing to join her on her drive to Green Bay might jeopardize every element of my new life, including my plans to go to the dance with her brother in just over twenty-four hours.

"I know, I know. I really don't want to drive to the mall alone, though. *Please?* We can drive down to Kenosha together, and I'll even buy you tacos on the way?" Olivia stared me down with those warm lagoon-blue eyes of hers, clearly accustomed to getting her way. I felt my insistence on attending the meeting beginning to slip from my grasp. I couldn't give in to her will; I *wouldn't*. If I folded on my intent to run for office, it would be a hasty decision that I'd regret all year.

I tried to suppress my rising annoyance with her for suggesting that her reluctance to shop alone had greater importance than my need to establish myself at school. "I would, Olivia, honestly, but I really want to run for class treasurer. It's just one meeting. It'll probably be over in twenty minutes, if you can wait."

Olivia sighed; she was cross with me but accepted that I wasn't going to cave. "Not even. Mr. Dean will blab for, like, forty minutes, and make you all suffer through a lesson about the electoral college and how our stupid Student Government elections at Willow High School compare to presidential elections in this country. I've endured it twice."

She dug the keys to her new car out of her pink leather purse and dangled them from one of her fingers. "Last chance to come with me to Green Bay."

"Wait a minute. You're going to the big mall in Green Bay?" I asked suddenly, the details of Violet's story at Olivia's birthday party returning to me. "Why would you do that? That's scary, Olivia. It's just like Violet's story."

"Oh my God," Olivia smiled, wrinkling her forehead. "You're not afraid to go shopping with me because of some stupid ghost story, are you? I've already looked for shoes at every store in the crappy mall in Ortonville. The dance is tomorrow!"

"No, of course not! That would be dumb." My real reason for not going to Green Bay was the meeting starting momentarily in Mr. Dean's classroom. "But you have to admit, it *is* scary that Violet said you'd be driving to Green Bay for shoes the day before the dance."

"McKenna, you are way too gullible. Violet's story was about a storm, and it's perfectly sunny outside. Candace has been checking the weather report all week to make sure the game won't be delayed. I will be *fine*." Olivia rolled her eyes and swatted me on the upper arm. "No tacos for you, then."

"I'll see you tonight," I said, hoping that I hadn't genuinely infuriated her. As I watched her saunter down the long hallway toward the doors to the parking lot, her long pale blonde hair hanging in a straight sheet to her waist, I realized there was a slim chance that Pete wouldn't even be waiting for me after school. That was how Olivia operated, if she was angry. Like a queen, moving all her pawns to suit her whims.

"Voting will be held on Monday of the week after next. All ballots will be counted that night. You have all of next week to promote your campaigns. The ballots will be tallied by a team of faculty members to remove any potential for cheating."

Mr. Dean droned on and on, having documented and created a strict process for every single detail of our student elections. At least I could relax a little now that I had seen the competition. No one was attempting to run against Olivia Richmond; that would have been sheer madness. Michael Walton was being challenged by Nicole Blumenthal, who was also his only real competition for valedictorian status. Jason Arkadian smiled weakly at me across the aisle of chairs, and then proceeded to doodle in his spiral notebook throughout the entire meeting. I recalled sourly how Mischa had told me the night we were in Olivia's pool that Jason had a crush on me, and figured it was safe to assume that he'd been cured of his crush.

Outside the classroom, a story below, I could hear the marching band loading its equipment onto the orange school bus that would deliver it to Kenosha. I remembered back to the big game against Kenosha the previous year, and how itchy and hot my navy color guard uniform had been in the atypical September heat on the night of the game. I wondered if Kelly and Erica, the girls with whom I had been closest friends on the color guard team, were boarding the bus for the long drive.

I stifled a yawn with the back of my hand. It was stultifying in the history classroom, and when I turned to see if the windows at the back of the room were even open, I was alarmed to see that storm clouds were rolling in. When I'd first sat down at the start of the meeting, the sky outside had been clear and blue. But now it looked unnaturally bright outside with a thick blanket of clouds covering the sun.

I immediately thought of Violet. Maybe I was being paranoid, but she'd conveniently excused herself from our plans to go to the football game earlier that day, as if she'd known details of her story were going to fall into place. But there was no time to be furious with Violet; I had to reach Olivia and beg her not to go to the mall.

Without wanting to attract the attention of Mr. Dean, I pulled my phone out of my purse and discreetly texted Olivia. Are you at the mall? Are you okay?

She texted me back five minutes later, when Mr. Dean was wrapping up the meeting, distributing handouts listing rules regulating in-school campaign advertising. Just got here. Took forever to find parking. Posters, buttons, and stickers were permitted. Stickers found stuck on school property, like lockers, would be scraped off by the janitors. Posters defaming any other candidates would not be allowed. Advertising materials making mention of any school faculty or staff, or using profanity, would not be allowed. It made my head spin to think that Mr. Dean had spent so much time imagining all the ways in which kids might underhandedly promote themselves just to win a school election.

Finally, the meeting came to an end. It was ten minutes to four, a full five minutes after Pete had said he wanted everyone to meet in the parking lot to depart for Kenosha. I was frantic with fear that the group had left without me, just as afraid of being left behind as I was that Olivia was breezily going through the motions that Violet had already told her would result in her death. I rushed down the stairs to the ground floor of the school and pushed through the doors that led to the student parking lot.

Outside, I was stunned by the strange energy of the afternoon. The cloudy sky was bright with ultraviolet rays, and everything in the parking lot was at a standstill. There was an electric charge in the air as if something was about to happen, something static and coiled, waiting to be set into motion. I looked around for Pete's black Infiniti, not seeing it in the first three rows of cars, and I fished my phone out of my bag to pretend to look busy. *Would they really have left without me? Are they on their way to Kenosha right now, laughing because they know I'm probably standing here looking for Pete's car?* I felt like I was breaking out into a light sweat. That might have been it, the end of my brief popularity, right there on that strange afternoon.

Suddenly, the door behind me opened, and I turned, expecting to see Candace or Jeff, but instead I was startled to see Trey Emory, wearing his usual scowl and army jacket. When our eyes met he looked as surprised to see me as I was to see him, and he straightened his posture. "Why aren't you on your way to Kenosha? Aren't you going to the big game?" Trey asked, sarcasm lacing his voice.

"I am," I said nervously, wishing he weren't there right then, at that very moment. "But I think my friends might have left without me. I was in this meeting, and it ran kind of late."

Trey studied me and shifted his weight from one ratty black Chuck Taylor to the other. "Well, leaving without you doesn't sound like something real friends would do."

I picked at my fingernail polish. My life had been much less complicated before I'd been inducted into Olivia's world. I could have been in Cheryl's mom's car at that very moment, singing Lamb and Owl songs at the top of my lungs, if things hadn't changed before junior year. "Why are you still at school?" I asked him, wanting desperately to change the topic.

Trey shrugged. "Detention. We were changing the spark plugs and wires in Coach Stirling's car in shop yesterday and . . . let's just say she wasn't happy with my work."

I could hardly believe my own ears. Coach Stirling drove a legendary piece of junk, a 1989 powder-blue Cadillac Fleetwood that was too enormous to even fit in one parking space in the faculty parking lot. The auto shop class was always working on it, giving Coach Stirling much-needed free tune-ups. "Geez, Trey! You can't just sabotage a teacher's car!"

Trey smiled innocently. "I wasn't intentionally trying to sabotage it. Maybe I just suck at fixing cars."

I thought of Trey's Toyota and how it was basically held together with a hope and a prayer. He was in the Emorys' driveway almost every Saturday, working on it. "Yeah, right. You probably could *teach* auto shop at this point."

He looked at his shoes, quite possibly blushing, and then added, "Well, maybe I decided to use Coach Stirling's car as the subject of an experiment because she doesn't like my sense of humor."

I was about to inquire further when suddenly Pete's black

Infiniti pulled into the parking lot, blaring music. Jeff sat in the front seat. Candace and Melissa, a girl I didn't know very well, sat in the back. "Are you ready, McKenna?" Jeff asked through his rolled-down window.

"Where were you guys?" I dared to ask.

"We stopped by my house to get umbrellas," Candace said from the back seat. "It's going to pour."

I looked up at the sky. The clouds were darkening, looking much more like storm clouds than they had just five minutes earlier. Had the similarities between the day's events and the elements of Violet's story about Olivia's death crossed Candace's mind? I really hoped that Olivia would abandon her mission to find shoes and drive to Kenosha before the sky got any darker. "Do you think the game is going to be canceled?"

"It's not raining in Kenosha. I'm checking my weather app," Jeff informed all of us.

Next to me, I saw Trey shrinking away toward his own car. I wanted to shout after him, but hesitated for a moment, hoping he wouldn't be annoyed with me for calling attention to him in front of the car full of popular kids. "Hey, Trey," I shouted against my better judgment.

He slowed down just for a second and turned, but kept walking backward, not wanting to slow his pace toward his car.

"See ya," I said weakly.

He waved quickly without saying a word, his hand low, lifted out of his pants pocket for just a flash.

I climbed into the back seat of Pete's car as Melissa moved into the middle to make room for me. "Hi," I said to Melissa.

"Melissa's going to the dance with Jeff," Candace said, explaining the presence of the girl with bright red hair and freckles.

"Has anyone heard from Olivia recently?" I asked. Fifteen minutes had passed since the last time she'd texted me, which made me nervous. Just then, my phone and Candace's buzzed in unison.

"Speak of the devil!" Candace laughed. We both checked our phones to find that Olivia wanted our input on two different pairs of cream-colored pumps she had found at the mall. "Totally the first pair," Candace commented, showing the pictures on her phone's screen to Melissa for approval.

I lowered my voice and said to Candace, "Think about it, Candace. Olivia's in Green Bay shopping for shoes, and it's the day before the dance." She looked at me with a confused expression before I continued, "And she drove there alone, in her *red Prius*. Isn't that kind of freaky?"

"What's freaky about that?" Melissa asked innocently.

Catching my hint, Candace blinked twice. "Oh. Right. Crap." Instead of texting her recommendation on which pair of shoes to buy back to Olivia, she tapped a long note into her phone and flashed me a distressed frown after hitting send. She inhaled deeply and said, "Better to be safe than sorry, right?"

An hour and about twenty heavy metal songs later, we were outside Oshkosh when it began drizzling. The rain put me on edge. Everything was starting to feel eerily similar to the story that Violet had told, like the entire afternoon was an extended moment of déjà vu. I focused on trying to imagine what it was going to be like once we got to Kenosha: the roar of the crowd, the smell of hot dogs, and Olivia waiting for us in the stands.

"You guys," Candace said, as if she was trying to motivate us to do something fun, "you know what would be so cool? If we stopped at the next rest station."

Pete and Jeff both groaned. I was secretly relieved because I had to visit a bathroom too, only I didn't have enough of a friendship established with Pete to request a stop. With much complaining about girls and their weak bladders, Pete pulled off the highway at the next rest stop and parked. The rain was falling more steadily, dancing on the roof of Pete's car and running in tiny rivers down its windows. Using the umbrellas brought from Candace's house, we all made a dash across the parking lot, running in between parked trucks. Pete intentionally jumped in a puddle to douse Jeff as he ran by, and Jeff yelled a curse word at him, the legs of his jeans soaked.

"It's totally raining," Candace said as we both washed our hands in the ladies' room of the rest station beneath glaring fluorescent lights. "They're going to cancel the game."

Melissa joined us a second later, stepping in between us to use the available sink.

"Who could we call to ask?" I wondered, not really wanting to drive all the way to Kenosha only to turn around and drive home again. At that point it would have been a huge relief to know that Olivia was driving home from Green Bay instead of to Kenosha, and to go home myself, since I was uneasy about the argument I'd had with my mom earlier that day about curfew.

Candace suggested, "Let's text Mischa. The cheerleading squad should already be down there."

The group of us reconvened in the small food court area of the rest station, where a handful of truck drivers sat, eating burgers and ignoring each other, as we waited for Mischa to text Candace back with an update about whether or not the game had been postponed. Through the wide glass doors of the rest station, we watched the rain shift into a heavy downpour, and a blinding flash of lightning crackled in the sky moments before an earsplitting clap of thunder shook the building.

"Call Olivia," I commanded Candace, my voice trembling. I was convinced that she was in danger. "She'll listen to you. Tell her she has to leave the mall right now if she hasn't already."

Candace didn't argue; she whipped out her phone and opened her list of contacts.

"Jesus," Pete muttered. "It's like the end of the world."

"There's no way the game is still happening," Melissa said, popping one of the cheese fries she had purchased into her mouth. Jeff helped himself to some of her fries, sliding into the hard plastic seat next to hers. The energy that we had carried into the rest station was steadily evaporating. Our clothes were damp, our hair was tousled, and the long drive ahead to Kenosha seemed more daunting the longer we sat still.

Candace pressed her ear to her phone, waiting for Olivia to answer, then checked its screen and announced, "Mischa." She answered it, stepping away from the rest of us for a few minutes to chat. My breath was becoming a little rapid the more I thought about Olivia by herself in Green Bay. I wished Candace would wrap it up with Mischa and call Olivia again. When Candace returned, she reported, "Game's off. It's being rescheduled."

A truck driver with a long scraggly gray beard wearing a Brewers baseball cap walked past our table on his way to dump the paper liner and napkins on his food tray into a nearby trash can. "You kids might as well sit tight for a while. There's a flash flood warning in effect. You shouldn't be driving on these roads right now."

Pete rolled his eyes once the truck driver's back was to us, but not one of us moved a muscle to get up from our table and return to Pete's Infiniti. None of the truck drivers at the rest stop appeared to be in a hurry to leave either. All of them patiently watched the lightning flash through the station's thick windows, drinking coffees and flipping through newspapers, content to wait the storm out.

Candace called Olivia again and left her a voice mail, sternly demanding that she call her back.

"I am completely freaked out," I told Candace quietly, no longer able to suppress my fascination and fear about how the afternoon was unfolding. We sat next to each other on a hard plastic bench one table away from Melissa and Jeff. I thought of Olivia's words in the hallway near my locker earlier that afternoon, when she had begged me to accompany her to the mall. She'd asked me if I was afraid to go to Green Bay with her "because of a stupid ghost story." This was no ghost story. This was something profoundly sinister, and it felt like it was happening with the momentum of a freight train. "Violet did this. She said all of this was going to happen. She *made* it happen."

"Agreed," Candace said without elaboration. She called Olivia again, who surprisingly answered this time. "Olivia? The game's postponed." She paused, pressing her hand to her free ear to block out the scratchy music playing in the rest station in order to hear Olivia better. "Where are you?" She paused again, still having difficulty hearing Olivia. "We're just outside Oshkosh, but we're turning around once the rain stops and driving home. Can you hear me?"

Candace pulled her phone away from her ear and looked at it angrily as if she intended to fling it across the rest station. "Her phone battery is dying," she told me, frustrated. "She says she's fine and she's still at the mall, but . . ."

Candace didn't have to finish her sentence for me to already know what would follow.

"Her car won't start."

Our eyes locked, and a chill ran through me so violently that I actually shivered. Melissa noticed the serious expressions on both of our faces and stopped chewing. "What's up with you two?" she asked.

"Nothing," Candace said sharply over her shoulder. Her mouth resumed the shape of a firm line, and she looked back at me.

"Do you think we should say something to Pete?" I asked. Pete and Jeff were playing video games on their phones, oblivious to our panic.

"Hell no." Candace shook her head. "They'd think we're nuts."

"Quite honestly, *I* think we're nuts too. But this is too crazy."

Candace looked like she was about to start crying, which rattled me even more. Candace Cotton—the girl who wasn't afraid of anything—was afraid. It made me feel a little better to be in her presence, because if *Candace* was willing to admit that the events of Violet's story were falling into place, I knew I wasn't being paranoid.

"What should we do? Should we call the police?" I asked, completely serious.

"Not the police," Candace said firmly, raising her phone again. She tapped the screen. "We're calling Violet."

She strummed her fingernails impatiently on the crumb-covered table where we sat as Violet's phone rang once, twice, three times and then transferred to voice mail. Candace frowned and held the phone up to my ear so that I could hear Violet's familiar outgoing message: "Hi! This is Violet! I'm not able to answer right now, so . . ."

Candace ended the call and hit redial. "This chick is *so* going to get it. Why the hell did we agree to play all those stupid games last weekend?" She waited again for Violet's voice mail to begin, her head cocked in annoyance, and this time left a furious message. "Violet. This is Candace. It's pouring rain, and Olivia's stuck at the mall in Green Bay. I think you can figure out why I'm calling you. You'd better call me back as soon as you get this."

I felt sickened with anxiety. We sat at the rest station as the storm raged on for another fifteen minutes. Finally, there was a sudden pause in the rain, and we all looked up at one another, surprised by how abruptly the pouring had ended.

"Should we make a run for it?" Jeff asked us.

"Olivia's stuck at the mall in Green Bay, and her car won't start," Candace informed the boys. "Since the game's canceled, we should go pick her up."

Pete said, "That's, like, an hour from here. At least. Why didn't she call me?"

Taking Candace's lead, I jumped in. "Her phone's dead, and we might get there faster than her parents."

Pete didn't need much convincing. "Let's do it. Maybe someone will let her charge her phone inside the mall."

We cleared our snack trays and stepped outside the rest station, surprised at how crisp and clean-smelling the air outside was after such heavy rain. Something kept us from rushing for the car; we stood outside the doors of the rest station for a moment with our collapsed umbrellas tucked under our arms, looking around in wonderment at the soaked parking lot.

One of the truck drivers—not the one with the beard who had cautioned us about the flash floods earlier, but an older one with an enormous belly—opened one of the rest station doors and leaned out of it to address us. "You kids might want to wait it out another five minutes or so." He looked up at the sky skeptically. "Smells like hail."

Pete smiled politely and responded in the voice he reserved for teachers and parents, "Thanks for the warning, but we have to be on our way."

The truck driver shrugged at us like we were just a bunch of dumb kids, and we began walking toward Pete's car. But we had barely gotten halfway across the lot when the first ball of hail struck the ground. The first few balls that I saw were thimble-size clumps of ice barreling down at the blacktop of the parking lot at an incredible speed, smashing to bits when they made impact with the ground and the cabs of trucks. Behind me, I heard Candace shriek, and in front of me, Melissa pulled the hood on her sweatshirt over her head to protect herself. I struggled to open my umbrella and gave up on it. Within seconds, the hail grew much larger—incredibly large, like little rock-hard Ping-Pong balls flinging down upon us from the sky. They hammered against the trucks in the lot and the hoods of parked cars, sounding like gun shots when they made contact. I felt hail hitting my back, my shoulders, and my head, and it hurt so much that I could barely think straight as all of us turned around and ran back to the rest station. It was difficult to even see where I was going as the hail accumulated on the pavement, slippery and crunching beneath my boots.

Bang! Bang! Bang!

Pete held the rest station door open for us as we dashed back inside, shivering and breathing heavily from the adrenaline. We stood there in clumsy silence watching the hail fall, just trying to calm down and make sense of the weather around us. The hail was coming down so steadily that we couldn't even see Pete's car in the lot.

"This is just nuts," Pete muttered to himself.

"It's, like, biblical," Jeff added.

When the storm came to an abrupt stop a few minutes later, we walked to Pete's car only to discover that a large ball of hail had struck the very center of the windshield and cracked it, sending ripples through it like a stone thrown into a pond. It left a dent that looked like an elaborate spiderweb at the point of impact. "Oh crap, dude," Jeff said to Pete.

Pete whipped out his cell phone to call AAA for a tow. "Great. Now we can't even go get Olivia."

Over an hour later, as we watched a tow truck drag Pete's car away through the small mountains of melting hail, we bickered over whose parents should be summoned to fetch us. Oddly, the storm clouds had passed over, revealing a peaceful blue sky that was quickly darkening as night approached. We hadn't heard back from Olivia yet, but Candace was adamant that everything was probably fine—quite possibly just to convince herself that was the case.

"She kept saying her phone was about to die. That's the only reason why she hasn't called," she insisted.

I felt in my bones that something very, very bad had happened.

It was the same way I always felt when I woke up from having my nightmare about Jennie and the fire, like something had changed and it was not only awful, but irreversible, too. Finally, I worked up the nerve to call my mom. I couldn't explain why, but as soon as I heard her voice, I began crying.

"McKenna, where are you?" she asked. As I suspected, she was in her office at the university, absolutely clueless about the storm that had just pelted most of central Wisconsin with hail.

"Outside Oshkosh," I said, trying to steady my voice. "We got caught in a really bad hailstorm and Pete's windshield was destroyed." Mom sounded baffled about why I was so emotionally distraught. "But you're okay, right? Why do you sound so upset?"

I couldn't tell her, obviously, that I had significant reason to believe that one of my closest friends was probably being violently killed just outside Green Bay at that very moment. And that my evidence to support this theory was entirely based on an uncanny paranormal story told by one of my weird friends, who may or may not have had psychic abilities. "I just really wanted to go to the game, and now it's postponed," I lied.

"Do you need me to come and pick you up? How are you kids getting home?"

I swallowed, and was about to request that she come and get me when Candace mouthed, *My mom is on her way.*

"I'm getting a ride home with Candace's mom," I said, kind of wishing my mom would come and pick me up anyway.

As it was just kind of the way things operated in high school, Pete's mom arrived almost an hour later to fetch him and Jeff, and she waited at the rest station until Melissa's mom arrived in a Mercedes. Then both moms went inside and purchased coffees while waiting for Candace's mom, who we all still thought of as Mrs. Cotton, even though she'd been Mrs. Lehrer for several years since she remarried. Pete's mom drove a huge SUV in which we all probably would have fit, but we were still at an age when everyone's parents wanted to drive all the way out of town to pick up their own kid. Finally, Candace's mom arrived, her heavy turquoise-and-silver jewelry jangling and clanging. After *she* insisted on going inside the rest station to get a coffee to keep her awake on the drive home with Candace's half sister, Julia, trudging along behind her, all three of our parents' cars departed the rest station in a motorcade. We drove back to Willow intentionally slowly since the streets were treacherously slippery from all the ice. By the time we were back within town borders, it wasn't even eight o'clock at night yet, but Candace and I were both yawning from the tension of the afternoon.

"Mom, can we drive past the Richmonds' house to see if Olivia is home yet?" Candace asked from the front seat as her mom's car rounded corners, taking us closer to Martha Road. I sat in the back with Julia, who had Candace's height but looked nothing like her.

Candace's mom had a throaty, gravelly voice just like her daughter's. "Oh, Candace, that's all the way on the other side of town, and the streets are so bad."

"It's really important, though," Candace insisted. "She hasn't texted me back in over two hours, and the last time I heard from her, she was stuck at the Bay Park Square mall in Green Bay"

Candace's mom made a right turn onto Martha Road, and just past Julia's head I caught a glimpse of the empty lot, silent and still as it always was, as we rolled down the block toward my house. "You can call her house when we get home."

Candace's mom slowed to a stop in front of my house.

Immediately, I noticed two odd things: Lights were on in my house, indicating that my mom was already home from campus, and the Emorys' house was completely dark. The Emorys' house was *never* dark on a Friday night. Trey's dad was always visible through the front window, watching television in the living room once he got home from work. Trey's brother, Eddie, was always using the game console attached to the television whenever Mr. Emory *wasn't* watching television. And the Emorys' kitchen light was basically on twenty-four hours a day. It was jarring to see the house so dark and empty.

"Thanks for the ride," I said, climbing out of Candace's mom's car.

"Call me *immediately* if Olivia contacts you," Candace ordered. Once inside my house, I couldn't resist the urge to text Henry to see if by chance he'd heard from his sister, which I knew was a long shot since he was at school and not planning to drive up to Wisconsin until the next morning. My anxiety grew when he didn't text me back. I waited until after Mom and I had finished eating pizza before I made the very bold decision to call the Richmonds' house out of concern, despite knowing that it would be really awkward if Olivia's parents answered the phone. I was prepared to apologize for interrupting their Friday night, and inquire politely about whether or not Olivia had made it home from the mall. My fears about Violet's grim story aside, there was still a legitimate possibility that Olivia was stranded in the parking lot at the mall an hour away, unable to call anyone for a ride home. So it wasn't so unreasonable,

I assured myself, that as a concerned friend I would call the house.

But no one answered.

I texted Candace one word: Anything?

And she texted back: Nothing. No answer. And no word from Violet.

I climbed into bed early, assuring myself that I'd be out late the following night. I wanted to believe that in just twenty-four hours I'd be dancing with Henry, Olivia would be fine, and I'd be amused at how oddly coincidental the day's events had mirrored Violet's story. Around midnight, I heard a car pull into the driveway next door, and sat straight up in bed to watch Mr. and Mrs. Emory enter their house through the side door with Eddie following behind them, rubbing his eyes tiredly. They were having a serious discussion, but with my window closed, their voices sounded muffled and indiscernible. It bothered me for some reason that Trey wasn't with them; where could he have been at that hour? For the first time it occurred to me that maybe Trey had a girlfriend I didn't know about.

About ten minutes after the Emorys arrived home and I finally began to drift off to sleep, the door to my bedroom opened and the shape of my mother's body appeared there, illuminated from behind by the light in the hallway.

"McKenna, honey? Are you awake?"

I struggled to pull myself free from the grip of sleep to focus on my mom. Something was wrong; I knew immediately. My mother never came into my room unannounced and never woke me up in the middle of the night.

"I'm afraid I have some really awful news, honey. There's been an accident."

CHAPTER 6

OLIVIA'S MEMORIAL SERVICE WAS HELD ON MONDAY, and school was canceled for the day so that everyone could attend. It was a somber occasion, almost unbearably long, as students, parents, and the Richmonds' extended family drifted in and out of Gundarsson's Funeral Home over the course of three hours. Mom insisted on accompanying me, even though I knew that hanging out in a funeral parlor was hardly how she would have preferred to spend her day off from teaching. The Richmonds, all tall and fair, gathered near the front of the large room, speaking in hushed voices, tapping the corners of their eyes with handkerchiefs. Olivia's casket, ornate and shiny, was closed. Next to it, a huge picture of Olivia smiling in her volleyball uniform was placed on an easel, with a few of her baby pictures pinned on top of it in a sort of hastily assembled collage. I had heard rumors that Henry had been forced to identify his sister's body at the coroner's office because it had been so mangled that Mrs. Richmond had passed out at the sight of it. He had greeted me with a painful smile when I'd first arrived, but after a few minutes of strained conversation, he excused himself to retreat back to his family's territory near the casket and avoided even looking in my direction.

Over the course of the weekend, I had aggregated snippets of the story from various sources. The headline on the Saturday-morning issue of the *Willow Gazette* had been TRAGEDY IN GREEN BAY: LOCAL TEEN KILLED IN COLLISION. The three sparse paragraphs about the crash claimed that two local teens from Willow High School had been involved in a crash just outside Green Bay when an eighteen-wheeler truck had hit them head-on during the hailstorm. The driver of the car in which Olivia had been riding hadn't been named, but had allegedly stumbled away from the scene with minor injuries. A picture of what was left of the car had run alongside the article. It was unrecognizable as a vehicle; it looked more like a gnarly knot of scrap metal, and the expression on the face of the state trooper who had been photographed next to the wreckage indicated that he was thinking the same thing that I was thinking: How was it possible that someone had walked away alive from that kind of an accident? The newspaper claimed that the truck driver involved in the crash was devastated; he hadn't even seen the other car swerve into his lane through the heavy hail. Cheryl had called me on Saturday afternoon to share the rumor that Olivia's body had practically been cut in half from the force of the collision. The shoes she had just bought at the mall were found nearly thirty feet away from the car, off to the side of the rural highway, in the woods. Not far, Cheryl added, from Olivia's severed arm.

Of course I wondered who had been driving her. In none of the tearful conversations I'd had with friends who'd called to talk had the name of the driver been mentioned. It didn't seem like anyone knew with whom Olivia had spent her final moments.

At the back of the room, just inside the doors, I lurked in a corner, watching quietly as kids from school and teachers drifted in. No one knew quite what to say to Olivia's parents, how to stand, where to put their hands, where to rest their eyes. Everyone was hungry for more details, myself included, but it was absolutely out of the question to talk about the accident at the memorial. Soft classical music played throughout the afternoon, pumped in through the vents along with chilly air. There were enormous floral arrangements on both sides of the casket; sent from the Lions Club, the Knights of Columbus, the PTA, the faculty union at the high school, and Olivia's dad's accounting firm. A hanging arrangement of pale pink bud roses and baby's breath draped over the casket's top, held together with silky white ribbon. It was probably not all that different from the corsage that Pete had planned to place on Olivia's wrist the night of the Fall Fling, the dance that had been canceled in light of Olivia's tragic death. Pete had arrived not long after me and my mom, staying just a few brief minutes with his parents before hugging Olivia's mom and dad and promptly leaving. He had nodded at me from across the room, his eyes red and swollen. Seeing a boy my own age who had quite clearly been crying made me feel very uncomfortable. His suit seemed to fit him perfectly, and I wondered if maybe it had been bought recently for the dance.

Tracy Hartford and her mother arrived early, their faces solemn and pious. They made a point of greeting everyone who entered and thanking them for coming, as if they were part of Olivia's family. In reality, Olivia barely even spoke to Tracy and thought she was an annoying busybody, but the Hartfords thrived on gossip and were certainly in their element that day at the funeral home. They asked everyone in attendance to sign the guest book, and they were so insistent about it, it was almost as if reaching a goal of signatures would bring Olivia back.

I couldn't remember having attended a memorial service or wake for Jennie, but presumably if there had been one, it had been in the very same room where we all gathered to pay our respects to Olivia. Willow was a small enough town that everyone was waked at Gundarsson's and buried either at our church, St. Monica's, which was where Jennie was buried, or the Jewish cemetery on the other side of town. Wearing my only black dress, two sizes too large for me, I picked the light blue nail polish off my thumbs and made small talk with people I recognized as they entered and left. Mischa and Amanda arrived with their parents, and Mischa and I hugged for what felt like five minutes even though we had been talking on the phone almost hourly since dawn on Saturday morning.

"Has Candace come yet?" she asked me. I shook my head.

Candace was having a complete and utter freak-out. As if it weren't enough to have unexpectedly lost her best friend, her whole-hearted belief that Olivia's death had been premeditated somehow by Violet was driving her to the brink of insanity. She had called me three times since Friday night, each time rambling hysterically about how she wanted to tell the whole world about what Violet had done because Olivia would have wanted it that way. It was terrifying to conclude that Violet somehow had either been able to predict with total accuracy what was going to happen with Olivia, or even more frighteningly, that she had caused the accident. But I tried not to emphasize that I agreed with Candace when I spoke with her. We weren't going to have any luck convincing parents or the police that Violet had anything to do with Olivia's accident. I hadn't heard a word from her since Sunday morning, and hadn't even received a response when I had texted her to see if she was okay on Sunday afternoon.

"Her mom admitted her to the hospital yesterday," Mischa confided in me. "Julia texted me. They were afraid she was having a nervous breakdown, and she's in the psychiatric ward."

I suddenly felt unbearably cold in the funeral parlor's frosty air. A certain and unshakable fear that we had brought this unthinkable tragedy upon ourselves nestled into the marrow of my bones. We had done something so childish and irresponsible by playing that stupid game, and now, if my fears were correct, Olivia had paid for it with her life. Poor Candace. Psychiatrists weren't going to believe her, of course. I imagined her as a patient, the patronizing looks on her attending physicians' faces as she wildly blabbed about the birthday party game, sounding absolutely crazy.

Light as a feather, stiff as a board.

"I thought maybe her mom would let her out to come to this, but maybe not," Mischa mused. "Maybe she's worse than I thought." It couldn't be discounted that Olivia's death had been a purely random coincidence. Even though it seemed pretty undeniable that Violet had known exactly what was going to happen, it was still hard to believe that it was true. There was simply no explanation for how she could have predicted everything, or had a hand in making all the events actualize.

"We're stepping outside for air," I told my mom, who was fiddling with her purse like she was ready to leave. Naturally, people couldn't help but stare at my mom, since many of the guests in attendance at Olivia's service had lived in our town long enough to remember the fire. Surely they were thinking that my mom had some kind of an obligation to offer words of comfort to the Richmonds, having herself lost a child in a freak accident. But my mom wasn't like that; even after eight years, her grief over Jennie's death was still very private. When she'd seen Tracy Hartford's mother approach her earlier in the afternoon, she had busied herself by pretending to read Olivia's prayer card. "You don't have to stay. I can get a ride home when I'm ready."

My mom looked like I had handed her a winning lottery ticket, and confessed to having some lesson plans to prepare at home. She accompanied Mischa and me outside to the parking lot, and we waited in silence, our backs pressed against the brick exterior of Gundarsson's, until she got into her car and drove off. It was cold out, significantly colder in just the ten days that had passed since Olivia's birthday party. Cold enough that I buttoned up my denim jacket and Mischa pulled her wool cardigan around her waist. We stood outside watching traffic pass on the highway in silence for a few seconds, our eyes adjusting to the bright, overcast day after having been in the dim funeral parlor for so long.

"My parents asked me about the game. Candace's mom called my mom and wanted to know what we did on Friday night," Mischa finally said, her voice flat and emotionless.

"Jesus, you didn't tell her, did you?" I asked, suddenly fearful that rumors were going to sweep the high school that we had been invoking spirits or worshipping the devil. My stomach felt upset, like I knew I was going to get in trouble, only I was far too old to be afraid of punishment. Primarily I felt embarrassed, because the game we'd played was so childish, for middle schoolers. It would be mortifying for the entire high school to find out that was how the most popular girls in the junior class had spent a Friday night.

"No! Of course not," Mischa exclaimed. She thought for a second, and then added, "I said we were telling ghost stories, but that was it. I mean, I feel bad kind of implying that Candace is lying, but she needs to get a grip! She can't just go around claiming that Violet had something to do with Olivia's death. She's going to make us all seem nuts."

"Have you heard from Violet at all?" I asked. "I've left her two voice mails, but she hasn't called me back."

A car entered the parking lot of the funeral home and both of our heads turned. It was the Emorys' car, and when it parked, Trey emerged with his parents, looking almost unrecognizable. It wasn't so much the black eye he had or the bright blue sling around his left arm that made him look so much like a different person, but the dark navy suit he wore with a silk tie. My immediate assumption was that he'd been in some kind of fight, and I wondered if he'd been out causing trouble on Friday night. I knew he sometimes hung out at Tallmadge Park with the heavy-metal guys from school, and every once in a while troublemakers from Ortonville would show up there looking to throw some punches. Our eyes met across the parking lot, and he looked away quickly as he approached the entrance with his parents.

"I cannot believe he's here," Mischa commented as the Emorys approached where we were lingering.

"Why? Because he wasn't friends with Olivia?" I asked.

Mischa looked at me as if I was crazy. "No, McKenna. Trey Emory was *driving* the night of the accident."

Time came to a standstill. My heart paused for a prolonged second as I tried to make sense of what Mischa had told me, working backward from the present to the beginning of Trey's involvement with Olivia's death. Trey had been with Olivia at the moment she died.

"We've talked on the phone, like, fifty times since Saturday morning and you never mentioned that," I said, sounding hoarse.

"I thought I told you this morning. He ran into Olivia in the parking lot at the mall and offered her a jump-start, and when that didn't work, he said he'd give her a ride back to Willow. Then the hail started."

The Emorys reached the entrance to the funeral parlor, and Trey strode inside without even acknowledging Mischa and me. Mrs. Emory recognized me and paused to greet me, and Mr. Emory stood loyally behind her, his hand on the small of her back as she leaned forward to peck me on the cheek. Mrs. Emory smelled like powdery perfume, one that was expensive and worn only on special occasions.

"Hello, McKenna," she said, sounding tired. "Is your mother here with you?"

"She already left," I said. "She had stuff to do at home."

"I'll stop by the house to say hi later," Mrs. Emory said wistfully, as if she and my mother were confidantes. Mrs. Emory was a little younger than my mom, and to the best of my knowledge they rarely spoke other than trading niceties in the driveway. She and Mr. Emory entered the funeral parlor, and Mischa raised an eyebrow at me.

"Who did you hear that from, about Trey?" I asked, my voice sounding a little strangled.

"Do you, like, *know* them?" Mischa asked suspiciously, distracted by my interaction with Trey's parents. Her eyes darted toward the doors of the funeral parlor, specifying that it was the Emorys to whom she was referring.

"Sort of. They live on our street."

That explanation seemed sufficient for Mischa to believe that I hadn't been holding out on her about us having some kind of secret friendship. "There's this girl, Megan, on my gymnastics team whose mom works in the emergency room at St. Matthew's Hospital in Suamico. She told me that Trey was brought in by an ambulance on Friday, and he was in shock. He couldn't even tell the doctors what had happened. He saw *everything*," Mischa told me, her eyes enormous. "They had to sedate him and take his ID out of his wallet to even figure out who to call. My stupid parents made us go to gymnastics practice last night even though we're, like, in mourning. So I only found out last night when Megan told me."

Mischa continued grumbling about her parents' insistence that she continue her training in preparation for the state sectionals in February despite the shock of Olivia's death. Her voice grew distant as my knees weakened with nausea. My heart ached for Trey and my feelings were even more hurt that he hadn't said hello to me as he had passed us on his way into the funeral home. Cheryl had told me that Olivia's injuries had been as terrible as those described by Violet in her prediction, and I couldn't imagine being inches away from that kind of gore. I thought of Trey's beloved Corolla and made the connection that it was the scrap heap I'd seen in the photo that ran in the town newspaper. That car, the one he'd spent so many weekend afternoons fixing, was completely wrecked.

But despite sympathy for him, I couldn't help but wonder—

what had Trey been doing in Green Bay at the mall on Friday evening after I'd run into him in the parking lot at school?

I was so caught up in thinking about Trey that I forgot if Mischa had said she'd heard a word from Violet. The sun began to set just after six o'clock, and Mischa's parents insisted on driving me home. On my way out of Gundarsson's, I finally submitted to Tracy Hartford's request for me to sign the guest book. Nearly every single page was covered in the neat penmanship of parents and drawings of kitties, butterflies, hearts, and unicorns. Michael Walton had been enough of a freak to write *junior class vice president* beneath his name. As I slowly signed my name in my best handwriting, I felt like I was making a promise to Olivia that I would find out why this happened. I remembered her trying to bribe me with tacos. If I had been a better friend, if I'd wanted her to like me more, if I hadn't been so adamant about running for office and trying to carve out a little independence for myself, I might have saved Olivia's life.

Or I might have died alongside her.

Mom had actually cooked a real dinner: a turkey meat loaf and baked sweet potatoes, a menu that consisted of foods from Rhonda's recommended list for me, showing that my mom cared more about the impact of Olivia's death on me than she had let on earlier in the day. We ate in silence, and she told me that Dad had called before I'd gotten home.

"Your dad's worried about you," Mom told me. "If you want to talk to a professional, he can make arrangements for you to see one of his old colleagues in Sheboygan."

I didn't look up. I continued stabbing at my turkey meat loaf with my fork. My feelings about Olivia's death were too complicated to share with a psychiatrist. I was upset about her loss, of course. But I was also being honest enough with myself to admit that after only three weeks of close friendship, I didn't really have the right to be completely devastated by her death. I didn't know Olivia all that well, not at all, and now I never would. My predominant feelings were of surprise, and of overwhelming indirect responsibility. My throat and chest felt raw from crying because of this sense of guilt, not because I couldn't bear the thought of going on with my life without Olivia in it. A professional psychiatrist couldn't possibly have understood how I felt, convinced that my participation in a stupid party game had led to my friend's death.

And worse: We'd *all* played the game. Violet had predicted *all* of our deaths.

Well, except mine.

For the first chilling time I wondered in terror . . . would Candace or Mischa be next?

"I'm fine," I told my mom before clearing my plate.

After I had changed into pajamas, Moxie scratched at my closed bedroom door to let me know that she wanted to run around the backyard one more time. I put on my slippers and my denim jacket and followed her to the kitchen. When I slid open the door to our small deck, I was startled to see Trey sitting on the steps, his back to me. He had changed out of his suit and was wearing his army coat and jeans again. He only budged when Moxie rushed toward him and attacked him with dog kisses, her tail wagging. His right hand moved up to her thick fur coat to pet her, and he turned to permit her to lick his face. He kept his left arm, still in its blue brace, pinned to his side.

Moxie's attention was caught by fluttering leaves at the far corner of the yard, and she trotted off as quickly as she could on her sore limbs to investigate. I hesitated for a moment before walking across the deck and sitting down on the steps next to Trey, leaving as many inches between us as the width of the steps would allow. The moon was a waning sliver of a crescent. Clouds slowly moved past it in what looked like nomadic caravans. There was simply nothing to say, I knew, despite the fact that my brain kept testing out greetings in my head, all of which I deemed unworthy. Even just simply saying, *Are you okay?* felt like it would come out wrong. Of course he wasn't okay; that much was obvious. I didn't dare look at him, not even out of the corner of my eye, because I knew if I got the slightest glimpse of his face I would be unable to stop staring at his swollen black eye. Mischa had said that Trey hadn't been able to speak at the hospital on Friday night. It was entirely possible that he wasn't speaking yet at all.

After a few minutes of silence, without saying a word, I reached for his hand and held it in mine. We sat there quietly in the cool night air, our hands locked between us on the wooden step. I could feel my heart beating against my own rib cage, and I struggled to think of anything I could say that might comfort him after what he'd experienced. I wondered if he felt responsible for the accident since the newspaper had said he was the one who had accidentally swerved into oncoming traffic. My heart ached with the desire to tell him that it wasn't his fault. There was nothing he could have done to prevent what had happened, but I couldn't explain to him how I knew that. If I hadn't been acting like such a selfish brat in wanting to rush off to the game on Friday, maybe I could have spared him from all this pain.

A lump rose in my throat. Seeing him like this, hurting so badly, made me desperately wish for a chance to do things differently. When I finally opened my mouth to speak, I said in a shaky voice, "Trey, I'm sorry."

He waited a long time before finally replying, "I'm sorry you missed the dance." Of all the things for him to have said in that moment, the last thing I was expecting was an apology from him about the cancellation of the dance. The dance, and all my romantic expectations for it, seemed like part of a different life, one I could barely remember.

"I don't care about the dance," I said truthfully. There were suddenly so many more things on the horizon that were more urgent than slow dancing with a guy I barely knew. Like trying to figure out if Violet had actually *murdered* Olivia in some roundabout way. "Right now, I care about *you*."

"Yeah, but you *did* care. Before Friday night, you cared," Trey said slowly, stating what he assumed to be a fact rather than phrasing his statement as an accusation.

I felt an obligation rising. I felt like I had no choice but to confess to him what we'd done at Olivia's birthday party, how we had summoned these events, how Mischa and I were trying to make sense of them, and how they were driving Candace mad. Now he was a part of it all, and I had to wonder if Violet had seen Trey in her vision of Olivia's death. But I couldn't be sure of Trey's state of mind, whether he'd be open to hearing my paranormal mumbo jumbo so soon after the horror of the accident.

"Nothing before Friday night matters," I said finally, deciding not to tell him anything about Violet's game just yet.

He turned toward me, and only when I felt his gaze on me did I dare turn to the left to examine him. His right eye was swollen nearly shut, and the bruising around it was an angry shade of purple. I hadn't noticed at Gundarsson's, but he also had stitches sewn in black thread, a single-file line of Xs, along his right cheekbone, and swelling along his lower lip. His eyes were blue, a dazzling aquamarine, I made note, recalling how I had neglected to check during our last late-night encounter.

"That's not true. A lot of things happened before Friday night that matter."

I was so taken aback by how seriously he had been hurt in the car crash, I couldn't say a word. It was a miracle he hadn't also been killed instantly. He never could have known when he'd offered Olivia a ride what awaited him on the highway, but *I'd* known. I squeezed his hand, remembering how he had touched my hair the previous weekend. "You're right," I agreed. On an impulse, I leaned over and kissed him gently on his cheek.

"*I'm* sorry," I whispered. "That you got mixed up in all of this."

His lips parted in question for a second, but I was already standing, my hand sliding out of his. "Moxie, come on, girl," I called, and the dog looked up at me from across the yard and began her lopsided hobble back to the deck. Even as I stood there, awkwardly waiting for my dog, I wondered if I had just blown a shot at having him kiss me, my first *real* kiss with a boy I *really* liked. But Trey wasn't supposed to be the boy who kissed me my junior year. It was supposed to be Henry at the Fall Fling, Henry about whom I would daydream.

None of this was supposed to be happening.

"Where have you been?"

In the locker room the next morning, Mischa and I found Violet in the farthest corner, changing into her uniform. Her complexion was pale, and her eyes looked sunken, as if she had suffered through the flu all weekend. When she saw us approaching her, her expression remained unchanged, and she looked away immediately, securing her combination lock on her locker. She sat down on a nearby bench to lace up her running shoes.

"Did you hear me? I've been texting you all weekend, Violet. What is going on?" Mischa put her hands on her hips and stood over Violet, fuming. For someone of such small stature, Mischa exuded a terrifying amount of power.

Other girls around us, also changing for gym class, looked over their shoulders at us. The entire high school was on edge that day. It was like the weekend of unexpected tragedy had pushed us all hard from behind—like a shove off a plane to force someone to reluctantly begin skydiving—right into a Tuesday schedule. Olivia's death had been mentioned in the announcements during homeroom, inspiring half the student body to spontaneously burst into tears before the day had even really begun. We'd all received text messages on Saturday morning letting us know that the Fall Fling had been canceled, and there were rumors going around about homecoming being rescheduled, too, or it being canceled completely.

When Violet looked up at us, both laces tied, her eyes were glassy with tears and she was grimacing, kind of like the unfulfilled urge to sob was causing her physical pain.

"I'm sorry, but what did you want me to do? I knew as soon as I heard about Olivia that you guys were going to be mad at me," Violet said.

"We're not mad at you!" Mischa yelled, certainly *sounding* mad. Now other girls were staring as they changed. We were creating a locker-room spectacle. "But you have some explaining to do, Violet, and I think you know why."

I stood behind Mischa with my arms crossed over my chest. Confrontation really wasn't my style, and I was a little terrified to accuse Violet of anything without having a better sense of exactly how much she had manipulated events leading up to the accident. I felt the tiniest little seed of an idea, of acting as sort of a spy to get closer to Violet, begin to grow in my head. If I could get to know Violet better and convince her that I was on her side, maybe she'd admit the truth to me. After Olivia's party, she'd confessed to me that she had visions of how people would die. Based on that alone, I reasoned that I had a better chance than anyone else at school at getting answers from her.

I uncrossed my arms and stepped in between Mischa and Violet. "We're not mad, Violet. Really. We're just confused."

"Let's go, ladies! I want to see you out on that track!" Coach

Stirling's booming voice entered the locker room, and seconds later she appeared around the corner of a row of blue lockers. "Portnoy! Brady! Suit up. Let's go."

Violet glared at both of us, and while Coach Stirling was still present to give her cover, she darted out the locker-room doors and onto the track.

Mischa set her tote bag down on the bench and pulled out her gym suit. "Why are you being nice to her? She knows something," she said, her eyes squinted. "I can tell that girl knows more than she's willing to admit."

I hadn't told Mischa or Candace about Violet's visions. Mischa was already so furious that it didn't seem wise to inform her now. She'd freak out that I hadn't told her sooner. Besides, I could use the secret Violet had shared with me as a basis upon which to build more trust. "She's not going to tell us anything if she thinks we're mad at her."

"This is *not* a matter of catching more flies with honey," Mischa snapped at me. "Olivia is dead!"

On the track, it was a perfect autumn day, the air scented with dry leaves and the sun still warm on my bare arms and legs as Mischa and I broke into a run to catch up to Violet, who was already at least one lap ahead of us.

"You can't run forever, Violet," Mischa warned her from behind.

Violet slowed to a jog and then a walk to allow us to fall into step with her. She looked straight ahead, avoiding eye contact with us, and pulled her earbuds out of her ears, letting them swing on long white cords to her knees.

"Why weren't you answering your phone all weekend?" Mischa demanded.

"What would you have wanted me to say?" Violet said, her voice high-pitched and wild. "I didn't know all those things were going to happen. It was a total coincidence, but as soon as I heard about it, I knew you guys were going to think I had something to do with it."

"Uh, yeah. Of course," I said as gently as possible, not wanting to upset her more. "Violet, how could we not? You predicted every detail of it."

"I didn't *predict* it," Violet insisted.

"Well, then what would you call it?" Mischa asked. "You knew what was going to happen, *how* it was going to happen, and exactly *when* it was going to happen. We're not paranoid, Violet. That's too many coincidences to be believed."

"Yeah, okay," Violet agreed sarcastically. Sarcasm was new from her. Her tone was so surprisingly biting, it didn't even sound like her. "I saw into the future at Olivia's birthday party and predicted this horrible accident right down to every last detail. Listen to yourself, Mischa. You sound psycho."

Mischa was quiet for a moment.

"I mean, if I really could see the future, I'd be working for the CIA to prevent terrorist attacks. And I'd play the lottery every night, and live in a castle with all my winnings. I mean, come on," Violet reasoned, gaining confidence in her voice. "Am I right, McKenna?"

She *was* right: It was ludicrous of us to suggest that she had magical powers. But at the same time, I felt certain that there was something not quite right about Violet. Somehow, she must have known that by confiding in me about her abilities—in the specific context of how it related to her knowledge of my sister's death—I wouldn't tell the others. She was providing me with the perfect opportunity to take her side. For the moment, even if it enraged Mischa, that was what I needed to do. "You're right," I admitted quietly. "But Violet, you have to admit this is all really weird."

"Yes, it's weird," Violet agreed. "Just try to understand how I feel. Olivia was my friend too."

She inserted her earbuds again and ran off ahead of us on the track.

CHAPTER 7

AFTER SCHOOL, I SAW MR. DEAN HAVING A conversation with Violet in the hallway as I collected my books. With Olivia gone and Candace in the hospital, I was reduced back down to my sophomore routine of walking home alone. Violet was nodding slowly, listening to every word Mr. Dean told her. I couldn't help but wonder if he was talking to her about Student Government. The election had been postponed because of Olivia's unexpected death, but only by one week. Voting had been rescheduled for the following Monday, so I had little choice but to get my posters in order once I got home that afternoon.

The next morning, I walked to school early, hoping with every step of the two-mile walk that no one from school, particularly Trey (who I hadn't seen at all the day before), would drive past and see me carrying my giant rolled poster boards. At school, I hung my posters with little loops of masking tape by myself, finding myself hanging them always a few inches from those belonging to Michael Walton, which I guessed was sort of a subconscious strategy. By the time I got back up to the hallway where my locker was located, kids were already starting to stream in through the hallways, and I noticed something incredible at the far end of the hall.

Violet was hanging up a poster above the drinking fountain, and Tracy Hartford seemed to be holding a few more pieces of poster board, assisting her.

I walked toward them as if in a trance. Sure enough, the poster that Violet was hanging up announced that she was running for class president. The poster featured a picture of her smiling face, with VIOLET SIMMONS FOR JUNIOR CLASS PRESIDENT neatly written in block letters drawn in red felt marker ink, colored in carefully. It was somehow far more stylish, even though simplistic, than my own posters, on which I had tried to obscure my lack of artistic inspiration with tons of glitter.

"What's this?" I asked as Violet smoothed the poster against the wall with her palm to flatten it there.

"Oh hi, McKenna. Mr. Dean asked me yesterday if I would consider running for class president since the election is so close at hand," Violet said innocently.

"She'd be a natural," Tracy said, smiling at Violet, as if anyone had asked her for her opinion.

"Really," I said, sure that I wasn't doing a good job of hiding the doubt in my voice.

"Well, I was class secretary at my old school," Violet said, tucking her hair back behind one ear. This was the first time I'd heard about Violet's involvement with Student Government at her old school in Illinois. "And, I mean, if Tracy's a shoo-in for class secretary here, it would be dumb for me to run against *her*. So if she's secretary and you're treasurer, we could have so much fun if I win."

"Is anyone else running?" I asked her rather impolitely. I was just so surprised that Olivia hadn't even been dead a whole week, and already Violet was running for her office. It was a cold, cold move, but I could see that Violet was already trying to innocently spin her ruthless ambition into a charitable service for the rest of her classmates.

Violet and Tracy exchanged uncomfortable looks, and Tracy rolled her eyes. "Well, of *course* Michael Walton wants to run for class president, but he was nominated for *vice president*, and it's too late to change the nomination."

I bit the inside of my cheek. Mr. Dean was the only teacher on staff who cared much about the Student Government, so he could have easily repealed any of the rules if it suited his fancy. "How did you convince him to let you run? You already missed the nomination period."

I'd had to collect five signatures to be allowed to run, which I'd obtained from Candace, Isaac, Pete, Mischa, and Matt at lunchtime on the Friday before the meeting. There had to be a reason why so many loopholes were being created for Violet, although it was an easy guess that her big blue eyes and long eyelashes were probably all it took to get Mr. Dean to make exceptions for her. The other possibility was that Violet was influencing Mr. Dean some other, more sinister way.

"No one other than Olivia sought the nomination," Violet said matter-of-factly, "so I was allowed to turn in my signatures this morning."

Just then, down the hall, Mr. Dean stepped out of his history class-room and nodded at all of us. He raised his hand in a friendly wave.

"Well," I said, still so confused about what was going on with Violet but getting an even stronger sense that the girl was just dangerous, "it *would* be cool if we were all on Student Government together." As I returned to my locker to gather my books for my morning classes, it occurred to me that I wasn't going to have to try very hard to become closer friends with Violet to gather information about her. Even though the thought of collaborating with her on Student Government projects all year sickened me, she seemed to be genuinely excited about the possibility of Tracy and me becoming her new best friends.

At lunchtime, it was noticed immediately by everyone at our table that Violet was sitting two tables away, across from Tracy Hartford. Mischa was fuming. "Who does she think she is? Did you see her posters? Does she think she can just pick up Olivia's life where Olivia left off?"

Matt put a hand on Mischa's back to calm her down. "She's just running for office. It's not a big deal."

Nothing could calm Mischa down as she glared across the cafeteria. "It *is* a big deal, and it's more than just running for office."

My focus on appearing unconcerned about Violet was interrupted by a boy wearing a green army jacket near the vending machines. It was, without a doubt, Trey, although how I hadn't noticed him earlier in the day, I didn't know. His back was to me as I watched him slide a wrinkled dollar bill into the vending machine with his right hand and punch a button to request a can of soda. The machine spat out the can as requested, and Trey took it with him as he trudged away, back down the stairs that led to the locker rooms.

I found myself wondering again if Violet had seen Trey in her vision of Olivia's death. She'd seen enough to know that Olivia hadn't been driving at the time of the crash. Had she known that Trey would survive?

Once again, I wondered what Trey had been doing in Green Bay on Friday. But now, just like everything else surrounding the accident, the coincidence that he'd come across Olivia while her car refused to start seemed awfully suspicious.

And Trey was the last person I wanted to suspect of aiding Violet.

On my long walk home, I paused about half a mile into my journey to change out of my stylish wedge oxfords and into my running shoes. A fat blister, watery and pink, was forming on the back of my left ankle. As I rounded my corner and passed the empty lot, I became overwhelmed with the hunch that something was wrong at home. I couldn't say what it was, exactly. It wasn't like a premonition or a vision of danger. It was just a slow suspicion, not so unlike how I'd sensed the blister forming on my foot half an hour earlier.

When I entered my house, it was oddly quiet. I stepped into the kitchen and opened the fridge as was my habit, before I realized that I hadn't heard Moxie shake her collar. Her days of meeting me at the door were long over since her arthritis had gotten so bad, but typically as soon as I got home I could hear her rising from whichever corner of the house she had been dozing in and shake out her fur and collar, jingling her dog tags.

But that day: no jingling. I slowly closed the door of the fridge, starting to feel terrible. I had no reason to cry just yet, but I knew already that the tears would come. First I checked the dining room, where Moxie sometimes liked to lie down next to the radiator. Then,

I peeked into Mom's room, *really* hoping to see a lump of black-and-white fur at the foot of the bed, where the dog often liked to snooze.

"Moxie?" I called down the hall, not knowing where else she might be. Moxie had her spots throughout the house, her favorite places to stretch out and rest, but I didn't find her in any of them. Finally, having already checked all her usual places, I stepped into my own bedroom. Moxie was curled into a ball on my bed with her head resting on my pillow, a position in which she used to sleep when she was still a puppy. Jennie and I had received Moxie as a gift from our parents when we turned three because Jennie was obsessed with puppies and had been asking for one. I sat down on the edge of my bed, not wanting to startle the dog if she was sleeping, but I already knew that she wasn't. I gently touched Moxie's soft head, and my fear was confirmed. She wasn't breathing, her chest wasn't rising, her nostrils weren't flaring in their little expand-contract pattern as they did when she was deeply asleep, dreaming about chasing creatures in the yard.

I can't believe this is happening, I thought.

I leaned forward and rested my head on hers, wanting that moment never to end, for Moxie to never be farther away from me than she was right there, on my bed. It wasn't possible for me to know at what time she'd passed away, but presumably she'd climbed up on my bed and drifted off to eternity at some point in the afternoon after my mom had left for Sheboygan. I thought about texting Mom to let her know, but couldn't find any words that wouldn't be too unbearably heartbreaking. It was entirely possible that this news was going to upset Mom so much that she wouldn't be able to drive home. So instead, after I kissed Moxie's head a few times and stroked her fur, I went to the garage by myself and decided to try to bury Moxie before Mom got home. It would be hard enough for her to accept Moxie's passing without having to see her immobile, not breathing.

In the backyard, I began digging a hole near the fence, where Moxie loved to dig holes, herself. After five minutes, my hands were becoming chafed from the handle of the shovel, and I was sweating. I paused for a moment to catch my breath, looking down at my progress, which was a hole little more than five inches deep. Behind me, I heard our gate open and close, and I saw Trey approaching me when I looked over my shoulder, carrying a shovel from his own garage. He was no longer wearing the bright blue brace on his left arm, and without saying a word he began digging where I was digging. I wiped sweat from my brow with the sleeve of my hoodie and wondered if his left arm was healed enough for him to be using it, but didn't dare ask.

"If you don't mind my asking, what are we digging for?" Trey asked a few minutes later when he paused to catch his breath.

"My dog died," I said as calmly as I could, not wanting to cry in front of him. I felt my nose threatening to drip as I suppressed my tears. The injuries on his face distracted me momentarily from my heartache over Moxie; the swelling had gone down but had been replaced by dark purple bruising along his cheekbone and around his lip and jaw. Trey didn't press me for more information; he just kept digging until we were both standing in front of a pretty sizable hole, about three feet deep.

"Do you think this is big enough?" he asked me. I nodded.

"Where is she?" Trey asked, looking past me, toward the house. I realized he was offering to go inside and retrieve her so that I wouldn't have to. I wasn't sure if he knew the layout of our house, but then remembered that all of the houses on our block were basically carbon copies. "She's on my bed," I managed to say without my voice cracking.

Trey went into the house while I stared ahead into space, daydreaming, watching my breath escape my mouth in barely visible white puffs as the day turned into evening and the warm sun disappeared over the horizon. I smelled fire and assumed that one of our neighbors was lighting their fireplace for the first time that autumn. The fireflies that had swarmed the yard just a few evenings ago were gone for the season. I swallowed hard; the thought that Moxie wouldn't live to see another summer and bark at fireflies ever again made my chest hurt. Trey returned a few minutes later, carrying Moxie's body effortlessly, as if she were weightless. I appreciated the care with which he gently set her down in the hole we'd dug, and arranged her paws as if he were trying to make her comfortable. I was on the edge of breaking into a tsunami of tears, knowing that it was strange to be so much more deeply saddened by the death of a dog than I was by the death of one of my own friends. Even assuring myself that Moxie was finally out of the constant nagging pain of her arthritis, and that maybe she was, at that very moment, looking down at me from heaven next to Jennie, didn't comfort me much.

"I'll cover her," Trey said finally, observing that I hadn't moved a muscle since he'd stepped back from the hole. Putting dirt on top of her was something I just couldn't bring myself to do, I realized. I wasn't sure if I would have found the necessary strength if Trey hadn't been there, or if having him there provided me with an opportunity to be overwhelmed by my sorrow. But either way, I turned my back and quietly cried as Trey filled the hole again with dirt from the small mountain we'd made.

"You can turn around now," he announced a few minutes later, when there was a soft mound of gray dirt over where the hole had previously been.

We both turned as we heard my mom's car pull into the driveway, and the engine shut off. She stepped out of the car, still full of energy from an enjoyable day of teaching on campus, and waved at us over the top of the fence.

"Hey, kids, what's going on?" she asked, stepping through the gate. Immediately, her smile fell when she saw us standing awkwardly in the yard with our shovels, the pile of dirt visible behind us. "What is this?"

"Mom," I started, "it's Moxie—"

My mom put her hand up to silence me, already knowing what I was about to say. She looked down at the ground near her feet to avoid looking up at us. "All right," she said abruptly, as if she simply couldn't stand to hear me say the rest. "All right."

"It was very peaceful, Mom," I blurted out, wanting to ease her pain in some way, but knowing that for Mom, Moxie's death was the equivalent of one of the few remaining pieces of Jennie that she had left to cherish being ripped away from her. She was already on her way into the house, shaking her head, and I imagined that she would disappear into her room and not emerge until morning, as she sometimes did during the second week of October, the anniversary of Jennie's death.

"Do you want to be alone?" Trey asked me.

I thought about it for a minute, and decided that I actually really did *not* want to be alone in my yard with a pile of dirt. I also did not want to be alone in my house, listening to my mom's sobs through the wall that separated our bedrooms. "No," I replied.

"Do you want to go for a walk?" he asked, looking kind of uncomfortable, shoving his free hand into the pocket of his jeans.

I agreed to go for a walk, and we put our shovels back in our respective garages. Not wanting to venture back into the house too far, I grabbed one of my mom's unfashionable heavy cardigans from a hook on the wall just inside our side door, and met Trey back on my front lawn a few minutes later.

Without exchanging words, we took a left at the end of Martha Road and began walking toward one of our town's small shopping centers. It was one of the few paths in town from my house that could be traveled entirely on sidewalk, as so many sidewalks within town limits withered off into ditches along rural highways, making it kind of difficult to take a long walk without having to worry about being mowed down by a speeding car. Dry, sweet-smelling leaves crunched beneath our feet, and the chirping of summer crickets was noticeably absent.

"So, I've been meaning to ask you," Trey began once we were a few blocks away from home. "Monday night in your yard you apologized that I had been *mixed up in all this*. What did you mean by that?"

Trey's words pulled me out of my fog over Moxie's death, and I tried to remember back to exactly what I had said when we were on my deck. Had I given him any reason to think that Olivia's death was related to anything else?

"I just meant, you know, that you were involved in the crash, that's all," I tried to explain, not especially wanting to think about Violet at such a sensitive time. But then I got to thinking: Violet had made mention of Moxie. She knew I had a dog. Was it crazy to think that Violet had played a part in Moxie's death? Other than her ongoing problems with arthritis, the dog really hadn't given any outward signs of health problems in recent weeks. The simple notion of Violet having done anything to bring on Moxie's death made me so angry I broke out into a light sweat despite the cool night.

"That's not what it sounded like when you said it," Trey insisted after a moment. "It sounded like you knew something about the crash. And it freaked me out, you know? Because right before that truck hit us, Olivia was going nuts in my car. She kept saying, *It's just like the story. You have to pull over. We're going to get hit.* Do you know what she was talking about?"

I remained silent, not sure if it was the right time to confess to him everything from Olivia's party. It hadn't even been a week since he'd survived the accident, so it was crazy to think he was emotionally ready to hear all the details of Violet's story.

He continued, "Because I really need to know. It's been driving me crazy, McKenna. It's all I can think about. What was she talking about? What story? How did she know that truck was going to hit us? She was so certain that we were going to be hit head-on that I was afraid she was going to open the passenger-side door and jump out of the car. She wanted me to pull over, but I couldn't see well enough to pull over because the hail was coming down so hard. So she grabbed the wheel, and then everything happened so fast."

We were on a long stretch of wooded road that preceded an intersection where a handful of stores were located, and very few cars were driving past us. It was almost dark out, and the few streetlights that lined the road were coming on. Somehow, the onset of night made it more difficult to tell Trey the truth. Talking about any of what we'd done after dark seemed like an invitation for more terrible things to occur. Nothing was safe in the dark. "Do you have any idea what she was talking about?" he asked again.

I took a deep breath, knowing there was no way to reverse things if Trey decided I was a total nutcase after I shared the events of Olivia's party with him. "Okay, all of this is going to sound completely insane. I will admit that. But there's something just so weird about it that it *has* to fit together somehow." I dared to look up at him to see if he seemed skeptical yet. He appeared eager to hear more, so I continued. "At Olivia's birthday party two weeks ago, we were up late and we decided to play a game."

"Just you and Olivia?" Trey interrupted.

"No, it was me, Olivia, Candace, Mischa, and Violet, that new girl at school from Illinois. Violet suggested that we play this game called Light as a Feather, Stiff as a Board. It's a dumb game, something that kids in, like, middle school play. But we were bored, so we said okay. The whole thing with this game is that one person is the storyteller and makes up this elaborate tale about how one of the other players is going to die. Then, at the end of the story, the other girls playing the game chant and raise the girl whose story was just told up with their fingertips."

"What do you mean, with fingertips?" Trey asked.

"Exactly that," I said. "Okay, I forgot to say that while the storyteller is telling the story, the girl who's the *subject* of the story is lying down on the floor. And at the end of the story, if the game works right, she's weightless. It's like a spell has been cast on everyone playing the game, and that girl can be lifted effortlessly until someone sneezes or laughs or something to break the spell."

"Okay, that sounds like some *messed-up* kind of game," Trey said. "I've never heard of a game like that."

"Yeah, well," I agreed reluctantly, "a lot of people say it's a game that invokes evil spirits, but that's just silly. My father says it's a form of group hypnosis. Everyone playing the game becomes hypnotized by the chanting. You can do a lot of seemingly impossible things when you're hypnotized, you know."

"So you guys played this weird game and someone predicted Olivia's death?" Trey asked.

I stumbled over a crack in the sidewalk in the dark, and he grabbed me by the elbow to steady me before I fell. "Yeah. But it was so, so much more than just predicting her death, Trey. Violet was the storyteller, and . . . I can't even explain it. She just told the story so convincingly. Right down to minor details. She knew all of it, about Olivia going to the mall to buy shoes, about it happening the night before the dance. She even knew that someone was going to offer Olivia a ride home in the parking lot after her car refused to start."

I saw Trey shiver beneath his army coat, and he looked ahead toward the strip mall, stone-faced. My heart was racing as I waited for his reply. I hadn't wanted to sensationalize the story, or lead him to believe that we'd willingly played some kind of scary paranormal game, but I'd been unable to control my blabbing and done exactly that which I'd tried to avoid.

"Did she predict *me?* Did she know it was going to be *me* driving Olivia home?"

I'd been wondering that, myself.

"She didn't say anything about you, Trey," I told him honestly. "But that doesn't mean Violet didn't know. She just didn't mention that part." I paused and carefully chose my words before asking the question that had been troubling me since I'd learned he had been the driver of the car involved in Olivia's accident. "What were you doing out in Green Bay the night of the accident?"

Trey looked at me with blank eyes, completely stumped. "I don't know. I must have gone out there to buy something, right? But I don't remember what. The emergency room doctors told me I might have some issues with short-term memory loss, but that's the only thing I'm having a hard time remembering. I really have no idea why I drove all the way out there after school on Friday."

Although he hadn't answered my question, it seemed reasonable enough that he would have forgotten his reason for going to the mall, considering the physical and emotional trauma he'd been through just a few days earlier. I let it go.

We reached the shopping center and walked across the parking lot slowly as Trey led the way toward Rudy's Ice Cream Shop, where a whole bunch of kids who appeared to be in around the fourth grade were spilling out of a minivan in their soccer uniforms.

"Have you guys told anyone about this? Like, parents?" Trey asked.

"Oh my God, no," I said. "I mean, Candace probably has, but she's in a psychiatric hospital. We would sound like idiots. Or lunatics. No one would believe us. Mischa and I confronted Violet, and she acted like the whole thing was in our heads. Maybe . . . maybe it is."

Trey stopped and lingered in front of the door to the ice cream store. "Do you want any ice cream?"

I did, but refused. "Nah. I feel gross talking about all this stuff."

Trey raised an eyebrow at me, like he couldn't believe I was turning down ice cream. "Well, what if I get a cone and you just have a lick?"

We ventured inside and waited in line behind all the rowdy kids on the soccer team. Trey ordered a double-scoop chocolate cone with rainbow sprinkles.

"I would never have figured you for a rainbow kind of guy," I teased him.

He replied with a smile, "I'm full of surprises."

Back outside in the parking lot, he handed the cone to me before he even sampled it. "The first lick is yours."

I licked the tiniest bit of sprinkles off the top scoop, and savored the sweetness on my tongue. The last time I'd eaten ice cream had been at Olivia's birthday party.

As I handed the cone back to Trey, I noticed a blue pickup truck driving past the shopping center. Its driver was Henry Richmond. My heart twisted in my chest. I hadn't said much to Henry at the wake because he'd been shadowing his mother closely and politely thanking guests for coming. I felt awful for not having made more of an effort to act kinder toward him that day, especially since I'd lost a sister too. But for that reason I knew that his grief was probably so enormous that words were not going to offer much consolation. We'd texted back and forth a few times, but I was self-conscious about it, unsure of how the cancellation of the Fall Fling impacted our somewhat new friendship.

Trey had noticed Henry driving by too.

"Is that guy your boyfriend or something?" Trey asked.

"No, not even," I replied, not wanting Trey to have any idea just how *much* I'd liked Henry just as recently as a few days earlier. "He had asked me to the dance because he knew I was friends with his sister, and I said yes because I wanted to go to the Fall Fling. That's all."

"Last year that guy used to call me a freak in the cafeteria. This year, I'm the person who hears his sister's dying words. High school is just . . ." Trey trailed off as if he'd forgotten the rest of what he wanted to say.

I had forgotten that Henry was the kind of guy who had picked on less-popular kids when he was still in school with us, which hadn't been that long ago. The realization made me feel protective of Trey, who I was discovering to be a lot kinder and more sensitive than I ever thought a boy my own age could be. It made me ashamed that anyone ever teased him at school, never mind that a year ago, I was teased from time to time too.

"So, you like him," Trey repeated, seeking some kind of confirmation from me.

"*Used to* like him," I said.

"When did it become past tense?" Trey teased.

I was pretty sure I knew what he was getting at, and I was eager to know if he was interested in me or if I'd just been imagining the closeness between us over the past week. "Recently," I said. "Probably right around the night those kittens were born, he lost his appeal." This was completely true. Despite everything that had happened because of the game at Olivia's party, Trey had been on my mind a lot, and not just because of my mom's pesky nagging.

Trey stopped walking and reached for my right hand. He laced his fingers through mine, and a car drove past us as he looked into my eyes. I knew then what he was about to do, and I wished I could slow down time because this was a moment I wanted to remember forever in perfect detail. He leaned forward and awkwardly kissed me. At first our lips did all the wrong things, our noses bumped and teeth clashed. I guess that's how first kisses between people usually go if neither person really knows what to do. But then after a few seconds, everything fell into place and Trey pulled me closer.

"Glad we finally got that out of the way," he said with a shy smile after we both took a step back.

"Really? What was it in the way of?" I teased.

"Everything," he replied perfectly, making my heart soar.

"So, let me ask you this," Trey said as we continued our walk back home, my hand in his. "When you guys were playing this game, did Violet tell the story of anyone else's death? Did she predict yours?"

I felt the darkness around us swell, and all the comfort and joy I had just experienced a moment ago, when Trey had kissed me, vanished. How could I have forgotten so quickly that death was right around the corner? It could claim me, or Trey, at any moment. "She predicted everyone's," I nearly whispered. "Except mine. She couldn't imagine any kind of a death for me, except . . ."

Trey looked at me with intense interest.

I continued, "She said she just saw fire. She saw Jennie's death. Not mine."

We walked for a block in silence as Trey thought about this. For the first time I wondered if my own death was imminent. Not even when Jennie had died had I so strongly sensed my own fragile mortality. Everyone dies, everything dies, but never before that moment on the sidewalk with Trey had I ever really wondered when my own death would occur. What was it that Violet had done to invite so much tragedy to unfold in a matter of days? Was it intentional? Did she have some kind of secret desire to kill all of us who had befriended her?

"How well do you know this girl Violet?" Trey asked, as if reading my mind. "She sounds like a pretty crappy friend."

I shared with Trey the details of the stories that Violet had told about how Candace and Mischa would die and confided in him about my plan to get closer to her in an attempt to figure out what exactly her deal was.

"This whole thing sounds really dangerous. It seems to me like this girl Violet needs to be banished back to the ninth circle of Hell more than she needs you as a friend," he said.

"But she likes me. And I suspect she thinks maybe there's something special about me because she wasn't able to predict my death. I really believe that getting to know her better is the only chance I have at figuring out if the rest of our predictions are going to come true too," I told him. The more I thought about my intention to get closer to Violet, the more I convinced myself I could be successful. And from what Trey had told me about Olivia grabbing the wheel of his car and forcing her own prediction to come true, it seemed urgent for me to figure this whole thing out before something bad happened to another one of us.

Trey volunteered to do some research into paranormal phenomena to see if there was an otherworldly explanation for Violet's power. We traded phone numbers, which was funny since we'd known each other our whole lives but had never texted before. I returned home feeling as if I were on a mission, which dulled the pain of not hearing Moxie trotting down the hall to greet me at the door.

As I got ready for bed, I wondered if Violet felt the least bit guilty about what she'd done, or if she was already fast asleep, completely unbothered by how she'd crushed Olivia's family. I envisioned Trey staggering away from the scene of the crash. And as I drifted off to sleep, I remembered Jennie waving to me through the flames in our front window as our house burned down. I had to do whatever it took to understand what Violet had done to Olivia. I'd never forgive myself if I didn't.

In the morning, it was strange to not be awakened by the sound of Mom pouring food into Moxie's bowl in the kitchen. When my alarm went off and I ventured out of my room, Mom's door was still shut. On my way out of the house, I hurriedly put Moxie's food and water bowls in a box in the garage so that my mom wouldn't have to see them when she got up. Unexpectedly, Trey was sitting on our front stoop, waiting for me. Without exchanging words, we embarked on the walk to school together.

Together, which felt right in every way.

I wouldn't read the article in the *Willow Gazette* about Olivia's wake and funeral until I got home. Beneath the headline A COMMUNITY MOURNS HIGH SCHOOL STUDENT, Willow High School junior Violet Simmons was quoted as saying, "No one can believe this has happened. Olivia Richmond was an inspiration to all of us and was one of my best friends."

Anyone in town who read that article in its entirety would have thought that Olivia and Violet had been friends their whole lives.

CHAPTER 8

CANDACE RETURNED TO SCHOOL THE FOLLOWING Monday, sedated, a little thinner, and humorless. It was only after she changed so drastically that I realized how much I had liked her previously, when she was like an explosion of sunshine and noise. Her schedule had been rearranged by her mother the previous Friday. Mischa and I had seen Mrs. Lehrer sitting in the principal's office with Mr. Bobek, the guidance counselor. Mischa told me that Candace's mom had called her own mother asking more questions specifically about Violet, and had informed Mrs. Portnoy that she was going to have Candace switched out of all the classes she shared with the new girl in town. Only after a week of intense psychiatric care and sedation had Candace stopped rambling about Violet's alleged evil powers and involvement with Olivia's death.

Whatever it was that Candace's mom had said to Mr. Bobek as justification for switching around Candace's required classes, it had resulted in me, Mischa, and Violet being called into the principal's office for a stern lecture. When an office runner arrived in my English classroom with a pink slip requesting my presence, I was genuinely surprised.

"Girls, I don't know what your religious upbringings have been, and to be perfectly honest, it's none of my business," Principal Nylander told us as he leaned back, way back, in his swiveling desk chair. The three of us sat on the brown couch in his office. I was in the middle, as was fitting, it seemed, trying to maintain a safe distance of a few inches from Violet, who sat to my left. I could practically smell the fury emanating from Mischa, on my right. "But when I hear accusations of students at my school playing games involving evil spirits, or even alleging to involve evil spirits, I feel personally obligated to step in."

My attention drifted to the window, to the rain falling and the puddles forming in the faculty parking lot. Principal Nylander and his wife were parishioners at St. Monica's, where we used to attend church before my parents divorced. To the best of my knowledge, the Portnoys rarely attended church other than on Easter and Christmas, so I couldn't help but feel like Principal Nylander was scolding me directly even though I knew that Violet and her family were regular churchgoers.

"Now, if any of you have questions about the afterlife, or about your creator, or, heck, even just about entertaining ways to pass time, I encourage you to contact a member of the clergy at your place of worship, a trusted teacher, or your parents. Messing around with occult practices is dangerous business," Principal Nylander warned us, pushing his wire-rimmed glasses farther up his little pug nose.

Back in the eerily quiet hallway, empty during the class in session, Mischa glared at Violet. "That was *excruciating*. I hope you're happy. And I read what you said to that journalist from the town paper. You had no right, do you hear me? *No right!*" She turned on her leather ballet flat and left me standing there, mouth hanging open, across from Violet.

"Oh. My. God," Violet said, her eyes enormous, her lips tilted into a semismile, as if Mischa's reaction was way over the top. "It's not like *I* ratted. I didn't say a word. It was *Candace* who started blabbing."

Sticking with my plan to befriend Violet, I remained there, watching Mischa walk down the hall. "I know," I assured her.

"Whatever." Violet's eyes narrowed as Mischa disappeared from view around a corner. "Her days are numbered, anyway."

I couldn't hide my reaction of surprised confusion from Violet as my face jerked back toward hers. I was sure I looked horrified by what she was suggesting. She immediately realized what her comment had just implied and quickly corrected herself.

"I *mean* her popularity," Violet clarified. "Without Olivia, Mischa doesn't stand a chance of staying popular. There are a ton of prettier girls at this school."

"You might be right," I heard myself murmuring, wondering if I was doing any kind of a convincing job of aligning myself with her.

Violet looked me over, scrutinizing my face. "You should sit with me and Tracy today at lunchtime. We can talk about Student Government stuff. I mean, the election is practically over before it's even begun."

"Maybe," I said hesitantly before catching myself. "I mean, of course."

I was eager to sit with Candace and hear her scratchy voice again. But if I was going to be successful in convincing Violet that I was on her side, I was going to have to make some sacrifices. Sitting with Candace and Mischa was not going to be an option. I had also wanted to meet Trey in the library, but meeting with him was going to have to wait; I couldn't be sure when I'd lose favor with Violet.

In my Spanish class, I texted Trey to tell him that I'd be having lunch with Violet and wanted to walk home together. I had agreed the night before to spend the lunch hour with him, researching evil spirits and games. He would understand why it was more urgent that I sit with Violet and listen to her talk for an hour. Mischa wouldn't be as accepting.

"God. I just want to transfer out of this gym class and into Candace's," Mischa was grumbling when I got to the locker room. She was changing into her gym suit already, in a different row of lockers from where Violet was twisting the dial of her combination lock. I set my canvas bag down on a bench and watched until I saw Violet exit the locker room for the stairs leading up to the gym.

"Listen, Mischa," I began. Even as I was opening my mouth to present my reason for not sitting with Mischa and Candace at lunchtime, the one hour of the day when Candace and Violet would be in the same room, I knew Mischa was going to be skeptical about my logic. "I've been thinking. The only way we're ever going to find out if Violet had any control over Olivia's death is if one of us stays friends with her."

Mischa glared at me. "She *killed* our friend, McKenna. I really cannot understand why you'd want to stay friends with her. I mean, am I missing something here?"

I pulled off my knit striped top and wriggled my gym shirt over my head. "I don't mean *really* be friends with her. I just want to try to find out what she did."

Mischa looked outraged when she glanced up at me from tying

the laces on her running shoes. "You must be insane. She's a murderer!"

Girls who had changed in the row next to ours looked over at us curiously as they passed us on their way out of the gym. "Look, we probably shouldn't talk about what happened to Olivia at all anymore at school," I said. "Do you have gymnastics today? Can we hang out and talk about this in private?"

"I'm going to Candace's house," Mischa informed me haughtily, and then added, "You can meet us there."

At lunchtime, I sat with Violet and Tracy and struggled to listen to their big plans for the junior class while out of the corner of my eye, I watched Pete where he sat at our old table, flanked by Matt and Isaac. I wondered where Mischa and Candace were, but then figured that perhaps Mischa had thought better of letting Candace observe me sitting with the enemy. Violet and Tracy rambled on and on about bake sales and initiatives to recycle the foil containers in which we were served everything from tater tots to lasagna in the cafeteria. I shared with them my big plan to start leaf-raking and driveway-shoveling services as a means of raising money for the class trip, and Violet's pretty face flushed with excitement.

"Oh my God, McKenna, that is such an awesome idea. You're a genius!" she exclaimed, flattering me more than I wanted to be flattered by her. Violet and I walked together to US History, and we passed Candace in the hallway, who glared at me as she watched us. Isaac stood protectively next to her at her locker, with one strong hand on her shoulder, and I hoped that Mischa had already taken the time to explain to her *why* I was spending time with Violet. The thought of Candace truly being mad at me upset me so much that

I could barely concentrate on Mr. Dean's lecture about Aaron Burr's historic duel with Alexander Hamilton.

After school, I slid out of the building without even stopping at my locker, where any number of girls with whom I did not want to speak might have noticed me. I met Trey down near the entrance to the library, in front of the vending machines, and we smiled nervously at each other. He pecked me on the cheek after neither of us knew what to do for a few seconds. It struck me as amazing all over again how cute he was even despite his stitches and bruises, and how it had taken me so long to notice.

"I have to walk over to the Sherwood Hills subdivision," I told him once we were outside, opening our umbrellas. "I'm going over to Candace's house to meet with her and Mischa."

"I have trigonometry with Candace," Trey informed me. "She was really spaced out. The teacher called on her once and she didn't even respond to her own name."

Candace hadn't even really looked like herself in school that day. She'd worn a cable-knit cardigan, floral button-down blouse, and a pair of pink corduroys that were, although tight, not at all her typical style. She looked, now that I was thinking about it, like her mother had dressed her for school.

"Did you find anything helpful in the library?" I asked. I had offered to look on Google when Trey had volunteered to do research, but he had shaken his head as if I were a foolish child and had insisted that the research begin in actual *books* found in the actual *card catalog*. Maybe it was silly of us to think we'd find an answer in a book, or *anywhere*, for that matter. But Trey seemed pretty certain that information of value would not be found online.

"Funny you should ask." He wiggled out of his heavy black back-pack and withdrew from it a hardcover book, its corners rounded from wear, covered by a faded paper jacket, on which the title was printed *Requests from the Dead*, by James W. Listerman. "I found this. I felt weird checking it out, so I just boosted it."

He handed it to me, and I didn't even bother scolding him for stealing the book. I examined it, trying to be careful not to let any of the slow rain falling come into contact with it, first checking its copyright page. It had been published in 1910. The book smelled moldy, and the pages felt fragile, like they might crack and crumble as I flipped through them.

"Wow, this is *old*," I commented. "Did you find anything good in here?"

"Definitely some promising stuff," Trey said. "Mainly that it seems like if old James W. Listerman knew what he was talking about, Violet might have made herself a deal with an evil spirit to serve as a medium. Like, a conduit through which other spirits can communicate, and share information with her."

"Why in the heck would anyone make a deal like that?" I asked.

"Well," Trey continued, seeming to have read more of the book than I had originally thought possible during a one-hour lunch break, "if Violet wanted something from someone—like Olivia, for example—then she might have struck some kind of deal with which-ever spirit she was able to contact. Or, if an evil spirit had some-how singled Violet out and made contact with her because *it* wanted something from her, and was harassing her about it, she might have been willing to agree to anything to make it end. Even killing people. We can't be sure unless we ask her. This book also says that spirits can be very deceitful and manipulative, so she may have been tricked. But obviously, don't ask her yet."

"Can I borrow this?" I asked, holding up the book.

He took the book out of my hands and tucked it into his backpack. "Not until I read it cover to cover. This is some really creepy reading material."

Trey walked me to the main gate of Candace's subdivision, and for a moment as we said good-bye, I wished I could put everything related to Olivia, Candace, Mischa, and Violet behind me and just walk home with Trey, back to a normal life that felt like mine. But I already knew that whatever Violet had started had ended my normal life forever, or at least until I knew for certain that I and the rest of my friends were safe.

"Finally," Candace said when she opened her front door and saw me. She sounded more like herself, and was smirking more like she used to before the accident happened.

"Hi," I said, entering the Cottons' huge home and enjoying how it smelled, unlike ours, like potpourri and fat, red, berry-scented wax candles. "You seem more . . . normal than you did at school today."

"That's because I take my meds in the morning and in the evening. Right around this time of day, the morning meds are wearing off," Candace explained. In her kitchen, Mischa was seated at the table, typing away on her phone, quite obviously concentrating on something intently.

"So. About this plan of yours to stay friends with Violet," Mischa said, looking up at me as I took a seat at the kitchen table. I hadn't noticed when I'd first entered the room, but Candace's half sister Julia was in the adjacent living room, stretched out on the couch, her bare feet dangling over the edge. "I don't like it. What if you're, like, some kind of double agent? Like, you're really loyal to Violet, but just spying on us?"

I looked at Mischa, and then at Candace, in disbelief. It seemed impossible to me that they'd accuse me of aligning with Violet when in actuality I was offering to stand by her against my every instinct to stay as far away from her as possible.

"You're kidding, right?" I asked. "I don't really want anything to do with her! I am almost positive she orchestrated Olivia's death, and had something to do with my dog's death too. I just can't prove any of it, and neither can either of you. So unless you guys want her to get away with it and keep doing whatever she's doing, *one* of us is going to have to gain her trust and find out what her plans are."

Mischa looked guilty and shrugged up at Candace. After a moment of hesitation, Candace appeared to be considering the logic behind my plan. She pulled out a chair and took a seat at the table. "What happened to your dog?"

I reluctantly confessed to them about the odd conversation I'd had with Violet on the track after Olivia's birthday party, the one in which she had guessed I had a dog and had described Moxie. Then I told them about getting home from school and finding Moxie dead on my bed.

"That sucks, McKenna," Mischa said, shaking her head. "I think she's evil. Truly evil. Check this out. At her last high school in Lake Forest, Illinois, *four* students died in weird accidents last year. And it gets freakier. One of the girls was killed in a hit-and-run accident, and she was the captain of the pom squad *on which Violet was a member*. One of the boys was a freshman, and Violet gave a quote at his funeral to a local newspaper saying that she used to babysit him when he was a little kid."

"What about the other two people?" Candace asked, suddenly very focused. She folded her hands on the tabletop.

"I can't make any solid connections yet, but I've only been looking for an hour. Violet's such a freak, she doesn't even have Snapchat. Anyway, it hardly matters. Think of how many times every day you cross paths with someone you don't even know so well at high school. They could have all known Violet any number of ways."

"Did Violet ever mention why it was that her family moved to Willow?" I asked, unable to recall her ever providing us with a reason for her sudden arrival in our out-of-the-way little town. Candace said, "She said it was for her dad's work." Mischa snorted. "Work? What work is there to do here?"

Mischa's mother was a real estate agent in Willow; at one point or another she'd negotiated the sale of almost every house in town. Mr. Portnoy owned several luxury car dealerships between Willow, Sheboygan, and Green Bay. Candace's mom managed the small nail salon at the Ortonville Mall, and her dad was a co-owner of a construction company in Green Bay. My own father had given up on opportunities that were within driving range of Willow and had headed down to Florida, where he'd gotten a better job at a state university. There simply weren't a lot of jobs in Willow that anyone's parents would uproot a family in another town to accept.

Our wonderment at what circumstances could have possibly delivered Violet into our forgettable little town inspired Mischa to begin making a list. The list essentially became my assignment. It was composed of things we needed to find out about Violet. Was she an only child? Had she attended any schools prior to the one in Lake Forest? I would be observing her, spying on her, casually questioning her, and reporting everything back to Mischa and Candace.

Of course, it had already occurred to me that Violet would *not* be happy if she were to catch on to what we were doing. Thankfully, Mischa and Candace seemed to share my concern about the danger involved, so we all agreed that for appearances' sake, we would refrain from acting like friends while at school. We would let everyone think that we'd had a big fight about Candace's refusal to be nice to Violet, and I'd communicate all my learnings to them over e-mail rather than by text message just in case Violet were ever to catch a glimpse of my phone.

We heard the automated garage door open, and Julia turned off the television instantly. Candace's mom entered the kitchen area, where we were all seated, from the garage, bringing a brief gust of perfume-scented cold air with her. She set beige plastic bags from the grocery store down on the kitchen counter. "Hey, ladies. What are we up to?"

"Just doing homework, Mom," Candace lied cheerfully.

"Have you taken your medication yet?" Candace's mom asked, opening the fridge to place a carton of soy milk in it.

Candace sighed so loudly it was more like a dragon's roar, and stood up from the table to retrieve her orange prescription bottles from the cabinet over the kitchen sink. Within minutes, her eyes seemed to cloud over, and the dazed and passive version of Candace was back.

Walking home from Candace's fancy subdivision, I felt more alone than I ever had during my sophomore year. My walk took me past the cemetery at St. Monica's, and I was tempted to step inside its gates not only to walk past Jennie's grave, but also to satisfy my curiosity about Olivia's. A sign on the front gate of the cemetery stated that it closed daily at sundown. Without consciously thinking through my actions, I began walking. As I passed the guard station, the uniformed guard looked at the watch on his wrist and told me, "I'm closing up in about twenty minutes, honey." I asked him for directions to where I might find Olivia Richmond's grave, and he had to look up its location on his computer. On a map, he drew a little line along the paths I should follow to find her plot, which happened to be in the opposite direction of Jennie's grave, located in the northeast corner of the cemetery. I walked as quickly as I could down the paths that led to the unmarked plot that was Olivia's. The headstone hadn't been placed yet, but it was easy to assume that it was Olivia's because the dirt covering it was still fresh and brown, and three arrangements of pink roses had been placed upon it.

I scratched my head and stood there on the path, not attempting to get any closer to the plot. It was impossible to connect my memory of giggling, whispering Olivia, her glossy platinum hair and fringy eyelashes, with this pile of dirt fifteen feet in front of me. Just like when Jennie had died, Olivia's death didn't have an element of finality. She simply didn't seem quite so far away.

That night, I tossed and turned until I finally found myself falling in and out of a strange dream in which my reflection in the mirror was that of my old self, my sophomore-year self, with a rounder face. My reflection was mouthing words, trying to tell me something, and finally I overcame my revulsion toward my own image and leaned closer to the mirror to hear.

"I'm still a part of you," my reflection told me. It reached for me, I felt its hand on my neck, and—

I woke up in a cold sweat, my heart beating wildly, and realized it was only one o'clock in the morning. It was nowhere near time to wake up for school, but too late to get out of bed and poke around the kitchen for a glass of water without alarming my mom. I calmed myself in the darkness and silence of my bedroom, and I wondered about the meaning of my dream. My father was a big believer in the psychological significance of dreams; ever since Jennie and I were little, he would ask us about our dreams and request that we retell them to him in detail. It occurred to me that maybe my dream wasn't about gaining weight and becoming the old McKenna again. Maybe it was about Jennie. If she hadn't died when she was eight, would she have lost weight and become pretty in the same timeframe as I had? Would she have lost weight and become popular even *before* I had?

As I wondered what it might have been like to have Jennie with me at Willow High School, I became keenly aware that I was not alone in my bedroom. A breeze blew in the light curtains that hung at the sides of the blinds over my window soundlessly. When it settled, the room felt suddenly unbearably cold, and it seemed as if I could almost feel something in my room inhaling and exhaling.

In, out. In, out.

I sat upright in my bed and remained perfectly still, wondering if whatever it was would leave me alone if it thought I had fallen asleep again. My eyes squeezed shut, and I convinced myself that there was *definitely* something there with me. It wasn't so much that I could *hear* its breathing, but more that I could feel the air pressure in the room falling and rising in the same way that Moxie's rib cage would expand and contract when she slept. The coldness of the room and the strangeness of the odd presence around me made the exposed bare skin on my arms, resting atop my comforter, prickle with goose bumps.

I am going crazy, I thought. *All this talk about evil spirits and predicting death is making me insane.*

Then, horrifyingly, over my bed, on the shelf where I arranged the music boxes I had accumulated as a little girl, I heard music begin to play. I squeezed my eyes shut, not wanting to see, but knew without even looking that the ceramic Minnie Mouse my father had bought for me at Disney World was slowly spinning in circles as it cranked out its mechanical tune of "It's a Small World." Next to it, a porcelain ballerina spun in circles on its platform to "Dance of the Sugarplum Fairy" from *The Nutcracker.* And on the end, a wooden jewelry box with a silver star on its lid must have opened itself to begin chiming out its version of "My Heart Will Go On." The medley of songs that I used to adore as a little girl all played together in a jumble without my having activated any of the statuettes. The eeriness of the music and spontaneous motion terrified me to the extent that I felt nauseous. I was too scared to even make a noise.

I tried to convince myself that I should just jump out of my bed and turn on the lights. The space between the edge of my bed and the wall on which the light switch was located was just a matter of a few feet. I could have been there in a fraction of a second if I could have just summoned the courage to throw back my comforter and make a run for it. Just as I had told myself I'd do exactly that on the count of five . . .

Five, four, three, two—

I felt with certainty a cold, damp fingertip press against my forearm.

Gasping in shock, I sprang from my bed, bolted across my room blindly and flipped the light switch. Before I even took the time to become too afraid to turn around I whirled, convinced I'd see something horrible hovering over my bed. But there was nothing. Absolutely nothing unusual, nothing out of place. My usual rainbow-striped sheets, a little faded from the washing machine. My stuffed bunny and stuffed dog next to my pillow, where they always were. The shelf over my bed displaying my music boxes was still in place. The music from the statuettes and jewelry box had ceased instantaneously. My bedroom was oddly, suspiciously, as boring as ever. Almost too calm, too normal.

I couldn't help but notice through my lowered blinds that the light in Trey's bedroom next door was on. Although I couldn't see the shadow of his body against his blinds, I assumed he was probably awake over there, and I hoped he hadn't observed that I'd turned my light on. Perhaps he was reading the mysterious works of James W. Listerman. Whatever he was up to at that hour, I was suddenly very self-conscious about the possibility of him noticing that I was awake next door. Part of me wished he were in my room with me to comfort me and assure me there was nothing to fear, but my dream had rattled me, and I was relieved that he couldn't see me so upset. I snatched my pillow off my bed and turned my light off, seeking a more restful night's sleep in the living room.

As I lay on the couch, comforted by the light from the lamp on the table beside me, filling the living room with warmth, my mind drifted into dangerous territory.

What if Violet wasn't the one delivering evil into our lives?

What if it was Jennie, and she had decided she wanted to switch places?

The more I thought about it, the more the theory seemed logical. If Violet was truly given visions of dead people by her spirits, what if the visions she had received for Olivia, Candace, and Mischa had been provided to her by Jennie? The mere thought that Jennie might have presented her own death as *mine* to Violet chilled me to the bone. But why would Jennie want to kill my friends? Had she lured Violet to Willow for this particular reason, or was Violet's delivery to our town just serendipitous to Jennie's purpose?

Before I fell asleep, I noticed out of the corner of my eye a framed photo of Jennie and me positioned over the television in an arrangement. The arrangement had been there for so long that I rarely studied the photographs individually; they were all moments in time at photographers' studios that I could kind of remember but had no reason to recall in detail. The one that caught my attention was of us both, taken right before our first day of kindergarten. It was a rare occasion when we were dressed identically, in pink smocked dresses with our hair in long brown pigtails. I remembered, after a moment, with clarity, how the photographer had positioned us in front of a tacky background that looked like autumn leaves changing color, had given us orange lollipops when were finished, and had led us in an overly enthusiastic chant of "Cheese!" But looking at the picture now, ten years later, I honestly couldn't tell which smiling little girl was me, and which was my deceased twin.

CHAPTER 9

S O, WHAT'S UP WITH YOUR CAR?" I ASKED TREY the next morning when we met outside my house to walk to school together. "Is insurance going to cover the cost of a new one?"

"Why, are you already in the market to upgrade to a guy who can drive you to school?"

I swatted him. "No! I'm just curious. I know how much you loved that car."

"Don't know. I don't think I'm going to be ready to get behind the wheel again for a long time."

We were in the middle of a long stretch of bad weather, with rain soaking our small town every morning. Trey insisted on holding an umbrella over my head as we walked. It hadn't occurred to me that it might be strange for him to ever drive a car again after the accident, which sucked because he loved fixing them so much. He seemed distant and uninterested in talking about cars, so I quickly changed the subject, not wanting to put him in a bad mood.

"So, did James W. Listerman have anything interesting to say about Violet?" I asked.

"Well, she told you she could hear voices, right? That spirits tell her things? That condition, if she's not lying and she is really able to hear things, is called 'clairaudience.'"

"Like clairvoyance, only hearing instead of seeing."

"Exactly," Trey confirmed. "Obviously, not everyone has that kind of ability, so Listerman's writings suggest one of two possibilities. Either Violet first discovered that she had the power to hear communications from spirits because one particular spirit who had known her during their own life reached out to her, or because she's close to someone that another spirit wants to reach, and can't."

A sweeping sensation of coldness filled my body. I wasn't ready to tell Trey that I thought there might be a possibility that Jennie was behind some of this. But what he had said certainly fit with my theory that perhaps Jennie had reached out to Violet in an attempt to get to me. When I thought about the night of the fire, I had to admit, if Jennie's spirit was behind all of this, I couldn't be angry. I supposed if I were her, I'd hold a grudge about being left to die too.

"So I guess the question is: Has anyone very close to Violet died during her own lifetime? Like a parent or a grandparent?" Trey asked. I had no clue how to go about trying to casually figure that out.

During gym, Coach Stirling did me the favor of selecting both me and Mischa as volleyball team captains, forcing us to select our classmates one by one until two teams had been formed for a gym class scrimmage. It provided us with an opportunity to suggest our imaginary rivalry. We glared at each other as we made our selections, and I enjoyed the look of pleased surprise that crossed Violet's face when I chose her first for my team. In a surprising twist of events, my team actually won both of the two matches we managed to squeeze into our fifty-minute gym class, which would probably have felt more meaningful if I'd cared at all about volleyball. The nasty expression on Mischa's face as we all headed back into the locker room made me have to remind myself that we were only *pretending* to fight.

At lunchtime, Violet, Tracy, and I worked on our speeches for the election. We were expected to give one-minute speeches over the high school audio system on Friday during homeroom after announcements. I had never really given much thought to public speaking, but now that it was suddenly and unavoidably in my future, it was pointless to deny that I was terrified. Violet wrote an outline for herself in her spiral notebook that was so concise and well crafted, I wondered if she had secretly worked on it all weekend and was only pretending to write down her first draft alongside Tracy and me. Tracy's speech was going to be based on her optimism about event planning. She wanted to promise future dances, a junior class Halloween party, and a junior class holiday party, and she seemed insistent on offering the idle promise of a junior class sleepaway ski weekend in Michigan. "How are we going to have *two* class trips in one year?" I challenged her.

"Well, *your* speech could be about extra fund-raising activities." Tracy smiled back at me viciously.

Perfect. *Way to calm my nerves about having to give a public speech in three days,* I thought grimly, *by requiring me to get the entire junior class psyched up to spend even more time this winter selling junk that no one in town wants to buy.*

It didn't seem like there was any natural way to begin my investigation into Violet's personal history. Only once at lunchtime did I look longingly over my shoulder at my old table, where Isaac and Matt were horsing around. Pete was forlornly eating french fries.

Mischa and her sister pretended not to see me watching. I had already been informed that Candace would be eating lunch for the foreseeable future in the nurse's office.

By Friday, although I'd been rehearsing my speech all week, I still didn't feel confident about reading it into the loudspeaker system from the principal's office. I hadn't slept well all week since the disturbance in my bedroom and was having difficulty keeping my eyes open in class even though nothing else had happened in my room since.

"And our last announcement of the day before I turn things over to our Student Government candidates for senior class office is that the administration has decided to reschedule the homecoming dance for next Friday, October fourth. The Ortonville Lodge has graciously offered to host the event. Tickets purchased for the originally scheduled dance will be honored, and tickets for the rescheduled event will be available for juniors and seniors to purchase in the cafeteria next week."

The freshman girl who had just shyly read the announcements stepped away from the microphone for the school's audio system in the administrative office to make room for Amanda Portnoy, who was ready to begin her one-minute speech. Amanda would be running for senior class president against Craig Babson, as she did every year. Even after three consecutive losses, Craig must have figured that the chance of losing a fourth time was worth the vindication he'd feel if he were to actually win during senior year and be able to include the position on his college applications. Amanda stepped up calmly to the microphone with her notes for her speech prepared on index cards.

My brain was still focused too closely on the mention of the homecoming dance being rescheduled for me to pay any attention to what Amanda was saying. How could Principal Nylander *possibly* think that was a good idea so soon after Olivia's death? Would a homecoming king and queen be named? I tried to imagine Principal Nylander standing at a podium at the banquet hall at the Ortonville Lodge, the only resort hotel for miles, announcing the winners. Who would people even vote for as queen now that Olivia was dead? I thought of her bare grave, not even marked yet with a headstone. It just felt wrong to me that life would be moving on so rapidly without her.

"First of all, I'd like to thank Principal Nylander for rescheduling the homecoming dance. Celebrating life and our time together as classmates is the best way for us to recover from the tragedy that our school suffered two weeks ago. We should never lose sight of the fact that life is short, and every moment counts," Violet was saying into the microphone. She was so cool, so collected, that her ad-libbed commentary about the homecoming announcement seemed rehearsed. All the senior candidates had delivered their speeches already, and I'd barely heard a word. I would have to step up to the microphone in fewer than five minutes, and I couldn't concentrate. The thought of having to actually put on the lavender dress that I'd bought for the Fall Fling—back when I'd still been dreaming of dancing with Henry under the disco ball—made me feel dizzy. Would I go to homecoming with Trey? Would Mischa and Candace boycott it? Would Pete dare to attend?

"McKenna," Violet whispered.

It was my turn. Tracy stood next to the microphone having just finished her speech, and was forcing a smile at me. I clutched between my fingers the index cards that I had written out for myself the night before and stepped toward the microphone, avoiding Jason Arkadian's stare. I hadn't heard a word of what Violet had said after she so eloquently made reference to Olivia's death as if she'd had nothing to do with it. Michael and Tracy's speeches had rushed past my ears without a single phrase standing out to me. All that was left was for me to read my notes off my cards, and then for Jason to step up to the microphone and quite possibly obliterate me.

"Ahem," I began, trying to focus. "I'm McKenna Brady and I'm running for junior class treasurer. As Tracy mentioned, we have a lot of exciting ideas for this year, but to keep them affordable for everyone to participate, it will involve the need to raise money. Rather than relying on fund-raisers that require us to sell candy or cheese or other things to our neighbors and family members as we usually do, as part of my campaign platform I'm proposing that we offer a series of services to our community that will involve a small time commitment from each of us instead of an obligation to meet an individual financial goal."

My voice was shaking, and I struggled to read my own handwriting on my note cards. I imagined how the entire school was reacting to my delivery at that point, nearly twelve minutes into Student Government speeches; I was certain that spitballs were being thrown and texts were being sent in every single classroom. But I had to press on, if not just to win the election, to avoid sounding like a complete fool.

"Some ideas that I have been considering are a lawn clean-up service during the fall, snow-shoveling service during the winter, and a booth at Winnebago Days where we can offer our own talents to Willow to make some money for our class trip as well as gain experience to put on our college applications." I hesitated, knowing that I was going to hate myself for what I was about to say next, but figuring if Violet had gone there, I had to too. "Everyone can agree that volunteering time after school or on a weekend sucks. But we deserve for our junior year to be a great time in our lives. Our class has experienced a great loss this year already, and we owe it to one another to commit to making the rest of this year as fun and memorable as we can. If you vote for me, I will work tirelessly to make sure that this year is one that we all remember fondly."

As I stepped away from the microphone, my hands were trembling. I could hear one of the office secretaries blowing her nose, and when I turned, I saw her dabbing at tears in the corners of her eyes with a tissue. She gave me a thumbs-up. Michael Walton patted me on the back with a friendly smile. Violet mouthed, *Good job*, to me silently. Tracy smiled impatiently and batted her eyelashes at me. She was really starting to bother me, especially because she had cozied up to Violet so quickly. She had no idea what she was getting herself into. Jason's speech focused on the need to start building up our class savings so that we could afford an impressive class gift when we were seniors. I felt a little bad for Jason, and wondered if it might have been a wiser move for me to have just flubbed my speech and handed him the election.

After school, Violet cornered me at my locker with her backpack already fastened over both shoulders. "You should come over to my house. We could bake cupcakes to hand out at lunchtime on Monday. Like a campaign promotion."

I thought about the history chapter I had to read later that night about the Constitution, and the Spanish verb conjugation exercises I had neglected to finish during study hall, but forced myself to grin. An opportunity to check out Violet's house was too tempting to pass up. Who knew when or if I'd have another chance? "Sure, that sounds great. I just have to text my mom and let her know I'm not going straight home."

Violet lived on the outskirts of town. We drove to her house after school in the white Audi her parents had recently bought for her. Her family's property was enclosed by a tall fence, and she punched a security code into an app on her phone to unlock the front gate. The house was set far back from the street down a long private road. It was nearly hidden completely by thick evergreens, with the sharp points of its Tudor roof poking out above the peaks of green in the distance.

"Wow, you live, like, in the middle of nowhere," I commented. I was already wondering how on earth I would ever give my mom directions later that evening to pick me up.

"Yeah, kind of sucks. It's so far from everything, even the grocery store."

The shade of the trees lining the private road made me feel like I was entering another world. The rain had temporarily subsided, and sunlight making its way through pine needles left patterns across the pavement. The heavy, wet scents of soil, pine, and decaying leaves crept in, and the chirping of birds overhead was dizzying.

After a bend in the wooded road, I could see the house emerge ahead of us. The road gave way to gravel, and turned in a circular drive wrapped around a grand fountain at the front of the house, where Violet parked. White cement steps led to the home's front door, and the house appeared to be three stories high, with elaborate latticework over its windows. Fluffy red geraniums grew in huge ceramic flower pots at both sides of the front door. The Simmonses' house was more like an English manor than any house I had ever seen before in Willow.

"How did your parents ever find this house?" I asked, not only for the purpose of information gathering, but also out of my own personal curiosity. Why would any family with enough money to purchase a lavish home like this one choose to live in Willow, Wisconsin?

"Well, it's not so much that they found the house. It was more like *it* found *them*." Violet sighed, pulling her keys out of the zippered pocket on her backpack. We climbed up the front steps. "It's the house my father grew up in. When my grandmother died two years ago, my uncle wanted to sell it, but my father really wanted to keep it in the family. I used to come here for summer breaks when I was a little kid, and I thought it was like a castle."

The front door creaked open, and the coolness of the front hallway reached us before we even stepped inside. I felt as if I was entering a museum as I walked into Violet's front foyer. Everything was polished wood, and an enormous staircase led from the hallway up to a magnificent second-floor balcony that overlooked the living room. An enormous Persian rug in rich shades of turquoise, mint, and fuchsia covered the dark wood floor in the living room, and the furniture all appeared to be antique, expertly reupholstered. As we entered and Violet kicked off her shoes, to our right I saw an ornately framed oil painting hanging over the fireplace. It depicted what appeared to be a family of four: a husband smiling politely in a dark suit, a wife with her hair curled delicately, and two gangly teenage sons. The woman, who I assumed to be Violet's grandmother, had her hands placed gently on the shoulders of her seated sons. Unlike in other portraits I'd seen in museums of wealthy families, Violet's grandparents were dressed modestly. Violet's grandmother wore what looked like a simple teal green silk blouse, open at the neck to reveal a delicate gold pendant instead of a thick rope of pearls or elaborate diamonds. Violet didn't look much like her grandmother, whose complexion was peachy and hair a dark shade of blonde in comparison to Violet's porcelain skin and raven hair. In the portrait, the grandmother smiled warmly, patiently, filling the room with a welcoming presence.

"This is amazing," I said, sounding more impressed than I intended. But it was. I had never in my whole life stepped into a house like that. I didn't even think that real, modern-day people lived in houses that enormous; it was like a house from a movie set in another time period. There was nothing spooky or haunted about it. The windows were enormous, filling it with cheerful sunlight despite the thick blanket of tall trees surrounding the house outdoors.

"Yeah, it's pretty great," Violet admitted. "Our house in Lake Forest was way smaller. This is fancy and all, but my parents spent a year remodeling it before we moved here." She hesitated for a moment, as if she were a little embarrassed by her next admission. "Technically, it's mine. My grandmother left it to me in her will. So it was my choice whether or not we should keep it in the family or sell it to developers who wanted to build condominiums on the property. My dad and my uncle got into a big legal thing over it, which was totally awkward. But my grandmother would seriously have rolled over in her grave if I'd let that happen. It's kind of a special place."

My heart beat a little faster than normal as we kicked off our shoes. Trey had asked me if anyone close to Violet had passed away recently, and a beloved grandmother who adored Violet enough to bequeath her an enormous mansion certainly counted. I had a hunch that Violet's inheritance would have raised James W. Listerman's eyebrows.

In the huge kitchen, Violet went on to tell me as she pulled several boxes of cake mix out of a cabinet that her father had been an investment banker back in Chicago, but that he had taken time after Violet's grandmother died to establish his own fund and take on private clients so that he would be prepared to work for himself in Wisconsin.

"There are eggs in the fridge," Violet told me, suggesting that I should go get them. "We can freeze the cupcakes today, and I'll frost them on Sunday." Violet's mother had a fancy automatic mixer, the kind that I imagined professional chefs had, and I wondered, as I opened the fridge and gawked at the abundance of food in there, what my mother would have made of the Simmonses' house. She wasn't easily impressed by wealth, but the Simmonses were quite obviously very, *very* wealthy.

While we mixed the rich chocolate batter and poured it into cupcake pans, I learned that Violet was an only child. She told me that her parents tried to have another child after her, but were unsuccessful, and for a long time their infertility issues put such a strain on their marriage that she was positive they were going to get divorced. She shared with me that back at her old school, she had a boyfriend named Eric, and they had decided to break up before she moved to Willow rather than try to keep in touch. The drive between Willow and Lake Forest took over three hours. They knew their relationship wasn't mature enough to last. Violet had been so upset about it that she'd deleted all of her social media profiles because she simply didn't want to know any details when Eric began dating anyone new. Maybe that was her subtle way of answering one of the questions on Mischa's list; I wasn't sure. If Violet had any supernatural way of knowing what was on the list, she was making a very smooth matter of answering the questions one by one—and keeping me wary of the danger I was in while I was a guest in her home.

Violet seemed so relaxed and open with me that it felt kind of like we were just normal friends hanging out under normal circumstances. In her sunny kitchen, as she heated the oven and moved from cabinet to cabinet, Olivia's death seemed like a faded memory. It would have been easy to forget that I was only there because my friends had tasked me with finding incriminating evidence supporting our theory that Violet had been responsible. That I was supposed to be digging for information.

"What about you?" Violet asked after the first batch of cupcakes had been gently placed on a rack in the oven. She was pouring glasses of diet soda for both of us. "Is that guy I've seen you walking to school with your boyfriend?"

My heart skipped a beat and my limbs went numb. I felt blood rush to my cheeks and I paused before replying, knowing that I had been caught off guard and would likely stammer. So many things ran through my mind: Had Violet really seen us walking to school together? Had she known Trey would be the driver of the car in the crash that would kill Olivia? I remembered Mischa and Candace teasing her on Olivia's birthday, suggesting that she and Trey would make a cute couple. Even though at the time, it had seemed like Violet genuinely had no idea who Trey was, the suggestion that they would be cute together filled me with jealousy now. In my head, I quickly scanned through what I knew to be factual about Violet and Trey's interactions; Violet knew who Trey was, but I had no proof that they had ever spoken.

"Trey's my next-door neighbor," I confessed, giving her only information that she would easily be able to obtain on her own. "We're sort of . . . friends. He has a weird reputation at school, you know? Like weeks ago when Mischa and Candace were talking about him, I didn't say anything because they wouldn't understand. We've known each other since we were really little."

"What about before him? Did you ever date anyone at school?" she probed, her eyes huge and innocent. For no particular reason other than a very strange suspicion, I got the sense that she was up to something. Like a lion slowing down its pace and dancing a little bit as it moved in on its prey. My mind was racing, trying to outrun her. I wanted to stoke her curiosity about my past, but not give her any details that she could use to endanger me. Moxie's death was still too fresh in my mind, and I hadn't even mentioned it to Violet.

"No," I said with a chuckle, figuring that if I was just totally honest with her I would at least avoid being caught in any lies. "I lost a lot of weight over the summer. Up until then I was not very popular. Boys did not give me a second look. Ever."

Violet blinked once, evidently surprised by my admission. Surely she must have known that I'd been heavier before junior year. Everyone at school knew that; anyone could have told her. "I never would have guessed that," she said, and I could tell she was lying. Maybe having a psychiatrist for a dad was an advantage I hadn't considered before. Dad could always tell immediately when someone was fibbing, and maybe I had gained that skill through my careful observation of him.

"So, what about homecoming?" she asked, changing her course. "Are you going with Trey?"

I shrugged, not wanting her to know that I didn't have an answer. Instinctively, I wanted to go to the dance because that was what everyone in the junior and senior classes would do, and I wanted to be like everyone else. But truly, in my heart, if there was a chance the dance would make Trey uncomfortable, I didn't want to go. The more I thought about it, if we were to go together and step out onto a dance floor, there would definitely be pointing and staring. "I don't know," I said. "I'm not sure if my heart's really in it right now. Everything was different a few weeks ago."

"Oh my God, McKenna!" Violet exclaimed. "You have to go! I mean, look. It's terrible that Olivia died. But this is still our junior year. Life goes on, you know?"

The baking cupcakes filled the house with a delicious aroma, and the sun outside the windows of Violet's kitchen began to set. Wearing oven mitts, I withdrew the first three trays of cupcakes, and Violet set the next three in to bake. When she leaned back from the heat of the oven, she winced in pain and her hand flew up to her chest.

"Ouch," she muttered. The locket around her neck had heated to a scalding temperature while she had been arranging the trays in the oven, and when she had leaned back, it had burned the skin on her chest, leaving a small red mark.

Elsewhere in the house, presumably a few rooms away, I heard a door open and close, and the clicking of high heels approaching on a hardwood floor. A well-dressed woman with smooth brown hair to her shoulders wearing a beige wool suit entered the kitchen carrying a briefcase. She was just as pretty as Violet, with the same bright blue eyes.

"Hi, Mom," Violet said, barely turning around to look at her mother. "This is McKenna. She's running for treasurer, and we're making campaign cupcakes."

"Well, that's very sweet," Mrs. Simmons said, smiling at me. "Have you lived in Willow long, McKenna?"

"My whole life," I replied with a hint of pride.

Violet drove me home later that evening, and I hated myself for feeling a little ashamed when her fancy white Audi pulled up in front of our plain one-story house. Over dinner I asked my mother if she knew of any influential families in town with the last name of Simmons, trying to get a better sense of who Violet's grandparents had been, and how they had come into their wealth. My mother, who had grown up outside St. Louis, had never heard of any Simmonses in town, and she encouraged me to call my dad, who had grown up in Ortonville. When I dialed his number, it went to voice mail, and even as I left a message I knew he wouldn't return my call that night. I should have felt proud of myself as I composed my e-mail report to Mischa and Candace with all my findings about Violet's life prior to her arrival at our high school. But instead, I thought of the sinister expression on her face as she had waved good-bye to me from the dark front seat of her car. I had unknowingly given her something that she'd wanted. I was sure of it, and just didn't know exactly what it was.

Later that night, as I was getting ready for bed and growing uneasy about the moment when I would have to turn off the lights, I received a text message from Trey. His message was one word: Homecoming?

I texted back after a moment of deliberation: Up to you.

When there was no reply after almost ten minutes, I looked at my bed with my hand resting on my light switch. I flipped the switch off and stood perfectly still for about three seconds before I admitted I was far too afraid to be alone in my room to actually fall asleep after the ghostly visit I'd received earlier in the week. So I decided to try sleeping with the light on and climbed into bed. Even with my comforter pulled over me, I felt like a weirdo closing my eyes when my room wasn't even dark.

I heard a soft tapping at the window, which made me jolt in fear. When the tapping paused and then began again, I rationalized that an evil spirit would probably not have the manners to knock before entering. I moved quietly to my window and raised the blinds. Trey was standing outside in a white T-shirt and sweatpants, shivering. Surprised to see him outdoors, I raised my window.

"What are you doing?" I whispered, not wanting my mom on the other side of the wall to hear us.

"Why is your light still on?" he asked.

"Because," I sputtered, "I'm afraid to be alone."

He motioned for me to lift the window, and I did, knowing that my mother would murder me if she knew that I was inviting a boy wearing pajamas into my bedroom at such a late hour. It took me multiple tries to lift the window screen, which was jammed because I couldn't remember ever before lifting it. Trey hoisted himself up and then climbed through silently. Once he was inside my bedroom and we'd lowered the screen and closed the window again, reality hit me: I had a boy in my room at bedtime. He looked around my small room in wonderment, as if trying to take it all in, even though he had been there recently the day he had retrieved Moxie for burial.

"Something weird happened the other night. It felt like there was something in here with me," I hurried to explain. I realized as the words were departing my mouth how preposterous I sounded, but a lot of strange things had happened in a short amount of time, so I didn't feel any need to justify myself. "Remember how the night we were outside with the kittens, you said it felt like someone was watching us? It was like that, only . . . creepier."

"I'll stay if you want, at least until you fall asleep," he offered in a whisper, continuing to look around my room as if I had a trap set somewhere.

"No—if you stay, I need you to stay until dawn," I requested, positive that whatever had interrupted my sleep the other night would just wait until Trey left if it intended to visit me again. I knew I was making a bit of a presumptuous request, asking a boy to spend the whole night in my room with me, but I was so terrified of falling asleep alone that I asked anyway.

"Okay." Trey shrugged.

I flipped the lock on my bedroom door just in case my mom

tried to open it in the morning, even though she rarely did that.

"Lights off," Trey commanded, "just in case your mom is curious why they're on. I don't need any weird lectures from my parents about adult responsibilities right now. I've had enough family time in the last two weeks to last me the rest of my life."

We both crawled into my narrow double bed, and it occurred to me once we were both lying parallel beneath my comforter that Trey might have come over with intentions in mind other than protecting me from evil spirits. But without even trying to kiss me or touch me, he set his head down on my pillow and put one arm protectively around me. Our eyes adjusted to the dark of the room, and I relaxed a little when I could actually see the whites of his eyes mere inches from mine.

"So, did you find out anything useful at Violet's today?" he asked. "Or did you guys just braid hair and eat Hot Pockets and do whatever girls do?"

"You mean like tickle each other with big feathers, and call cute boys and then hang up?" I teased.

"Was that *you* who kept calling?"

I shared with him all of what I'd learned, which had seemed important while I was in Violet's kitchen, but seemed embarrassingly insignificant now that I was repeating it all back. However, my mention of Violet's grandmother's passing, and the inheritance of the magnificent house behind the trees, sparked Trey's interest.

"So, this grandmother . . . she recently died?" Trey asked in a low voice. "That could be something."

"It sounded like she died two years ago. Violet said her parents spent a whole year renovating the house."

Trey mulled that over. "So the timing is right. Was she especially close to her grandmother?"

I tried to remember Violet mentioning anything that hinted at noteworthy closeness between herself and her grandmother, but came up dry other than Violet's insistence that the house was a special place. "She must have been. I mean, the grandmother left the house to Violet, and it sounded like her uncle was pretty upset about that."

"So, that book from the library says that oftentimes a spirit will use an object from their own life to connect to the medium," Trey mused aloud. "Is there anything that maybe Violet's grandmother gave to her that might be some kind of a channel for communication?"

I tried to clear my mind to form a picture of Violet. In my head, I envisioned her long hair, those long lashes . . . but then I became distinctly aware of the breathing sensation I had experienced on Monday night.

In, out.

I dug my fingernails into Trey's arm and whispered hoarsely, "Do you hear that?"

His eyes were huge, staring straight into my own. "I don't hear anything, but I feel it."

He pulled me closer to him. We both lay in silence for a moment before I asked, "What should we do?"

Trey shook his head very slowly, almost too slowly to notice. "Nothing. Let's see what happens."

The room, as it had the night before, became bone-chillingly cold. I felt the tip of my nose turn to ice, and could see steam escaping from Trey's nostrils in tiny puffs. The breathing sensation in the room was growing stronger, and I gripped Trey's arm more tightly. It felt as if the energy was being sucked out of my body as the presence pulled me toward the ceiling lightly, and then released, again with the steady rhythm of . . . *Inhale. Exhale.* I was paralyzed with fear, thoroughly expecting to feel the same fingertip that had pressed against my arm making an indentation again that night. Why had I been so stupid as to think I'd be safer with Trey? He was as defenseless as I was against this *thing*, whatever it was, that presumably Violet had unleashed upon me. My stomach tied itself in knots and I knew the window of time during which I might have found the courage to make a dash for the light switch had already passed. There was nothing to do but wait for this terror to run its course.

I heard a low rattling. Trey dared to sit up slightly to look across my room, and a moment later, I did too. The shelf over my desk was vibrating. It was barely noticeable at first, but in less than a minute it was shaking so much that I feared it would fall from the wall at any second, clatter down to my desk, and wake up my mom. It was the shelf where I kept my CDs, most of which had been given to me by my dad when I was still in middle school. I rarely listened to any of them, since I downloaded all the music that I kept on my phone. Trey and I both watched the shelf thrashing against the wall; we could see the screws holding it in place against the drywall visibly being pulled out from the force. Suddenly, one CD in a plastic jewel case fell from the shelf and landed on top of my desk. The shelf ceased moving immediately, and the coldness that had just filled my room disappeared. If it weren't for that single misplaced CD, it would have been easy to think that perhaps we had just imagined the past few minutes of strange phenomena in my bedroom. Trey and I sat, frozen in fear, for a long, gut-wrenching moment before either of us dared to move. I was sure that at any second my mother would come knocking on my door, demanding to know why such a racket was coming from my room at such an odd hour. But as my ears strained to hear what was happening in the house beyond the four walls of my bedroom, I was surprised to hear nothing at all but the clock ticking on the mantelpiece over the fireplace in the living room. The house was at peace.

"What the hell was that?" Trey asked me.

I released my grip on his arm and realized that my fingernails had broken the skin. Red semicircles were left behind where my nails had dug in. "Sorry," I said. "I don't know what *that* is. But it's the reason why I was going to sleep with the lights on tonight."

"That's what happened in here the other night?" Trey asked me, shaken by the event.

"Not exactly like that, but yeah."

Trey pushed back my comforter and walked over to my desk. He flipped on the small desk lamp and held up the CD that had been dislodged from its place on the shelf. "Death Cab for Cutie," he read off its cover, holding it up for me to see. "So the ghost haunting you has crappy taste in music."

"Watch it, now," I warned. I knew without budging from my bed exactly which CD it was: a single of "Soul Meets Body" that my dad had sent to me from Florida after I'd heard a snippet of the song playing at a restaurant while I was visiting him. He'd used the Shazam app to find the name of the song, armed only with the handful of lyrics that I could remember. I couldn't remember the last time

I'd listened to the song, and was at a loss if whatever kept entering my room at night intended for me to find any significance in it. Trey lifted the CD as if to place it back on the shelf, and I immediately said, "No!" I feared that restoring it to its position might be ample reason for whatever spirit had just visited us to return. Trey set the CD back down on my desk.

"The lamp stays on," he stated before climbing back into my bed with me. This time, when he wrapped his arm around me, I felt sure that we wouldn't be visited again that night. I noticed that his feet were bare and freezing cold when mine tangled with his at the bottom of my bed. "So, whatever that just was, it's done this before?" he asked.

"It didn't shake my furniture, but I think it touched me."

"Geez. I don't think that was anyone's grandmother. I mean, old people don't listen to Death Cab for Cutie, right?"

I hesitated before confessing what had been on my mind all week. "It might have been Jennie."

"Your sister? Why would your sister be haunting you? And why after all these years?" he asked.

I wanted to tell him about the day after the fire in the hospital, about how my parents had believed that I'd died in the fire and Jennie had been saved, but couldn't bring myself to say the words.

"I think it might be whatever spirit Violet summoned when you guys were playing that game. We need to find out more about that grandmother. If it isn't her who came after Olivia and is now terrorizing you, then maybe it's some other spirit that used her to set up a channel with Violet."

We both fell quiet for a few minutes, and his breathing steadied. I wondered if perhaps he'd nodded off to sleep. "I'm glad you're here," I whispered. "I'm starting to think I'm going crazy."

"You're not going crazy," he murmured, sounding tired. "Whatever is going on here, it's very real. I think we need to figure out a way to communicate with that thing, whatever it is, and tell it to get lost." He kissed me on the forehead. When I woke up in the morning, the sun was up, and the light bulb in my desk lamp had burned out at some point overnight. Trey had already slipped across the lawn back to his own room, and cool morning wind was blowing in through the open window. I thought about the words he had uttered right before we both fell asleep. A shudder rippled my body. Just about the last thing I wanted to do was invite that thing to come back.

CHAPTER 10

N O ONE AT SCHOOL WAS SURPRISED THAT VIOLET, Michael, Tracy, and I were elected to the junior class Student Government when the winners were announced on Tuesday morning, except, perhaps, me.

"Congratulations," Dan Marshall told me at our lockers after school. Dan was friends with Jason, and I genuinely hoped that Jason wasn't too upset about the news of my victory.

As I gathered my books, I noticed Trey down the hall, approaching from the other end, where most of the seniors' lockers were arranged. The sight of him sent an excited shiver up my spine. Feeling his eyes on my body even from so far away made my heart beat faster. He'd never walked right up to my locker before—giving people a reason to gossip. But the day I was named treasurer, he did. He placed his hands on my hips and he planted a soft, slow kiss right on my mouth. The closeness of his body to mine made my head spin. I could taste the wintergreen flavor of his gum on his lips, feel the warmth of his skin through the sleeve of his jacket.

"Excuse me," I heard Dan next to me mumble as he stepped out of our way, closed his locker, and left us alone. Dan was a nice guy.

When Trey and I parted, I caught a few kids staring at us in surprise.

"Congratulations, Madame Treasurer," Trey teased me. "I can't believe I'm hooking up with a government official."

On the walk home, I was elated. My peers—the very same jerks who had called me names not six months earlier—had voted for me. *Me.* I had actually won what could be considered a popularity contest. The scary spirit that had visited me twice in my bedroom hadn't made another appearance since the night it knocked the CD off my shelf, which was a huge relief. That afternoon, as Trey and I walked home swinging our arms happily, we allowed ourselves to believe that the paranormal activity Violet had brought into our lives had passed. The leaves on the trees lining the rural route taking us back to Martha Road had shifted from shades of vibrant green to warm hues of gold and persimmon, and it would only be a few more weeks before the branches were bare and snow would start falling.

My excitement about my victory was short-lived, however. When Trey and I reached my house, my mom's car was parked in the driveway, which was a bit curious, since she was typically lecturing on Tuesdays and didn't get home until late. We found her in my living room, home from the university early, with a little surprise for us. "I know, it's crazy," Mom admitted, sitting on the floor with a wiggling black-and-white mutt puppy. The puppy was gnawing on a rawhide bone that was as long as its own body. "The house is just so empty without Moxie. And you'll be leaving for college before I know it."

"But, Mom . . ." I trailed off. The beautiful little dog, with her liquid cocoa eyes and her salty puppy smell, overwhelmed me with sadness. All I could think about was how Violet had known about Moxie without ever having seen her. My mom had the best intentions having brought an innocent little animal into our home to keep her company, but she had absolutely no idea the danger into which she might have just put this dog. She had named the puppy Maude. I didn't want to fall in love with Maude, didn't want to feel her cold, wet nose against my hand, didn't want to care about her in the least, or I feared the second I did, she'd be vulnerable to Violet's game.

"Do me a favor, hon, and go get Moxie's food and water bowls and leash from the garage," Mom requested of me.

I sighed and stepped through the door off the kitchen. We primarily used our attached garage for storage. Mom only parked the car in there in the winter, and inevitably the first frost required her to spend an entire Saturday reorganizing boxes to make space for it. Trey followed me, and I looked around for a moment, clueless, not having any recollection of which box I'd tossed Moxie's food and water bowls into the morning after she died.

"Maybe . . ." I lifted one box off my father's giant old workbench and peered inside. It contained nothing but Christmas decorations. I then recalled putting the bowls into one of the boxes on the low shelf near the lawn mower. When I lifted a box that had its top cardboard flaps already half-opened, intending to set it down on the floor so that I could see its contents, the bottom flaps of the box gave way and everything packed inside of it came clattering out to the floor.

Before I even realized what I was looking at, I gasped.

What had hit me directly on the foot was one of the Lite-Brite toys that Jennie and I had fought over so many years ago. Plastic colored light bulbs rained down upon the cement floor around my feet.

I remembered that the Lite-Brites were some of the few toys that had survived the fire, boxed up by the volunteers for the Red Cross who had picked through the charred remains of our old house. But the sight of the toy wasn't what startled me.

It was that the colored plastic light bulbs pressed into the black screen had been arranged, unmistakably, to form the letter *V.*

"Holy crap," Trey whispered, looking over my shoulder and instantly understanding why I was freaking out.

"It's a sign, Trey," I babbled, on the brink of tears. "It has to be. This box has been in here for years, at least. I don't even remember playing with this toy since the fire. It may have even been Jennie who played with it last. I can't think of any reason why either of us would have designed a letter like this back when we were eight years old."

"Okay, so maybe it's a sign. But a sign from who?" Trey asked. "Obviously it's a *V. V* for Violet. You know, since last week we've both been thinking that whatever came into your room was coming after you. But what if whatever it was . . . was trying to warn you? Or protect you?"

"That doesn't make sense. None of this makes sense! Why did Olivia die? Why did Moxie die? Why did *that* CD fall off my shelf? It's too disconnected," I rambled.

"Well, maybe it's not *all* connected," Trey reasoned. "No one ever said that paranormal spirits had to be good project managers. Maybe Moxie just died of natural causes because it was her time. Maybe Death Cab for Cutie fell off the shelf because it was already closest to the edge."

I tried to catch my breath and calm down, not wanting to alarm my mom if she could hear us talking in raised voices from where she was cooing at the puppy in the living room. "I can't take this anymore," I exclaimed hoarsely. "Every time I think this is over, something even weirder happens."

Trey leaned against my dad's workbench and ran his hands through his dark hair. "I think we have to turn the tables on this thing, McKenna. I'm not happy about it because I'm not particularly enthusiastic about getting into this any deeper than we already are. But like it or not, we're in it."

"*I'm* in it," I clarified. "I'm playing the game. I'm the one trying to get into Violet's head."

"I'm the one who was in the car with Olivia," Trey reminded me. "She knew this was real. In the last moments of her life, she *knew* that this was real and that something was coming for her, and I chose not to believe her. I need to know why it took her and not me, too. I'm in this as much as you are."

We both fell quiet for a moment, and I knew without even asking him that we were both doing the same thing: listening, waiting, determining whether or not we were really alone. This had become our shared habit over the last few days. Barely breathing, afraid to even look too closely at shadows, knowing that at any second, it might be back.

"So . . . how does your boy James W. Listerman think we should reach out to it?" I asked.

After Trey declined my mom's offer for dinner that night and walked across our yard back to his own house, Mom asked me, "When was the last time you called your father?"

I groaned and slumped in my chair. I hated when she nagged me about keeping in touch with my dad. We texted all the time, and he called me on weekends, but for one reason or another, Mom liked to micromanage my relationship with him. "I don't know! I texted him and told him that I won the election this morning. Does that count?"

My mother lifted the pot of pasta boiling on the stovetop and carefully shifted it over to the kitchen sink, where she poured out the hot water into a colander. A puff of steam formed over her head and clouded the window over the sink. "You've had a stressful couple of weeks. It wouldn't kill him to have some idea of what's going on in your life these days. He's expecting a call from you after dinner."

I ate my spaghetti in silence, fuming about having to talk to my dad, and about my mom bringing a defenseless puppy into the house.

"Your mother tells me you have a boyfriend," my father greeted me when he answered the phone, without even saying "hello."

"She exaggerates," I informed him. "I'm just going to the homecoming dance with Trey Emory from next door. Remember him?"

My father claimed to remember, but he was probably lying. I didn't think he made much of an effort to remember the life he left behind in Willow.

"In all seriousness, McKenna, your mom called me today to tell me you've been having a rocky junior year so far. It sounds like you've been going through some pretty heavy stuff."

I hesitated before replying. My dad was a pretty knowledgeable guy, so there was a strong likelihood that he might have been able to provide some valuable insight about the game we'd played at Olivia's party, and the possibility of another explanation for Violet's seemingly paranormal abilities. "Actually, do you remember when you taught me about group hypnosis, Dad? Like about how the military makes soldiers chant to get them psyched up for combat?"

My father remembered.

"Well, what about in cases when the chanting makes something happen?" I suggested. "Like, do you know that game Light as a Feather, Stiff as a Board? When a girl tells a story about one girl dying, and everyone else lifts her up with their fingertips?"

"McKenna, do you mean to tell me that instead of underage drinking and experimenting with drugs, you and your friends have been playing silly horror games?" my father asked with a heartfelt laugh.

"Dad! This is *not funny*. One of my friends is *dead*! Mom told you that, right?"

The line went silent as my father considered my outburst. "You're right, McKenna. I am truly sorry for being insensitive; that's a terrible loss for someone your age to suffer. Games like the one you mentioned can be explained a variety of ways. The simplest explanation is that a young woman your age—when her weight is evenly distributed and lifted from several points—may not seem so heavy. That effect combined with the distraction of chanting, or even the possible light hypnosis of the game's participants from the chanting, can make the body seem weightless. You have to let go of the idea that some kind of . . . supernatural power had anything to do with your friend's death. I don't know how to put it more plainly. People die in car crashes all the time. If you're having difficulty with grief, I'd be more than happy to arrange to have you talk with someone at the university."

All of my dad's former colleagues at the University of Wisconsin–Sheboygan, were the kind of psychiatrists who treated the criminally insane and researched new medications to control schizophrenia.

"No thanks, Dad," I declined. But then I had an idea. If group hypnosis was what my dad claimed was responsible for our belief that we had levitated one another, then maybe hypnosis was responsible for all the weird stuff I was still experiencing. Maybe I was still hypnotized! Maybe we all were, and that was why Candace had gone so far off the deep end. Thoughts assembled in my head with the rapidity of machine gunfire. Was there a possibility that Trey and I were wrong about Violet, that there was an alternate explanation? "But actually, my friend Candace is having a very hard time dealing with Olivia's death. She might need to talk to someone."

My father was thrilled to offer up the services of his former colleagues. He told me he would e-mail me the names and contact information of psychiatrists he recommended.

"One more thing, Dad. When you were growing up, did you know of any families in Willow named Simmons?"

He paused and actually thought about my question for a minute. "Give me a moment here, McKenna. You're asking me about ancient history. Simmons . . . Simmons. I can't recall having any friends or classmates named Simmons. But I'm pretty sure there was a really well-to-do family in Willow back then by that name. They had something to do with construction. When the library expanded, the new wing was named after them."

Owning a construction company certainly seemed like a possible way for Violet's grandparents to have amassed enough wealth to afford that big house out in the woods. At least it was something for me to go on. If Dad was right about the library, I could start my research around the building's expansion.

That night, wrapped in Trey's arms, I shared with him my plan to use Candace as my guinea pig. If I could convince her to visit the psychiatrist and have removed whatever hypnotic spell she might have been under, I could determine if it improved her overall state of mind. And if it worked for her, then I would have good reason to believe that it would work for me.

"And if it doesn't help Candace, then you'll believe this is real and not in your head?" Trey asked.

I nodded. "Maybe we're all still under some spell. If we are, then I'm probably just perceiving every little thing that's happening as part of this."

Trey pushed my hair back from my face and said carefully, "What about the thing in this room? *I* wasn't hypnotized, and *I* believe that was real."

I knew what he was saying was true, and it somewhat disproved my theory, or maybe my hope, that everything that had been happening was a trick of the mind. Trey had just had a severely traumatic experience, and even though he'd been present during the last haunting in my bedroom, I needed to be absolutely sure that I wasn't going nuts. Messages from Jennie on a long-lost toy in the garage? Things were getting too serious for my brain to handle. "I know, Trey. But it's been over two weeks. We jumped so quickly to the conclusion that ghosts and evil spirits were responsible that maybe we just . . . should have taken a moment to be rational."

Trey leaned in and kissed me on the lips. "Rational," he whispered. "If you're ready to be rational, and stop believing in ghosts, then I might say—*rationally*, of course—since I've been a little in love with you since around the seventh grade, and we've been sharing a bed for the last few days, that it might be a *rational* next step for us to do more than cuddle."

His warm palm slid beneath my T-shirt and traveled upward as his eyes remained fixed on mine, seeking confirmation that his touch was welcome. "It's okay," I assured him in a whisper. I buried my fingers in the dark mop of hair on his head and pulled his face closer. His mouth connected with mine, igniting a sense of certainty in my heart that no other person in the world would ever understand me better than he did. We kissed as if we had been separated, desperately missing each other, for a very long time—which was kind of the case, even though I'd always known exactly where I could find him. In the haze of our attraction, I forgot about the hailstorm, about Olivia's death, and just desired—

In unison, we both became aware at the same time that the breathing sensation in the room was back. "Just kidding," Trey muttered. He jumped off me in a fraction of a second.

I clutched my comforter tightly, pulling it up closer beneath my chin. We both sat upright, looking around the room for some kind of evidence of the disturbance that we both felt. Across the room, on the doorknob to my closet, my attention was caught by my student ID, which I kept on a lanyard and often hung there at night. It was moving, ever so slowly, around the doorknob. As if a hand I couldn't see was revolving it around the knob in a jerky, unsteady circle.

"Trey, do you see that?" I whispered, surprised to see my breath trail through the cold air in my bedroom as white steam.

"Yeah," he said faintly. "I see it."

The steel frame of my bed began rattling ever so slightly, and what began as a barely noticeable vibration rapidly grew stronger. I could see the movement of the footboard, and hear the frame's joints making metallic clinking noises.

In, out.

"Holy . . . ," Trey murmured, inching closer to me, watching the footboard at the other end of my bed move. I didn't dare turn to look, but I could sense the headboard behind my pillow moving too. The clanging was growing more violent. The footboard was pulling away from the rest of the bed, then snapping forward, its left side rocking up and down at a different pace than its right side. I began to seriously wonder if the screws holding my bed frame together might become loose enough from so much motion that the whole frame might fall apart, letting my box springs and mattress fall to the floor.

"Is it trying to throw us off the bed?" I asked Trey, terrified. "I think so. Maybe if we jump off, it'll stop."

My mind immediately went to the dark, scary gap between the floor and the bottom of the bed. One of my greatest childhood fears was that there might be a monster lurking down there, patiently waiting to grab my ankles with cold, wrinkled hands the moment my feet graced the ground. Jumping off the bed seemed to me as terrifying as *staying* on the bed. But the entire bed was beginning to rock and shake, and it was making so much noise that my mother simply *had* to hear it.

"Okay," I agreed.

"On the count of three . . . three, two, one."

Trey threw back the comforter and we both hopped off the mattress and onto the carpeting. Before we even landed on the ground, the bed frame stopped vibrating, and the clammy, sickly feeling that washed over me whenever the spirit was in my room had vanished. Immediately, I felt like a complete idiot, standing in my bedroom in the dark, out of breath from fear, having sweated a damp pool into the back of my T-shirt purely from terror. Trey and I stared at each other from opposite sides of the bed, shaking our heads, trying to recover from the shock of the experience. It was by far the spirit's most aggressive episode, and I could only assume that it had not taken kindly to our make-out session.

"Whatever that thing is, it didn't seem to appreciate us fooling around," I said in a very quiet voice.

"Yeah, not a romance fan. Point taken," Trey said.

Suddenly, I heard the door to my mom's room open farther down the hall. "McKenna? What's going on in there?"

My eyes shot wide open in panic. *Hide!* I mouthed at Trey, who looked around wildly. There would be absolutely no logical excuse I could give her for his presence in my bedroom at nearly three in the morning, especially not when he was barefoot, wearing nothing but sweatpants. Instinctively, he dodged toward the window, and I shook my head and hands wildly.

"Don't! It'll be too loud," I insisted. I had closed the window after he'd climbed through, and the frame always squeaked when it was raised. I pointed under the bed. "There!"

He looked at me with pleading eyes for a moment, surely imagining the same scary possibilities in those few inches of darkness that I had just considered before leaping off the bed. But after a brief hesitation, he got down on his knees and wiggled beneath the bed on his stomach. My mom knocked on my door firmly before jiggling the locked doorknob, and said, "McKenna, open this door. What on earth are you doing in there?"

Thinking fast but not necessarily coherently, I grabbed my earbuds off my desk and stuck them in my ears. With my phone in one hand, I opened the door to my room, instantly feeling guilty when I saw my mom standing in the hallway with her robe wrapped tightly around her. "Hi," I said foolishly.

"Do you want to tell me what all that racket was about just now?" she asked, sounding cross. I could hear the puppy down the hall stirring and whimpering in her crate.

"What racket?" I bluffed, blinking my eyes innocently.

My mother peered into my room suspiciously, reached in through my doorway, and flipped on the light. "The clanging and knocking around I just heard in here. It sounded like you were jumping on your bed." I tried very hard not to think about Trey under my bed, and hoped he was holding his breath, curled into as tiny a form as possible so that my mom wouldn't discover him in my room. For the first time it occurred to me that maybe I should be more afraid of my mom's wrath—if she were to find out that Trey had been sneaking in through my window every night—than of the evil spirit occasionally paying me a visit.

"Oh, sorry," I ad-libbed, taking my earbuds out of my ears. "I was listening to music because I couldn't sleep. I guess I was dancing a little more than I realized."

My mother looked at me with a very dubious expression. "Get some sleep," she told me sternly, "and don't lock your door. I shouldn't have to tell you how dangerous that is in a house fire."

I sighed loudly as she walked back down the hall to her own

room, and although I closed my door, I stood behind it, listening with the light on, before even addressing Trey again. As I suspected, I heard my mom return down the hall, her bare feet padding on the hardwood floor, moments later. Maude scampered behind her on their way to the kitchen.

"What's happening?" Trey whispered from beneath the bed. "She's letting the puppy outside," I whispered back, hearing the sliding door in the kitchen open, and the puppy's claws scratching across the deck as she scurried over it on her way to the grass to relieve herself. I waited until I heard my mom reenter her room with Maude and settle in for the rest of the night before I turned off my light. Trey rolled out from under the bed and we both looked at my pile of blankets, confused.

"Do you think if we both get back into bed, it'll come back?" Trey asked.

I shrugged. My honest suspicion was that it would. "Maybe I should go," Trey said, looking at my empty bed and scratching his head.

"No!" I insisted, *really* not wanting to be left alone in the room. We ended up stacking my pillows on my bed to look like my body, and piling blankets on top of them. The two of us lay down on my floor on the far side of my bed, where my mother wouldn't automatically notice us if she were to open the door, and kept a safe distance of a few inches in between our bodies, not wanting to take any chances again. For safe measure, I set the alarm clock on my phone to wake me up far in advance of when my mom would normally check on me to make sure I was getting ready for school. "You realize that we are sleeping on the floor," Trey told me before I nodded off. "This is officially *completely* insane."

It *was* undoubtedly insane. But even still, there was a part of me that was hopeful that the shaking of the bed could be explained by some logical, natural phenomenon. There were two things I was certain I had to do in order to move my investigation forward in both directions: explicable and inexplicable. First, I would find a way to get Candace to agree to a psychiatric appointment in Sheboygan. And second, Trey and I would attempt to make contact with the spirit directly, if that was really what was disrupting our lives so forcefully, on our own.

Hank's Hobbies and Crafts was the only toy store within the town limits, and it was as unlikely to keep a Ouija board in stock as the fertilizer and feed store. The only toy store for miles that might carry an item such as a Ouija board was the big store at the mall in Green Bay. I couldn't ask Trey to drive there with me, knowing that the last time he was there, in that parking lot, was the day he'd offered Olivia a ride home with him. Obtaining the Ouija board was going to be my solo mission, and I hated the thought of it. My hope was that my mother would let me borrow the car, but I had, of course, not considered the impracticality of my request. Since earning my license I had never yet driven the car alone, and Mom had never taken out an auto insurance policy for me. I had been covered on her policy while I was a student driver, but now that I had my own license tucked away in my wallet, I no longer had coverage. "If you can wait until Saturday, I'll give you a ride," Mom offered cheerfully at the breakfast table.

I was totally failing in my request to borrow the car under the guise of needing to buy more things for the rescheduled dance. "Homecoming is *Friday*, Mom. Going to the mall on Saturday does me no good."

"Then I'll pick you up after school and we'll go tonight," she said, taking a sip of her tea.

"No, that's okay," I quickly refused, not wanting for her to witness my strange purchase. My mom could never find out that I was buying weird occult toys.

She studied me across the breakfast table with one eyebrow raised. "You and Trey have been spending a lot of time together recently. Is there anything going on that I should know about?"

I rolled my eyes. How typical of her to think that my need to go to the mall was somehow related to teen sex. For just a moment, I felt a little guilty that Trey had been spending every night in my room, but then I reminded myself that there was really nothing at all romantic about clinging to each other in fear until dawn, startling awake at every single chime of the clock in the living room and unexpected creak in the floorboards anywhere in the house. It was almost humorous how *little* fooling around we were doing. "Mom, there is *nothing* going on between me and Trey that you need to know about. I promise, okay? It's just that I've had my license since August and eventually I would like to be able to run errands by myself."

"Well, then maybe it's time for us to talk about you finding a part-time job," my mom countered. "Car insurance for a teenager can be a couple hundred bucks every few months. I highly doubt your dad is going to increase his child support payment to cover that. In fact, I'm sure he'd be willing to send you a bike helmet if you would agree to ride your bike to school."

I sighed and cleared my empty cereal bowl from the table. Finding a part-time job just to drive to the mall to buy a Ouija board was not a solution I could consider just two days before homecoming, mere hours after a presumably evil spirit had rattled my bed frame. I was going to have to find another way to get myself to Green Bay, which was not going to be a simple feat considering there was no public transportation in our area of Wisconsin that would transport me farther than Ortonville.

"Not gonna happen," I informed Trey on the sidewalk ten minutes later as we walked to school.

"She won't let you borrow the car?" he asked, glancing over his shoulder back at our house.

"I'm not covered on her auto insurance," I said. "I'm going to have to ask Mischa or Amanda to drive me."

Trey twisted his mouth a little and then said, "Or we could borrow my mom's car after school and say I'm driving."

All day long at school, my stomach tied itself in knots as I imagined having to drive alone to Green Bay. I wasn't even sure I knew the way entirely from memory; when someone else was driving, I knew where to turn, but it might be different when I was the one behind the wheel. I didn't know if Trey's mom's car had a reliable GPS, or if I'd have to keep a map open and handy in the front passenger seat just in case I flubbed the directions.

"So, do you think that would be okay?" I was pulled out of my daydream abruptly back into real time in the cafeteria by Violet, who was looking at me expectantly for a response. Tracy, across the table from us, sucked diet soda through a straw, her cheeks hollow, as she, too, waited for my reply.

"I'm sorry, that what would be okay?" I asked.

"That I'd go stag to homecoming," Violet said, clearly repeating something she had just explained in detail when I wasn't listening. "Mark can't come with me to the dance this Friday. St. Patrick's has an away game that night, and he'd never make it to Ortonville in time."

It seemed very much like Violet was telling me all of this more for my information than because she was seeking any validation. Without either of us saying a word to this effect, I already knew the tables had been turned on popularity at Willow High School. Violet was junior class president; she could go to homecoming alone, naked, and screaming "The Star-Spangled Banner" at the top of her lungs, and no one would dare to say a negative thing about her. I was no longer teetering on the edge of popularity, one foot in and one foot out, as I had been the night of Olivia's party, either. I had my own Student Government office, a real (if maybe still a little secret) boyfriend, and secret ties to Mischa and Candace, who were still admired by freshman and sophomore girls even though they were fading into the background of the junior class.

I swirled my kale salad around on my cafeteria tray. "Oh, I mean, of course. Why would that be a problem? You're class president. You have to go, and at this point, I don't know which guys in our school would even be, you know . . ."

I trailed off, not wanting to complete the sentence in my head, which went a little something like, *crazy enough to date you*. But she and Tracy both looked up at me quizzically, urging me to finish. "Popular enough to go out with you," I said, covering my own hide. My response seemed to meet with approval from Violet and Tracy.

"It's true," Tracy agreed, stabbing at macaroni and cheese with her white plastic fork. "I mean, the hot senior guys are taken, and it's slim pickings among the juniors."

For a second, I thought I saw Violet catch Pete's eye across the cafeteria. He looked away immediately, and I wondered if I had seen anything at all.

CHAPTER 11

THAT DAY AFTER SCHOOL, TREY'S MOTHER GAVE him the keys to her gray Civic. She looked reluctant to trust him, but pleased that he was volunteering to get back behind the wheel. I buckled into the passenger seat as he fired up the engine, kind of hoping that he'd miraculously overcome his fear of driving and get us all the way to Green Bay. But instead, he drove around the block and then pulled over. He took a deep breath as the engine idled, and wiped sweat from his brow.

"Enough?" I asked gently, seeing how hard it was for him to steer the car.

Without saying a word, he unbuckled his belt and threw it off of himself. He jerked the parking brake and climbed out of the driver's-side door. I took a deep breath and prepared myself for a first in my own life: driving in a car all alone. I stepped out of the car, prepared to walk around its back to take my seat behind the wheel. Surprising me, Trey sat down again in the passenger seat and suggested, "Maybe you could just drop me at the Starbucks in Silver Springs and pick me up on your way back from the mall."

Without him saying so, I inferred that he really did not want to

209

be in the mall parking lot again so soon after finding Olivia there on the night she died. I agreed and ran through my checklist of tasks before pulling away from the curb. Engine on? Check. I peeked in my rearview mirror and my side mirror and then eased onto the gas pedal. Oddly, the car didn't move.

"You might want to release the parking brake," Trey gently reminded me.

It had been over two months since Dad had taken me for my license in Florida, and another three months before that since I'd driven regularly when I was practicing during my sophomore-year driver's ed class. I was shamefully out of practice at driving, and feeling very unqualified to transport myself all the way to Green Bay and back in a car that was a lot fancier than any I'd ever driven before. But Trey and I had agreed: We needed that Ouija board. It was our best shot at contacting Jennie or any other spirit who might be cooperating with Violet. There was simply no other way we were going to obtain one. Buying one online would have required me not only to ask my mom for permission to use her credit card, but also to deal with her curiosity when the box arrived at the house. I was going to have to drive to Green Bay alone, whether I liked it or not, because making contact with a spirit had become imperative.

I abandoned Trey at the Starbucks as he had requested, and pulled out of the parking lot, back onto the rural highway. Fortunately, there was a lull in the slow, dreary rain that had fallen all day, but even that did little to ease my fears about the wet leaves everywhere on the flat stretch of highway ahead as I drove, other than relieve me of the need to locate the windshield wiper controls on the dashboard of Mrs. Emory's car. The drive to Green Bay was a

boring, unremarkable journey punctuated by few things more exciting than barns painted dreary colors, and out-of-date billboards
marketing morning radio shows and local car dealerships. I was
thankful that at least it was still light out, but knew that the drive
back to Willow would be infinitely more difficult for me in the dark
no matter how quickly I shopped. Nervously, I tinkered with the
car's satellite radio, and succeeded in filling the car's interior with
Mrs. Emory's preferred honky-tonk country-western music. I was
too anxious about keeping my eyes on the road to bother trying to
find a more appealing station.

Parking was tricky, and to avoid a collision due to my sloppy
turning, I parked farther away from the mall's entrance than I probably needed to, in a space fairly far from other cars. Once I stepped
outside Mrs. Emory's car and clicked the doors locked with the automated key chain, I breathed a sigh of relief and then looked around.
I was standing at the very place where Olivia must have realized that
Violet's prediction was coming true. For a minute, I stood in the lot,
hugging my purse to my chest, wondering why in the world Olivia
hadn't just waited out the storm at the mall. She must have sensed
when her car wouldn't start that she was in danger.

Inside the mall, I entered the store walking briskly, on a mission.
I walked down the board game aisle feeling like a total creep, trying to ignore the mothers shopping with young children for games
like Connect Four and Chutes and Ladders. My eyes reviewed the
stacked board games for sale on the shelves, and I started to wonder
if I had just forced myself to drive all the way to Green Bay in vain,
when I should have been at home catching up on homework. But
then, on the top shelf, at the bottom of a stack of boxes of Stratego,

I saw a white box with the word OUIJA printed across the top. It appeared to be the only one in stock.

"That'll be twenty-three dollars and fifty-four cents," the teenage girl behind the cash register told me, snapping her gum and smirking. I hated that girl immediately for her knowing smirk, and I fumbled around in my wallet to hand her exact change. It was annoying that she would dare to assume why I was buying such a silly toy. I was eager for her to just put the box into an opaque white plastic bag and let me be on my way as mothers with quarreling children were lining up behind me, impatiently waiting to pay for their Barbies and Tonka trucks.

"Here you go," I said quickly, handing her cash and a handful of coins.

"We sell a lot of those this time of year," she informed me, handing over my receipt.

Of course—Halloween! Buying a Ouija board in early October wasn't so odd, after all. I rushed back to the parking lot with my purchase under one arm, and tossed it in the back seat before I strapped myself in with the seat belt. In the split second after I inserted the key into the car to start its engine, I became paranoid about driving home in the dark with an occult communication tool for talking with the dead in the car behind me.

Get it together, McKenna. There's no other way to get home but to drive there.

I took my time switching music channels until I found a station playing pop music that I knew by heart, and carefully maneuvered my way out of the parking lot. I fumbled with the headlights, putting on the high beams even though it wasn't completely dark yet, and turned them back down to low beams after someone angrily honked at me on the highway. All the way back to Silver Springs, I drove slowly, terrified of missing a turn or streetlight and getting lost in the woods, feeling the weight of Mrs. Emory's car anchoring me to the road. As I pulled into the lot at Starbucks, Trey waved at me through the window, holding a large white paper cup, and met me in the lot so that I wouldn't have to suffer through the ordeal of trying to park in a tightly jammed space.

"You got it," he said, sounding relieved upon seeing the bag in the back seat.

"I got it," I confirmed.

He reached into the back seat and pulled the bagged game into his lap to examine it. "So, where should we test this thing out?"

"Hey, could you put that away? It's freaking me out," I said, feeling a surge of relief pass through me as we drove past the familiar sign along the highway that read:

WILLOW POPULATION 4,218

In my head, I subtracted one from that number of residents. "Seriously, McKenna. Now that we have it, where should we see if it works? We can't try it in your room. If by some incredible long shot, this piece of junk, manufactured by"—he examined the box again, reading the logo—"Winning Moves, is actually able to channel communication from paranormal spirits, and those spirits happen to be *loud*, we'd better not be under your mom's roof."

"Where, then? Your basement?" I asked, braking at a light.

There was a little more traffic now that we were within town boundaries.

"Possibly," Trey considered the option. "Although getting you down there might be tricky unless you come over after dinner and we say we're going to do homework."

I eased onto the gas again as the light turned green, and we drove without talking until I turned left onto Carroll Road, the block before ours. It was already after six o'clock, and it would be close to eight by the time I finished dinner at home and helped to load the dishwasher. "Okay. Homework at your place it is. But can you do me a favor? Take the board inside with you. If my mom finds it, the questions will never end." I pulled over to the curb so that we could switch seats to prevent Trey's mom from suspecting that I had been the one driving all the way to Green Bay and back.

As he sat down in the driver's seat, he said, "I remember why I went to Green Bay that night. It was to buy spark plugs for Coach Stirling's Cadillac. I must have seen Olivia in the parking lot or something when I was driving by on my way to AutoZone."

"But you don't remember actually running into her?" I asked. I didn't want to let on how relieved I was that he'd remembered why he'd been so far away from our town that night.

He shook his head. "I remember her telling me that her car wouldn't start. But I don't remember exactly how I ended up in the parking lot."

Throughout dinner, Mom attacked me with questions about whether or not I had tried on my dress for homecoming recently to make sure it still fit, which earrings I'd be wearing, if Trey would be driving me to the dance on Friday, and what time I expected to be home. It was kind of baffling that she was putting so much more consideration into my attendance at the homecoming dance than I was; I didn't have the right answer to any of her questions because Trey and I hadn't really made an action plan for getting to the dance yet.

After I cleared my place, rinsed dishes, loaded the dishwasher, and set it to run, I threw my backpack over one shoulder without even peeking inside of it to see which books I'd carried home. At the front door of our house, I called over my shoulder, "I'm going over to Trey's to do homework!"

The Emorys' basement was nothing like the one at the Richmonds' house. It was one giant unfinished construction project, with wiring peeking through drywall, and a non-functioning toilet standing in a corner on the cement floor that had been intended for a bathroom renovation that Mr. Emory had never completed. A bare light bulb hung from a wire that dangled from the ceiling, and a stained plaid couch had been pressed up against the wall near the stairs. Mildewing board games were stacked on a utility shelf. The entire basement smelled like decay, and the air was damp against my face. I suspected there were way more spiders down there than I wanted to know about.

Trey and I plunked ourselves down on an old rag rug with our legs outstretched, our backs pressed against the plaid couch. He opened the game board between us. The sight of it made me shudder. The word YES was printed in its upper left corner, and NO was printed in its upper right corner. The letters of the alphabet were printed in two orderly arcs, and numbers were assembled below them. Beneath the numbers, GOOD BYE was printed in capital letters.

Trey placed the plastic planchette on which we would rest our fingers in the center of the board over the word OUIJA, which appeared in between the YES and NO in opposite corners. "Kind of cheaply made, right?" he asked me shyly. "This thing might only be capable of contacting extremely tacky spirits."

"Ha ha," I replied dryly.

We could hear his parents watching television in the living room upstairs, but it seemed as if they were in another dimension. I couldn't say why, but that Ouija board on the floor terrified me. I was afraid to place my fingertips on the plastic guide; a sense of doom was washing over me, as if we were about to throw open a gate to allow terrible things from another world into our neighborhood. "I don't know about this," I admitted quietly. "It seemed like a good idea yesterday, but what happens if we contact something and we don't know how to control it?"

Trey leaned over and planted a soft kiss on my cheek. "The book says that this is our world, and we have more power than they do here. Truly evil spirits might resort to crazy tactics to try to scare us, but we have to remember that we belong here, and they don't. James W. Listerman wrote that we have to be very authoritative when we're communicating with them. Tell them who's boss."

Telling spirits capable of nearly tossing me out of my bed with sheer force that we were in charge seemed ridiculous. I wished there was a fireplace in the Emorys' basement like the one at the Richmonds' so that if things got out of control, we could toss the game into the flames, which seemed to be a viable method of disposal in horror movies. I followed Trey's lead by placing my own freezing fingertip alongside his. "We should warm it up first," he instructed, and used his own force to gently move the planchette around the board in circles. After a minute or so of this, I looked over to him to suggest that he should take the lead.

Trey nodded at me and cleared his throat nervously. "We are try-ing to reach the spirit that is visiting McKenna's bedroom on Martha Road," Trey said in a firm voice. "But only kind, well-meaning spirits are welcome here."

I felt a very subtle vibrating sensation beneath my fingertip, and I couldn't be certain if Trey was trying to scare me or not, but the planchette seemed to be channeling some kind of faint energy. It circled the board in a wide arc, coming to rest over the word OUIJA at the bottom. "We're supposed to start with easy yes-and-no ques-tions," Trey informed me. "Is there someone here with us?" he asked the board.

The planchette, in a slow and wobbly trajectory, made its way toward the upper left corner and stopped with its pointer touching the Y in YES. I winced. Trey looked over at me for permission to con-tinue, and I reluctantly nodded, sensing that the tip of my nose and my lips were freezing cold. The temperature in the basement seemed to have dropped at least twenty degrees during the last minute.

"Are you the spirit who has been trying to make contact with McKenna Brady?" Trey asked carefully.

My heart skipped a beat as the planchette trembled but didn't move. "It's already on YES," I whispered. "Ask it something else."

"What can you tell us about Violet Simmons?"

The planchette dragged our fingertips toward the center of the board, hesitated, and then moved up toward the NO in the upper right corner.

"What does that mean?" Trey asked me under his breath, not directing his question to the board. "'No'?"

"Maybe it's too complicated to answer this way," I suggested, but then the planchette began moving again. First, it slowly dragged its way over to the *F* in the top arc of letters. Then it shifted a little more over to the *E* and came to a rest.

"E," Trey said. "I think I might know where this is going."

The planchette, as expected, then moved its way down to the second arc of letters, and hovered with its pointer touching the *V.*

"Evil. We've got it," Trey assured the spirit. He looked at me and nudged me with his elbow. "Ask it something."

There was one question on my mind, but it was too terrible to ask. If the answer was what I feared it would be, there could be no turning back time to a place when I believed Jennie was at peace, wherever she was. There would only be the knowledge that her existence persisted past the point at which her body died in the fire, and that she was still trailing me through my life, I feared, with jealousy. I *really* did not like the notion of leaving Trey's basement and walking back to my house knowing that Jennie was around me, watching me, *after* me. After a moment's hesitation I realized that Trey was studying me, waiting for me to speak, and surely he knew the question on the tip of my tongue.

"I'll ask," he assured me. "Are you Jennie?"

The planchette rocketed up to the right corner of the board, and landed on the NO.

I breathed a deep sigh of relief, and the air in my lungs rushed out of me with a giant *whoosh*. It was both an enormous relief and a heartbreaking tragedy that my twin, my other half, wasn't the spirit trying so hard to reach me.

Which left really only one relevant question: Who *was* trying to reach me?

Reading my mind, Trey asked, "Okay . . . who are you?"

The planchette slowly, steadily, led our fingers across the board until it came to rest pointing at the letter *O*.

Trey's fingers flew off the planchette, and he shook his head. "No way. No way," he muttered.

To remove any possibility that we were misinterpreting the board, the planchette began moving with only my fingertip on it toward the board's *L*.

"Let go of it," Trey commanded.

I raised my fingertips, and as soon as I did, the planchette moved rapidly all on its own to the letters *L-I-V-I-A*. I gasped in horror. How was it moving on its *own*? I felt like I couldn't even believe what I was seeing to be real.

Trey asked, "Are you the spirit visiting McKenna's bedroom?" The planchette slid over to the YES.

"The Lite-Brite," I asked hoarsely, "was that you?" The planchette slid upward and landed on the NO.

We both watched the planchette where it had come to rest on the board for a moment, holding our breath for another sign of motion. "Maybe she's gone," I suggested. At the sound of my voice, the planchette slid over to the *S*. I clung to Trey's left arm, barely breathing, as the planchette spelled out:

S-H-E-K-N-E-W-E-V-E-R-Y-T-H-I-N-G.

"Jesus," I murmured.

"Will more people die?" Trey asked. I could see steam escape through his lips in the frosty air that surrounded us.

The planchette delivered the response we both feared most.

YES. GOOD BYE.

219

* * *

That night, hours after I had said good night in a stiff voice to Trey's parents and walked across our yards back to my house, and Trey had crept through the window, I rested my head on his chest and stared at the wall.

"What do we do about Violet?" I asked, knowing that Trey wouldn't have an answer. "How do we stop her?"

"I don't know," Trey said, holding me protectively close, with a grip like an iron clamp.

"Why would Olivia reach out to me, and not Mischa? They were closer friends. Is she trying to protect us? Is she just out for revenge against Violet?"

The answers that Olivia had provided to us created even more questions. One thing was certain: Olivia wasn't going to visit us in my room that night, but even knowing that we wouldn't be troubled by her interruptions wasn't enough to put either of us in a romantic mood. It seemed to be more and more the case that we were going to have to bring an end to Violet's plans before another one of us died. And this time, because Trey and I knew it was coming, if we couldn't prevent it from happening . . . we'd be partly responsible.

The staff at the Ortonville Lodge outdid themselves, lavishly decorating their grand ballroom, usually used for hosting sales conference banquets for Realtors and lawn equipment retail executives. Flowers had been donated by the same florist in Willow who had supplied most of the arrangements at Olivia's wake, and they had placed clusters of orchids and carnations dyed blue throughout the ballroom, filling the entire space with fragrance. A disco ball dangled overhead, hung from a crystal chandelier, and streamers crisscrossed from one corner of the ceiling to the other. An enormous table had been set up for the DJ, with speakers tucked into all four corners of the room. A photographer had decorated a corner of the hallway leading to the ballroom with a gazebo and backdrop of clouds, and couples posed for pictures, choosing fun props from a box offering flower leis and grass skirts. The theme for the dance, chosen by the senior class, was Tropical Paradise. Given that we were dancing in a ballroom in central Wisconsin to Top 40 hits, hearing the chilly autumn wind whistle through the hotel windows, the theme was a bit ironic. But no one seemed to care how absurd it was that we were pretending to hold our school dance in Fiji. "How authentically Tahitian," Trey quipped at a snack buffet offering popcorn balls dyed lavender with food coloring, and water chestnuts wrapped in bacon, served on little toothpicks.

The usual suspects were all in attendance at the dance. Coach Stirling surprisingly wore a tea-length gray dress and shoes that were not sneakers. Mr. Dean wore a brown suit with a paisley tie. Principal Nylander brought his wife as his date, as he usually did, and our town was so small that everyone knew Katie Wayne from the freshman class was babysitting the Nylanders' two kids that night. I felt a twinge of embarrassment for my old friends, Cheryl, Kelly, and Erica, who had intentionally bought identical dresses. They'd come to the dance together, dateless, as a threesome. I would have been with them, sitting at their table in the far corner giggling over cups of punch in a matching forest green dress, a year earlier.

Mischa wore her hair up and looked like a tiny fairy in her hot pink strapless gown when she entered the ballroom on Matt's arm, with Candace and Isaac right behind them. Candace looked sedate and serene in a teal gown with spaghetti straps, her hair curled like a movie star's around her shoulders. The moment I saw them, I felt a twinge of resentment toward Violet, because I knew they had probably all driven to the dance together with Amanda and Brian. I had to remind myself that I had volunteered to be the one who remained close to Violet, even if it meant missing out on group fun.

Trey and I lingered to the side of the ballroom, silently watching everyone with our hands locked together tightly beneath the table, where no one could see. A few chaperones had questioned me with their eyes when we entered, clearly indicating that they considered us to be somewhat of an odd pairing. Trey had surprised me with a white rose corsage; I had no idea when he had the time to choose it or pick it up at the florist since we'd walked home from school together, but I suspected his mom had something to do with it.

All day long, I'd had a throbbing headache and a suspicion that something significant was going to happen at the dance. Everyone had been rowdy in classes all day in anticipation of the night's big event, but I'd been lost in daydreams, caught off guard when I'd been called on to describe the weather using the future tense in Spanish. When I'd arrived home from school, I was annoyed rather than happy to find my mom home from work early, eager to help me prepare for the big night. I'd snapped at her when she suggested that I curl my hair and allow her to do my makeup, and then had ultimately given in. After all, she had agreed to drive me and Trey to the dance, and to pick us up.

"There she is," Trey informed me, trying to be discreet, as he nodded in the direction of the ballroom entrance.

Violet, looking downright gorgeous, stood nervously in the wide doorway to the ballroom, lit from the bright hallway behind her. Her hair was loose and wavy, and her light blue minidress fit her perfectly. More than one guy turned his head to check her out, and a moment later she was joined by Tracy and Michael, who looked more handsome than usual. Tracy and Michael had struck up a rather unsurprising partnership since the student election had begun, and they actually looked kind of cute together as a couple, despite their combined annoyingness. Tracy had made an impressive effort, with her hair pulled back tightly in a French twist, showing off her long neck. But it was Violet who, without any real competition, stole the show.

Eventually, after fetching cups of punch and saying hello to other students, both girls made their way over to the table where Trey and I sat, and I did my best to greet them cheerfully.

"Oh my God, McKenna! You look so pretty!"

I blushed, mostly because the lavender dress I'd bought such a long time ago hardly seemed suitable now that the night of the dance had finally arrived. I felt like I'd been a different person completely when I'd bought it, and I had cringed at home when I looked in the mirror. Mom had insisted on my wearing her amethyst earrings to match, and while the dangling gems felt extravagant for me, they were nothing in comparison to the excessive jewelry Tracy had piled on. She had jewel-encrusted combs in her hair, chandelier earrings almost reaching her shoulders, and an enormous cocktail ring on her left hand. Violet wore her gold locket, as always, but with a dainty pair of diamond earrings.

We exchanged compliments on one another's dresses and gossiped halfheartedly about the dresses worn by some of the more popular senior girls. I nodded but didn't contribute to the conversation when nasty comments were made about Cheryl, Kelly, and Erica. Amanda Portnoy looked phenomenal in a gold sequined dress that definitely had not been bought at any of the stores near Willow. I couldn't help but wonder how magnificent Olivia would have looked, had she lived to attend the dance.

It took a while for people to loosen up enough to venture out onto the dance floor, but once they did, they were ready to party hard. Isaac challenged Coach Highland, the boys' football coach, to a dance-off, and everyone was clutching their guts with laughter. The DJ played Kool & the Gang's "Celebration," which no one could resist, other than Trey and me. We remained fixed in our seats, communicating entirely with expressions, watching. Waiting.

"Guys, come on and dance! It's a party!" Tracy yelled at us, red in the face from jumping up and down during "Rapper's Delight." She grabbed me by the hands and attempted to drag me off my chair onto the dance floor.

"Nah, I'm not a good dancer," I refused.

"Come on, Trey! Tell your girl to get on her feet!" Tracy encouraged Trey, as if they were friends.

Trey was not the kind of guy to welcome false friendliness, even if he looked far less intimidating that night in a suit than he normally did. "McKenna doesn't want to dance," he stated firmly.

"Well, you're missing out!" Tracy cautioned us, ignoring his bitterness and trotting back out onto the dance floor with a smile, where Michael, clapping his hands, was waiting for her.

Trey nudged me and nodded his head in the direction of where Pete and Violet had struck up what appeared to be a friendly conversation near the punch bowl. Pete appeared to be telling her that she looked nice, and she was shrugging her bare shoulders bashfully and flirtatiously placing one hand on his forearm. Pete looked hot as always, wearing a different suit from the one he'd worn to Olivia's wake. He'd left his jacket on the back of a chair somewhere, and had a pink carnation tucked into the breast pocket of his white button-down shirt. My heart was pounding with fury as I looked around to see if Mischa and Candace were witnessing what I saw, but when my eyes found them in the crowd, they were oblivious, dancing together.

Pete. So maybe snaring Pete was part of Violet's motive. Trey raised one eyebrow at me. He was thinking the same thing.

At nearly ten p.m., Principal Nylander stepped up to a podium carrying two envelopes, and the DJ cut the music after a slow dance ended.

"Attention, everyone! Attention!" Principal Nylander said, tapping the microphone to make sure it was working. The crowd on the dance floor calmed down, and Trey and I shifted our chairs so that we could watch the principal's speech. He cleared his throat. "I'd like to thank all of you for joining us tonight and showing some admirable school spirit. Now, I know our school year has already been marred by tragedy, but tonight the good time we're having in each other's company shows that the students of Willow High School have the strength to celebrate the life of our lost friend, Olivia Richmond, and move forward with positivity."

There was light applause; people were a little surprised that he had chosen to mention Olivia by name.

"Now, we were a little surprised when we tallied the votes for homecoming court this year. Quite a number of you wrote in Olivia Richmond's name, and we felt it was the right thing to do in her memory to mention that and acknowledge your votes."

Whispers filled the ballroom. Principal Nylander hadn't specified whether or not Olivia had actually won. No one knew exactly what to expect next.

"However, while we all acknowledge that Olivia was very much a beloved member of our high school community, in the interest of moving forward into the future, it brings me great pleasure to announce this year's homecoming king and queen."

Now excitement was building. Chatter in the ballroom swelled in volume, and Trey and I exchanged confused looks. *How could any other girl have received votes?* I wondered. I'd written in Olivia's name, and so had everyone I knew. Amanda, who had been the previous year's homecoming queen when she was a junior, looked outraged where she stood across the ballroom, saying something directly to Mischa.

Principal Nylander tugged the first envelope open, flanked by Coach Stirling to his left, and Mr. Paulson, the wood-shop teacher, to his right. He leaned forward to speak into the microphone again, reading off of the piece of paper that he had removed from the envelope. "This year's homecoming queen is . . . Violet Simmons."

I couldn't control my reaction: I lurched forward to my feet and my jaw dropped open. Trey stood behind me and placed his hands on my shoulders to keep me from leaving our table. The crowd erupted into jubilant applause, and I had to remind myself that no one but me, Trey, Mischa, Amanda, and Candace really had reason to be upset by Violet's win. To everyone else in the junior class, Violet was just the mysterious new girl who had been close friends with Olivia. For them, it was probably perfectly natural that she had received the most votes after Olivia.

But for us, it was plainly obvious that Violet might have been the only person in the entire junior class who had voted for herself, and that *one* vote had probably been enough to earn her the title of queen. In disbelief, I watched as the crowd of students closed in on Violet. Girls with happy tears in their eyes patted her on the back and urged her toward the front of the ballroom. Violet had covered her mouth with her hands in surprise and was shaking her head as if she just couldn't believe that her name had been called. It was impressive acting, indeed, since it was unlikely that she was truly surprised.

"Congratulations, Violet. And next, our homecoming king is . . . Peter Nicholson. Congratulations, Pete!"

Principal Nylander was beaming proudly at the crowd as Pete rose to his feet from the chair on which he was sitting, urged by the other guys on the basketball team. He, unlike Violet, appeared to be embarrassed to have won anything, and impishly took his place standing next to her. After greeting her with a shy smile, he looked down at the floor, his hands fidgeting nervously.

"Way to go, man!" a male voice yelled from the crowd, causing Pete to reluctantly nod in acknowledgment.

"Something's going to happen," Trey said, grabbing my arm. "Do you feel it?"

I did feel that something was about to occur, but I couldn't explain how. The room still felt warm, but the hairs on my forearms were standing on end. Something about the whole experience of standing next to Trey and hearing applause felt like déjà vu. Then a nauseating feeling washed over me as I heard the first chords of a song I'd never expected to hear that night. Trey reached for my hand and squeezed, realizing in unison with me what was happening. "Soul Meets Body" by Death Cab for Cutie filled the ballroom of the Ortonville Lodge as Pete put one arm loosely around Violet and they bowed to be crowned. After Principal Nylander placed gaudy plastic crowns on both of their heads, they looked up to face the applauding crowd, and tears of joy were falling from Violet's eyes, stained purple from her eyeliner, glistening beneath the spotlight shining down on her. I felt like I was in a dream, where everything that was happening was wrong, and all I could do was watch.

Through the crowd, I saw Mischa and Matt. Our eyes met, and she looked furious, angry enough to cry. Matt had his arm around her shoulders and was stroking her cheek, whispering in her ear, trying to calm her. The boys in the senior class, in their Sunday-best suits, were chanting and hollering with their fists in the air, "Kiss her! Kiss her!" Pete turned to Violet, smiling uncertainly, not wanting to disappoint the crowd. I tried desperately to remember how much of our suspicions about Violet we had shared with Pete after the accident and realized that we might not have told him anything at all, wanting to spare him more emotional anguish. It was very possible that he just thought Candace's rambling was an effect of her own grief over Olivia's death.

Trey shook his head slowly as Coach Stirling and the wood-shop teacher placed sashes over Pete and Violet's shoulders. Only as Pete took Violet's hand in his and raised her arm over their heads in victory did I notice Isaac struggling to hold Candace back. She was writhing with anger and yelling toward the back of the crowd, but I couldn't hear what she was saying over the volume of the music. All the care she had put into her appearance was overpowered by her animalistic rage. She looked monstrous, clawing at Isaac to release her, her face red. He lost his grip on her arms and she rushed for the podium, moving so quickly that she nearly tripped over her own heels. As she tumbled toward the front of the ballroom, shoving anyone standing in her way off to the side, she looked like a roaring cannonball, ripping through the crowd too fast for anyone to really put together was happening. She barreled into Violet, knocking the podium over on its side as she and Violet both hit the floor. Violet hadn't even seen her coming; she'd been too busy waving dreamily to the rest of the students at the dance.

"Holy . . ." Trey trailed off.

The dance immediately turned into a scene of chaos. Teachers swept in, pulling Candace off of Violet. Pete and Coach Stirling helped Violet back up to her feet, and as she regained her balance she realized that her nose was dripping blood all over the front of her baby blue dress. Her crown had been knocked to the ground in the tussle, forgotten behind the podium. Melissa, the girl who had been along for the drive with us to Kenosha the night of Olivia's accident, dashed to the banquet table and returned with a stack of soft white napkins to press against Violet's face. Pete concerned himself with Violet and cast an angry glance at Candace as Mr. Paulson dragged her away. Several teachers called for ambulances and police, so within minutes, sirens could be heard outside. No one within the ballroom knew quite what to do; everyone was looking around in helpless surprise. The music had been silenced, and the entire grand ballroom was filled with the curious murmurs of confused teenagers.

"Let's go." Trey motioned for me to follow him, and then led me by the elbow through the double doors that returned us to the hotel's lobby. Hotel guests looked in wonderment at all the baffled teenagers spilling out of the ballroom in their evening attire. Candace had been dragged out to the front of the hotel and was being held back by Mr. Paulson and one of the physics teachers. Through the hotel lobby's floor-to-ceiling windows, we could see the two of them, grown men, struggling to restrain her as she tirelessly thrashed in an attempt to break free of them. We watched, stunned at her behavior.

"She definitely doesn't seem like she's under hypnosis," Trey observed.

It was true; Candace seemed more *possessed* than hypnotized. A paramedic gave her an injection of something, presumably a sedative, and she fell slack about four seconds later, her knees buckling beneath her. The paramedics caught her before she hit the sidewalk, and gently positioned her on a rolling gurney before sliding it into the back of the ambulance.

"Somebody call an exorcist," grumbled a senior girl passing behind us, returning to the dance from the ladies' bathroom down the hall. We were lucky to have made our way to the front lobby quickly, because behind us, other chaperones and hotel administrators were preventing other students from leaving the ballroom, urging them to stay calm until the medical professionals had an opportunity to attend to Candace. Isaac was among them, and his attempts to explain that Candace was his girlfriend didn't gain him access to the lobby. "Stay calm, everyone," we heard Principal

Nylander commanding everyone over the microphone in the ball-room. "The night is still young." Trey and I watched as the ambulance carried Candace away, trailed closely by two police cars. Behind us, we heard the music resume, and homecoming continued on as if nothing had happened.

As far as our classmates were concerned, all they had witnessed was an explosive catfight, one started by a girl who was off her rocker. I was stunned. Olivia's ghost had been haunting my bedroom to warn me about this. She had brought that song to my attention so that I would realize something important was going to happen, and I was furious with myself for not understanding the clue.

"I just don't get it," I complained to Trey after we were herded back into the ballroom by Coach Stirling. "What comes next?"

"Candace's death in the game. How did Violet describe it? Is there any chance she's going to die on the way to the hospital, or *at* the hospital?" Trey asked me.

I had to think back to remember the details of the story that Violet had concocted for Candace. "It was drowning. On a beach. In deep water. She said fish would eat off Candace's face."

Trey put his arm around me and pinched my shoulder tenderly. "There aren't really any beaches in Wisconsin, silly, other than rock beaches around the lakes. Olivia must have wanted us to take notice of something else. Maybe just that Violet wants Pete? That much is pretty obvious."

Violet and Pete were slow dancing at that very minute. They weren't dancing very closely together, but they did appear to be having a friendly conversation, which was reason enough for us to be curious. Violet still looked pretty, even despite the bloodstains down the front of her dress, which club soda had done little to remove. I wondered if Violet had ever originally made plans to go to the Fall Fling with Mark Regan, or if her mention of that had been part of her longer-term plan to kill Olivia and steal Pete.

"See that?" I heard a voice behind me and turned to find Mischa taking the seat next to mine, glaring across the ballroom at Violet. She was risking the credibility of our fake fight by speaking to me, but she was in no mood to care. "It's Pete. She wants Pete. I think she killed Olivia just to go out with him."

As if her head was guided by a mystical power, Violet looked directly over at us at that moment and made eye contact with me. Her expression toward me was one that suggested I was in trouble rather than one of curiosity as to why I would be conversing with my alleged adversary. Whether she instantly was able to discern that my entire fight with Mischa had been phony, or assumed that we were in the process of restoring our friendship, I couldn't tell. It was just clear that she wasn't happy to see us together.

Mischa glared back at her and snarled, "Oh, look at that! Someone's not happy that we're friends again. Too bad. No more sneaking around, McKenna. I want that girl to know that you're *my* friend too. It's too dangerous for you to get close to her."

I had to agree with Mischa. Violet was quite obviously outsmarting us all. It was everything: the popularity, the Student Government victory, the boyfriend . . . all of it. I just needed some kind of a breakthrough to better understand why Olivia had needed to die to make it all possible.

CHAPTER 12

MAUDE THE PUPPY SAT OUTSIDE THE BATHROOM door and barked at me as I scrubbed off my makeup at home in the bathroom later that night. "I don't know what's gotten into her. She was quiet all night," Mom said, studying the little dog. Maude looked up at me and barked, and turned to my mother as if to say, *See?*

"Crazy dog," I said gruffly and walked down the hall to my room.

An hour later, when Trey tapped on my window, he announced, "I'm not sure I should keep staying over here. My parents know something's up."

My breath caught in my throat with both fear and panic. "What do you mean, they know? Do they know you're coming *here*?" I looked through my window over to the Emorys' house, which was dark and silent for the night.

"They know I'm going *somewhere*. My mom sat me down tonight and told me that they didn't want to bug me before the big night but that they're concerned about my well-being and have noticed that I'm sneaking out at night." He sank onto the edge of my bed, not

233

wanting to get too comfortable, looking to me to confirm whether he should stay or leave. "Crap," I uttered. It was already quite late. I could hear crickets in the backyard and the ticking clock on the mantel over the fireplace in the living room. "Maybe it'll be okay. Maybe because I blew it with her last clue, she'll leave me alone."

"Are you sure?" Trey asked, not believing me. I didn't really want him to leave but was already highly suspicious that his parents knew exactly where he was going every night, and I didn't want them to approach my mom with the news. The warmth of his body in bed next to mine had grown familiar, and I was a little terrified that Olivia was going to be enraged that I hadn't figured out what she had wanted me to do at the dance. He took both of my hands gently in his, and ran his thumbs over the tops of my fingers. "I don't really want you to sleep here by yourself."

I looked around my dark room, up at the shelf holding my music boxes, and the other shelf holding my CDs, and shrugged. "I can sleep in the living room. I think it's safe out there."

Once Trey reluctantly left and scrambled back into his own room through the window, I grabbed my pillow and a blanket and rushed out of my room as quickly as I could. As soon as I was situated on the couch in the living room, I could hear Maude down the hall in my mom's bedroom softly whimpering to herself. Then I began thinking about how on reality TV shows about ghost hunts, oftentimes pets could detect paranormal activity that humans couldn't see with their eyes, and I started freaking myself out.

In the morning, my fear that Maude had sensed Olivia's spirit was up to something in my room was confirmed when I peeked in there just after sunrise. At first everything in my room appeared to be in place, just as I'd left it, but then I nearly jumped out of my skin in surprise when I noticed one word written on my mirror in plum-colored lipstick. It said:

NOHI

That morning, Mischa borrowed her sister's car and we drove to the hospital in Ortonville to visit Candace. I hadn't given up on my hope of trying to determine if she was under hypnosis, although her behavior at the homecoming dance had strongly suggested she wasn't. We talked lightheartedly about homecoming and about boys, but primarily to distract ourselves from the severity of our situation. She told me that she thought Trey and I made a very cute couple, even though she never would have guessed that brooding loners were my type.

"You have to admit he's weird," Mischa insisted, "but he *is* hot. I'll give you that."

"Okay, he's weird," I agreed, "but so am I."

Mischa told me that I'd missed a somber trip to Bobby's after the dance. Matt had driven her home in his dad's car after Violet, Pete, Melissa, Jeff, Tracy, and Mike had shown up. Mischa hadn't been in much of a mood to party after that.

"I mean, seriously, who does she think she is? I asked Matt to talk to Pete, but they're not really friends. I guess if he actually likes Violet, there's not much we can do about it, but I mean, God! It's just so messed up that she'd go after Olivia's boyfriend and it hasn't even been a month yet," Mischa rambled.

The nurse at the front desk in the emergency room told us that under no circumstances would we be allowed to visit Candace, because she had been admitted to the psychiatric ward and we weren't immediate family members.

"This is really, really important," Mischa insisted. "It's, like, life or death."

"I'm sure it is, honey," the nurse told us patronizingly, "but it'll have to wait until she's released."

Fortunately, we saw Candace's mother in the parking lot before we drove away, and bolted out of Mischa's car to intercept her before she reached her own car.

"Mrs. Lehrer!" Mischa called.

Candace's mom stopped before opening the driver's-side door to her car and seemed startled to hear her name called. She appeared to be exhausted, with bags under her eyes, and was dressed far less fashionably than she usually was, wearing a washed-out sweat suit. She carried a cup of coffee from the hospital cafeteria in one hand, and her car keys dangled from the other. "Oh hi, girls. I'm sorry, it's been a long night. I didn't recognize you just now."

"We really need to see Candace," Mischa pleaded.

"I don't think the hospital is going to allow that. Candace is having a difficult time and can't have any visitors. She is still obsessed with the notion that this girl Violet at school has some kind of evil powers because of whatever game you guys played at Olivia's house a few weeks ago. Her doctors seem to think that game has become the fixation of whatever psychosis she's suffering. I don't think it would be beneficial for her to see any friends from school."

"My dad is a psychiatrist," I piped up. "He said you should take Candace to the University of Wisconsin in Sheboygan and have her examined by one of his former coworkers. He gave me the name of someone." I handed her the e-mail from my dad that I had printed out, which included contact information for Dr. Felipe Hernandez. Candace's mom inspected the sheet of paper before tucking it into her purse.

"Thank you, McKenna, and thank your dad, too. I'm at my wits' end with all of this. I just don't know what to do for her anymore. Candace's dad and stepmom are driving up from Green Bay this afternoon, and I should have a better idea tomorrow of what's going to happen next."

On the drive back to Willow, I grappled with the decision of whether or not to tell Mischa about all the weird occurrences in my house, and about the Ouija board connection that Trey and I had made with Olivia. I really wanted to share, but didn't want to end up in the room next to Candace's in the psychiatric ward of the hospital. But still, if there was a chance that Mischa was receiving messages from Olivia, then maybe *her* messages, combined with *my* messages, would lead to some kind of understanding about what we needed to do to stop Violet.

"Have you been noticing anything weird lately at your house?" I asked with trepidation. I heard my phone buzz in my handbag with a text message, and ignored it. Violet had been texting me all morning, wanting to see if I would join her and Tracy for a movie that afternoon, and I hadn't gathered the energy to respond yet.

"How do you mean, weird?" Mischa asked. "My sister is basically a terrorist. *That's* weird."

"Like . . ." I drifted off, suspecting that approaching this territory was probably a bad idea. "Just unexplained occurrences, uneasy feelings. General strangeness."

Mischa took her eyes off the road to shoot me an *are you kidding me?* look. "What are you freakin' talking about, McKenna? Are *you* losing your marbles too? I'm not sure if I can handle both of my best friends being wackos."

"I'm not, I'm not," I insisted, embarrassed by how flattered I was that Mischa acknowledged me as one of her best friends. "Just . . . there's this word that keeps popping up in my life and I can't explain it. Does 'nohi' mean anything to you?"

"It sounds Japanese." Mischa shrugged. "Like, '*kodomo no hi*' is 'Children's Day' in Japan."

It was hard to hide my dismay. That didn't seem like much of a clue, and it didn't sound like Mischa had been observing any strange things like I'd been. While Mischa could surprise with me the wide variety of trivia she stored in her head, there was no chance Olivia had learned how to say anything in Japanese before her death. Acquisition of knowledge had not exactly been one of Olivia's interests.

"Really?" I asked. "So as far as you know, that word doesn't have anything to do with Olivia at all?"

We had stopped at a red light before an intersection, and Mischa stared me down. "I don't know what you're talking about, McKenna. Are you trying to tell me that you think you're getting messages from Olivia . . . from the other side?"

I took a deep breath. "Before Candace went completely off her rocker, did she tell you that it freaked her out that Violet knew about her half brothers, even though Candace couldn't remember ever mentioning them to her before? I told you guys what Violet said to me on the track before Olivia died, that spirits *tell* her things. So I know it's far-fetched, but maybe Olivia is a spirit now, and she's trying to tell us things. There's been some weird stuff happening at my house, and it's not just me—Trey's seen it too. I think Olivia is trying to warn us. I think . . . more bad stuff is going to happen."

The light changed from red to green, but Mischa hesitated before accelerating. "You are seriously, seriously bugging me out."

We drove a few more blocks before Mischa asked, "What kind of bad stuff do you think is going to happen? Are more of us going to die, like Olivia?"

I stared out my window at my little town as we passed through, not wanting to say the words on the tip of my tongue. There was the florist, the feed shop, the pizza place that reliably delivered through snowy winters (Federico's was its rival pizza restaurant across town and offered only takeout during winter months), and as we passed the public elementary school, I said, "Mischa, we have to stop at the library. I need to see something."

Without asking me any questions, Mischa turned right into the parking lot of our small brick public library, just a little farther down the road from the elementary school. I'd been going there with my mom my whole life, and had never before paid much attention to the back wing of the library, which rose to two stories and featured enormous floor-to-ceiling windows. Now that I was taking a closer look, that wing of the library, which had been added onto the original structure a decade before I was born, dwarfed the original structure and had been designed in a far more modern style. It was obviously an addition to the original building, and very little effort had been put into making it look like a natural extension.

"I don't get it. What are we looking for?"

I pointed to the wing of the library and turned to Mischa. "Guess whose grandfather paid for that wing of the library. I have reason to believe it might be named after him too."

Mischa squinted her eyes at me. "Get out."

Inside, we were both stupefied to see the phrase THIS WING OF THE LIBRARY WAS MADE POSSIBLE BY A GIFT FROM THE HAROLD J. SIMMONS FAMILY along with the year 1984 on a copper plaque fixed to the wall near the entrance to the wing on the first floor. I ran my fingertips over the name of Violet's grandfather slowly. This was the wing of the library that contained the children's section, and upstairs on the second floor, nonfiction books about art, history, and drama were arranged. Mischa and I wandered into the wing dreamily, even though we had walked those rows of books hundreds of times since we were kids. "Wow, Violet's family must be *crazy* rich," Mischa commented, looking upward at the second floor of the library, which overlooked the reading section of the children's area. "I never really thought about the *library* too much, but this could not have been cheap to build."

We sat down at the row of computers in the media lounge and searched for Violet's grandfather's name. The results were so abundant that we couldn't possibly read through all of them. He had owned an architecture and construction firm, just like my father had remembered, and there seemed to be hundreds of search results about contracts for his firm and buildings they had constructed from the shores of Lake Superior all the way down to Chicago.

"Ooh! What about that one!" Mischa pointed to a headline on the screen that read, WILL DISPUTE OVER SIMMONS ESTATE SETTLED.

I clicked on the link, and Mischa drummed her long fingernails on the table where we sat, earning herself an irritated glance from the man sitting at the computer next to ours, while we waited for the old news article to load on our screen. Our eyes devoured the story as a picture and paragraphs of text loaded. It seemed to be the case that when Violet's grandfather passed away, fourteen years before her grandmother died, his will was contested by his former business partner, claiming that he had been jilted out of his half of the fortune. Harold Simmons hadn't left Arthur Fitzpatrick anything, not a dime, and he was adamant the will Mr. Simmons had left behind was a forgery, updated and signed just a few weeks before his unexpected death. Harold Simmons's widow, Violet's grandmother, claimed that all of the initial capital for the construction business had been fronted by Harold, and that all profits were contractually his own based on the agreement that the men had made when they began the company. She was insistent that Arthur Fitzpatrick was owed nothing more than the generous salary he had been paid during the time when he'd worked with Mr. Simmons.

"Scandal," Mischa whispered.

The battle raged on in court for three years until finally a judge ruled in favor of Mr. Fitzpatrick, awarding him a sliver of the land, a fraction of the business profits, and a contract to complete one of their larger unfinished jobs with his newly formed company. The story ended with quotes from Mr. Fitzpatrick as well as Violet's grandmother Ann Simmons.

"Finally, the court has delivered a fair ruling. I am eager to put this matter behind me, and look forward to a bright future for Fitzpatrick & Sons Construction," stated Mr. Fitzpatrick outside the Shawano County courthouse.

"Mr. Fitzpatrick may have been awarded what he wanted, but I

will not rest until my family's property has been restored to its rightful owners," Mrs. Ann Simmons retorted.

I sat back in my chair, a little winded. So Violet's grandmother, who had left her magnificent estate to Violet, had died with a grudge. None of these facts at face value explained any of what Olivia had been trying to communicate to me, but at least I finally felt like I was getting somewhere. I texted the link of the article to Trey, and Mischa and I continued searching for more information. Arthur Fitzpatrick developed the land that he won in the dispute in less than a year after the court's ruling. It was turned into a condominium community, sold off lot by lot. It reminded me of what Violet had told me about her uncle wanting to sell the land on which their mansion was built to be developed as condominiums too, and how her grandmother would have rolled over in her grave if that had happened. Mr. Fitzpatrick died of natural causes five years before Violet's grandmother did the same. We finished reading his obituary in the *Ortonville Courier* and both shook our heads. He had been survived by a wife, several children, and grandchildren, but by the time of his death had relocated to California.

"This might not even have anything to do with the grandmother," I announced, not wanting us to get our hopes up that we were onto something big. "Violet could just be evil, plain and simple."

Mischa looked unconvinced. "The grandmother was out for vengeance, and we don't know if she ever got it. And now Violet lives in her house. The entire family is just mean. That's *something.* That's more than we knew an hour ago."

We discussed researching the possibility of any kind of historical connection between the Simmons, Richmond, and Portnoy families, or any connection between Arthur Fitzgerald and any of my friends' families, but after a few quick web searches turned up sparse results, Mischa sighed. "My mom's parents came here from Russia after World War II. My dad grew up in Minnesota and moved here when they got married. I really don't think there was ever any connection between the Simmonses and my family. I mean, if the Simmonses had anything to do with *any* family in town, it would be Tracy Hartford's. Her grandfather was a district judge for, like, a billion years. If we have to read through all these property deeds and stuff, I'm going to die of boredom. I'm getting a headache just thinking about it."

Mischa had far too short of an attention span to ever qualify as a legitimate detective. We shut down our library research and drove to her house to try to determine our next move. I texted Violet back with a lie, saying that I was visiting my grandparents and wouldn't be able to join her and Tracy for a movie until Sunday. I just wanted one afternoon to myself, one afternoon to gossip about the homecoming dance and be a normal junior in high school.

When we arrived at the Portnoys' house, Amanda summoned us up to her room, calling out to us as soon as she heard the garage door open into the kitchen. "Mischa! Get up here! Have you seen this?"

We scrambled up the stairs to Amanda's room on the second floor, which was practically wallpapered with pictures of YouTube stars. She sat at her desk with her back to the door, completely engrossed in something on her phone.

As we entered the room, we saw that she was looking at highly unflattering pictures of Candace attacking Violet at the dance the night before, shared with her on her Instagram. "God, look at that. Candace looks like a maniac." Candace's hair was a blur, her face was flushed with rage, and her expression could only be described as demonic. "Who posted those photos?" Mischa asked defensively.

"A bunch of idiots from the football team. I already asked Brian to have them untag Candace. But, God, like, what's *wrong* with her?" Amanda clucked her tongue. While the pictures were horrific, the comments were worse. They were mean-spirited, brutal, and many had been posted by girls and boys alike who Candace had probably considered to be her friends. "I feel so bad for Candace. I know you guys like her, but her high school life is totally *over*."

Mischa motioned for me to follow her down the hall to her room. "I can't believe I didn't think of this before. What if we try to find kids from Violet's old school and ask them about her?" Mischa suggested, her eyes sparkling. It seemed like a great way of finding out if anyone had thought Violet had something to do with the four kids who'd died in Lake Forest the year before. Mischa wasted no time in searching for memorial pages for the two deceased kids whose names we knew. The parents of the girl who had been captain of the pom squad at Lake Forest High School had set up a private group called "Remembering Rebecca." We were unable to see any of the posts, but could browse the members of the group, and I asked Mischa to stop scrolling when the photo of a guy our age whose name was given as Eric appeared on screen.

"Hold it right there," I commanded. "That guy. Violet told me that she dated a guy named Eric and broke it off when she moved here because of long distance."

Mischa looked at the picture of the handsome, smiling jock skeptically. "Violet said her old school was really big. Don't you think there would be a lot of Erics in a big school?"

I couldn't explain how, I just had a strange feeling that we were looking at a picture of *the* Eric, the one who'd dated Violet. "Well, *this* Eric cared enough about Rebecca Shermer to join her remembrance group on Facebook. It would kind of make sense that Violet was friends with Rebecca Shermer if she was one of the kids who died, right? And if Violet was dating Eric . . ."

That afternoon, Mischa composed slightly mysterious messages to several kids who had posted to the remembrance pages for Rebecca Shermer and Josh Loomis, the freshman who Violet had once babysat, and to Eric. She explained that she was a student at Violet's new school in Willow, Wisconsin, planning to throw a surprise party to celebrate Violet's Student Government victory. She asked everyone she contacted to reply with discretion to maintain the surprise, and urged those who couldn't attend in person to send along best wishes that she claimed she would print out and include in a card to present to Violet at the party. I had to admit, it was a pretty brilliant plan for Mischa to have come up with. It was improbable that anyone would say they'd want to attend the party in person and drive all the way up from Illinois, and we would be able to tell a lot about how people perceived Violet from their responses. Best of all, it was unlikely that anyone would reach out to Violet and tell her that people at her new school were inquiring about her past. Mischa also sent a request to join the "Remembering Rebecca" group, but we knew it was not too likely that Rebecca's parents would admit anyone to the group whose name they didn't recognize.

"Check this out," Mischa told me hours later over the phone as I watched television with my mom. "I've gotten three responses so far. Molly Vega said, 'I don't really know Violet that well. Good luck with the party.' Then, Mike Goldsmith wrote back and said, 'I don't have anything nice to say about that girl.' And then . . . wait for it . . . Keeley Alden said, 'I would advise you to stay as far away from Violet as you can. Sorry you're stuck with her now, but at least she's not at our school anymore.'"

"Freaky," I said. My mother looked up at me from her newspaper at the other end of the couch with vague interest.

"And that guy? Eric? The boyfriend, right? He wrote back and said, 'I don't want anything to do with Violet Simmons. Don't ever contact me again.' And he just updated all of his privacy settings so I can't see anything on his profile anymore."

So we weren't the only ones who had discovered Violet to be a bit of a bad-luck charm. Unfortunately, no one from Violet's old high school wrote back to Mischa with any specifics about why she was so disliked. We didn't have any concrete evidence that she had ever led any other students in a game like Light as a Feather, Stiff as a Board, so whatever she had done at her old school to earn such a negative reputation remained unknown.

After another restless night sleeping on the couch, I agreed to see a movie with Violet and Tracy at the small mall in Ortonville on Sunday afternoon despite a stern warning from Mischa. I feared finding myself alone with Violet, feared being in a moving vehicle with her. It was very likely there would be some kind of reprimand in store for my having communicated with Mischa at the dance on Friday night, and I was afraid the longer I put off apologizing, the more severe the punishment would be.

"Is your nose okay?" I asked, trying to sound as chipper as possible as I climbed into the back seat of Tracy's car. Violet's nose appeared to be fine, but it looked like she had bruises beneath her eyes, heavily masked with porcelain-colored concealer. She and Candace must have bumped heads pretty hard when they'd hit the floor.

"Yeah, it's okay. Not broken, just sore," Violet said from the front passenger seat.

"I'm so sorry about that. Candace is just . . . out of control. She's in the psych ward again. Who knows when she'll be released," I said, feeling rotten to the core for sounding like I was glad that Candace had been locked up.

"Yeah, geez. I know. My dad wants to have her thrown out of school. She's a danger to herself and other students," Violet said absentmindedly, flipping through stations on the radio.

I held my comment.

As we reached the corner of Martha Road, and the empty lot was just outside Violet's passenger-side window, Tracy commented, "Isn't that where your old house used to be?"

I felt as if the wind had been knocked out of me. Of course it *was*, and I passed the corner of my own street every day, but I couldn't remember the last time someone had so ignorantly asked me outright about the fire. The empty lot looked unassuming, over-grown with long, dying yellow grass, as it always did. "Uh, yeah," I said uncomfortably. "My parents bought a house down the block rather than rebuilding."

"God, I would buy a new house too. Who would want to live on the site of a fire like that? I mean, ew. It's, like, a perfect plot for a horror movie," Tracy said, furthering my belief that she was the most insensitive girl in the world.

When we arrived at the mall, we were fifteen minutes too late to see the romantic comedy that Tracy and Violet had used as bait to get me out of the house. Violet studied the movie times for the theater on her cell phone with a wrinkled brow, insisting that she couldn't understand how the wrong time for our original selection had been listed on the theater's website.

"We're probably just missing the previews anyway," Tracy said with a shrug, but when we attempted to buy tickets for the movie that had already started, the pimply teenage boy at the counter refused to sell them to us for that screening. It was a crowded Sunday afternoon at the theater, and families with young children swarmed around us as we tried to decide what to do. Our options were to buy tickets for the next showing of *The Scent of Love*, starting almost three hours later, or to see one of the other films playing that afternoon: the kiddie cartoon or blockbuster 3-D action flick, both beginning within the next half hour. "I guess I could see *Brethren*," Violet said. "At least there are hot guys in that movie."

Brethren was a high-velocity action movie set in the Middle East about a group of hotshot special operative agents who take on a ridiculous assignment to assassinate the head of a terrorist organization. We bought our tickets and each took a pair of cardboard 3-D glasses out of the bin in the theater's lobby. The movie was terrible, but exactly the kind of movie that would earn millions of dollars at the box office. I started to lose interest after the first twenty minutes, when it became clear that the subplot about two of the special-ops guys not getting along well was going to ruin every critical scene with cheesy one-liners meant to be funny. Halfway through the movie, the special agents planted a bomb in an open-air market that caused a rapidly spreading fire at nightfall, moving from stand to stand, incinerating everything in sight as hot desert winds assisted in its expansion. The swirling fire on-screen, the crackling of flames and popping of wood throwing sparks, was simply too much for me. *It's just a movie*, I reminded myself, but I felt my breath growing short and could have sworn I smelled smoke. Sweat broke out on my forehead, and my heart was racing. I felt like I couldn't get any air into my lungs, and I was getting light-headed. Tearing off my 3-D glasses, I stood, and without even excusing myself, I stepped over Violet and inched my way out of our row of seats, desperate to get outside and away from the roar of the blaze.

Once out in the hallway, I wiped the dampness off my face with the sleeve of my cardigan. The silly jingles of the video game machines left unattended in the hallway to cycle through their game trailers comforted me as my breathing returned to normal. In the ladies' bathroom, I splashed cool water on my face. Even after I felt calm enough to return to my seat, I waited a little longer, studying my reflection in the mirror. It was crazy to wonder, but had Violet intentionally made us miss the screening of *The Scent of Love* so that instead we'd have to see *Brethren*? Had Violet known about that horrible fire scene from the trailer, or from commercials? She must have known how traumatic it would be for me to see a scene like that, especially in 3-D. I found myself dreading my return to my seat in the theater, childishly wishing once again that I could just call my mom to ask her to come and get me.

Moments before I reached to open the heavy door to reenter

the theater, I heard my phone buzz in my bag. I saw Mischa's name appear on the screen, and I retreated back down the hallway to talk to her in privacy.

"I figured it out," Mischa said over the phone.

"Oh, yeah? What?" I asked, feeling like somehow Violet could hear us even though she was in the middle of the crowded movie theater.

"Candace called me. She's feeling better and she's being released tomorrow afternoon. And guess what? Her father decided she needs a change of scenery. He's taking her to the Big Island," Mischa said, sounding very pleased with herself.

"Oh my God, Mischa," I said, feeling nauseous, my stomach lurching. "Waves! She could drown at the beach."

"I know. Don't you get it? Nohi. It must have been a message from Olivia. It means no *H-I*. No *Hawaii*."

CHAPTER 13

THAT EVENING, I GREW INCREASINGLY UNEASY AS the sun began to set. The sky turned from pink to gold and then began to darken, and I suspected that since Mr. Cotton had put events in motion to take Candace to an area where she could potentially drown in deep waves just as Violet had predicted, Olivia's spirit was going to turn violent. It was making sense now to me why Olivia had wanted me to be alarmed at homecoming by the song she had singled out: I was supposed to have prevented Candace from attacking Violet. Because the attack had led to her trip to the psychiatric ward, and her hospitalization had inspired her dad to book a vacation. I saw it all clearly now; I was failing to protect Candace so completely that I was actually helping Violet's prediction manifest.

"Turning in soon?" Mom asked in the living room after bringing Maude inside from her last wild frolic in the backyard for the night. Her tone suggested that I *should* turn in, seeing as how it was a Sunday night and I had school in the morning.

I was pretending to be thoroughly engrossed in a television news program about a serial killer who had lived in La Crosse. "Yeah, I just want to see the end of this," I assured her.

"Are you sure you should be watching something so troubling right before bedtime?" she nagged me. "You don't want to give yourself bad dreams."

Avoiding eye contact with her, I said, "I'm not having nightmares. I'm sleeping just fine."

"Then why have you been sleeping out here on the couch?" She raised an eyebrow skeptically at me before disappearing down the hall. "Good night, sleep tight. Don't let the bedbugs bite," she called.

When the show finally ended, I turned off the television and was startled by the absolute quiet in the house. I turned on the light in the hallway and switched off the lamp in the living room, already creeping myself out with thoughts about what might await me in my bedroom. Since Maude had shown an interest in whatever paranormal activity Olivia was stirring up in my bedroom, I had started keeping the door closed. While it kept the puppy out of my room, it created a moment of panic for me each and every time I had cause to open it and peer inside. In that fraction of a second before I was able to flip on the light switch, my heart always stopped beating in distressed fear of what might await me on the other side.

I leaned forward, putting my ear to the door to listen for any strange sounds coming from my bedroom, and then, hearing nothing suspicious, I reached for the doorknob. My hand recoiled and snapped back to my chest before I even realized what had happened; I gasped in surprise because the doorknob was scalding hot to the touch. My fingertips felt singed, but when I looked down in the darkness expecting to see blisters rising, they appeared to be fine. There was nothing about the appearance of the doorknob that would have suggested that it was hot. I tapped it again lightly with the tip of my index finger, and finding it still to be alarmingly hot, I weighed my options.

I considered trying to sneak out the front door and over to the Emorys' house, but the front entrance of our house would definitely be too noisy. The side door in the kitchen, with its busted spring, would also create a noticeable amount of noise. There was no way out of the house through the garage unless I used the automatic door opener, which would definitely wake my mom out of a deep slumber. Before I even took a look in my bedroom, I knew there was no way I could sleep there for the night, and the thought of sleeping exposed, on the couch, and irking my mother more, was also not appealing. If it was Olivia playing games with me, simulating a fire in my bedroom just a few hours after I'd been terrified by a fiery movie scene was downright cruel.

So I made the decision to cross my bedroom as quickly as possible, slip out the window, and dash over to Trey's. Using the bottom of my T-shirt to protect my hand, I turned the knob and threw the door open, finding my bedroom to be suspiciously quiet and cool. I quickly closed the door behind me, tiptoed across the room as fast as I could, climbed through the window, and lowered the screen again. Wearing only socks on my feet, I unlatched the gate in the fence surrounding our backyard and opened the gate to the Emorys' yard. I knocked on Trey's window lightly with my knuckles, hoping he was still awake. The room behind the blinds was already dark. Just as I began to panic because he wasn't answering and a cold wind was blowing, the window lifted, and he smiled at me.

"McKenna Brady! Why, what a nice surprise," he joked.

"Can I come in?"

It was disorienting to be in Trey's bedroom in the dark. He bashfully cleaned up a pile of dirty underwear on his floor and tossed it into the back of his closet. The room had a salty, safe smell about it, like dirty sheets or old gym shoes. As we crawled into his narrow bed and he lowered his flannel sheet over me, he warned, "You definitely have to wake up and go home early in the morning. If my parents find you in here, your mom will kill you, and then you'll be a ghost who haunts me."

"Olivia's angry at me. I really messed up at homecoming," I confessed. I told him about the hot doorknob, and about how Candace would be flying to Hawaii with her father in two weeks, right after midterms.

"The book says that the more acclimated a spirit becomes, you know, as a ghost, the more comfortable they become with their powers," Trey explained matter-of-factly. "She's probably just trying to find more effective ways to communicate with you."

I snuggled beneath Trey's blankets again alongside him and said suddenly, "Violet tricked me into seeing a movie today with her and Tracy, and there was this scene with an out-of-control fire that really upset me. Okay, maybe she didn't know that scene was going to be in the movie, but I think she *did* know. Am I totally paranoid?"

"Maybe a little paranoid," Trey told me, wrapping one arm protectively over me. "Lots of movies have scenes with fires in them."

"Yeah, but this particular scene was intense. I had to leave the theater and collect myself, and all afternoon I've been wondering this same thing, this same thought again and again: Why me and not her?"

Trey studied me for a moment, concerned, and asked, "Why Jennie and not you?"

I nodded, unable to say anymore, afraid that I'd cry.

"Don't you remember anything about the night of the fire?"

I didn't know how Trey thought he might remember details from that night that I didn't. I was the one who'd been engulfed in flames, who'd choked on smoke and watched the roof cave in.

"The reason you weren't killed in the fire with Jennie?" He searched for some kind of recognition in my expression.

"You actually remember that night?" I asked. It wasn't completely impossible that Trey would have remembered it; after all, it had happened at the end of his street and was probably the only noteworthy thing that had happened in our small town during his entire childhood.

"I remember a lot about that night," he insisted. "My mother woke me up because she smelled smoke. I remember watching her run through the front door and down the street in her robe, and the night sky above your house was glowing because of the flames. She had told my dad to keep me in the house, but after a few minutes he put my coat on me and we followed her to the corner, where your old house used to be. You were standing outside in the street with your dog, barefoot, in your nightgown, just watching the flames climb higher and higher. The dog was going nuts. She was barking her head off, and wouldn't let anyone near you. I remember thinking it was just so weird to see you standing there alone. I'd always thought of you and Jennie like a pair, you know? Like two socks that go together."

"You knew it was me standing there, and not Jennie?" I asked, surprised.

Trey nodded. "Of course. I could always tell you apart. Jennie's posture was different. Her eyebrows were a little heavier. She bit her fingernails down to the quick."

Unbelievable, I thought to myself, that Trey had known instantly that I'd survived and Jennie hadn't, but my own parents hadn't been able to tell the difference between us.

"I don't think I'd ever seen one of you without the other before that night. You could ask my mom about it, if you want. Back then she used to tell anyone who would listen that the dog must have gotten you up and led you outside."

I tried so hard to remember that night, but my memories were what they always were: little more than the unbearable tightness of smoke in my chest, the roar of the flames, and a sense of urgency that I needed to get outside. Had Moxie awakened me? Had she run through the screen door, as she was fond of doing when she was a puppy—she'd figured out how to stand on her hind legs to press the handle with her front paws and open the door—to inspire me to follow her out onto the lawn? I really couldn't recall. I didn't remember much about even being in the street, other than the moment when I saw my mother's silhouette emerge in the doorway, the wall of orange fire behind her. If Trey's mom was right and Moxie had nudged me awake, then why me and not Jennie? Would Moxie have gone back into the house to rouse Jennie if the flames hadn't risen so quickly? There had been a gas leak in the basement, the fire department had determined during their investigation. That was why the whole house had gone up so quickly, and it could have been started by anything, even a tiny spark from static electricity.

"So if you're wondering why you made it out and not Jennie, the answer is Moxie. For whatever reason, she was able to wake you up, but not your sister. It's as simple as that, McKenna. You can't question it."

I lay quiet for a moment, thinking about life and the energy of the universe and how something as simple as the sensitivity of my skin to a dog's wet nose had probably made the difference between life and death for my twin and me.

"We kept her here with us, you know," Trey told me. "Moxie. We had her here for two or three weeks while your family stayed somewhere else. I kept hoping you'd move away forever so that she'd just be my dog."

I shook my head in surprise, touched that he had cared enough to remember my dog with such kindness. No wonder he had been so sweet about helping me bury her. "I didn't know that," I admitted. The weeks following the fire were a blur for me. I distinctly recalled missing school. After our time in the hospital and Jennie's funeral, Mom and I went to Missouri to stay with my grandparents for a few weeks while Dad stayed in Willow at a motel and dealt with the insurance paperwork. I remembered very little about those weeks in Missouri other than the most random details: a red patchwork quilt spread over the brown plaid couch for me, turkey sandwiches with thick mayonnaise prepared by my grandmother, and my mother disappearing behind a closed door to her childhood bedroom to cry for hours on end without my seeing it. But now that I was trying to remember it all, I was sure of it: Moxie hadn't been with us.

"Sorry," I apologized. "That we didn't move away forever."

"Don't be sorry about that," Trey teased, nudging me with his arm. "If you had moved away forever instead of into the house next door, I would have been watching someone else get undressed for the last few years."

My eyes shot wide open and my jaw dropped. "Trey!"

"Probably some gross, hairy guy," Trey continued tormenting me. He leaned over and took my face in both of his hands and kissed me right on my protesting frown.

Strangely, Candace returned to her old self that week at school. It was as if the promise of a trip to Hawaii had pointed her mania in a different direction. In the cafeteria, she rolled her eyes at Violet and didn't appear to be affected by the taunts and jeers of lower classmen who had heard about her homecoming rampage. I continued to sit with Violet, Tracy, and Michael at lunchtime but made no attempt to hide my friendliness toward Mischa and Candace. With midterms approaching and the leaves beginning to fall from every tree in town, I busied myself with preparations for our first junior class fund-raiser of the year. It was my goal to organize a weekend yard cleanup service, which I had decided to call "the junior class rake sale." I created a series of posters encouraging classmates to sign up for six-hour shifts to help our class "rake in the money" for the ski trip that Violet was organizing for January. The amount of money that we needed to raise by the end of January was fairly daunting. Wealthy kids at our school probably could have asked their parents to write checks to cover their costs, but everyone else could raise the majority of the cost of their trip by working their shift. No one liked doing manual labor, but I was hopeful that people would take advantage of the opportunity to pay for their trip with a few hours of hard work.

To my great surprise *and* relief, the sign-up forms were nearly full by Wednesday afternoon at lunchtime after having been posted in the cafeteria for only three days. It definitely seemed like kids were open to working off their fee to go on the trip; the big remaining question was whether or not people in town would be interested in hiring high school kids to clean up their leaves, mow their lawns, and trim their hedges. We lived in a town where everyone's family had thousands of dollars' worth of lawn equipment in their garage, so it was a gamble whether or not anyone would be willing to pay for assistance.

Candace's mom checked Candace out of school from the principal's office on Thursday to drive her to Sheboygan to meet with my father's former colleague Dr. Hernandez. Candace had actually been looking forward to the examination, hoping that Dr. Hernandez would take her side on the topic of the sedatives and antidepressant drugs she had been taking for the last month. She was insistent that the drugs were dulling her senses and making her feel stupid, and was eager to be free of her prescriptions. Mischa and I walked Candace to the first floor before lunchtime and watched through the slats in the blinds on the windows of the principal's office as she greeted her mother. They exchanged pleasantries with the office administrators before stepping back into the hallway. Mrs. Lehrer shifted her oversize sunglasses from the top of her head back down over her eyes in an attempt to avoid the stares of curious teenagers as soon as she was back in the busy high school hallway. Candace held perfect posture as she strode toward the high school's western exit, a set of double doors leading to the guest parking lot, not especially caring who observed her leaving school midday with her parent.

All afternoon, I was lost in thought during my classes, wondering if, when Candace resurfaced later that night, she would be able to provide some kind of logical, reasonable explanation for everything that had happened in the last few weeks. Even despite all the proof that I'd gathered, I was still holding out for some kind of plausible reason for all the weirdness I had witnessed. My father had taught me that logic was the greatest defense against doubt, and while I was certain that what I'd seen with my own eyes was real, I desperately wanted a reason for it not to be so. Not surprisingly, Candace reconnected with Mischa that night before calling me. Mischa had already texted me the disturbing message, She's in total denial, ten minutes before my phone rang. I smiled politely at my mom and crept down the hall to my room to speak in privacy. "So, what's the word? Are you bonkers?" I teased.

"Totally not bonkers. Easily distracted and suffering typical symptoms of grief, but I'm afraid that's all," Candace sighed. "Sorry to disappoint."

I didn't want to press her for more information and risk upsetting her, but at the same time, I was desperate to hear more about the psychiatrist's assessment of the circumstances of Olivia's death. "Did he ask you about Olivia and the accident?"

"Duh. Of course he did. We talked for a while about the emotions people go through when someone close to them dies. All of it made total sense. I realized when I was trying to tell him about Olivia's party that I don't even really remember too well what happened that night. I still think Violet is shady. But, I mean, how similar was her story about Olivia's death to what actually ended up happening?"

I couldn't believe my ears. It was as if Candace had been brainwashed. She took a deep breath on the other end of the line.

"I am open to the possibility that I may have imagined a lot of the details that were upsetting me most."

A million objections sprang to mind, but I kept myself calm, not wanting to disrupt whatever solace she had achieved during her meeting with Dr. Hernandez. "I don't think you really imagined all of it," I commented gently. "Mischa and I were there too, and we've both thought for the past few weeks that Violet was involved in Olivia's death. Did he say anything about the possibility that we were all hypnotized into thinking weird things because of the game?"

Candace paused, and then said, "Honestly, McKenna, I don't think it's healthy for me to dwell on that game any longer. I just want to get my midterms over with and fly to Hawaii. That's all I want to think about: getting a tan. And I don't think it would be such a bad idea for you to talk to a psychiatrist too. Don't take this the wrong way, but you might very well have some unresolved issues from your sister's death."

Naturally, I bristled at that and couldn't stop myself from wondering if this was speculation on Candace's part or if Dr. Hernandez, who I'd never met but who surely knew all about me, having worked with my dad, had formed that opinion of me. Our conversation drifted to a close, and Candace asked if I was prepared for that weekend's fund-raiser. I was surprised that the rake sale was even on her mind. Candace had been generally so checked out of normal high school life for the last few weeks, I doubted that she read the posters on the walls or listened to morning announcements.

Although I'd hoped my dad's psychiatrist friend could have provided me some kind of plausible explanation for what we'd been experiencing since playing the game, now I regretted recommending that Candace visit him. She seemed to be completely oblivious to the danger she was in, even when I pointed out to her that beaches in Hawaii fit perfectly within the story Violet had told for her at Olivia's party. One way or another, Mischa and I were going to have to find a way to talk Candace out of going on that trip.

As Candace seemed to be distancing herself from Violet's involvement with Olivia's death, the disturbance in my bedroom had been growing stronger all week. I had taken to keeping myself awake until the wee hours of the early morning with my lights on, waiting until I was absolutely certain my mom was asleep and that my trot down the hall with a blanket to the living room couch wouldn't wake her. Sleeping over in Trey's room on Sunday night had been enough to scare me out of attempting it a second time soon; either the alarm clock on his cell phone had failed, or Trey had absentmindedly turned it off after its first ring, and we'd overslept. The sound of his mom knocking loudly on the door had sent me diving beneath the comforter, certain that a very uncomfortable and oddly baseless conversation with my mom about sex was in my not-too-distant future.

On Friday morning, my mother was waiting for me with her hands on her hips in the kitchen when I surfaced for orange juice after a restless night.

"When I got up this morning, one of the burners on the stove was on, and it looked like it had been burning all night," she said in a barely controlled, angry voice.

Already having a good idea of who was to blame for the oven being turned on, I feigned interest in the stovetop and noticed that an area around the burner in the front left corner was darkened from heat.

"Sorry," I said, not sure what to say. "I don't even remember the last time I turned the stove on."

I knew better than to flat-out deny my own involvement; there were only two of us in the house, and if I blamed Olivia's ghost, my mother would cart me off to the insane asylum to have my head checked faster than I'd be able to say, *Just kidding*. I was not surprised that Olivia had managed to tinker with the gas stovetop, seeing as how she was probably annoyed that I was foiling her attempts to harass me in my bedroom. I had taken down all the shelves and framed photographs in my room, and had boxed up my music boxes and CDs. In frustration, Olivia was obviously trying out her strength in different areas of the house, and it occurred to me that I should probably fear that she might try out her tricks in my mom's room.

"Honestly, McKenna," my mom said in wonderment, staring me down. "What is going on? You're up at all hours of the night, doing absentminded things like this. Are you sleepwalking? I am really concerned."

"I don't think I'm sleepwalking," I said, not sure how to get myself off the hook for this kitchen disaster. "But I guess anything's possible. I honestly don't remember turning the burner on. I didn't cook anything yesterday."

Mom was not buying my act of innocence for a second. "Maybe this whole Student Government thing was a bad idea. If you're under too much stress, then something has got to give."

"It's not too much stress," I assured her quickly. "I'm enjoying it." But even as I was speaking the words, I knew I was trying to convince myself as much as her.

That night, Trey told his parents he was sleeping over at a friend's house, and crept through my window with his backpack. He looked around at my stark walls in wonderment, shaking his head. "It looks like you're moving out," he commented. Olivia's spirit was strangely quiet, not causing any disturbances at all. It was so eerie, I half expected to open my bedroom door in the morning and find the rest of the house missing.

In the morning, my alarm clock sounded at dawn, and I left Trey sleeping in my room when my mom gave me a lift to the shopping center where juniors would assemble for the rake sale. Violet and Tracy were already there, waiting and sipping lattes in Tracy's car. Mom and I had brought with us a table with folding legs and posters that Violet, Tracy, Michael, and I had made during the week, and Violet and Tracy walked across the parking lot to greet us as Mom pulled the table out of the trunk.

"Hi, girls," my mom said, unfolding the legs of the table. I could tell that she had no idea which girl was Violet and which girl was Tracy. I made fast, bashful introductions, eager for my mom to drive away before volunteers from school began to arrive.

"This was such a great idea of McKenna's. She's really a genius at thinking up ways to raise money," Violet gushed.

My mother looked at me with a quizzical expression. "I don't know where she gets it from. Certainly not from my side of the family."

Thirty minutes later, there were a handful of students roaming around the parking lot for their shift, and holding signs along the roadside to catch the attention of cars passing by. It was nine in the morning, and our services were officially available for the day, at least according to the hours of service we'd written on our posters, and the story that had been written about us in the *Willow Gazette*. Kids had arrived carrying rakes, hoes, bush pruners, and gardening gloves as they had been instructed, and were now just eager for some customers. I tried to happily greet everyone who had arrived for our first shift and felt a little guilty as I saw Erica's mom's black SUV pull into the lot. Erica's mom greeted me by loudly announcing, "McKenna! You've lost so much weight! I never would have recognized you!" I blushed furiously, wishing that Mrs. Bloom hadn't reminded everyone in the parking lot that I had been thirty pounds heavier the previous October.

By ten in the morning, several cars had pulled into the lot to book services for the day. I staffed the reservation table with Tracy, and Violet kept track of which kids we would assign to each appointment. In pairs of two, kids accepted slips of paper on which we had written the address and phone number of the house where they were being sent, and drove off to mow lawns and trim bushes. Fortunately, our town was small enough that we knew by name most of the people who requested our services. We sent Jeff Harrison and Tony Fortunado from the basketball team over to the Highlands' house to clean the gutters of the coach's in-laws. Sarah Chaney and Crystal Blomquist went to the home of the owner of our town's largest grocery store to plant orange chrysanthemums and marigolds. A husband and wife with a handful of young children stopped by and asked for three kids to come by, claiming they had an acre of property and could use all the help they could get. It felt like a gift to be actually busy, for once occupied with something other than ghostly business.

Taking me completely by surprise, Trey surfaced in the parking lot around one o'clock when the afternoon shift was beginning.

"Hey!" I exclaimed. "You're not even a junior."

He pecked me on the cheek and clarified, "Oh, I'm not here to work. Just to flirt with girls."

I blushed and reached out to hold his fingers. With the exception of me, I had never witnessed Trey flirting with *any* girls before.

"Your mom went into your room after she got back from dropping you off," he told me in a low voice, taking a step closer to me.

"Oh God, did she see you in there?"

"No, of course not, but she was going through your stuff," he continued, and waited for my reaction.

At first I was furious—who wouldn't be?—but then I remembered our conversation the previous morning, and realized she was probably being a diligent mom, making sure I wasn't hiding drugs in my room. I quickly tried to think through the inventory of stuff in my room to make sure there wasn't anything in there that might spark concerns. The Ouija board was hidden in plain sight in the Emorys' basement on their shelf of mildewing board games. I had never kept a diary at any point in my life, and since Trey usually crept through the window already in his pajamas, he had never accidentally left any possessions behind before returning home.

I sighed. "I guess there's not much I can do about that. I'm giving her plenty of reasons to be worried about me."

"That's not the part that's weird," Trey said. "She left the door open when she left, and Maude came in. This freaked me out so much: The dog sat down and just stared up at the ceiling, blinking and watching. She knows something's in there."

This chilled me; I so desperately wanted Maude to remain safe from the spirits trying to interact with me. "Was she barking?"

"Not at all," Trey said. "She just sat there, like she was watching TV. She barely even noticed when I left."

Mischa arrived not long after Trey bought an ice-cream cone and walked home. She was dropped off by Amanda, almost half an hour late for her shift, and walked across the parking lot directly toward me, ignoring everyone else. "I'm here," she announced. "But please, please don't make me talk to *her*." She gave Violet an evil sideward glance across the lot, where Violet was grinning and having the time of her life talking with Jeff and Tony about their morning of lawn work.

I tasked Melissa with taking over my duties with Tracy at the card table, prepared to take the next job that came in and put in some manual labor personally. Mischa and I both watched in agony, our conversation abruptly ending, as we noticed Pete's car enter the parking lot. As expected, he climbed out of the car and shyly approached Violet, placing one hand lightly on her shoulder and kissing her suspiciously close to her mouth.

"Unbelievable!" Mischa muttered, tightening her grip on the handle of her rake. "So she really is after him. She even *looks* different than she did back when she first moved here. I remember on the first day of school thinking she was kind of shy and could work it a little more. She's wearing different clothes now, and more makeup."

I had noticed that too. Maybe before Olivia's death, Violet had been holding back a bit, not wanting to overthrow the queen. But now that the queen was out of the way, she wasn't the least bit shy anymore about batting her long eyelashes and making it abundantly clear that she was the cutest girl at Willow High School.

Pete's flirtatious interaction with Violet wasn't the only surprise of the afternoon. The very next car to pull into the lot was a black Mercedes driven by none other than Mr. Richmond. Olivia and Henry's dad was classically handsome, and he whipped off his aviator sunglasses in a smooth, practiced move as he stepped out of his car. He smiled directly at me and Mischa where we lingered near the card table, looking like a catalog model with his cleft chin and broad shoulders, wearing a classic navy cable-knit sweater and khakis.

"Can you girls tell me where a fellow can get some help with yard work around here?" he asked us in a deep, playful voice that made me wish my own dad were more like him and less like a beach bum having a severe midlife crisis, teaching two classes a week when he wasn't repainting his boat.

"You came to the right place," Mischa said in her special, perky voice reserved for parents.

Since Mischa and I had already committed to taking on the next task that came in, we climbed into Mr. Richmond's back seat and made small talk about school all the way to the Richmonds' house. Mischa had been close friends with Olivia far longer than I had, and Mr. Richmond asked her a litany of questions about her parents, her sister, and far-off plans for college. My mouth twisted into a frown when I saw Henry's pickup truck parked in the driveway. We hadn't been in contact since the wake, but I'd heard he'd dropped out of school to spend the semester in Willow with his parents. Naturally, the Richmonds had a perfectly landscaped front lawn, so the most we could do to earn our wages for two hours was rake the leaves that had fallen from the trees near the curb, and weed in between the bushes and fluffy goldenrod planted around the perimeter of the house. My heart was heavy as I pulled weeds near the ground-level window on the side of the house through which Pete had kissed Olivia on the night of her birthday. I fought the urge to peer through the hazy window to the Richmonds' basement, not wanting to see the location where we had played Violet's game and relive those moments in my head.

Inside the Richmonds' home, I was overcome with emotion simply from the familiar potpourri smell in their front hallway. Even though Mr. Richmond had just welcomed me into the house moments earlier, I still felt like a sneaky intruder, trying to be as quiet as possible, cringing at the sound of my own footsteps. Just as I was about to reach for the light switch in the bathroom on the first floor, I wasn't sure what inspired me, but I felt a sudden and irresistible urge to sprint up the stairs to the second floor and use the bathroom adjoined to Olivia's room. The house seemed silent and empty, and although Henry's car was parked in the driveway, I thought it might be possible that he had gone somewhere with his mother. Once the notion of going into Olivia's room entered my head, I couldn't shake it. It was as if I was magnetically being drawn to that corner of the house. After standing in the bathroom in a state of suspended anima-tion for at least thirty seconds, I finally spun on my heel and darted upstairs, my heart pounding.

I was surprised to find the door to Olivia's bedroom wide open. Late-afternoon sunlight flooded the room through the windows, and

I marveled at how unchanged it looked since the last time I was there. Olivia's white comforter was still spread across her queen-size bed. Her stuffed Gund teddy bears still flanked her pillows like guards. A bottle of amber-hued perfume waited patiently on her dresser, and I impulsively lifted the heavy glass bottle to my nose. Pictures of Olivia, Mischa, and Candace were tucked into the wooden frame around the mirror attached to Olivia's dresser. In one picture, Olivia smiled brightly in Pete's arms, and I realized it was a photograph taken at homecoming the previous year. The piles of clothes that had been on the floor the night of Olivia's birthday had been put away, and a stuffed unicorn, the kind that could be won by throwing darts at balloons at Winnebago Days, was set on the white wicker rocking chair in the corner. Standing in the center of the room, it seemed as if Olivia was simply not home instead of not alive, as if she could walk through the door at any second and ask what I thought I was doing in her room.

Ignoring my bladder, I dared to open Olivia's closet to peek inside, and saw the eggshell-colored strapless dress that Olivia had bought at Tart hanging in clear plastic wrap on the rack, singled out from the other, familiar clothes as if no one had altered anything in Olivia's closet since the morning of the big game. I thought of Maude at my own house, staring up at the ceiling, and realized why it felt like Olivia might catch me red-handed in her room any second. Because it was very likely that her spirit *knew* exactly where I was.

"What am I supposed to do next, Olivia?" I asked aloud, quietly, looking around her bedroom. "I don't know how to prevent Candace from going on the trip with her dad. You have to give me some kind of sign."

I used the bathroom quickly, not even bothering to turn on the light. When I turned on the faucet to wash my hands, I observed that the squirt bottle of liquid lemon-scented soap that used to be in there had been replaced by a crystal dish of white soaps shaped like hearts. Then, the conundrum: Wash my hands with a brand-new, unused novelty soap and leave evidence that I'd been in Olivia's room, or simply not wash my hands? After two hours of raking leaves and digging through dirt, I genuinely wanted to wash up. On an impulse, I washed my hands quickly with one of the creamy little white hearts, and then, feeling like a criminal, I wrapped the remainder of the soap in a tissue and stuck it in the pocket of my jeans. I bolted down the stairs, *really* not wanting any of the Richmonds to catch me snooping in Olivia's room. Outside, Mr. Richmond already had the engine running, ready to drive us back to the shopping center.

CHAPTER 14

LATER THAT NIGHT, AFTER VIOLET DECLARED
the day a success (twenty-two juniors had raised their funds
for the ski trip, and the weatherman's prediction that it might
rain in the late afternoon had not come true), I accepted a ride
home with Amanda and Mischa. "I've been thinking," Mischa
announced, "about what you started telling me last Saturday. If
you've been able to make a connection with Olivia, then I want to
talk to her too."

I thought of the Ouija board in Trey's basement and decided
it might not be a terrible idea to let her try. After all, Olivia had
been better friends with Mischa than she had been with me. Perhaps she'd be able to give Mischa clearer directions, although I
couldn't help but wonder, if that was the case, why Olivia had
been lurking in my bedroom instead of taking up ghostly residence at the Portnoys' house. "Can Trey and I come over tomorrow night? I have to work the rake sale all day, but we'll be done
by five."

On Sunday evening, Trey and I walked across town to the
Portnoys' in the dark rain carrying the board, in its box, tucked into

a shopping bag. He rolled his eyes dramatically while I spoke with the guard at the station who stood watch over the entrance to the Portnoys' gated community.

"We're here to visit the Portnoy residence," I announced. "I'm McKenna Brady." The guard nodded and phoned the Portnoys to confirm that we were expected guests.

"What are these gates supposed to be keeping out?" Trey mused aloud. "People who don't live here, like us?"

I smirked, understanding his point, but not wanting to alarm the guard. There was relatively little crime in Willow, so the entire purpose of a gated community was lost. The gate served to represent a barrier between the wealthy on the inside and the less wealthy on the outside, as sort of a physical reminder to the rest of the town that *we live here, and you don't.*

The guard waved us through and we entered the community on foot, walking another two blocks past sprawling mansions with manicured lawns until we reached the brick home in which the Portnoys lived. Mischa met us at the front door, eating ice cream directly out of the gallon carton, causing me to experience a strong pang of resentment toward her for having such a tiny frame. "Let's go up to my room," she suggested. "My parents are out."

We climbed up to the second floor, and walked past Amanda's room toward the end of the hall. Mischa's room was decorated entirely in shades of purple, with lavender carpeting and a rich violet velvet comforter on the bed.

"Have you guys used this thing before?" she asked skeptically as we sat down on the floor and Trey opened the board.

"Yes," I admitted. "Only once, to try to contact whatever was creating such a commotion at my house. We are pretty sure it was Olivia who responded to us."

Mischa made a grunt that suggested she was satisfied with my answer. It was still early, not even dinnertime yet, but already night outside due to the early setting of the sun, a sign that winter was fast approaching. "Should we turn off the lights or something?" Mischa asked.

Trey nodded. Mischa plopped down in between us after flipping off the light switch on her wall, and the three of us set the tips of our index fingers on the planchette. "Is this going to be scary? Should I, like, go to the bathroom first?" Mischa asked in all seriousness.

"You should announce that we're looking for Olivia. Just also say, *Only kind spirits are welcome here*," Trey instructed Mischa, irritation with her frivolity audible in his voice. He was being patient and cordial for my benefit only.

"Okay," she said, taking a deep breath and repeating after him. The three of us sat on our knees in breathless silence for nearly a minute, our fingers resting on the immobile planchette, waiting to be spooked by sudden movement. But everything about the setting felt wrong. It was too busy with the noises and energy of life: The heat coming through the vents was audible; a dog barked down the street.

"I don't think anything's happening," I announced. "Maybe you should try, Trey."

I could tell that Trey suspected the same thing I did—the Portnoys' house was just not the right place to summon a spirit—but he indulged us and in a firm voice said, "We request to speak with the spirit of Olivia Richmond. We only welcome kind, well-intentioned spirits."

We waited another minute, and Mischa's patience expired. She leaned back on her heels and crossed her arms over her chest. "This is totally unfair and ridiculous. I don't even believe you guys that you spoke with Olivia before. And *that* is really messed up, if you'd lie to me."

Trey ran his hands through his hair, and the annoyance that I had sensed bubbling in him since we were at the guard station finally boiled to the surface. "We did communicate with Olivia, but to make this work, everyone has to be very—"

Unexpectedly, with my finger remaining alone on the planchette, it began darting across the board. Trey and Mischa both fell silent immediately, watching my hand jerk from one corner of the board to another. The sudden movement took me by surprise too, but even when I attempted to pull my hand back, I couldn't. My finger felt affixed to the planchette, a slave to its will.

"What's happening?" Mischa asked in a terrified voice. "Is this a joke?"

"No! I can't lift my hand!" I exclaimed. The fear in my voice convinced her that I was not fooling around. The planchette came to rest pointing at the letter S. "Do you see that, Trey? S."

Mischa reached forward in an attempt to place her finger back on the planchette, and Trey grabbed her arm to stop her. "Don't," he warned.

It jerked my fingers after a moment toward the letter T.

Then O.

It came to rest on the letter P.

Mischa pressed her hands over her mouth in surprise, and her eyes were enormous.

"Stop what?" Mischa gasped. I felt her fingernails digging into my right shoulder. "Stop playing with this board? Stop Candace from going to Hawaii? Stop trying to reach Olivia? Stop messing with Violet?"

But the planchette didn't specify. It dragged my finger as we watched in silence to the *N*, the *O*, and then, finally, the *W.*

"What's it doing? What does it mean? Stop *what* now?" Mischa shrieked.

"Is this Olivia? Are we talking with Olivia?" I asked the board desperately.

The planchette came to rest alarmingly at NO.

I swallowed hard, bracing myself for the answer I next expected. "Are we speaking with Jennie?" The planchette circled lazily around the board for a painfully long time before resting once again at NO. I was more afraid than I was disappointed that we hadn't reached my sister. Twice now we'd tried to reach her, and twice we'd failed.

Mischa inquired, "Who else could it be?"

"Who are you?" Trey demanded.

The planchette inched over a few centimeters to the illustration of the moon in the top right corner of the board, and then stopped moving. "The moon?" I asked. "What is that supposed to mean?"

During a long, dramatic pause, the planchette remained still, and I wondered if the spirit had left us without saying good-bye. But then I sensed it vibrating beneath my fingertips, seeming to gather energy as if it were a car revving its engine. I was relieved to discover that I could lift my fingers and did so, intending to break the connection. "I'm not sure what's happening," I told Trey and Mischa. "It's doing something."

The plastic heart-shaped pointer began revolving on its own, gaining speed until it looked like a spinning wheel going so fast that its shape blurred.

Trey muttered, "Uh oh."

"Has it done that before?" Mischa asked.

Before either of us could answer, the planchette rocketed off the board and hurled itself directly at Mischa. Its pointed end hit her in the throat and tumbled down to the floor as Trey and I watched in terror. Her hands flew to her neck, and her eyes shot wide open in surprise until she realized she wasn't hurt. Although it had hit her pretty hard, the planchette hadn't even left a mark on her skin.

Then she whispered, "Guys? I don't want to play anymore."

An hour later, after we had boxed up the Ouija board, Mischa was fuming that only I had been able to make any kind of a connection with a spirit.

"It's not fair! We were all *trying*. What makes you so special that they only want to talk to you?"

I didn't have a response for her. It didn't comfort me much that the spirit world had chosen *me* as the lucky recipient of its messages that night. Especially because whoever had contacted us had not been Olivia, which meant that there were other spirits involved who, one way or another, knew about me even though I had no clue about the significance of the moon they had tried to suggest. "Maybe because of, you know . . ." Mischa frowned as if I ought to have known exactly what she was insinuating. "Your sister. Maybe she's, like, a conduit between us and them. Maybe it's easier for spirits on the other side to reach you because she's there, with them."

She'd stopped short of saying that identical twins split from the same egg. Because I'd been raised Catholic, I was well aware of the argument within the church of whether or not twins share a soul, since Catholics believed that souls were formed at the moment of conception. If there was truth to this, then half of my soul, Jennie's half, was dead. This logic scared the crap out of me, but it also suggested that every identical twin who had ever died before their twin could expect to suddenly become a portal for messages from the afterlife. That was ridiculous, but out of all the explanations for why Olivia had been haunting my room and why the Ouija board worked best for me, that seemed to me like the most probable.

Trey cleared his throat, suggesting to Mischa that she should pipe down.

"My sister's been dead a long time," I said, "and I've never had any mix-ups with ghosts before this year. We bought the board hoping to be able to communicate with her, but so far, no Jennie."

But Mischa's question gnawed away at me for the rest of the evening. Why did spirits connecting with us through the Ouija board always seem to want to communicate exclusively with me?

That night, I lay in Trey's bed staring up at the ceiling, unable to sleep. Why hadn't Jennie ever reached out to me? If it hadn't been too complicated or strenuous a thing for Olivia to manage, then why hadn't Jennie been able to figure out how to make contact?

CHAPTER 15

ON TUESDAY MORNING, WHEN SCHOOL RESUMED after Columbus Day, Mr. Dean shook my hand and told me with sincerity that my rake sale had been a huge success and was a shining example of precisely the kind of ingenuity for which he'd spent twenty-one years of his career waiting. The glow of his compliment faded before I even took my seat. I was woefully unprepared for the impending midterms, and knew it. Not even the promise of a ski adventure in January was enough to corral my thoughts during classes, when I was supposed to be paying attention. Every kid in school seemed to be buzzing with a little extra energy that week; on Friday, the annual Winnebago Days carnival would open on the western outskirts of town near the lake and seniors would prowl through the crowd, marking freshmen with red lipstick *F*s on their foreheads as an act of high school initiation. The carnival brought with it each year a small, strange crime wave, and the roar of rock music blasted from the carnival's janky rides, which would carry over the flat land of our town for miles. Every year, I could hear Def Leppard jams from a distance as I tried to sleep in my own bedroom. My mother was not a fan of Winnebago Days, claiming that it was little more than three-day plague of riffraff and litter upon our town each year.

"What if we break her legs?" Mischa wondered aloud during gym on the track as we walked our laps, wearing our fall jackets over our gym uniforms. Our eyes followed Violet on the other side of the track as she ran, with Tracy struggling to keep up with her.

"Violet's legs? What would that accomplish?"

"Not *Violet's* legs," Mischa corrected me. *"Candace's."*

I stopped walking on the track and shook my head in disbelief. "What are you talking about? Are you proposing we just hit Candace with baseball bats? Why would we *break her legs?*"

Mischa shrugged. "Well, if she has casts on her legs, then she won't be able to go in water. Maybe we can't prevent her from going to Hawaii, but we can do something to keep her from swimming."

I resumed walking, noticing Coach Stirling keeping an eye on us where she paced, carrying her clipboard, close to the double doors leading to the gym. "You have lost your mind. I don't want to get thrown out of school, or worse, go to jail."

"Well, we have to do something!" Mischa exclaimed. "She's leaving on Saturday!"

Glumly, I mulled over our options and couldn't think of a single action plan that seemed like it might prevent Candace from boarding her flight. "Mr. Cotton isn't going to cancel his expensive vacation plans because a couple of hysterical teenage girls ask him to."

"Of course not! God! I'm not stupid," she snapped. "But maybe we can convince her to refuse to go." She raised her hand to her eyes to block out the sun as she surveyed the boys, who were kicking soccer balls around on the football field. "And by *we*, I mean someone she might actually listen to." Isaac Johnston was among the boys doing soccer drills. He'd been sidestepping Candace since her freak-out at the homecoming dance. In my opinion, there was even less of a chance that Isaac would help us save Candace's life than of us convincing Mr. Cotton to cancel the trip. But I knew better than to discourage Mischa once she put her mind to something.

After gym class, Coach Stirling barked at me as she passed me in the locker room, "Brady! Stop by my office after you've changed. I need to have a word with you."

I couldn't even guess what it was that the coach wanted to discuss with me; I had never shown much athletic aptitude, and I did my best to avoid her attention.

"Hi," I said, knocking lightly on the door frame of her office, where she sat at her desk, watching ESPN coverage of the WNBA online. She turned at the sound of my voice and closed her laptop.

"McKenna. What is going on here?"

She sounded concerned, and I wasn't sure what exactly gave her reason to believe there was anything going on with me at all. "I'm not sure what you mean, Coach," I said innocently. "There's nothing going on with me."

She had summoned me to her office to express concern about my weight loss and issued me a hall pass to check in with Nurse Lindvall. Because I didn't want to be hauled off to a mental institution like Candace, I couldn't explain to the nurse that I was eating plenty but probably looked haggard from the stress of dodging evil spirits and dreading the gruesome death of a close friend in the very near future. I didn't have to wonder what had sparked Coach Stirling's sudden concern; I was sure that Violet had approached her claiming to be worried about my waning health. Making faculty and staff at Willow High School doubt my mental stability (just like they doubted Candace's) was a fantastic way to ensure that they would never take seriously any accusations I made about Violet.

Nurse Lindvall asked me to return every Friday morning before homeroom for the rest of the fall semester to weigh in. I had to hand it to Violet for being a strategic mastermind; she'd found a way to turn the bags under my eyes into her own advantage. When we passed in the hallway she smiled knowingly at me, confirming my assumption that she was responsible for Coach Stirling's unnecessary intervention.

As the week progressed, I began having terrible dreams about beaches and Hawaii. It was impossible to know if it was Olivia inspiring the dreams, or if my own subconscious was working overtime as Mischa and I finalized the details of our scheme to keep Candace from going to Hawaii. When I would open my eyes in the morning and roll over to look through my window toward Trey's house, often I would see him already awake, standing there, checking on me. A ukulele tune that I was pretty sure I had never heard before in my life other than in my Hawaiian dreams began playing on repeat in my head constantly. It blasted through my brain, roared between my temples, destroying any chance I had of concentrating on the days of review in preparation for our midterms, and at an even louder volume on Friday, when I sat in front of computer screens in my classrooms, staring slack-jawed at the tests I could not complete.

During my Spanish midterm, I felt the weight of a hand on my shoulder and looked up to see my teacher, Mrs. Gomez, studying my screen. Forty minutes of class had passed, and I had only filled in responses to the first five questions on the test. "Is everything all right, McKenna?" she asked me quietly so as not to disturb the other students, hard at work on their midterms.

"I have a headache," I managed to sputter through the ukulele chords in my head, which were blurring my vision and making my ears ring.

"Nurse's office," Mrs. Gomez commanded.

So I found myself back in Nurse Lindvall's office for the second time that week, outstretched uncomfortably on the cot, trying to drown out the imaginary music in my head with ibuprofen while I stared at the white ceiling above. While I could barely focus on anything, I felt the nebulous sensation of having failed my midterms closing in on me. Failure and falling semester grades would be a concern for the following week, after Winnebago Days, after Candace boarded her flight with her father and half brothers bound for Hawaii. I could worry about my grade point average after Candace arrived back to her mom's house in Willow safely. I made no mention of my performance on my midterms to my mother after school, not wanting to give her even more reasons to worry about me.

That night, I walked through the Winnebago Days carnival with Trey, our arms entwined. The roars coming from the Tilt-a-Whirl, the blasting music, and the smell of kettle corn were sensory overload, and I appreciated all of it for distracting me from my fears. "I think, for safety's sake, we might be wise to avoid all rides," Trey told me as we both stood in front of the rickety-looking Ferris wheel, hesitating before stepping into the line to buy tickets. We saw Violet climbing into a passenger car with Pete. She was wearing tight bright red jeans and a white leather jacket that looked new, her long dark hair hanging straight down her back. Jeff and Melissa climbed in after them to share the ride, and a tattooed carnie closed the door to the car behind them before the Ferris wheel rotated slightly so that the next passengers could board. They looked like the perfect group of popular high school friends, without a care in the world. Of everyone watching them in line, only Trey and I knew that a complicated murder had brought them together.

In a town as small as Willow, it was a surefire bet you would encounter just about every single resident at some point during an event as big as Winnebago Days. We saw Principal Nylander at one of the game stands, trying to toss a quarter into a glass jar to win his daughter a stuffed lion. We saw and ignored Tracy and Michael making out at a table near the grill where hot dogs and hamburgers could be ordered, and Coach Highland and his wife and young children swaying to the music near the stage that had been set up for a performance by Norwegian Wood, a local Beatles cover band.

Several times we passed by the small booth that I had arranged as part of the junior class fund-raising effort, where Hailey West and Paul Freeman were drawing caricatures of people for a small fee to put toward their ski trip costs. I knew I should have been very pleased to see Hailey and Paul so busy with customers, but my Student Government obligations seemed like too much to handle that weekend. I was grateful that the booth was too tiny for me to stand by and oversee operations. Near a table where the PTA was selling tickets to a raffle, for which the prizes included hand-sewn quilts and salon services from the local beauty parlor, I saw Henry Richmond staring straight up at the Ferris wheel, watching Pete and Violet flirt and giggle against the night sky. I could only imagine what was running through his head, observing his dead sister's beloved boyfriend moving on to a new romantic prospect barely a month after Olivia's grave had been dug. I wasn't sure if Trey saw what I saw, or that I wanted him to if he didn't, but the expression of hurt on Henry's face affected me like a slap across the cheek.

"Do you want me to win you a mirror with a painting of Elvis on it?" Trey offered jokingly as we passed a game stand where fancy mirrors could be won by throwing darts at balloons. We were both in quiet, sullen funks, and I adored him for trying to lift my mood.

"Nah," I refused, "that would just be one more fragile thing in my room for ghosts to break."

Trey pulled me closer to him with the arm that hung around my shoulders and kissed my forehead. "You know, there's a chance that Olivia's death was a freak coincidence, and Candace will be home next weekend, safe and sound."

I wanted to believe him—I did. But he had been in that car with Olivia. He had heard her last words.

"I know you don't really believe that," I replied, squeezing his hand.

When we stood in line for cotton candy and Violet tapped me on the shoulder from behind to say hello, I felt an irresistible urge to confront her. If not for Candace's sake, then for Henry's.

"This carnival is so much fun!" she gurgled. Pete, next to her, smiled his classic handsome smile.

It took me a second to remember that Violet was a big-city girl, and she'd probably never been to a small-town traveling carnival before in her whole life. "Enjoy it; it's the only thing that happens here all year," I muttered. I hadn't really been inclined to go that night, but Winnebago Days was unavoidable, and I had to check in on the booth at least once each day.

"Have you guys gone on the Ferris wheel yet? It's amazing! You can see the lights in Ortonville from up there!"

I tried to force a smile. I had managed to be civil, sometimes even friendly, with Violet in the week since homecoming. "We may go on later. I am a little afraid of the rides at this carnival. Every year at least one breaks down and there's some kind of crisis."

Violet looked to Pete to confirm, and he shrugged in agreement. She swatted him playfully and said, "Pete! You didn't say a word about that when we got on the Ferris wheel!"

"It's mostly safe!" he insisted.

We stepped up to the man selling cotton candy and Trey opened his wallet to buy us each a puffy light blue ball of sugar.

Violet's delight with the carnival was unnerving me, making me want to scream at her that she had no right to be enjoying herself, having so much fun, so soon after Olivia's death, and with Candace on her way to a setting that matched her own prophesied death. "You know, Candace is going to Hawaii tomorrow with her dad," I casually mentioned, my eyes boring into Violet's.

Violet raised an eyebrow, but without acknowledging that she understood what I was insinuating, she replied, "I heard. I have to admit, I'm a little jealous. It's getting cold early this year. I wouldn't mind a week in the tropics."

I glared at her, shaking my head. Mischa had been right. She was simply coldhearted. Her ambivalence about Candace's life ignited a wild rage within me, something that I had been suppressing up until that point either out of a naïve hope that Violet really hadn't had a hand in Olivia's death, or out of fear of her power. But in confronting her in that line, I noticed that Violet couldn't bring herself to make eye contact with Trey. I wondered again if she had known it would be Trey driving the car in which Olivia would die, and why she hadn't warned him. Or why she hadn't mentioned him to the rest of us when she had told Olivia's story.

Trey and I agreed to walk over to Bobby's for milkshakes with Erica, Kelly, and Cheryl before walking back home. They were all in especially giggly moods, presumably because a guy who was a senior was in their midst. Trey was noticeably friendlier with them than he had been with Mischa, and for that I was truly appreciative.

The next morning Mischa pulled into my driveway at six, before the sun was even up, just as we'd planned. We didn't know when Candace's plane was departing, so we figured we needed to intercept her as early as possible, and I didn't want my mom to give me the third degree about going to a friend's house at such an odd hour. Technically, I assured myself, I wasn't sneaking out without permission since it was morning and not night.

With a sour sense of dread in my gut, Mischa and I drove straight to the Johnstons' house. Isaac was sitting on his front stoop just as he'd promised us he would be, although he made it clear when he climbed into the back seat of Mischa's little Volkswagen GTI that he was not thrilled to be helping us.

"This is so stupid," he grumbled. "You guys do realize that Candace is insane, don't you? Like, nuttier than squirrel shi—"

"That's disgusting and insensitive to mentally ill people," I interrupted him.

"Oh, well then. I guess I should apologize to both of you, because you're obviously as out of your minds as she is," Isaac snapped.

Mischa reached over her shoulder from the driver's seat and handed him a jewelry box. "Here. Don't lose this, or my mom will disown me."

Isaac rolled his eyes at her and cracked the box open to take a peek at the small diamond ring it contained. "I can't believe you talked me into this." Exasperated, Mischa backed out of his driveway. "You don't actually have to marry her! You just have to profess your love for her and propose like you mean it. It's a matter of life and death. Just take our word for it."

"Let's just do this already. I want to go back to bed," Isaac muttered, leaning back and fastening his seat belt.

I had my doubts that our plan was going to be successful too, but I remained quiet as we drove to Candace's house. All week at school, Mischa and I had been trying to convince her that it wasn't safe to go to Hawaii, but we were up against the mood stabilizer she was taking in addition to the nearly daily counseling she was receiving. Her psychiatrist had convinced her that facing her fear of water was the healthiest way to overcome her obsession with Olivia's death, and nothing we'd said to convince her that we shared her belief that Violet had killed Olivia made its way through her dazed optimism.

Having Isaac ask her to elope with him—as extreme and desperate a measure as it was—was the only tactic Mischa and I had come up with that might work. After all, we didn't need Candace to actually marry him. We just needed her to get into Mischa's car with us so that we could whisk her away for a few hours—long enough to make her miss her flight and inspire her parents to put her back in the hospital. It was a cruel plan, and if we pulled it off, I knew I'd feel guilty for the consequences. But at least Violet's prediction for Candace wouldn't come true. We'd be buying ourselves more time to decipher what Violet had done to us.

"One more time. Candace comes outside the house, you tell her you love her and want to marry her so that you can have a legal say in all her mental health treatment," Mischa said, laying out the plan again for Isaac's benefit. "We tell her we're driving to a wedding chapel in Wisconsin Dells, she gets in the car, and we take off."

All the lights were out at Candace's house when we parked alongside the curb. Isaac once again announced how stupid he thought this whole thing was before he texted Candace, requesting her to come outside. We waited for her response in silence, all of us knowing that there was a chance she wouldn't reply since she was both heavily medicated and not on great terms with Isaac since the dance.

"Try again," Mischa urged Isaac. "Tell her it's imperative that she come outside."

"Impera—how do you spell that?" Isaac asked.

When a few more minutes passed without a reply, I suggested that we resort to old-school measures and toss gravel at her window. We inched our way around the side of the house and stood beneath what Mischa believed was Candace's bedroom window. I tossed a twig upward at the window and flinched at the sound it made, fearful that Candace's mom or stepdad might pull back the curtain. But a minute passed, and Isaac grunted in annoyance.

"We're gonna be here all day." He withdrew a quarter from the pocket of his jeans and flung it. It made a sharp noise as it ricocheted off the window, much louder than any of us would have expected.

"What are you doing?" Mischa hissed at Isaac. "Do you want Candace's mom to call the cops?"

Just then a window ten feet away opened and all three of us looked over in surprise at Candace's younger sister, who stared out at us from above. "What's going on?" she asked.

"Go get Candace, Julia," Mischa commanded. "We need to talk to her."

Julia rubbed the sleep from her eyes. "She's not here. She already left for her vacation."

My heart stopped beating as the full impact of what Julia had said landed on me. Candace was already gone. We had missed her. Time felt as if it were slipping into slow motion. "How?" I asked, close to tears. "I thought she was leaving today."

"Their plane left super early this morning, so her dad picked her up after dinner and she slept at his house," Julia explained. "They're supposed to land at like eleven our time? So, you could call her then."

Mischa paced in circles, pulling at her hair. "No! No! No!"

"We could call the airline and say there's a bomb on the plane," Isaac suggested, suddenly sensing how dire the situation was. "They'd probably have to land, then."

"Yeah, and then the FBI would probably come and arrest us!" Mischa shouted. "God, Isaac!"

I thought back to Violet's grisly description of how Candace's body would be found, and I shuddered. I hoped with every fiber in my being that Violet was wrong about Candace, or at least about her drowning at this age, on this trip.

That night, as I sat in my living room in front of the television with *The Iliad* in my lap, Candace texted me a picture she'd taken in Honolulu on her layover before her flight to Kona. The sun was setting in Hawaii, the sky shades of rose and coral over the tops of palm trees. All I texted back was Please stay away from the beach.

Monday after school, my mother was waiting for me with her arms folded over her chest.

"Sit," she commanded as I entered the house, pointing to a chair in the kitchen.

I had, not surprisingly, failed my Spanish midterm, as well as (a little more surprisingly) my midterms for Calculus I and chem lab. I had gotten a C on my English midterm, which secretly I was a little happy about, because I hadn't bothered finishing *The Iliad*. Perhaps I'd just read farther than a lot of other kids to have earned my C on the bell curve. But my grades were a complete reversal of my entire academic career up until that point. I had been a straight-A girl all the way until junior year.

"Well, during my Spanish midterm, I had a really bad headache and Mrs. Gomez sent me to the nurse," I said nervously, picking at my fingernails. "She told me in class today that I could retake it."

"You *will* retake it. Mr. Bobek called me this afternoon to tell me that all your teachers are concerned about you. This is your *junior year*, McKenna. A year from now at this time, you'll be sending out college applications. This is not the time to be letting grades fall."

I listened patiently as my mom continued on for a while about the burden she faced in paying my college tuition, my need to win a scholarship, her resentment of my weight loss bringing unfair scrutiny about her parenting abilities upon her by the staff at my school.

"So you tell me, McKenna. Where do we go from here?" she asked, staring me down, her arms outstretched and hands folded on the kitchen table. "Do you need to see a therapist every week?"

I looked at my feet. The only response that came to mind suddenly seemed so perfect—maybe if I'd failed to prevent Candace from going to Hawaii, I could convince my mom that I needed to meet her there. I blurted out, "Candace Cotton's parents took her to Hawaii because she's been having such a hard time with Olivia's death. I think I could use a change of scenery—"

"I absolutely agree with you there," my mother interjected. "I don't know how many times I've asked you what's happening this semester. You're secretive about your friends, about what you and Trey are up to every day after school, about why you're sleeping out here on the couch nearly every night. I've already spoken with your dad, and you're going to be spending the week of Thanksgiving with him and Rhonda this year."

Spending an entire week away from Trey in less than a month felt like it would be impossible to survive. I had to fight the urge to snap at her about snooping around in my room, since that would only make her more suspicious about how I'd known she'd gone in there at a time when I had been almost a mile away. "Fine," I said, in a weak voice.

"Your father wants to talk to you this evening. He's home now," my mother informed me.

I called my father from my room, not wanting Mom to overhear our conversation. Even despite going into my room for privacy, I left my door open a few inches because I was fearful that if I closed it, anything could happen while I was on the phone.

"So, what's all this failure business about, McKenna?" he asked me. "Your mom said you tanked your midterms and your gym teacher thinks you have an eating disorder."

In the background on his end, I could hear seagulls cawing and distant voices. I presumed that he and Rhonda were stretched out at the beach watching the sun set, or lounging on their boat with their neighbor. I struggled to remember what life was like when Dad lived at home with us, in the pre-Florida days. Enough time had passed that I really could no longer imagine how things would be different if he were tinkering around in our garage instead of over a thousand miles away.

"I don't know," I muttered. It felt like the most honest thing to say. I *didn't* know. I didn't know if Candace would live, didn't know how the letter *V* had been assembled on the Lite-Brite in the garage, didn't know if Arthur Fitzpatrick and the will of Violet's grandfather had anything to do with the game we'd played on Olivia's birthday, didn't know why Violet hadn't been able to predict a death for me.

"Level with me, kid. Are you having problems?"

"Just some problems sleeping," I admitted.

"So, what is it? Is all this Student Government stuff too much work? Is that kid next door pressuring you into things you're not ready for?"

"God, Dad, *no*! Trey isn't pressuring me for anything."

We talked for almost forty minutes, but I still couldn't find a way to tell him what was really going on in my life. He informed me that he'd be purchasing a plane ticket for me, departing from Wisconsin on the Saturday before Thanksgiving, and I'd be spending nine whole days in Tampa. Rhonda wanted to drive down to Key

West while I was visiting and go on an alligator swamp tour. I looked out my window, where the cold autumn night air was picking up dry leaves and spinning them in miniature tornados across the Emorys' driveway. It was difficult to imagine cruising through a hot swamp in four weeks, wearing a tank top.

The next morning, the high school was buzzing with gossip because Violet had not only tried out and made the pom squad, our school's version of cheerleading, for the basketball team, but the girl who had been junior varsity captain during our sophomore year, Hailey West, hadn't even made the team this year. Mischa and I exchanged eye rolls in the hallway, not even needing to utter words on the topic to know that we were thinking the same thing. Somehow, Violet was making all of this happen for herself.

Violet's junior year was shaping up perfectly. What else could she want from us? I wondered. There was nothing Candace had that Violet could possibly envy, so I couldn't determine what Violet might gain from Candace's death.

I turned down Violet's offer to come over after school to watch television and bake cookies, claiming that I was informally grounded until I brought up my grades, which wasn't a total lie. Her disappointment was palpable, but I didn't feel the least bit regretful. I knew all she wanted to do was hear herself talk about her new romance with Pete, and her excitement about her pom squad uniform. It occurred to me that her invitation was oddly timed, and was perhaps a strategic tactic to try to reel me back into her clutches while Candace was out of town. I remembered my first impression of Violet back in September at the start of the school year: how she had seemed so meek and unsure of herself, nervously twirling her long dark hair around her fingers. Had that been an act? Had she intentionally been trying to convince us that she was shy and quiet to gain our trust?

Our lunch table crowds merged that week. Violet's new status as Pete's girlfriend entitled her to join him at the table formerly ruled by Olivia. Tuesday, she and Tracy shifted over, carrying their lunch trays without explanation or apology. Mischa, having at least the sense to acknowledge that angering Violet might put Candace in greater danger, slid down to the other end of the table with Matt to be as far away from her as possible without actually sitting elsewhere. Matt and Mischa had been together long enough for him to follow her social cues; he kept his interactions with Violet brief but polite.

During classes, Mischa's and my phones buzzed in unison with carefree messages from Candace. We received and reviewed photos and quick notes about food she ate at the breakfast buffet in the resort where she was staying, and at the festive luau her family attended on their second night. She sent pictures of plates filled with lomi-lomi salmon, kalua pork, fresh pineapple slices, and macaroni salad. There were pictures of dancers in grass skirts and Candace's discarded purple lei on the dresser in her hotel room after a night of fun, and pictures of her half brothers stomping across black dried lava in the volcano park.

And then on Wednesday, the messages stopped abruptly.

What are you up to today? I texted Candace nervously on Thursday morning when I woke up.

I became frustrated when she hadn't replied by the time Trey and I began our walk to school, even though it was still the middle of the night in Hawaii.

I knew it was paranoid and silly, but my heart was beating

irregularly from fear. Reality seemed to be operating on an abnormal timeline on Thursday, with periods slowing down and then speeding back up. I had an unshakable feeling that exactly what Mischa and I had been expecting was actually happening, but of course, without hearing anything from Candace, there was no way of knowing. Her phone battery could have been dead; she could have had bad reception; she could have decided she was having too much fun to keep in contact with us. Whatever the case may have been, it was impossible for me to focus on anything other than my irrepressible suspicion that events were occurring that were far beyond my control.

By the time I sat down in homeroom, I realized that the saccharine ukulele music that had been tormenting me for the past two weeks had curiously stopped. I had grown so accustomed to tuning it out, it was a surprise to listen for it and not actually hear it in my head. It was an enormous relief, like putting down a heavy book bag after carrying it on a long walk home, but it was still concerning. The end of the music could have meant any number of things, but for me it signified even more greatly that I had lost contact with Candace.

When I passed Violet for the first time that day in the hall, she smiled sadly at me before waving, and I wondered if she had any idea what Candace was going through at that very moment. She was wearing a beautiful gray cashmere turtleneck sweater over a black skirt with leather detailing on it that made her look enviably more punk rock than she actually was. Clothes like that couldn't be bought at any malls within driving distance of Willow; she must have bought all her clothes online. During gym class, Violet chose me first to play on her volleyball team and tugged gently at my ponytail. "Your hair looks really pretty lately," she complimented me. "It's getting a little darker now that it's fall."

"Thanks," I muttered.

She smiled at me weakly, and for a second it seemed as if she had something more to say, but then changed her mind. Coach Stirling blew her whistle to order both teams to their respective sides of the net, and the moment was lost.

Changing in the locker room after gym, Mischa was fraught with worry. "Still nothing since Tuesday night," she told me in a hoarse whisper, not wanting Violet to overhear. We had both been receiving the same messages from Candace, so that didn't surprise me. "I sent her ten text messages yesterday, and she didn't write back at all. I'm starting to really, really freak."

I asked, "Do you remember the name of the hotel where they're staying?"

Mischa didn't remember, and we spent our lunch break Googling resorts in the Honaunau Bay area trying to find anything that sounded familiar. The Kohala Orchid Village and Kohala Lani Halili both seemed like contenders. We requested bathroom passes from the lunch-room monitor, and from the otherwise empty ladies' restroom we called the front desks at both hotels hoping to leave a message for Candace in her room.

"Hello, I'd like to leave a message with the Cotton party," Mischa said in her most mature voice after dialing the number to the Kohala Orchid Village. She nodded at me a moment later, and then returned her attention to the phone. "Oh, I'm so sorry. I must have the wrong number."

We had better luck with the Kohala Lani Halili. The concierge there connected Mischa to what we hoped was the suite rented by Candace's dad. In a shaky voice, Mischa said, "Hi, this is Mischa Portnoy calling from Willow to leave a message for Candace. Me and McKenna just wanted to say hello and we hope Candace is having fun. Please text us as soon as you get a chance to let us know you're okay."

"Weird hotel voice-mail system," Mischa informed me as she ended the call on her phone.

But the afternoon lagged on without a response.

When the bell rang at three fifteen, ending the school day, Mischa nodded off her sister in the parking lot, taciturnly announcing that she would be missing yet another gymnastics practice. We walked to my house while Trey served detention for mouthing off in Advanced Physics. "Would it be weird if we called Candace's mom to see if she's heard from Candace today?" Mischa asked.

We both agreed that the answer to Mischa's question was *yes*, it would be totally weird.

My mom had left a note for me saying she had gone to campus to offer in-person office hours, and that she would be bringing home dinner. We turned on the television and chatted through a music video show on cable until Mischa grew bored and began flipping through channels. It was only then that we caught the tail end of a commercial for the evening news, during which a pretty brunette newscaster was saying, "A teen feared swept out to sea at a popular resort in Hawaii. More details at five."

My heart seized and my limbs felt icy instantly. Mischa gasped as if someone had just punched her in the solar plexus, knocking the wind out of her. Just like that, a second later, the news segment was gone, switching unapologetically into a commercial for an energy beverage. Our lower jaws fell, leaving our lips hanging agape.

"This can't be happening," I whispered, my chest feeling too tight to even inhale normally.

"This is it, McKenna. It's her! It's happening again!" Mischa's voice sounded choked, hoarse with hysteria. She was trembling on the edge of the couch, her lower lip quivering, a layer of tears cresting over her eyes released to her cheeks by a blink.

My mind scrambled to justify an alternative reason for the broadcast we had just seen. We obviously couldn't wait until five o'clock to find out more information, so we checked our phones like maniacs, searching hashtags on Twitter. Major news sites were only offering basic information about the story, and it wasn't even a front-page headline feature yet. The press was stating that an American teenager was missing after disappearing from a beach on the Big Island of Hawaii, and authorities were hoping for a happy outcome. No names were given, and no news outlets even confirmed that the missing teen was a girl. There was nothing at all conclusive about the story having anything to do with Candace, and yet it was just too great a coincidence. We discussed once again whether or not to call Candace's mom, and decided against it, not wanting to upset Mrs. Lehrer if, indeed, she knew there was a search on, or alternately be the bearers of bad news if by some chance she hadn't heard about what was happening in Hawaii. My blood felt cold in my veins. I did not want to admit, for Mischa's sake, how grave my sense of doom was becoming.

Trey knocked on the front door before entering when he got out of detention, having already seen the headline for the news article online at school.

"Any word yet?" he asked, already aware that we were both freaking out while we waited for any kind of communication from Candace. He set his doodle-covered backpack down next to the couch and sat beside me.

"Nothing," I informed him.

He rubbed at his nose and then suggested, "Have you tried, you know, contacting her?"

Mischa blew up at him, her face flushed. "Of course we have! We've been texting her for two days, Trey!"

Trey shrugged and added, "I meant, you know, with the board. Just in case she's not exactly able to respond to text messages right now."

"That is just *morbid*, okay?" Mischa snapped. "We need to remain positive right now! We don't know anything for certain. Maybe Violet wanted Olivia dead so she could get her hands on Pete, but why would she be so mean to Candace?" I had a very, very bad feeling that Candace's disappearance meant that Violet wanted more than just what she'd taken from Olivia. The purpose of her game was about something much bigger, although I couldn't guess what it was. All three of us pretended for a few minutes to focus on the tacky reality television show in front of us, but the air in the living room grew thick with our thoughts. We all watched the minutes pass on the digital clock on the cable box, counting the seconds remaining until five o'clock.

"Trey," I said softly.

"I'll get the board," he agreed, jumping up off the couch.

Since Trey's mom was home and might wonder about him hanging out in his basement with two girls, both younger than him, and I was reluctant to introduce any additional spiritual activity to my own bedroom, we put on our jackets and walked briskly to the corner. It had been my own suggestion that we try fishing through the spiritual world for Candace from the abandoned lot where my old house used to stand. It seemed like if there was any chance at all that we'd be able to contact Jennie, it would be there, the very spot where she had passed away. That evening, my concern for Candace outweighed my fear of the abandoned lot. I had a sickening, chilling feeling before we even set the board out in the weeds that we already knew what had happened to Candace.

"Are you ready?" I asked Trey and Mischa both as we sat down around the board in the long grass. The sky was pale yellow above us. We could hear the occasional whiz of a car passing on the rural highway behind us, the pitch that the noise made shifting due to the Doppler effect as the cars sped farther along on their way out of town. We knew we were mostly hidden by the overgrown weeds in the lot, and paid the traffic no mind.

This time, Mischa seemed solemnly prepared to communicate with the dead. Her nervous, giggly antics were a thing of the past, and she looked as exhausted as I felt. The three of us placed our fingers on the planchette and moved it around slowly to warm the board up. I did the talking. "We are hoping to contact the spirit of Candace Cotton, if she has indeed crossed over to the other side. We welcome only kind spirits."

We waited. The wind blew gently, whistling around us among

the bare branches of the trees on Martha Road. For a second, I smelled a little glimmer of winter in the air, the chill, the hint of fires roaring in fireplaces farther away in town. Then I felt the planchette slowly energize beneath my fingertip, and looked up to see that Trey and Mischa sensed it too.

"It's here," Mischa whispered.

The planchette coasted to the letter *Y*, and then came to a stop. "Ask if it's Candace," Mischa urged.

But I hesitated, because it seemed like whatever spirit had contacted us through the board already had a message it was intent on delivering. The planchette slowly, deliberately moved from letter to letter, spelling out two words:

Y-O-U-N-E-X-T.

CHAPTER 16

"I T WAS A RIPTIDE. THERE WASN'T ANYTHING ANYONE
could do. *A riptide.*"

Candace's stepmother sounded like a broken record the day of
the wake. She was obviously very emotionally shaken by the events
of the last few days, and while Mischa and I both wished she would
just stop talking, neither of us felt empowered to put an end to
her tirade. She looked like a younger, thinner version of Candace's
mom, athletic and stylish, in a blue-and-white wraparound dress that
seemed inappropriately informal for a wake. Mr. Cotton, quite possibly the only person who stood a legitimate chance of silencing his
wife, seemed to be in a daze, picking at his fingernails, nodding to
acknowledge everyone arriving at the funeral home but barely saying
a word to anyone.

Candace's mom, on the other hand, was simmering in a corner,
nearing her boiling point. The veins in her neck stood out like metal
rods supporting her head, and her sisters swarmed around her like
bees, attempting to calm her. "We never even saw her fall underwater! The tide just took her out to sea. Who would have known?"
Candace's stepmother continued on, despite Father Fahey, the priest

from St. Monica's, who was scheduled to deliver a short service later that evening, trying to quiet her down. "I mean, who would ever think a *riptide* might carry someone away from a resort that costs six hundred dollars a night?"

"Shut that woman up!" I heard Candace's mom say from her corner. Her sisters swooped in, circling her more tightly.

Mischa, Matt, Trey, and I sat on the same floral couch Mischa and I had occupied during Olivia's wake. Candace's memorial was very different from Olivia's, which had been somber and respectful. A second memorial for a high school student, following Olivia's by less than two months, seemed to be more than the good graces of our town could handle. By late in the afternoon, it was evident that the Richmonds would not be arriving to pay respects, probably because it would just be too difficult emotionally to set foot in Gundarsson's again so soon. Just like at Olivia's wake, the casket was closed, and the flower arrangements were so abundant that the funeral home director had run out of places to put them. A few were in the hallway, flanking the entrance to the parlor where everyone was gathering for Candace's memorial. Her extended family seemed endless, with tall relatives of all ages comforting one another and fetching cups of coffee from the lounge area. The wake was held on Wednesday, and classes had been suspended at Willow High School for the day so that students could attend, but because of Candace's erratic behavior in the weeks leading up to her death, the turnout was significantly less than the number of students who had shown up for Olivia's wake.

"Candace's mom is going to knock her stepmother over," Mischa muttered, impressed by the potential for violence within the Cotton family.

"I don't think I need to see that." I got up from the couch, smoothed out the skirt of my black dress, and moments later Mischa stood to follow me out into the hallway and toward the lounge. I felt awkward seeing Candace's mom under such terrible circumstances. She had been holding herself together pretty well since the morning she found out that Candace had drowned. My mom had driven us over to the Cottons' house early on Saturday morning to see if there was anything we could do to help. At that point, officials in Hawaii had told Candace's parents to brace themselves for bad news as they expanded their search for the body. I either hadn't known or hadn't remembered this, but at one point when Jennie and I were very little, Mom and Candace's mother had played together in the Willow ladies' bowling league. We had been there, in Candace's kitchen when the call had come from Hawaii confirming that Candace's body had washed up at low tide, nearly two miles from where she had disappeared. "Well," Candace's mom had said with unnerving composure, "now we know."

In the lounge, we found Julia picking at a tray of cookies with some cousins her own age. She wore a short dress with a layer of black lace over it, which seemed a little provocative for a girl who was thirteen years old. I wondered for a second if that dress had been bought for a school dance. Surely no one had ever thought at the time that the dress was purchased that Julia would end up wearing it to her older half sister's wake.

"How's it going, Julia?" I asked as I poured myself a cup of coffee.

"I'm okay," Julia replied, her eyes looking a little puffy. If she remembered Mischa, Isaac, and me waking her up the morning Candace had left for Hawaii, she made no mention of it.

Violet did not attend Candace's wake, which wasn't surprising, but on the other hand, it kind of was. I wondered if she'd dare to show her face the following morning for the prayer service before the burial. Mischa's parents had denied her request to be permitted to spend the night at my house after the wake, and although my mom would probably have let me spend the night at hers, I wanted to stay close to home and Trey. Olivia's spirit had mysteriously left my room quiet since the previous Wednesday when Candace had stopped texting me, and it was a source of wonderment for me why she had decided to stop pestering me. If the original haunting had been intended to prevent Candace's death, I had failed, and maybe her abandonment of my room meant that Mischa wasn't in danger. Or maybe Olivia's spirit was preoccupied with welcoming Candace's spirit to the other side. I couldn't know the reason, but I had a strong suspicion that my room hadn't experienced the last of the supernatural activity. There would be more, but there was no way to know when to expect it.

That night, as I tried to decide what to wear the next morning for Candace's prayer service, I had a breakdown. Two months earlier, I had been convinced that it was going to be the best year of my life. I had hoped that Candace and Olivia would be the kind of friends I'd keep in touch with forever. We could have been roommates at college, bridesmaids at each other's weddings, godmothers to each other's children. Now, both of them were dead, and I had every reason to believe that Mischa would be dead soon too. Then I'd be completely alone with the memory of what Violet had done, and the guilt of not having been smart enough to stop her.

Doubled over with sobs, I wondered how anything in my life

would ever be okay again after all of this. I might never escape from Violet's game. Ghosts might follow me around for the rest of my life. I fell asleep with the lights on and slept soundly through the night. When I woke up in the morning, my face was still sticky with tears.

It was Halloween, and Candace's body was scheduled to be lowered into the ground that day.

My mother drove me to back to Gundarsson's that morning for the prayer service, and opted to stay with me rather than wait in the car. All things considered, she was being great about the whole situation, and hadn't asked me questions about the issues Candace had been having after Olivia's death. She'd allowed me to stay home from school every day so far that week, which I would have appreciated more if I hadn't been shocked into a state of pure panic by the reality of Candace's death matching Violet's prediction. A cold, restrictive sense of dread had taken over me. My body felt stiff. This time there was no "maybe" about it: It was certain that we were under some kind of hex or curse.

Even though I didn't have the energy to think about what my next steps might be while still mourning Candace, I knew that Trey and I were going to need help in bringing an end to this. The enormity of taking on Violet and whatever was helping her in the spirit world was simply too much to consider on that rainy morning of Candace's funeral.

Tracy arrived at the prayer service as some kind of an ambassador from Student Government, blabbing about how it was her social responsibility as class secretary to pay her respects. She also stated that Violet had been home sick from school all week with a severe cold and couldn't pay her respects, even though she really wanted to be there. As Tracy nonchalantly told us this, I sensed Mischa's muscles tighten next to me, like a cat about to pounce. I may have been going through the motions of the week in an emotionless void, but murderous fury was raging inside of Mischa. And of course it was. We both knew now what was in store for us.

Mom stood next to me in the cemetery at St. Monica's as Father Fahey led the small crowd that had gathered in a few prayers at the gravesite. Trey stood on my other side, loosely holding my left hand, letting his long dark hair cover most of his face. Isaac Johnston wiped a few tears from his eyes and shook his head when the casket was lowered. I wondered now if he remembered how Mischa and I had told him that preventing Candace from going to Hawaii had been a matter of life and death.

On the drive home from the funeral, we passed parents trick-or-treating with their children. Seeing kids outside in costumes and jack-o'-lanterns on doorsteps was a cruel reminder that the world was going about its ordinary business even though Olivia and Candace were no longer a part of it. Back at home that afternoon, I changed out of my black dress and tights and directly into my plaid pajamas and crawled under my blankets even though it was still light outside. In the back of my mind, I knew it was an hour when parents weren't even driving home from their jobs yet, and the high school marching band was still practicing out on the football field, yet all I wanted to do was close my eyes and block everything out. I wanted to wake up in another town, in another life, another existence entirely, in which I had never gone to Olivia's birthday party and become a part of this nightmare.

You next.

Who next? Who had the spirit in the empty lot meant? It had denied that it was Olivia, denied that it was Candace. Was I vulnerable? Was I protected from the game because Violet hadn't been able to see my death? But even that wasn't exactly true; Violet had said she'd seen fire. What would that do to my mother, to lose her surviving daughter in a fire?

In the middle of the night when I stirred awake, Trey was there, and the lights were on.

"Can't be too safe," he told me when I blinked around, trying to figure out what time it was.

"Whatever was in my room is gone for now," I assured him. "If it was really Olivia, we failed. We didn't put the clues together fast enough. Now they've got Candace, too."

Trey looked at me intently, directly into my eyes, and after a long moment asked, "The night you played the game, whose turn was it after Candace?"

"Mine."

He nodded. "We're getting help, and we're ending this thing."

On Friday, my mother stood in the doorway and informed me that she was driving to campus for her class but would be coming back immediately afterward, handling her office hours over Skype from home. She didn't have to spell it out for me because I already knew: Next week she would expect me to return to school.

Trey's mother drove him to school and he immediately doubled back on foot, knocking on our front door incessantly until I rose from my bed and met him, still wearing my pajamas. "Get dressed," he ordered. "We're walking into town to meet with someone."

I didn't ask questions, simply tugged on jeans and a sweatshirt and followed Trey through the brisk morning air on a long walk through town. It was a foggy day, which was common weather for Wisconsin in the fall. School and regular life felt a million miles away. Mischa hadn't sent me an e-mail or text message since before we knew for certain Candace had died, but I strongly suspected that she was being kept home from school all week too. Nothing felt real. I wasn't thinking clearly. I was in a state of distractedness, following orders I could barely hear.

"State your business," a female voice addressed us through the security system at the back door of the brick rectory building behind St. Monica's church. Trey and I stood, shivering, on the cement staircase leading up to the rectory, which housed the church's administrative offices and the priest's living quarters. Standing there, I suddenly felt very exposed in the overcast daylight, the dead eyes of plaster statues of the Virgin Mary and St. Augustine upon us. I hadn't felt as if I had been in danger on the walk over from our neighborhood, but now that we were standing at the perimeter of the sanctuary of the church grounds, I felt an urgent need to step inside.

"We're here to ask for Father Fahey's help in a personal matter," Trey stated, gripping my hand a little more tightly. A surveillance camera was affixed above the rectory door in plain sight, presumably because the rectory hosted a soup kitchen and from time to time, people not quite right in the head turned up on this very same doorstep demanding help. We were asked for our names, which Trey supplied, and then we were buzzed in.

"Jim, two teenagers are here to speak with you," a gray-haired secretary wearing a knit vest over a floral polyester blouse announced into her desk phone as soon as we entered the rectory. She sat at a cluttered desk behind a glass window with a slot in it just like a teller's window at a bank, and pointed at a wooden bench across from the window where she expected us to take a seat.

We sat down quietly and unzipped our jackets in the warm hallway. Down the hall and through a doorway, in what was presumably the rectory kitchen, we smelled soup and could hear the clattering of dishes.

"What's the nature of this personal matter?" the secretary asked us through the window, her hand over the mouthpiece of the phone.

"It's private," Trey shot back, glaring at her.

A moment later, she set the phone back down on her desk and told us, "He'll see you now."

When we stood and walked to the end of the hallway, she buzzed to release the lock on the door and we passed into the cozy kitchen of the church offices. Father Fahey stood at the stove in a brown wool cardigan stirring soup with a wooden spoon. A monthly calendar with a big picture of the Duomo in Milan hung on the fridge, along with a number of church bulletin newsletters held in place with magnets. A cuckoo clock hung on one wall, fixed above a framed picture of Jesus with a tear rolling down one cheek.

"So, a private personal matter," Father Fahey said as we entered. I felt like an overgrown giant the moment we stepped into the small room, and the old man nodded us toward the chairs around the kitchen table. "Let me guess. You're truly in love and you want to get married, but your parents think you're too young. Or you're truly in love and you've given in to sins of the flesh and now you're in a predicament and you need my advice on what to do."

"Neither of those things, sir," Trey said, holding out a chair for me to sit down at the table. "My girlfriend and her friends from school played a game involving the occult, and now something evil is killing them, one by one." From his backpack, he pulled out his copy of *Requests from the Dead* and set it down on the kitchen table.

Without even turning to face us, Father Fahey slowly turned the gas knob on the stovetop to its off position. When the roar of the boiling soup quieted down, we could hear that a small radio on the kitchen counter was tuned in to morning talk radio. "You're talking about Candace Cotton and the Richmond girl, I presume."

"Yes," Trey confirmed.

"And what makes you think that their deaths had anything to do with occult forces rather than simple, random acts of nature?" he asked patiently. "We live in a society that believes blindly that there must always be a fair cause for suffering. When bad things happen to us and people we love, we find comfort in the idea that there is a just reason for those bad things. We believe that time will reveal those reasons, because we cannot understand that in this universe, events occur at random. We cannot question God's will."

"We all played the game on Olivia's birthday. There's a new girl at school from out of town, and it was her idea. She made up stories about how we would all die, and they're all coming true, right down to small details. And since Olivia died, something has been haunting my bedroom. It was trying to leave us clues before Candace died.

It was trying to warn us about what was going to happen to her." My admission was embarrassing, and I tried to sound as mature and serious as I could.

Father Fahey put the metal lid on his pot of soup, and turned to face us, crossing his arms over his chest.

"Follow me," he ordered.

The basement of the rectory was paneled and carpeted, but it still felt damp and unfinished. Father Fahey locked the door behind us as we began our descent down the staircase leading to the lower level of the building. "Just part of our security routine here at the church. You're perfectly safe, and I'll explain everything when we get downstairs."

At the far end of the basement, past a Ping-Pong table, a long table surrounded by chairs, and a set of utility shelves stocked with boxes labeled SUNDAY SCHOOL SUPPLIES, Father Fahey unlocked a plain-looking wooden door with a bowl of holy water set on a table next to it. He dipped his fingers in the bowl and made the sign of the cross, and encouraged us to do the same. "I served both of you at your First Communions. I know you're familiar with this routine."

We both made the sign of the cross obediently, and followed Father Fahey through the door. My heart was beating rapidly at that point since I didn't have any idea what to expect on its other side. In the split second before Father Fahey flipped on the light, I was imagining a scary spiral stone staircase leading even farther down toward the earth's core, taking us to dungeons or secret chambers filled with torture devices. But all that we saw on the other side was a large, relatively plain room, with two orange couches, a long brown table, heavily stocked bookshelves, and what looked like a medical examination table in the center of the room.

"Forgive me for the dramatic evacuation to the basement," Father Fahey apologized, taking a seat in the corner upon a chair that looked like it belonged in a library. Trey and I sat down on the couch across from him, and I relaxed a little when I realized I could still slightly smell the soup upstairs and could hear a warm stream of air coming from the central heating vents. "We have two elderly priests who live on the second floor above the administrative offices. Father Nowicki, you probably remember; he said mass often when both of you were still in Sunday school. He suffered a stroke two years ago, and his visiting nurses tend to him all day. We also care for Father Adeyimi, a missionary from Africa who is recovering from heart surgery. You must understand that the elderly and very young children are especially susceptible to evil, and I can't afford to expose them to anything you may have brought with you. So it's safer for us to discuss things of this nature down here, hence the lock on the door so that we aren't interrupted."

I must have looked horrified and surprised by this, because it had never occurred to me that spirits might be following me around. Or that churches had secret, windowless rooms in their rectories.

"Spirits cling to strength that they find compatible with their needs," Father Fahey explained. "You mentioned upstairs that something has been haunting your bedroom. Make no mistake. It is manifesting its powers in your bedroom because it has figured out how to manipulate the energy in that space. But it is haunting *you*."

Father Fahey's words stunned me. I had never been spoken to by an adult so directly before about such a frightening idea. He was making no attempt whatsoever to sugarcoat the situation for me, or to assure me, as grown-ups were often likely to do, that things weren't as bad as they seemed.

"Can you *see* it? Is it here with me?" I asked, alarmed. Instinctively, I leaned forward and looked over my shoulder.

The priest shook his head patiently and folded his hands in his lap. "I don't have any magical powers, Miss Brady. I'm just a simple man of the cloth. There's no magic wand I can wave in front of you to reveal if there's a bogeyman behind you. But as I said before, spirits latch onto the energy of people. You may have no awareness that something's following you, but there's a chance that it's with you at all times."

Trey fumbled with the book in his hands and mumbled, "We started doing some research after Olivia died. We thought maybe Violet, this girl at school, made some kind of a deal with a spirit and she's been delivering souls to it."

Father Fahey strummed his fingers on the end table next to his chair and considered that. "Sounds plausible. But in exchange for what? Why would Violet be in service to this spirit? What's it giving her in exchange for her cooperation?"

"Popularity," I suggested. "She's new in town and she went from being kind of shy and quiet to suddenly the class president and captain of the pom squad. *And* she's dating Olivia's old boyfriend. It's like she just stole Olivia's whole life in a matter of days."

"And this girl was involved in the game that you played?" Father

Fahey asked, suddenly appearing to be a lot more intrigued by our allegations now that we were in the basement. He leaned forward, resting his elbows on his knees.

"She was the one who told the stories about how we'd all die. It was her idea to play the game," I offered.

The priest mulled this over. "So this girl recently arrived to town, led all of you in this game, and you claim the manner by which both the Richmond girl and the Cotton girl passed away match up with details presented in the game?"

I nodded solemnly, wondering if he was drawing his own conclusion that Trey and I were nuts. Trey held up the book he had brought with us again. "This book suggests that maybe Violet has ties to the spirit world through an object."

"Yes, well, that's oftentimes how these things go," the priest agreed, easing back into his chair again. "However, don't allow yourselves to think that it will be an easy task to identify the object. Sometimes when a spirit passes and feels like it has unfinished business among the living, it fastens onto an object of significance, and is able to exercise control over living souls through it. This isn't always necessarily a practice of evildoing; sometimes the spirit of a parent or grandparent will maintain a presence among the living to keep watch over a child they're leaving behind. But more often than not, a spirit will resort to trickery or harassment to enlist a living person to execute their intended actions here in our plane of existence. Destroy the physical object, and destroy the connection. The *catch* is going to be figuring out exactly which object it *is*. There's a good chance this girl being manipulated doesn't even know which object in her life is connecting her to this force."

Trey squeezed my hand. This is what we had come to hear: that there was a way to end Violet's game. Even if the solution was going to be difficult and dangerous, we knew we had to pursue it.

"But I must warn you, guys," Father Fahey continued. "From the sound of it, this girl Violet seems to have an arrangement with a very powerful spirit. This thing isn't going to be easily overthrown, and if it's viewing the living through Violet's eyes, then it's probably already aware that you're suspicious of it, and she'll be wary of you. You're going to have to be very cautious in your approach."

Father Fahey asked me to repeat for him as best I could remember the stories that Violet had told at Olivia's party, and he took extensive notes as I tried not to leave out any details. Trey chimed in during my retelling of Olivia's story, as his real-life experience had followed Violet's predictions during the car crash. I hesitated after finishing Candace's story, and said, "It was my turn next, but when Violet tried to tell my story, she couldn't come up with anything good. She said she could only think of something having to do with fire, but it didn't feel right."

"Interesting," Father Fahey commented, adjusting the frames of his glasses. "There could be any number of possibilities for that, but if part of this spirit's successful acquisition of a soul is linked to the prediction of death, then maybe a soul on the other side stepped in to protect you."

"Jennie," I mumbled. Of course Father Fahey knew that I'd once had a twin. He had baptized us, and delivered the eulogy at Jennie's funeral service.

"If you remember back to your catechism classes, you'll recall that we believe all souls who have passed into heaven and purgatory are part of God's spiritual union. The *church triumphant*, which is how we formally refer to souls who have been admitted to heaven, can be called upon by the living for help with their lives on earth," Father Fahey explained.

I tried to think back to Sunday-school lessons I attended as a kid at St. Monica's after church services, but I couldn't remember learning anything about relying on the help of the dead. Trey, a much more critical thinker than me, was already summarizing what the priest was telling us and drawing his own conclusions.

"So, basically, you're saying that believing in ghosts is a fundamental part of our religion," Trey said dubiously. "And that ghosts can meddle with us whenever they want."

Father Fahey smiled, seemingly pleased with Trey's interpretation of his lesson. "I didn't use the word 'ghost.' But in our faith, we believe that souls are eternal. A soul that has been dedicated to God remains dedicated to God and can intercede in heaven on behalf of the living."

I continued with my memory of Olivia's party, concluding with the premonition of Mischa's death by choking. I never would have thought that night at Olivia's house on her birthday that I would end up in a church basement, resuming my religious education—yet there we were, doing exactly that. Then, in the spirit of full disclosure, Trey told Father Fahey about all three times we used the Ouija board, and the priest shook his head disapprovingly.

"I strongly urge the two of you to dispose of that as quickly as possible. You have no way of controlling what kind of energy passes through something like that. It's a horrible shame those instruments of evil are sold as novelties in toy stores. They are highly dangerous tools and should not be handled by children."

If any adult other than Father Fahey had referred to us as children, we probably would have rolled our eyes.

"But if Violet is possessed, how else are we supposed to gain any kind of advantage over her? I mean, we need some kind of guidance," Trey objected in our defense. "We're, like, helpless against her."

"Violet is not *possessed*. Possession has to do with demons, and demons are very different from spirits. Demons rarely have goals other than just to deliver messages and torment. Why, in fact, demons are fairly straightforward to remove," Father Fahey stated, waving his hand toward the table in the center of the room. For the first time since we'd taken our seats in that room, I realized its true purpose. The room must have been used for exorcisms. Upon closer examination, I observed there were ties attached to the table, like seat belts, at points where they might fasten over the chest and legs of anyone reclining on the table, restraining their movements. The walls were bare, devoid of any object that might be torn off and flung across the room. The sudden knowledge that possessed people had been brought to this space, and that demons had been released right into the very area where we were sitting, made me shiver. "There's no need to be afraid," Father Fahey consoled me, noticing my discomfort. "It's a very straightforward process. And a fairly common one too, I'm sorry to say."

Trey looked around the room suspiciously. "This room is used for . . ."

"Exorcisms. Yes," Father Fahey said nonchalantly. "I don't mean to alarm you, but every church has their own process for dealing with such things. It's a community service provided, although one not frequently discussed. This room is thoroughly cleansed after every use, and I'll admit it's been a while since the last time we had an appointment down here. The devil's strength is in fear, and the more we give in to our fears, the stronger he becomes. Spirits with vengeances, however . . ."

He trailed off, and then took off his glasses and rubbed the bridge of his nose with his fingers. "Spirits can gain their power any number of ways. Souls can take a lot of anger with them into the afterlife, as well as a lot of ambition and intelligence. Because they're halfway between here and"—he waved his hand toward the ceiling and then toward the floor—"everywhere else, they can linger where they are for as long as they want. They're the only ones who can banish themselves into eternity, and unfortunately for us, sometimes those with axes to grind overstay their welcome."

"So there's no way to really get rid of them? No ghostbusters, no magical chants, no pointing them in the direction of the light?" Trey asked, sounding hopeless.

Father Fahey shook his head, a little amused by Trey's question. "You've seen a lot of movies."

We shared with him as much as we knew about Violet, her grandmother's quarrel with Arthur Fitzpatrick, Violet's life prior to her arrival in town, and her inheritance of her grandmother's mansion. I could hear desperation in our voices as we tried to make sense of it all, and I wondered if the priest could tell just how urgently we wanted his help. How badly we needed someone older and wiser to instruct us, or to at least believe us that with one misstep on our part, either Mischa or I would die next.

"Well, I can tell you this," he said, sitting back in his chair and folding his wrinkled hands over his belly. "When spirits latch onto a servant in our world, they can only see and experience our world through that servant's eyes. If they have any weakness at all in this situation, it's that: limited vision. From what you've shared with me, I would suggest that you focus on destroying whatever that object is that connects Violet to the spirit controlling her. It won't rid her, or any of us, for that matter, of the spirit forever if it chooses to continue to try to find a channel back into our world, but it will be a significant enough setback that it will slow the spirit down in achieving its goal. I wouldn't bother trying to figure out the spirit's goal in an attempt to bring an end to this. That could take you far too long; it could be far too dangerous."

I cocked my head in confusion, not sure if I understood the priest correctly. "But if we destroy the object, how will that bring an end to the curse on me and Mischa? Wouldn't that just prevent Violet from pulling more people into this in the future?"

Father Fahey said, "The object serves as the connecting thread between Violet and the spirit, but it also serves as the means by which the spirit's will is released into our world. Separate Violet from this object, or destroy it, and you will interrupt this curse."

"So how do we know which object?" Trey asked. "Can you help us figure this out?"

At Trey's request, the temperature in the room seemed to change, and Father Fahey shifted position. "I'm terribly sorry, but other than offering advice, I can't help the two of you at all in this matter. I'm the managing director of this parish, the only priest still capable of saying mass and running administration. My responsibilities to the people of this town and the people who reside in this building are too great for me to risk any kind of . . . spiritual contamination."

I felt my chest ache and my throat begin to close as if I was going to start crying. Trey and I were really alone in this miserable mess. The only person in our town who believed us, and who we could imagine might possibly be able to help us, was refusing to do so. We were going to have to figure out how to save ourselves, or more specifically, me and Mischa, on our own.

That night after Mom got home, Candace's mom surprised us with a visit. Mom put on a pot of coffee, and Candace's mom handed me a plastic bag after taking a seat in the kitchen.

"Candace's father brought this back from Hawaii," she explained as I accepted the bag. "Candace apparently bought these for you and Mischa on their first night of the trip."

I peeked inside the plastic bag and saw inside of it what looked like a cheap toy ukulele. The plastic bag was from a gift shop in Hawaii, and a crumpled receipt was at the bottom of the bag. I thought of the music that had filled my head and distracted me in the days before Candace flew to Hawaii, and then throughout midterms. It had been my strongest warning from Olivia, and I hadn't acted on it.

Candace's mom stayed in our kitchen, sobbing and talking to Mom, long after I'd turned in for the night and tucked the ukulele into the box in my closet where I'd stowed all my other problematic possessions. I could smell cigarette smoke, the reassuring scent of company, and guessed my mom was probably counseling Candace's mom about losing a child. Not long after I heard the clock chime midnight, Trey texted me asking if I wanted him to come over, and I assured him that I was okay and that he should stay in his own room for the night. The sadness wafting off of Candace's mom seemed to fill our whole house, settling in my bedroom and surrounding me as I fell asleep.

On Monday, I woke up at dawn without the help of an alarm clock and dressed for class, not the least bit happy about returning to school. Before homeroom, I walked directly toward Mr. Dean's classroom and entered boldly while Trey waited for me in the hallway with his books.

"Mr. Dean?" I asked, causing him to look up from the papers he was grading at his desk. "I have some bad news. I didn't do so well on my midterms, and I'm resigning from my position as class treasurer to focus on bringing up my grades."

Mr. Dean's expression was one of absolute astonishment, but I stuck to my story. As I twisted the combination lock on my locker and mumbled, "Good morning," to Dan Marshall, I thought of how wildly my priorities had changed since the beginning of the year. In September, securing my popularity had seemed more important than anything. Now I had just willingly abandoned my foothold in the world of popular people without fear of how Violet would react. Senior year was going to be a complete roll of the dice, if I lived long enough to experience it.

Mischa and I agreed that at lunchtime that day in the cafeteria, we would abandon our old lunch table and sit elsewhere.

We wandered through the cafeteria together with Matt, our empty trays in our hands, and eventually, after considering nearly all of the kitchen's options that day, I stepped into line behind Mischa with a turkey sandwich.

"That's all you're having?" I asked, noticing that she had returned her tray to the stack and was carrying nothing but a carton of skim milk.

"I'm not hungry," she claimed.

After she paid and stepped into the seating area to wait for us, I stepped forward to pay for my sandwich at the register, and Matt, behind me, said quietly, "She won't eat. She hasn't eaten anything solid in days."

"Why?" I asked, holding out my hand for the cashier to return my change.

"She's afraid of choking," Matt said, concerned.

We ventured out into the seating area, the salty stench of deep-fried tater tots and spicy chicken patties clinging to our clothing and hair. When we found space at the end of a table of sophomores and sat down, they looked at us as if we were bonkers. Across the cafeteria, I sensed heads turning in our direction and didn't wonder too much what Pete, Jeff, and Isaac were thinking about our sudden departure without explanation. I would leave it to Violet and Tracy to explain. I watched Mischa, who sat across from me, as she unwrapped her straw and tucked it into her carton of milk.

"You have to eat, Mischa," I warned her. "Chew slowly if it makes you feel safer, but come *on*. You can't just *stop eating*."

Mischa blinked and casually brushed away either a tear or a stray eyelash. "That's easy for you to say. *You* weren't predicted to choke to death. *You* don't have nightmares about not being able to breathe—"

Mischa stopped short and when I looked over my right shoulder, I saw Violet standing behind me. Her posture and gestures were aggressive, but her voice was intimidated and unsteady. True to what Tracy had said at Candace's wake, she *did* sound stuffed up, as if she had been suffering from a bad cold, and her nose was pink and dry from the heavy use of tissues.

"Why are you guys sitting over here? There's room at our table," she said. She was wearing a beautiful brand-new sweater with a stylish cowl collar, multicolor cashmere flecked with strands of fine gold thread. A sweater like that could not have been inexpensive, and it served as yet another unwelcome reminder that the Simmons family was wealthy. "And Mr. Dean said you quit Student Government. I don't get it, McKenna. We had such great stuff planned for this year."

"You killed Candace," I said firmly in a voice low enough to prevent the sophomores at the other end of our table from hearing us. Although I knew the time was right to confront her as Trey and I had discussed, I still wished he wasn't so adamant about avoiding the cafeteria during our shared lunch period so that I wouldn't have to address her alone. We had decided that it might be easier to distract her from our true intent by making sure she was aware we were angry. The time had come for all of our sneaking around to end. "Not to mention Olivia, too, but that goes without saying."

I fought the urge to look away from her and as uncomfortable as it was, I watched as she turned beet red and struggled to find words to respond. Her ankle twisted, her lips mashed together, her fingers tightened where her hands were placed on her hips. Her discomfort with confrontation was as evident as was mine with being assertive.

"McKenna, you know that's irrational. I was nowhere near Hawaii when Candace died. And I wasn't anywhere near Olivia when she died either. A human being cannot control the weather. I can't control the *ocean*."

Feeling my pulse begin to race with anger, I steadied my nerves before replying, "We all know now that you are very much in charge of what's happening to us. We have something very special planned for you, and we're waiting to see what you do next."

Violet opened her mouth to speak, but no words came out. Her eyes darted from mine across the table to Mischa's. After a moment of hesitation, she regained her composure. "Is that some kind of threat?" she asked haughtily.

"You'd better believe it is, Violet," I bluffed.

"We'll kill you," Mischa blurted, taking me and Matt both completely by surprise. "If you die, the spell is broken. I'm not afraid to kill you to save my own life."

Trey and I hadn't told Mischa about going to visit Father Fahey, or our plan to determine which object belonging to Violet served as her connection to the spirit. Her comment about killing Violet was completely out of left field, but it served a perfect purpose: distracting Violet from what Trey and I had in mind. Violet's face drained entirely of color. Her expression faded to one of absence of emotion, and she turned on her heel to return to our former table. We didn't watch long enough to see the reaction of everyone else sitting over there to her explanation as to why we weren't accompanying her. "Are you *crazy*?" I asked Mischa. "She can go to the principal and say you're threatening to hurt her! She could go to the police!"

"Fine," Mischa said firmly, taking a sip of her milk. "I'm serious.

I will throttle her with my bare hands. If I'm going to die, then I want her dead too."

Matt put an arm around her shoulders and kissed the side of her face, but I could tell by Mischa's tone and calmness that she was not kidding around.

In gym class, I attempted to be sent to the nurse's office by claiming I had cramps, but Coach Stirling thwarted my efforts by informing me that moderate exercise was as good a cure for cramps as Tylenol. Earlier that week, before Mischa's return to school, her parents had done what Candace's had done for her and switched around her entire class schedule so that she could avoid Violet in every class other than lunch. I wished I could be more honest with my parents about what was happening at school and ask them to do the same thing for me, but I knew if I asked my mother to change my schedule I would face an endless assault of skeptical questions. I changed into my red-and-black gym suit in the row of lockers other than the one I usually used to avoid Violet and Tracy. I pulled on my gray hooded sweatshirt as an afterthought, because it was starting to get cold out.

On the track, I ran at my own slow pace, avoiding the eyes of everyone around me. I focused on the lyrics of the song playing on my phone until I unmistakably heard my name called.

"McKenna!"

Violet was behind me, trotting to catch up with me. Quickly I noticed that Tracy was halfway around the track, running, so I took out my earbuds and listened.

"What?" I asked.

"Why are you suddenly so mad at me?" she asked, sounding earnestly bewildered about the change in our friendship since the previous week.

"This isn't sudden, Violet," I told her sternly. "I was willing to consider the possibility of coincidence when Olivia died. But not now that Candace is gone too. I'm onto you, I know what you're doing, and I think you're sick. You're going to sit back and laugh as all of us die."

"No," Violet said, shaking her head. "That's not true. I don't have any control over what's happened. I feel terrible about Olivia and Candace dying. You have to believe me."

I was so furious at her contemptible insistence on her own innocence, I wanted to spit at her. "Tell me one thing," I said, standing and facing her, not caring who saw us arguing on the track. "When it was my turn, why couldn't you see my death?"

Violet blanched. She blurted, "I don't remember. That was *months* ago."

"You *do* remember, and you know exactly why!" I accused. Violet looked around wildly, but I was staring her down, demanding an answer.

"Because you're already dead," she finally said matter-of-factly.

Her answer stunned me so profoundly that my jaw must have dropped.

"I don't know how to explain how it works when it does. I just start having a vision, and during yours I saw you in the fire. I watched you die," she stammered.

Before I'd even processed enough of her response to be curious about the visions she'd mentioned, I fired back, "You didn't see me,

LIGHT AS A FEATHER

you idiot. You saw my twin. She's the one who died in the fire."

Violet's eyebrows rose in reaction, as if I'd just pressed the final missing piece into a puzzle. "A twin! Your sister was your twin!"

I began walking again, once again afraid to reveal information about myself that she could use against me. Numbly, my fingers jammed my earbuds back in my ears, and music blasted out the frantic reaction in my head.

Already dead.

I could hear Violet calling my name as I broke into a run, but didn't stop.

As unlikely as it seemed to me, it was totally possible that every time Violet had heard a rumor about the fire that had destroyed my house, Jennie had been referred to as my sister rather than as my identical twin. My theory about the possibility that Jennie and I had shared a soul, and that therefore I was half dead, suddenly seemed a lot more correct. But if I were already half dead, was I exempt from the curse?

The thought that I may have been truly immune to the curse made my core glow with joy. If Violet had no power over me, then I wouldn't have to worry about what might happen to my mom if I suddenly died, or about Trey's reaction. Suddenly, the promise of ongoing life made the morning air all the more fresh, the sunlight all the more warm, the music in my earbuds all the more spectacular. But almost as fast as relief flooded my nervous system, I remembered that Mischa was not immune. And I still didn't have the slightest clue how to go about saving her.

* * *

After school, Mischa and Trey met me at my locker. Mischa was planning to invite herself over to my house to do homework to avoid having to go to gymnastics practice with her sister, who was waiting for her in the parking lot, presumably with her engine running.

"Just wait for me right here," Mischa instructed outside the west doors of the high school, right before she darted off in her black suede blazer through the cars in the lot toward her sister's hatchback car. Trey and I watched as the sisters argued, and finally Amanda threw her car into reverse and pulled out of her parking space. She shouted some parting words at Mischa, which appeared to have been along the lines of, "Wait until Mom and Dad find out."

Mischa shrugged when she rejoined us near the doors to the school, adjusting the strap of her stylish leather messenger bag over her shoulder.

"Is everything okay?" Trey asked.

"Fine," Mischa said in a singsong voice. "My sister just doesn't understand that gymnastics doesn't really seem very important to someone who's about to die."

A moment after those words left Mischa's mouth, the red doors of the high school behind us opened and we found ourselves face-to-face with Violet. There was a moment of awkward, sickening silence as the four of us all examined one another.

"Hello," Violet finally said sheepishly to us, and then turned and raised a hand to shield her eyes from the sun as she looked across the busy parking lot for something.

"I believe you owe Trey an apology," Mischa piped up, preventing Violet from just dashing off without further acknowledging us.

Violet looked at her, startled. "For what?"

"You knew it was going to be Trey driving the car the night that Olivia died," I intervened. "And you didn't even say a word."

Trey looked at his feet, uncomfortable for having been pulled into our fight.

Violet batted her eyelashes wildly, and said, "I don't know what you're talking about," but I could tell by the tone of her voice that she knew exactly what I was talking about.

"Don't be ridiculous, Violet. Trey knows; he knows everything." I took a step toward her, studying her, trying to determine what item on her person might have been given to her by her grandmother. Her vintage Louis Vuitton leather Speedy handbag? The charm bracelet around her wrist? Could the key to our troubles be as elusive as a bottle of perfume, a mist of magic that Violet sprayed on each morning? "With one phone call to him, you could have prevented Olivia from dying. All you had to do was tell him, and you could have saved her life. Olivia *knew*, you know. Trey said right before the truck hit, she was begging him to pull over. The last moments of her life were spent in terror, and that's all on you."

Accusing her so directly seemed to have an emotional impact on her. She probably hadn't thought too much about how her inaction had resulted in the death of two friends. She had probably been so concerned with issuing her predictions that she had overlooked her own responsibilities as a moral human being.

"You have to believe me, guys. I didn't know it was going to be him," Violet said, her eyes pleading with us for mercy. Her voice was almost shrill; she was so desperate that I not doubt her. "They didn't show me his face."

"Why should we believe you?" I snapped. I didn't buy her claim that whatever had allowed her to watch Olivia's death had obscured Trey's identity from her. "If you had warned him, Olivia would still be alive."

"But that's just *it*," Violet sputtered. The doors to the school behind her opened, and a flood of freshman boys rushed past us toward an idling minivan driven by someone's mom. Violet waited until the minivan pulled away before she continued, "I can't *warn* anyone. I can't change what will happen. They don't let me see enough to try to stop it."

The impact of everything she had said to us was all at once so shocking I didn't even know how to continue interrogating her. And I found it odd that she was implying that there were multiple spirits who kept her informed instead of just one. I was speechless for a second as my thoughts tried to assemble everything Violet had just said in my mind. I tried to remember Father Fahey's guidance: *Don't try to figure out the spirit's motivations. Just focus on the object connecting her to it.*

"What do you mean, *they* let you see things? *Who?*" I asked. "And you knew. If this has happened before, then you knew that Olivia was going to die!" My lips were forming words, but I was trying to scour her with my eyes. Was it an object in her bag that we couldn't even see? Would Mischa and I have to break into her gym locker to search the contents of that leather handbag? Was it something she kept hidden away in her bedroom? No . . . my hunch was that it was something she had brought with her to the Richmonds' the night of Olivia's party.

Violet's eyes flooded with tears that rolled down her cheeks, and she made no attempt to wipe them away. "I didn't know, not for sure. I never know exactly what will happen."

Mischa's temper was flaring. "What are you even *talking about*, Violet? You're not making sense! Who shows you things?"

Violet took a deep breath and looked around the parking lot suspiciously. Rap songs blasted through the closed windows of cars, doors slammed, and horns honked at the corner where kids impatiently waited their turn to leave the lot. "I'll tell you whatever you want to know, but not here."

"You'd better," Mischa warned. "Because *you* were the one who suggested we play that stupid game in the first place, and I think you owe us a lot of explanations."

The track was abandoned at that hour, although through the trees that separated the fields, we could see and hear the football team practicing for their game that weekend. Violet had told Tracy she was going to hang out with us and declined a ride home, and throughout our walk from the parking lot down the cement path leading to the football field, we could hear Tracy furiously text messaging Violet through the buzzes emanating from Violet's bag. We stood near the small row of bleachers, and I shivered inside my denim jacket, wishing that we'd have the luxury of at least one more week of warmth before winter settled in for the season. Trey sat down on the lowest cold, aluminum bleacher seat, but Violet remained standing, clutching her little leather bag, kicking at the dry grass beneath her feet as she spoke. "They started showing me things a while ago. I don't even remember exactly when it started," Violet began quietly. "Don't ask me who *they* are, because I don't know. Spirits. Ghosts? Friendly ghosts, evil ghosts? I don't know.

"I've never felt afraid of them, and they've never hurt me. Certain situations make it easier for me to see what they want me to see, like the game, for example. It's hard to explain any of this, really. They tell me things, but I don't really hear voices. They let me see things, but it's not the same as seeing these bleachers."

"What kinds of things do they tell you to do?" I asked. A gust of wind stirred the dry leaves on the trees surrounding the track.

The question made Violet uncomfortable, and she picked at her fingernails before replying. "Talk to certain people. Ask them about their lives. Offer to read their palms."

I immediately felt sick. It sounded like she had been doing this for longer than we suspected. Who knew how long this had been going on, how many lives had been taken?

"Like Josh Loomis and Rebecca Shermer?" Mischa asked with one eyebrow raised.

Violet didn't look the least bit surprised to hear those names from her past mentioned.

"I guess." She shrugged. "Look, I didn't realize at first that what happened to them was connected to me. Josh was always a sickly kid. It's terrible to say, but no one was really surprised that he died after having an asthma attack. They didn't tell me that if I read his palm I'd be opening the door for it to happen. That's what it's like, in my head. It's like a door opens and things just start moving through it."

I couldn't help but roll my eyes at her. The way in which she'd so easily shifted into Olivia's life convinced me that she could very much control these predictions if she wanted to. "Didn't you realize after he died that *you'd* made it happen?" Mischa asked, not buying any of Violet's innocent act.

"No! Not at all. Imagine if you were in my shoes. Would you really put two and two together? It's like . . . What if the lady who works the cash register in the lunchroom died tomorrow? Would you ever think that her death was linked to a hamburger that you bought, or the five-dollar bill that you handed her? No!"

"And then what about Rebecca? Did you figure it out when she died? Or did things not click into place until the third funeral, or the fourth?" Mischa snapped.

Violet straightened her posture and threw her shoulders back, growing defensive. "Hey. Rebecca was *my friend.* I'm not a monster, you know." Two enormous tears made their way over her lower eyelids and spilled down each cheek. She wiped them away with her fingers quickly, and blew her nose into a tissue she withdrew from her coat pocket. "I don't even know who hit her, to this day. The police never caught the guy. . . ."

"So, I have to know. Did your parents move you away from Lake Forest because of all the problems you caused there, or because of the estate here to settle in Willow?" I asked. For just a fraction of a second, Trey looked up from the bleachers and glanced at Violet. As soon as her eyes met his, Violet looked away out toward the fence circling the track.

"The things that happened in Lake Forest were *not my fault,*" Violet insisted. "I haven't committed any crimes!"

Mischa snorted. "The way we see it is that you brought this on," Mischa accused, taking a step forward and stabbing her fingertip into Violet's chest. "You killed Olivia, you killed Candace, and now I'm probably next. The last time I checked, murder *is* a crime. *You* have to make it end."

I was a little afraid of Mischa. She was acting wild, but then again, if I had still believed my death was next in the lineup, I might have been acting with a greater sense of urgency too.

"I don't think you get it, Mischa," Violet said, smiling nervously, digging her hands into the pockets of her coat. "I can't change what they showed me. I didn't *kill* anyone. I don't know how to make it all stop."

This brought Mischa no comfort. She folded her arms over her chest and stared Violet down. "I don't want to choke to death now or ever. And if I'm going to die, I'm comfortable taking you with me. I want to be clear with you. If you don't make this stop, I *will* kill you."

I was chilled to the bone by Mischa's conviction and tried not to turn and stare at her. To my left, I could hear the huffing and puffing of her angry breathing. The truth was that she had considerable upper-body strength from gymnastics training for ten years. If she wanted to hurt someone, she could. If she wanted to kill someone, and wanted my help, I wasn't sure how I'd respond. While I believed Violet in her claims that she didn't know how to bring the game to an end, I didn't believe her charade of innocence entirely. I believed she was being guided through this confrontation. She was being told what to say, how to throw us off.

Violet's eyes darted beyond us; surely she was wondering if we'd chase her if she made a run for it across the track back toward the parking lot, where the late bus would be arriving momentarily to pick up kids who'd stayed at school an extra hour for extracurricular activities. Maybe her spirits controlled her words, but they couldn't control her thoughts, and she was probably thinking in that moment that if Mischa lunged at her, she would be a goner. "How do you propose I do that, Mischa?" she asked. "I don't know how many times I've told you guys, I can't stop this."

"Then summon your spirits. Make them fix it," Mischa demanded.

Violet's voice quivered. She was on the brink of crying. "It doesn't work that way, I swear," she insisted. "I can't just summon them. They only come to me under specific circumstances, or randomly, when they feel like it."

Mischa and I exchanged determined looks. "You mean, like if we were to play Light as a Feather, Stiff as a Board," Mischa suggested. Violet shifted her weight from one leg to another. Beneath her, gravel that had drifted over from the track into the grass on which we stood crunched. She said finally, "Yes. Or if we held some kind of a séance. But even *that's* not a guarantee. They don't take requests. They just arrive, show me stuff, and leave."

Mischa's plum-stained mouth was set into a firm, serious line. "Then we play the game again to bring them back, and you tell them that they made a mistake."

Violet looked at me as if to object, and then carefully said, "But the game won't work again. They already showed me your death. If they arrive again they might just show a repeat, or they might get angry."

"We'll play the game on Trey. They haven't told his story yet," Mischa suggested.

I gasped in objection. There was no way I was going to risk Trey's life.

Trey looked at the gravel, and Violet shook her head slowly. "They don't have a story for him."

"Then McKenna. They didn't show her death," Mischa reminded us both.

Violet's eyes flew wide open in terror, and she looked to me to save her. As much as I didn't want to participate in the game again, it wasn't an ideal time to inform Mischa that Trey and I had other ideas on how to topple Violet's power. "Okay," Violet agreed. "Tomorrow."

"Not tomorrow," Mischa shook her head. "Tonight. Be at my house by eight o'clock. I want to deal with this as soon as possible. I could be *dead* by tomorrow, remember?"

"I can't tonight!" Violet objected. "It's my mom's birthday, and we have a bunch of people coming over. I can't sneak out."

"Then fine. Tomorrow. My house."

Violet's lower lip trembled a little bit before she agreed. "After the basketball game. It's only the second game of the season. I have to be there."

Mischa's arms flew out at her sides in exasperation. "You're saying a basketball game is more important than my life!" She looked to me and Trey for help, but I couldn't inform her that we had no intention of ever playing any games with Violet again while Violet was standing right there, listening. A buzz came from within Mischa's bag, and she checked her phone to find a text message from Matt. After reading it, she said, "Okay. Tomorrow after the game, if that's the best you can do. We'll all be here tomorrow night in the stands, so don't even think about disappearing with the pom squad to go to Bobby's or something. We'll be waiting for you." Mischa turned and walked toward the gate leading back to the parking lot, through which we could see Matt pull up in his mom's Honda to pick her up. "Do you think she'll really kill me?" Violet asked me after Mischa passed through the gates and climbed into Matt's mom's car.

"She might," I mumbled. Things might have been different right after Olivia had died. But Candace's death had changed everything. I felt it as sure as I felt the wind blowing: Mischa was doomed just like my other two friends had been. "Look, I'm not really thrilled about playing this damn game with you again, but I'm willing to try, because I actually care about Mischa when obviously you don't, Violet."

Violet looked down at the ground again and startled me with a loud, uncontrolled sob. When her eyes met mine again, they were filled with tears, and her nose was pink. "I didn't want to tell Mischa this, but her plan isn't going to work."

I already knew that playing the game wouldn't work to break the curse, as did Trey, but I put my hands on my hips. The cold November wind blew through my light jacket, making me wish I'd done as my mother had instructed and dug my winter coat out of the back of my closet that morning. "And why is that?"

"Because," Violet began, "I told you. They couldn't show me your death. The door was already closed. If we try again, they're going to be really mad."

"We're done here," Trey announced to Violet. "You're going to miss your bus."

Trey and I walked home without saying much. "That girl's crazy," he muttered as we reached the corner of Martha Road. "Don't pay attention to her saying stuff about you being dead. She doesn't know what she's talking about."

"I know I'm not dead. I'm right here," I insisted. "But I've been thinking that maybe Jennie and I shared a soul, you know? One soul, split in half, and that's what Violet's seeing when she tries to read me."

Trey kept shaking his head. "Everyone has their own soul, and yours is perfect. We really can't believe anything she says. I was watching her reactions on the track. They, or *it*—or whatever is behind this—is telling her what to say. She was waiting for direction from them every time she opened her mouth. It was like she was reading from a teleprompter."

"What about the object?" I asked, still considering the destruction of the object to be a safer course of action for us than resuming Light as a Feather, Stiff as a Board. But to avoid initiating the game again, we were going to have to figure out the object, *and* destroy it, before evening the next day. "Any ideas?"

"I've got nothing," Trey said. "My only guess would be something she keeps in her purse, because she kept it pretty close to her the whole time we were talking."

At dinnertime, Mom asked me a ton of questions about my day, quite obviously trying to be a more involved parent. I was distracted as I provided her with adequate answers about my classes, my thoughts lost in musings about objects and the afterlife. Maude was being a general nuisance throughout the meal, first begging for a sample of chicken potpie and then scratching endlessly at the sliding back door leading out to the deck. "All right, already!" Mom exclaimed finally, flipping the switch on our kitchen wall to flood our backyard with light and sliding open the door so that Maude could race across the yard.

Almost an hour later, I put on my shoes and my jacket to try to lure Maude back into the house after she refused to return inside when Mom called her. "There must be a rabbit back there or something," Mom theorized.

In the yard, even despite the light shining over our deck, my eyes adjusted to the darkness before I could see Maude's dark body in the far corner of the yard, digging away at something. It was freezing cold outside, with frost settling on the grass, and I cursed the puppy for dragging me out of the warm house. When she saw me approaching, she became very excited, running in circles around her digging spot, not far from where Trey and I had buried Moxie, happily yapping at me. "What are you doing back here, you bad girl?" I asked. As I grew closer, I noticed that the hole she had dug, which she was so anxious to show me, wasn't very deep. It was about a foot in width, and oddly shaped. Standing right over it, I realized that the puppy had somehow scratched a hole in our grass that looked unmistakably like a heart. Maude barked at me enthusiastically, as if she was telling me, *See?*

And then clarity hit me like an unexpected slap across the cheek. The sweaters.

Since the weather had turned cold, Violet had been wearing new sweaters every day. All of them—thick wool and creamy cashmere—covered her neck. There had been loose cowl-necks and tight turtlenecks, ribbed crewnecks and an ivory funnel-neck that had shown off her figure, even before Candace's death.

They had been covering the gold locket that she had so plainly displayed during warmer weeks of the school year. Whether she had subconsciously been obscuring it with knitwear to put the locket out of our minds, or had been intentionally piling on sweaters in the hope that we'd forget that she had worn it every day at the beginning of the school year, I wasn't sure. But I had forgotten about it entirely, until Maude had reminded me. I thought back to the bowl of heart-shaped soaps in the bathroom at the Richmonds' house, and how I'd been compulsively inclined to use them. And then I realized whether I was "dead" as Violet claimed or not, I had just as much help on the other side as she did, if not more. It was possible that Jennie, Olivia, Candace, or even Moxie had guided Maude outside to trigger this visual cognition.

It was that locket, that *heart-shaped* locket, connecting Violet to all of this trouble. I was absolutely sure of it.

CHAPTER 17

TREY AND I HAD A DEADLINE NOW. WE HAD TO get our hands on that locket before we played the game again with Violet at Mischa's insistence. In any scenario I could imagine, the most opportune time to snatch that locket would have been in the girls' locker room before gym class. Since Mischa was no longer in my gym class, and since Violet would instantly know we were up to something if she were to see Mischa appear in the locker room with me before class, I would have to attack her alone if we couldn't think of a better plan. For obvious reasons, the idea of attacking Violet on my own was daunting. What if I reached for it and the clasp didn't break? Or if something even more horrific happened, and the gold chain sliced through the skin on Violet's neck? I felt with certainty that we were on the brink of closure with Violet, but surely she must have felt it too.

I heard my phone vibrate on my bedside table at five in the morning and instinctively sat up to answer it. It was Mischa, in an inconsolable state. Next to me, Trey sat up and rubbed his eyes. I patted him on the shoulder and told him to go back to sleep.

"Do you ever think about what it's like to die, McKenna?" Mischa asked me. Her voice was raw, and sounded like she had been crying for hours.

"Sure," I confessed. "All the time. I've wondered that for a long time. I think it's peaceful. The whole bit with the white light full of grace, and drifting toward it, and then feeling total serenity and contentment. I believe in all of that." I didn't tell her that I believed all of that because I had to, because without that I couldn't stand to wonder what pain and horrors Jennie had endured as she'd left behind the life we'd shared.

"I don't believe that," Mischa countered. "When my grandmother died, my father told me that all life consists of is a series of neurons firing in our brains that make us perceive energy around us. When we die, and those neurons stop moving around, there's nothing left. Just blackness. Nothingness. That's what becomes of us when we die."

There was a long pause, and I tried not to let her words make too much of an impact on my thoughts. The notion that everyone I had known who had already passed away had just been hurtled into a void was too painful to consider.

"We know that's not true. Olivia reached out to me. *She* wasn't in a state of nothingness," I offered.

"What's going on?" Trey asked me groggily. I shooed him away, knowing that Mischa's emotional state would only annoy him.

"I don't want to be an angry ghost. I want to stay with my parents and win a medal at the GK U.S. Classic, and I want to go to college in La Crosse and marry Matt and be a mom. How did all of this happen? Why did we play that stupid, stupid game? I want to take it all back! I don't want to die, McKenna!"

I could hear the sincerity in her plea, and I didn't have a simple response for her. It wouldn't be fair to assure her that she wouldn't die. Olivia and Candace already had. "We're trying, Mischa. We're trying."

As I climbed back into bed, I wondered if she'd eaten any solid food at all yesterday. If we didn't find a surefire way to prevent the death that Violet had foreseen for Mischa, she might just die of starvation anyway.

Even with Trey's arm wrapped around me, the now-familiar fall and rise of his chest against my back, both of us enveloped in the smells and textures of my childhood bedroom, I sensed that all the security I had known most of my life was about to be torn away. I tried to assure myself that it was just Violet's spirits trying to scare me out of doing what I knew needed to be done. But deep down in my heart, I felt certain that I was on the edge of a precipice. Once I pushed back the blankets and climbed out of my bed in the morning, my life would never go back to normal again.

The parking lot of the high school was packed by six p.m., even an hour before the basketball game against Angelica High School was scheduled to begin. I hadn't confronted Violet in the locker room that morning before gym class because Trey had thought it would be too risky to attempt during the school day, but he and I knew as we arrived at the game that we needed to get our hands on Violet's locket *that night*. I pulled into the lot behind the wheel of Mrs. Emory's Civic with Trey in the passenger seat beside me. Mischa sat in the back seat, defying Matt's order to stay home and away from this situation. As far as she knew, we were at the game solely to prevent Violet from disappearing afterward without making good on her promise to play the game again. Trey and I had discussed the complication of Mischa joining us at the game and had decided it would be in her best interest, and ours, to refrain from telling her about the locket and our plan to steal it from Violet. She was behaving so erratically that there was no telling what she might do if things were to go wrong. We also knew that our plan was basically nonexistent, and that we were just going to have to be ready to spring into action at any point during the game when an opportunity presented itself, whatever the consequences.

As soon as I pulled cautiously into a space at the less-crowded back of the lot, still not entirely trusting my driving skills, Trey said, "Look."

Violet's white Audi was pulling into the lot. As it turned down one lane to navigate toward an empty spot closer to the west entrance of the school, we saw Violet, in profile, behind the wheel. She was wearing her black-and-red pom squad uniform, and after parking, she applied lip gloss. She checked her reflection in her rearview mirror and stepped out of the car, throwing her duffel bag over her right shoulder and casually locking the car behind her with the remote on her key chain. Her long dark hair, tied back in a ponytail, swung from left to right as she strode into the high school and disappeared behind the red doors.

"Ugh," Mischa snorted. "She has the nerve to be in a good mood."

But Trey and I ignored her and taciturnly shared the same thought: She was already wearing her uniform. If she stopped by the locker room now, it would just be to stow her bag and dash off into the gym to warm up with the rest of the team. I would need her to be preoccupied down there for at least a few minutes to be successful, to catch her off guard and tear that locket off of her. The element of surprise was going to be critical for me.

"Let's go," Trey said. "I can't believe I almost graduated without ever attending a school basketball game."

I rolled my eyes at him, knowing that a few weeks ago he would *never, ever* have voluntarily attended a school sporting event.

Inside the west doors of the school, we were greeted by two nerdy freshman girls seated at a card table, selling tickets. "Tickets are five dollars each," the girls told us happily, stamping our hands with a red rubber PAID stamp. The halls were strangely empty, since it was evening, and unlit to deter kids from Angelica High from exploring our small school building during the game. A small roar of festivity was already coming from the gym, where dance music was being pumped over the sound system, popcorn and sodas were being sold, and parents from out of town were finding seats in the bleachers. We pushed our way into the gym and looked up into the bleachers for inconspicuous seats where fans of the home team would be sitting, where Pete's parents had already spread out their coats and bags with his younger brothers and Jeff's mom was making adjustments to her video camera in preparation for tip-off.

My limbs already felt cold and numb with anticipation for the game to begin. We climbed the bleachers and sat nearly all the way at the top in a corner, where we hoped Violet might not notice us while performing dance numbers with the squad. Even after we sat for a few minutes and absorbed all the activity in the gym, none of the pom squad members from either school had drifted out onto the hardwood.

"Where is she?" Trey wondered aloud.

"Probably in the locker room, hanging out and warming up. Usually, the teams share the girls' locker room," Mischa informed us, having unique insight on the situation of teams sharing our school resources as a member of the cheerleading team during football season. "At least for home football games, that's what happens. The cheerleading squad from the visiting school uses the locker room at the same time as us, and we just try not to talk to each other."

My stomach clenched at the thought of having to walk into the locker room and receive curious stares from girls on not only the Willow pom squad, but the Angelica pom squad too. More witnesses. More people trying to stop me if Violet cried out for help. More trouble for Trey to get into if he were to follow me in there and potentially observe girls from the visiting high school in a state of undress.

"Do you think the pom squad will have to go down into the locker room again during the game?" Trey asked Mischa innocently. The music playing over the loudspeaker in the gym faded out and a new bass-heavy dance song came on, signifying the entrance of the Willow pom squad, which danced out onto center court and took formation. Violet, whose snug uniform fit her perfectly, stood in the center with her hands on her hips, beaming proudly. The rest of the team took their positions behind her, locking their overly exuberant smiles into place and tilting their hips.

"Probably after halftime to freshen up," Mischa mused as the dance routine began.

After halftime. That made sense. The home team's pom squad would presumably perform a rousing routine for at least five minutes. The opening routine was scandalously risqué. I could hardly believe I was at a high school basketball game in Wisconsin with all of the grinding, flashing, and chest popping going on. More than one dad wolf-whistled, and moms whispered disapprovingly in the bleachers. The rhythm of the music filled the entire gym, and the fans in the bleachers began stomping along with the beat. Violet loved the reaction of the crowd and her new, truer identity was in full bloom. There was no trace of the shy wallflower we had met in September out on the basketball court that November evening. The girl who led the dance routine that day seemed taller than the Violet we knew, more poised than her, radiating confidence. She seemed like a girl who had everything she wanted, and was afraid of nothing. She seemed, I shuddered to think, invincible.

Throughout the routine, I kept waiting for Violet to spot us up in the bleachers and to lock eyes with me. Since sitting down in the gym I'd had an unshakable feeling that Violet knew we were present, and why we were present. When I went down to the locker room later, she would be expecting me. Things wouldn't be as simple as Trey and I were hoping. There was absolutely nothing I could do, as that music played and the pom squad girls continued to shake their rear ends, as well as their pom-poms, to prepare. And yet her eyes never drifted up to where we had perched. The routine ended with Violet's polished back handspring and midair Chinese splits, and as applause filled the gym, my eyes were focused on one thing only: the glimmer of light reflecting off of a gold chain around her neck.

She was wearing the locket. It was just tucked underneath her tight black polyester team sweater, *almost* entirely out of view.

Trey had seen that glimmer too, and he gently elbowed me.

The pom squad sat down on the lowest bleacher, a few feet away from where our varsity basketball team took seats after they entered the gym to a round of applause. From our vantage point, we could look directly down upon Violet's dark head, and watch her giggling and sharing secrets with the girls on her team. At tip-off, when Jeff and Pete strode onto the court to face the two forwards from Angelica, she sat up straight, paying close attention, her clasped hands held up to her mouth in anticipation. When Pete shot for his first basket of the evening from nearly midcourt and made it, Violet was on her feet in less than a second, arms in the air, cheering. When the ref called a foul on an Angelica forward who had accidentally tripped Pete as he dribbled the ball, she furrowed her brow and expressed her frustration to the girl sitting next to her, a senior named Annie whose brother was on the team.

At the end of the first quarter, Willow was leading by nine points, and parents left the bleachers to visit restrooms and buy sodas while the coaches for both teams gave their athletes a pep talk. The pom squad from Angelica performed its first routine, and then the pom squad from our school stood and chanted a very quick cheer.

In less than five minutes, the ref blew his whistle, summoning both teams of tall lanky boys back out onto the court. I hadn't ever sat through an entire school basketball game because the marching band and color guard only performed at football games, and I was barely able to keep up with the rules of the game.

Fifteen minutes later, as the second quarter came to an end, Angelica had somehow managed to catch up and tie the score.

The pom squad from our school stood and filtered out of the gym through the doors on the other side of the huge room, the doors that led to the hallway by which the stairs leading to the locker rooms, weight room, and track were accessed.

"Bathroom break," I announced to Trey and Mischa, knowing that if Violet was on the move and the halftime show was our best chance to confront her, I'd be better off out of the bleachers, nimble and on my feet in the school's hallways.

"Me too," Trey said, putting his green coat back on rather than leaving it in the bleachers.

I looked helplessly at Mischa, wondering what we'd do if she insisted on joining us, but she just shrugged and continued drinking her diet soda.

The acoustics of the hallway were a welcome change from the bone-rattling bass and echoing footsteps of the gym. Parents gossiped to our left in the line for soda and popcorn, and beyond them, the hallway curved around the outer perimeter of the gym toward the staircase down to the locker rooms. In the other direction, vending machines glowed and buzzed, and beyond them the hallway led to the west entrance to the school, where we had entered and bought our tickets. "Over here," Trey urged me quietly, pulling me around the side of the last vending machine in the row as the pom squad rounded the corner. Cautiously, we leaned forward to catch a glimpse of the team as they entered the gym. Music was starting for their halftime routine, and we crept forward, lingering in the doorway through which they had just passed to watch them assemble for their routine. The girls' backs were toward us, and they formed a V shape in the center of the court, each girl crouching down on her knees, balancing her forehead on the floor, waiting for the bass to start booming. In succession, as the music picked up, each girl unfolded her body and climbed up gracefully to her feet. A dance remix of "Cry Out" by hip-hop artist Tiny J shook the gym with its bass line. Once all the girls were standing, they began dancing in unison and the crowd went wild.

Trey turned to me and refocused my attention. "We should get downstairs and wait."

I nodded and looked out onto the basketball court one last time. Violet had thrown her arms in the air dramatically and spun around just in time to look directly at me where I lingered in the doorway, as if she had known where I was the whole time I'd been standing there. Her face was as expressionless as a plain piece of paper, and a moment later she continued her dance routine as if she had never noticed me, but I understood. She knew the time had come. She knew I'd come for her. My heart beat in my chest like there was a wild animal trapped in my rib cage trying to escape. The look in her eyes told me that if I didn't come for her, she'd be coming for *me*.

"I don't know about this. I don't think waiting in the locker room is the right approach anymore," I mumbled to Trey nervously as he tore me away from the doorway and guided me down the hallway toward the stairs leading to the locker room entrance. Parents and teachers hovered near the doorway as the performance continued, paying us little attention as we moved farther down the unlit hall.

"It's the safest, McKenna. It's a small space with only two ways in and out. I'll go with you," Trey tried to convince me.

"She knows, Trey," I protested, hearing how hysterical my voice sounded, and hating it. "She knows we're going to be down there. I'm scared!"

Trey put both of his hands on my shoulders in an attempt to calm me. "McKenna, listen to me. This is *it*. All we have is this one chance. *Everything* depends on this. You *know* that. Mischa's life depends on us getting that locket away from Violet, and we have to do it right now!"

The music booming from the gym was scattering my thoughts and making it impossible for me to visualize what I knew we needed to do: descend the stairs, pass through the entrance to the girls' locker room, lurk somewhere out of sight like the shower stalls until we heard the pom squad enter, and then attack. That had been the plan in my head since the night before, when I had thought it through in such detail that I imagined feeling the warm sharpness of the metal chain against my palm as I tore the locket from Violet's neck, smelled the lemony cleanser scent of the locker room, and saw myself sprinting away from the locker room, locket in hand. But that was where the fantasy ended. Father Fahey had said we needed to *destroy* the locket. How were we going to destroy something made of gold in a parking lot? How had we overlooked that critical detail until now?

"It's not right, Trey. The setting's just not right. She can break away from me and go out the other exit, onto the track. I'll never catch her. She's faster than me, and then I will have blown it. I'll never have a second chance if I attack her with so many witnesses and she gets away," I rambled. His expression was one of such deep disappointment; I longed to trust his instincts, but everything just felt wrong. He looked so amazing in that moment, his pale eyes pleading with me, his mouth so pink and full, I was overwhelmed with wonderment that we had been sleeping in the same bed more nights than not and had done little more than kiss since the end of September. I fought the almost irresistible urge to forget all about Violet and drag him back to his mother's car in the parking lot to tear his clothes off, to finally give in to the surge of desire for him I had been suppressing for weeks. As if something else was operating my body, I saw my own hand rise and stroke his smooth cheek, my thumb press upon his full lower lip.

"McKenna, what are you . . ."

I didn't *know* what I was doing. It was as if my thoughts were being supplanted by something or someone else. Like I was being operated by some other force. And then I realized that probably was *exactly* what was happening. The spirit that controlled Violet was trying to distract me from what I had to do, and it was doing a darn good job of it.

"Sorry," I said, turning crimson and regaining control of my thoughts. I must have seemed like a complete nut, first being panicky and cowardly and then coming on to Trey so strongly. "Something is messing with my head. I don't want to wait for her downstairs. Really, I think it's a bad idea."

In the gym, I could hear the song winding down. Applause was rising and feet were stomping in the bleachers. The sound inside my ears was deafening. I felt as if my eardrums might explode, and in that moment I wanted nothing more than to run from the high school and get out into the parking lot, away from the brain-aching noise. "McKenna," Trey said firmly, shaking me.

Before I had a chance to really get a grip on myself, the pom squad was exiting the gym. In single file, they rushed out, led by

Shannon Liu, a senior still glowing from the excitement of the performance. The entire team jumbled together in front of my eyes like a wild octopus with twenty bare tan legs and long hair of every color, until my eyes settled on the girl at the heart of the group: the gorgeous girl with the ice-blue eyes. Violet.

Without even thinking through exactly what I was doing, without even giving her a fraction of a second to look up and see me and Trey lurking in the shadow of the hallway, I sprang forward. I moved too quickly for Trey to hold me back, too quickly to even entertain the possibility that by acting so impulsively and recklessly, I was jeopardizing everything. Not a word left my lips as I threw the entire weight of my body at Violet, knocking Stephani deMilo out of my way and sending her crashing down onto the tile floor. I tackled Violet, pushing her backward, and as we both hit the floor I grabbed for her locket, gritting my teeth as I felt my fingers wrap around the gold chain that disappeared beneath her sweater.

"Hey! No! Help!" Violet cried out as soon as she realized what had happened. I was on top of her, pinning her to the floor with my knees pressed against her shoulders. I was sure that I was hurting her, but didn't have time to care.

The chain was surprisingly strong, although the gold looked delicate and old. I tugged on the chain hard enough to break the clasp, I was sure, and yet just as I felt the metal about to snap, I felt strong hands under my arms, pulling me backward. I was yanked off of Violet with such force, I felt the locket slip through my fingers in an instant, and gaped at it as I saw it—the embossed heart dangling by the delicate gold thread—snap back into place over Violet's sweater.

"What in God's name?!" Coach Simon yelled from behind me. I

recognized the voice of the boys' basketball coach even though I had never exchanged words with him before. Even before my feet found the ground and stabilized so that I could stand on my own, behind me, Trey tackled Coach Simon from the side, knocking him to the ground. I fell over with them since Coach Simon still had a strong grip on my arms, but I regained my balance faster. Back on my feet and suddenly liberated, I turned to see Trey struggling to keep the tall, balding coach down on the ground.

"Run, McKenna!" Trey yelled.

And so I turned back to my left and saw Violet climbing up to her feet.

There was commotion everywhere—other teachers and parents rushing toward Trey and me—but nothing was going to stop me. With determination unlike any supply of energy I had ever sensed before in my life, I charged toward Violet like a tiger, blowing past the other girls on the pom squad. She darted just fast enough to escape my grabbing fingertips, and she ran toward the staircase leading to the locker room entrance at top speed. I was steps behind her, skipping stairs to catch up to her, and clumsily missed a step. With a sickening feeling in my stomach because I knew every part of my body was about to start hurting *a lot*, I crashed into Violet from the back, sending her tumbling forward. She fell face-first down at least four steps, and then bounced down two more, buffering the fall with her arms outstretched as her knees tucked around to one side. With more velocity on my side, I fell over her, surely hurting her back and shoulders as I tumbled forward, and I rolled down the rest of the stairs tucked into a ball, feeling every single stair jut into my rib cage until I hit the floor at the bottom.

I took a deep breath, sure that the warmth that I felt on my forehead was blood, and before I even gave myself a moment to adjust to the terrible pain setting in along my back and ribs, I saw Violet collect herself and sprint toward the locker rooms. Hearing footsteps and concerned voices calling out to me from the top of the stairs, asking if I was okay, I struggled to get up on my feet. With no time to lose, I ran toward the locker room. My left hip crashed into the door frame as I entered, releasing another blinding jolt of pain through my body. I didn't wait for the pain to swell along my left side, and followed Violet into the cool, calm locker room, losing sight of her the moment I entered as she dashed behind a row of blue steel lockers.

I rounded the corner carelessly, only realizing after I stood there, unsure of where she'd gone, that she could easily have been waiting for me, ready to bash a garbage can or something over my head. For a second, I stood perfectly still, barely daring to breathe, desperately trying to hear any noise that might have indicated the direction in which she had darted. That second passed, and I heard nothing but the footsteps and voices of girls and parents following us into the locker room. I had to move quickly; I couldn't risk being detained by parents. Since the moment that locket had grazed my fingertips, I knew I needed to feel it in my grasp again. It felt as if my skin was hungering for it, craving it.

To my right, I saw the row of blue bathroom stalls past the small walled-off square that served as Coach Stirling's office. It was possible but not likely that Violet might have stepped into a stall to hide from me, but I couldn't afford to waste a few seconds checking. To my left were the white-tiled blocks of showers, their walls definitely tall enough to hide Violet if she had stepped into one to dodge me. Beyond the showers were the rows of lockers and then the double doors, locked from the inside at night, leading out onto the track. Having no option but to keep moving, I headed for the last cube of showers after a moment's hesitation, hearing the voices of other people from the gym chasing me into the locker room.

As soon as I stuck my head into the shower area, I heard light footsteps ahead of me and darted back out of the shower block just in time to see the double doors swinging closed. I bolted with all my might for those doors, finding a new burst of energy, leaving the locker room just as the girls from the pom squad filtered in, hot on my trail.

Outside, my ears adjusted to the quiet night. It was cold enough to startle me, cold enough for the air to smell sharply like snow. Ahead of me by at least ten feet, I saw Violet booking it for the gate that led to the parking lot. She glanced over her shoulder only once, dark hair flying. Reaching the fence, she grabbed at the gate that was all that kept her from sprinting across the parking lot, and found it surprisingly stuck. From behind her, I saw plainly what it took her a second to realize: There were a padlock and a chain securing the gate, presumably to keep visitors from using the high school track at night. I could hear Violet snarl in frustration as she ran her fingers over the lock for a split second and then wasted no time doing what I never expected her to do: climb the fence in her tiny pom-pom skirt.

"Oh, geez," I muttered to myself. I slowed myself down to an abrupt stop at the bottom of the fence just as Violet was two steps into her ascension toward its top. I reached up and grabbed her left foot with the intention of pulling her back down to the blacktop, but instead of faltering, she held on to the fence more tightly. I pulled harder a second time and was taken by surprise when she jumped down from the fence to knock me over with a fierce, raging look in her eyes. I fell backward hard, hitting the blacktop and instantly knowing I had bruised my tailbone. While I was down, Violet delivered a brutal, powerful kick to my gut, completely knocking the wind out of me. I gasped for air and rolled over onto my hands and knees as she began scaling the fence a second time, and before even catching my breath, I was back on my feet, reaching for her again in an attempt to pull her down.

Only this time, I caught her by surprise. This time, it was her body that hit the blacktop with an unpleasant *thud*, and her head that smacked against the ground. It was as her eyes blinked slowly, refocusing as she tried to figure out what had just happened and how badly she had been injured, that I reached for that gold chain around her neck and pulled with all my might.

This time, she howled, "OW!" and her fingers flew to the back of her neck, where undoubtedly the chain had dug into her sensitive skin before the clasp snapped off.

With the locket clutched tightly in my right hand, I was scaling that fence as fast as I could, still very aware of Violet's dazed state on the blacktop below me. By the time I reached the top of the fence, other girls from the pom squad had caught up to us, and while half of them bent to help Violet back onto her feet, the other half childishly shook the bottom of the fence in an attempt to make me fall. I threw one leg over the top and took two small, careful steps down before I decided to abandon caution and jump. I landed firmly with a *thunk* that sent pain snaking up my back from my tailbone, and wiped a dark trickle of blood out of my right eye. I wasted a fraction of a second looking over my left shoulder only to see that Violet's fury had returned, and she was violently pushing back her teammates intending to help her. One foot in a black leather dance shoe slipped into a hole in the aluminum fence, and within seconds, Violet had reached the top, as if a supernatural force were lifting her.

Now it was my turn to run, to run as fast as I could. The only thoughts in my head as I ran were nebulous, imprints of colors suggesting the immense physical pain I felt. I had the keys to Trey's mom's car in the right pocket of my black jeans, but the only way to get across the lot to the Civic was to weave through parked cars. There was a possibility that Violet would reach the car faster than I would, and even if she didn't, I didn't like the idea of driving out of the lot on my own without Trey. From there, I wouldn't know where to go, or what to do with the locket.

Fortunately, just then, through the west doors of the school, Trey ran out, followed by Mischa. Trey spotted me, and then saw Violet chasing me, and he broke into an impressive sprint and tackled Violet from the side, knocking her over. "Don't get up!" he warned her as he dashed behind me toward his mother's parked car. Parents and teachers from both Willow and Angelica poured out of the school through the west doors and had witnessed Trey's assault on Violet. Coach Simon was among them, holding a bloodied handkerchief to his nose. Several mothers rushed toward Violet, who obeyed Trey and made no effort this time to get up. As I anxiously transferred the locket from my sweaty right palm into my left palm so that I could jam the key into the car door, I looked up to see the disarray we had caused in the parking lot: pom squad girls crying and shouting angrily on the other side of the fence near the track, parents weaving through parked cars toward me and Trey, Mischa standing alone on the stairs leading to the west entrance, her arms wrapped around herself.

"Don't look, just drive!" Trey commanded. I climbed into the driver's side of the car and started the engine so that I could open the lock on his side. He popped into the car and slammed the door shut seconds before the heavyset dad of one of the basketball players reached the car and yelled, "Out of the car right now, you two! You are both in a lot of trouble!"

I tried to block out the man's voice, and set the locket down on the plastic divider behind the transmission lever. Trey fastened his seat belt and said confidently, "Let's go."

I backed out of the parking spot as fast as I could, a little impressed with my own driving skills until I heard the crunch of metal and realized I had backed out a little too overzealously and had clipped the back corner of the car next to me. Without checking to see how bad the damage was, I floored Mrs. Emory's Civic toward the entrance of the parking lot in the wrong direction so as to not waste time. I made an illegal right turn, and could see the angered father through the passenger's-side window, his face red, his hands packed in fists. Near the doors to the high school building, concerned parents were helping Violet limp back inside.

CHAPTER 18

"WHERE DO WE GO?" I ASKED TREY, TERRIFIED, barely even stopping at the stop sign at the end of the block before throwing the car into a hard left turn without signaling. My pulse was racing. I felt like I was sweating flakes of ice. My palms felt so slippery I feared I might not be able to control the car.

"We have to destroy this thing," Trey muttered, picking the locket up to examine it. "How do we destroy a gold locket?"

At the next corner, I turned right and merged into traffic, heading toward the rural highway that was our best bet for getting out of the town limits quickly. Almost immediately after I felt the warm rush of relief from mixing in with other cars driving at normal speeds, I heard the sirens of several police cars behind us. Someone at the high school had called the cops, and they were coming after us.

"Oh God!" I exclaimed. "Do you think I should pull over?"

"Um, you just assaulted a fellow student, I just punched a teacher, and you just drove away from the scene of an accident. I *really* don't think you should pull over right now," Trey advised me.

"Right," I agreed, impulsively switching lanes and cutting off someone to my left who honked angrily at me. I wanted to put as many cars as possible in between us and that police car behind us in traffic.

Using his minuscule, chewed-down fingernails, Trey managed to pry the locket open and made a sound that was a mix of *oops* and *whoa*. I took my eyes off the road for a split second to see that there was a small lock of golden hair, the color of honey, in the locket. It had uncurled the moment Trey had parted the two halves of the heart, and was stretched out, tickling his palm.

"I don't know if this is gross or cool," he muttered.

I thought instantly of the portrait in the Simmonses' hallway, with Violet's grandmother, her blond hair perfectly coifed, smiling so gracefully. My memory of that patient smile suddenly seemed eerie. In the painting, Grandmother Simmons wasn't welcoming guests into her living room with that smile. She had been telling me, through the cracked paint, that her patience would outlast mine. The Simmonses were trouble, and I'd made the mistake of crossing them.

We were greeted by two more police cars when I turned right onto the rural highway leading out of town. Upon seeing our car, they flipped on their sirens and the swirling red and blue lights on the tops of their vehicles filled the night with color.

"I really don't like this," I told Trey, my voice shaking. I was already starting to wonder if anyone had called my mother to inform her that there was a wild police hunt for my capture in progress.

"Just keep driving." Trey scratched his head, thinking, and said, "The lakes. If we can make it as far as County Highway up past the airport, we can toss it over the side of the suspension bridge at White Ridge Lake."

That was *far* from where we were. The drive up to Shawano Lake and the smattering of smaller lakes around it in the densely forested area would take almost thirty minutes, driving *fast*. I wasn't sure my nerves and driving ability could hold out that long. The rural highway was only four lanes—two lanes eastbound, as we were, and two lanes westbound. If the police attempted to obstruct our passage, I wouldn't have the first idea of how to react. What was equally concerning was that we had less than a quarter tank of gas.

"Trey, I don't know if we're going to make it that far," I said, too scared to even cry.

"Think about Mischa," Trey encouraged me. "We have to at least try."

"But do you think throwing the locket into deep water is going to be enough to actually destroy it?" I asked. I would have felt a lot better if we had made the preparations to throw it into a vat of acid or an incinerator hot enough to melt precious metal. But it was eight o'clock on a Tuesday night in suburban Wisconsin; how the heck would we ever come across either of those options? "Gold doesn't rust."

"I think," Trey hypothesized slowly, "if we just put it in a place where Violet will never be able to get her hands on it again, we'll be in much better shape than we are now. And if it's the hair that holds the power, that's easy to deal with right now."

He fished around in the pocket of his coat until he found a book of matches.

"Trey! I'm driving!" I shrieked, overcome by my fear of fire. I didn't want to smell burning hair or see smoke in the car with me while I needed to be focused on the outrageous speed at which I was driving down the rural highway, passing occasional cars while three police cars with sirens blaring chased us.

"This is the police. Pull over."

The police officer riding shotgun in the car closest behind us had rolled down his window and was barking out orders to us using a bullhorn.

"It's okay," Trey assured me. "If I burn the hair now, we'll be halfway done with the job even if the gas runs out."

He was right, so I took a deep breath and tried my best to ignore him as he lit the edge of the golden lock. The hairs curled and blackened quickly, filling the car with a sickening, sweet odor and a ton of smoke.

"All done," Trey said, lowering his window just enough to slide his left hand through so that the remaining ashes could blow off into the wind.

"You are under arrest. Pull the vehicle over to the side of the road."

Ahead of me by about forty feet in traffic was a logging truck, piled high with freshly cut trees secured with an elaborate network of cords and hooks. It was taking up more than one lane, and passing it was going to be impossible without swerving into oncoming westbound traffic.

"What do I do, what do I do?" I asked Trey.

Trey placed a steady hand on my right thigh to calm me down. "Watch for a gap in oncoming traffic, then dip into that lane and gun it."

Listening, I watched, and then he added, "And pray like hell there isn't a car right in front of the truck when we get around it."

I took a deep breath after a blue Volvo station wagon whizzed past us on the left, and I threw Trey's mom's car into the oncoming lane and hit the gas. Almost a hundred feet ahead of us, cruising at the same speed we were, a maroon Kia was approaching us, threatening to hit us head-on if I wasn't able to pass the logging truck and merge back into the eastbound lane. For some unfathomable reason, the driver of the logging truck picked up speed, and I didn't think I was going to be able to get ahead of him before the Kia smashed into us.

"Jesus!" I screamed. At the very last second before impact with the Kia, I realized that if I tried to cut off the truck driver at the speed at which he was traveling, he'd clip the back of our Civic. I swerved farther left into the second westbound lane, narrowly missing an oncoming Jetta. My stomach lurched as I heard the horrific *whur* of gravel beneath our spinning wheels. We had veered onto the side of the road, but fortunately I had recovered the car before it had spun off beyond the gravel, into the tall grass and pine trees.

"Oh my God," Trey whispered, his voice full of vibrato from the bumping along of the car over the gravel. He was clutching his car seat with both hands, the locket still tucked in the palm of his left hand.

"We're good. I've got this," I exclaimed, unable to believe that we hadn't been annihilated by one or both of the oncoming cars we had just dodged, both of which had slammed on their brakes after we passed them, skidded, and were halted in the middle of their respective lanes. With no immediate oncoming traffic in either westbound lane, I hit the gas again once getting back on the pavement, not wanting to floor the car while still on loose gravel. We soared in front of the logging truck, and its driver skidded to a stop. Behind us, we heard the distant squealing of brakes as the police cars also desperately tried to avoid slamming into the back of the truck.

Unlike in chase scenes in movies, the ties holding the logs in place on the back of the truck did *not* tear open, causing mayhem and destruction to the police cars. But the distraction did give me enough time to pass a Chevy truck ahead of us on the highway and gain a sizable lead on the police.

"That was awesome, but I think later, when we have time, I'm going to wet my pants," Trey confided.

I forced a smile. I'd only had my license since August, and at this point I was pretty sure that after my mad dash for White Ridge Lake, I'd never be licensed to drive again.

It was less than a minute before we heard the sirens soaring behind us again, and the situation became only slightly more dire when there were two more police cars waiting for us at an intersection about two miles before we entered the lake region. At Trey's urging, I blazed through the intersection without stopping, and the two new police cars joined in the chase after us.

"These two are a little late to the party," Trey quipped.

I almost wanted to cry with relief as we passed the smallest body of water in the cluster of lakes that were located north of Shawano Lake, the much larger body of water to the south. Ahead of us, I could see the lime-green metal of the small bridge that spanned the expanse of White Ridge Lake. We were so close. *So close.*

And then the Civic rolled to a stop.

The gas tank needle was jiggling to a stop above the E, indicating that our luck had run out and we were finally completely out of gas. It was probable we'd driven the last mile entirely on fumes.

"No, no, no!" I yelled, slapping my palms against the steering wheel in frustration.

"No time to waste. Let's go," Trey urged me. He handed me the locket before rocketing out of the passenger side of the car. I followed his lead, hearing the police cars slamming to screeching halts behind us, no doubt leaving streaks of black rubber on the asphalt.

"This is the police! You are under arrest! I command you to stop and put your hands above your heads!"

I ignored the commands of the police as Trey and I ran the last few feet toward the small bridge with all the energy we had left in us. We ran to its center, and I hesitated just for one second, looking down into the lake's gray depths. The lake looked unusually dismal that night in the pale moonlight, with black trees, barren of their leaves for the winter, crowning the lake's edges. Feeling the weight and the cool metal of the locket in my right hand, I leaned back, and whipped the gold necklace as far as I could into the gentle ripple of water below. It sank beneath the dark surface without even making a splash, and moments later I felt the strong hands of police on my arms, handcuffing me. I turned toward Trey on my left, who was also being handcuffed and led back toward the police car. He was smiling that perfect smile of his, that precious, rare smile that only I ever got to see, the smile he had reserved for me alone since we were little kids.

It was over, at last.

EPILOGUE

OUR UNASSUMING LITTLE HOUSE ON MARTHA Road looked surprisingly different when I came home for winter break. It was smaller than I remembered it being just a few weeks earlier, when I'd watched it shrink out of view through the back windshield of our car. For the first time, I noticed that the shingles on the roof could use some attention, the brown paint on our shutters was peeling, and the little metal mailbox mounted next to our front door was rusting in one corner. I knew it wasn't the house but rather my perspective that had changed during the time I'd been away, but it was still unsettling to see my childhood home for the first time with fresh eyes.

Mom had put forth an unexpected, uncharacteristic amount of effort and had decorated the front bushes with glimmering white Christmas lights. I fought a swelling of homesickness rising in the pit of my stomach, reminding myself that there was no reason to miss home when I was right there, where I belonged. It was pointless to dwell on the fact that I'd be headed back to Illinois in just ten days. "Nice," I commented from the front seat of the car as we pulled into the driveway. I meant it. The lights looked really cute, and it was touching to see her getting into the holiday spirit for a change. I couldn't recall Mom ever even taping up cutouts of Santa in the front windows before. It made my chest ache a little to even think it, but maybe my being sent away had been good for her.

"They were Glenn's idea," she said, blushing a little.

Somehow, miraculously enough, Mom had struck up a bit of a flirtatious friendship with Maude's vet in the weeks since I'd been away at boarding school. As it turned out, they had been classmates together at the University of Wisconsin–Sheboygan in the graduate veterinary program, and Glenn was recently divorced. Considering all the many, many laws Trey and I had broken on our little crime spree in November, I had gotten off somewhat lucky when the district judge had sentenced me to attendance at a therapeutic boarding school. My new school was pretty horrific, but even more than the uniforms, bad food, uncomfortable beds, and strict curfew, the worst part was not having any control over my own private communications. Cell phones weren't permitted on the campus of the Sheridan School for Girls, and neither was unmonitored Internet use. My only communication with Trey had been ten-minute phone calls on Sunday nights on the pay phone in a very public hallway in my dormitory.

Trey had been sentenced to a military academy way up north. There literally weren't any programs in the state of Wisconsin for girls who had gotten into as much trouble with the law as I had, so my mom had been given the choice of two schools: one in Illinois and the other in Minnesota. She had begged the judge to reconsider, claiming she had absolutely no explanation for my behavior on that fateful Saturday other than the severe post-traumatic stress of suffering the loss of two close friends in just two months. The judge hadn't bought her pleas on my behalf, and even worse, the middle-aged male judge had seemed touched by Violet's overly dramatic, tearful recollection of the events of November fifth. But there was no shortage of military-style behavioral correction facilities for boys in Wisconsin. Trey's parents had chosen the first on the list provided to them by his attorney, eager to appease the court and move on with their lives.

There were butterflies in my stomach as I entered the house, knowing it would only be a matter of hours until Trey arrived home the next morning. We had barely had time to hug good-bye before being sent away to our respective schools back in November, neither one of us daring to risk additional contact in the face of more punishment. The house smelled as it always had: faintly like coffee and toast. Maude had grown considerably; her head now almost reached my knees.

"I bet it's nice to be home," Mom said. I hadn't been completely honest with her about how unpleasant my life at Sheridan was. Many of the other girls were there because they'd gotten pregnant, gotten busted shoplifting, had beaten up their foster brothers and sisters, or had repeatedly run away from home. Before I'd left Willow, Trey had coached me on how to survive the experience, advising me to keep to myself, avoid making friends, and follow orders. Keeping my head down and ignoring girls whose primary thrill in life came from antagonizing others was exhausting. But there wasn't anything my mom could do to make things easier for me, so there was no point in making her worry more than she already did.

"So nice," I agreed.

"Is there anything special you'd like for dinner?" Mom asked.

There were a million special things I wanted for dinner, anything other than the bland roast chicken legs and meat loaf served at Sheridan. "Pizza from Federico's would be awesome. But really, anything would be fine," I replied. I still felt so guilty about what I'd put her through that I didn't feel comfortable making any requests.

"Pizza sounds good," Mom said. She headed into the kitchen to order from the landline. "Bring in the mail, will you?"

I opened the front door and reached into the mailbox to grab the envelopes inside. It looked like the usual assortment of stuff, including a weekly flyer from the grocery store, a water bill, Mom's credit card statement, and two Christmas cards in red envelopes. But lastly, at the bottom of the stack, there was a slightly oversize beige envelope addressed to me. I came across it as I entered the kitchen with Maude following behind me and wondered who had sent it.

Mom asked, "Mushrooms and spinach?"

I was so intrigued by the envelope that I'd barely heard her question. My name on the envelope had been written as "Miss McKenna Brady," and no one I knew referred to me as "miss." Although the return address in the top left corner of the envelope was in Willow, I didn't recognize the name of the street—which was weird. The postmark was from Willow too. With her hand over the mouthpiece of the phone, Mom was waiting for my answer. "Oh. Yeah, sure," I replied.

I set the mail down on the kitchen table and carried my bags and the strange envelope addressed to me down the hall to my room. Once in my bedroom, I sighed with relief at the familiarity of my own bed, my books, and my desk. Nothing looked different, although a lot had changed in Willow since I'd left. Mischa had been transferred at her own insistence to St. Patrick's, and she had been writing me letters detailing her painful adjustment to life under the rule of nuns. Amanda was still at Willow, since she was only one semester away from graduation, but I had a feeling she limited how much information she shared with Mischa about school gossip. Cheryl sent me long, handwritten letters covered in stickers and illustrations of things going on at the high school, but she didn't concern herself with the lives of the popular people. She had started dating Dan Marshall, and most of her letters were about their dates and how much she liked him.

I sat down at my desk and inspected the envelope, having no idea who could have sent it. Everything related to my court case was always sent to my mom, and I didn't think anyone in Willow aside from the Emorys, Mischa, and Cheryl even knew I was being allowed home for Christmas. Since there had been quite a bit of local news coverage about the car chase, I guessed the letter might have been from someone who wanted to threaten me or voice their support for Violet. I probably should have brought the envelope to my mom's attention before I tore it open. But curiosity got the better of me.

Inside was a printout of a calendar that detailed the phases of the moon. It was fastened with a paper clip to several printouts of news articles from the Internet.

At first glance, I wondered if someone had sent me my astrological birth chart or something related to astrology. Two dates were circled on the lunar calendar in red ballpoint pen—September 13, which was positioned under the "Full Moon" column, and October 27, which was positioned in the first column on the left side of the chart beneath the headline of NEW MOON. Next to this red circle, someone had written *Oct. 23*.

I shivered. This was the date on which Candace's text messages from Hawaii had stopped. The day her half brothers had watched her walk straight into the Pacific Ocean. What I'd been sent wasn't some kind of horoscope. It was some kind of a clue.

The first article clipped beneath the calendar was about the accident in which Olivia had died, printed out from the *Willow Gazette* website. On it, the date of the accident, September 13, had been circled in red pen. The second article, also from the *Willow Gazette*, was about Candace's disappearance in Hawaii, giving the date of her death as October 23. I referenced the lunar chart again, trying to understand what was being implied by the numbers. Both Olivia and Candace had died about six weeks apart. Olivia had died fifteen days before the new moon, which had occurred on September 28. Candace had died on October 23, four days before the next new moon, on October 27. What could that possibly mean?

The other pages in the packet were from the Lake Forester section of the *Chicago Tribune* website. They were obituaries of four teenagers with the dates of their deaths also circled in red ink. The first two names, I recognized: Rebecca Shermer and Josh Loomis. All four of the kids who had died in Lake Forest a year ago had died within four consecutive months, and all also shortly before new moons.

Breathing heavily as if I'd just awakened from an intense nightmare, I tossed the papers down on my bed, not even wanting to touch them. Who would have sent me a puzzle like this? Who would have known I'd be home for Christmas break, and that the deaths of kids in Lake Forest were related to the deaths of kids in Willow? If whoever had sent me this was implying that there was an order to what Violet did, a pattern to it, I didn't want to know. Mischa hadn't died before the new moon in November; we'd saved her. The last thing I wanted was to get tangled up in Violet's lies again and land myself in even more trouble.

My mother knocked on my doorframe, surprising me so badly that I flinched. "I thought you might appreciate having this back while you're home," she said. She stepped into my room and handed me my phone, hesitating for a second and then adding, "No more trouble, McKenna. I need you to promise me."

"I promise," I said solemnly, meaning it.

As soon as Mom left, I called Mischa. I needed to hear her voice and know that she was safe. She answered on the first ring. "Oh my God! Are you home?"

"Yeah," I replied. "This might sound like an odd question, but did you send me an envelope full of freaky moon stuff?"

"Moon stuff? No. But I'm so glad you're back because you're never going to believe this. Amanda told me that Violet's been doing tarot card readings during study hall, and she's been telling people how they're going to die."

On unsteady legs I rose from my bed and walked to my window. I looked across the snowy patch of land between my house and Trey's. His blinds were closed, and I wasn't sure if we'd be permitted to see each other when he arrived home the next morning.

The faint melody of "It's a Small World" trickled out from under my closet door, and my blood ran cold. I'd packed up all my music boxes and stashed them in the closet in the fall. There was no way any of them had been wound up in weeks. A sense of dread washed over me. Trey and I had failed. Violet was still playing games, and Olivia's spirit was not pleased.

★ GOOD BYE ★

ACKNOWLEDGMENTS

Although the list of people I need to thank for inspiring and assisting me on this project is very long, I should begin by thanking Courtney Greenstein for inviting me to her Halloween party in the fifth grade. It was the first time I'd ever played Light as a Feather, Stiff as a Board, and obviously the experience made a lasting impression on me.

I owe great thanks to the entire team at Wattpad for their invaluable support. Allen, Eva, and Ivan have created a platform for community and expression that has added a new dimension to the experience of consuming fiction and has connected me with readers eager for ghostly thrills. My Wattpad fans, who crack me up with their comments and amaze me with their fan art. Ashleigh Gardner, Caitlin O'Hanlon, I-Yana Tucker, Abby Ho, Alysha D'Souza, Kelly Steen, and so many more Wattpad staffers (past and present) have accompanied me on this journey since the very first chapter. Special thanks to Monica Pacheco, who encouraged me to return to Willow after I'd spent a long time away. Also, a giant shout-out to Aron Levitz and Eric Lehrman for overseeing this project's development in Hollywood, and to Kelsey Grammer for his commitment to this story and his enormous generosity in shepherding it along.

I don't know where to begin thanking Jessica Smith, Rebecca Vitkus, and everyone at Simon Pulse for their dedication, collaborative enthusiasm, appreciation for the idiosyncrasies of small Midwestern towns, and willingness to deal with my overuse of prepositions.

My wonderful friend Robin Epstein, for being the world's best listener in addition to being a great storyteller herself.

And, of course, Jenny.